Praise for Anne Perry and her William Monk novels

Corridors of the Night

"[A] suspenseful, twisting narrative." —*Historical Novels Review*

"Anne Perry has once again evocatively and meticulously conjured up Victorian London. . . . This is one of her best as she continues probing . . . the dark impulses that haunt all human souls." —*Providence Journal*

"Pulls no punches and depicts Victorian London in all its corrupt glory." —*Bookreporter*

Blood on the Water

"Riveting . . . one of [Anne] Perry's most engrossing books." —*The Washington Times*

"Victorian London comes alive in Anne Perry's tension-filled mystery." —*BookPage*

"The [William Monk] series is renowned for its accurate and often devastating presentation of Victorian London—a world of stark polarities between rich and poor." —*New York Journal of Books*

Blind Justice

"[Perry's] courtroom scenes have the realism of Scott Turow." —*Huntington News*

"Perry again delivers searing social criticism with well-drawn continuing characters." —*Booklist*

"Gripping . . . In an intriguing switch of focus, Ms. Perry tilts away from her customary championing of the underdogs of Victorian England with a reminder that the aristocracy was also at risk, with everything to lose." —*The Washington Times*

A Sunless Sea

"Anne Perry's Victorian mysteries are marvels." —*The New York Times Book Review*

"Much more than a whodunit, this book [is] possibly the author's best yet." —*Publishers Weekly* (starred review)

"Unexpected twists and revelati⬛⬛⬛⬛⬛⬛⬛⬛⬛⬛⬛⬛⬛⬛⬛ Anne Perry deception and wit." ⬛⬛⬛⬛⬛ *reporter*

REVENGE IN A COLD RIVER

ANNE PERRY

REVENGE IN A COLD RIVER

A William Monk Novel

BALLANTINE BOOKS • NEW YORK

2017 Ballantine Books Trade Paperback Edition

Copyright © 2016 by Anne Perry
Excerpt from *An Echo of Murder* by Anne Perry
copyright © 2017 by Anne Perry

Published in the United States by Ballantine Books, an imprint of Random House, a division of Penguin Random House LLC, New York.

BALLANTINE and the HOUSE colophon are registered trademarks of Penguin Random House LLC.

Originally published in hardcover in the United States by Ballantine Books, an imprint of Random House, a division of Penguin Random House LLC, in 2016.

This book contains an excerpt from the forthcoming book *An Echo of Murder* by Anne Perry. This excerpt has been set for this edition only and may not reflect the final content of the forthcoming edition.

LIBRARY OF CONGRESS CATALOGING-IN-PUBLICATION DATA
Names: Perry, Anne, author.
Title: Revenge in a cold river : a William Monk Novel / Anne Perry.
Description: First edition. | New York : Ballantine Books, [2016] |
Series: William Monk ; 22
Identifiers: LCCN 2016023121 (print) | LCCN 2016028841 (ebook) |
ISBN 9781101886373 (trade paperback) | ISBN 9781101886366 (ebook)
Subjects: LCSH: Monk, William (Fictitious character)—Fiction. | Private
investigators—England—London—Fiction. | Murder—Investigation—
Fiction. | London (England)—History—19th century—Fiction. | BISAC:
FICTION / Mystery & Detective / Historical. | FICTION / Historical. |
FICTION / Mystery & Detective / Traditional British. | GSAFD: Historical
fiction. | Mystery fiction. | Suspense fiction.
Classification: LCC PR6066.E693 R45 2016 (print) | LCC PR6066.E693 (ebook) |
DDC 823/.914—dc23
LC record available at https://lccn.loc.gov/2016023121

Printed in the United States of America on acid-free paper

randomhousebooks.com

246897531

Book design by Karin Batten

To Priyanka Krishnan

REVENGE IN A COLD RIVER

1

WILLIAM MONK STEPPED OUT of the boat and climbed up the stone steps from the river, leaving Hooper to tie the vessel to the bollard and follow him. As he reached the top, the November wind struck him with chill, although it was a clear day. Or perhaps it was the figure of the customs officer McNab, waiting for him with one of his subordinates, that made him so aware of the cold.

How long had they known each other? He had no idea. In the coach accident nearly thirteen years ago, in 1856, his entire life up until then had vanished. He knew of it only through deduction, and other people's memories. He had bluffed it brilliantly. A handful of people closest to him knew. Each one of them, in a sense, held the quality of his life in their hands.

McNab hated him. Monk did not know why, but he knew very well why he hated McNab. McNab was behind the failure of the gunrunning arrest that had ended in open battle on the deck of the smugglers' ship, and Orme's death. He just did not know exactly how McNab was involved well enough to prove it. It was months ago now, but Monk still grieved for Orme, who had been his mentor, right-hand man, and above all friend, since the day Monk was appointed as commander of the Thames River Police.

McNab was waiting for him now, a solid man with his feet planted firmly on the dockside, the wind tugging at his heavy coat. He turned as he caught sight of Monk, and his blunt face assumed an expression of anticipation.

"Morning, Mr. Monk," he said loudly enough for his voice to carry above the distant sounds of chains being hauled, the slap of water on the steps, and the shouts of bargees and lightermen out on the tide. "Got one for you!"

"Good morning, Mr. McNab," Monk replied, stopping beside him and looking down at the lumpy outline under the canvas tarpaulin in front of him. The message that had brought him here had said that a body had been pulled from the incoming tide.

Monk lifted the tarpaulin off the corpse. It was a middle-aged man, fully dressed in well-worn working clothes. He was very little bloated from the water, and Monk judged he had probably been in it for only a few hours. His face was vacant-looking, but not disfigured, apart from a couple of bruises and a little swelling. Obviously that had happened before he died. Monk did not need the police surgeon to tell him so. When the heart stops, so does the bleeding, particularly into bruises.

Monk leaned forward and felt the thick, sodden hair. His fingers moved slowly, searching for an injury, either a lump, or a soft depression where the skull might be broken. He found nothing. He opened one of the eyelids and saw the tiny red spots in the white of the eye that indicated a lack of oxygen.

Monk looked up at McNab to see if he had noticed the spots, and saw in his face a moment of unguarded satisfaction. McNab smoothed it away instantly and his face became expressionless again.

Strangled? There were no marks on the throat; the larynx was not broken or crushed. Drowned? It was not uncommon in the Thames.

The water was deep, filthy, and ice cold, the current fast and treacherous.

"So why am I here, Mr. McNab?" Monk asked. "Who is he?"

"No idea," McNab answered quickly. His voice had a slightly rasping quality. "Not yet. Thought you ought to be sent for before we do anything. Wouldn't like to damage the evidence . . ." He let the remark hang unfinished. Then he gave a small, satisfied smile. "Let you look at him a bit more closely, like."

Now Monk knew that there was far more to this than he had seen yet. McNab was waiting for him to find it or, better, to have to be shown.

He took the tarpaulin off the rest of the corpse and let it lie on the stone of the dockside. He looked at the hands and feet. The hands were whole, quite soft, without calluses and with nails clipped short, carefully. Not a manual worker. He felt the upper arms through the cloth of the woolen shirt. No heavy muscles.

The man's boots were ordinary brown leather, cheap but serviceable. No tears in his trousers. His coat seemed to be missing, or perhaps he had not been wearing one at the time he fell into the water.

McNab was still smiling, very slightly, and watching. It brought back to Monk some long-ago memory of buzzards sitting on high fence posts watching for small vermin in the grass.

What had Monk missed? A drowned man with soft hands . . . With difficulty, and no help from McNab or his colleague, he turned the man over, laying him on his face. Then he saw it: the neat bullet hole through the back. If there had been any blood or powder burns the river had washed them away.

Had he been wounded before he went into the water, perhaps fatally? No, because those tiny red blood dots in his eyes said he had struggled for breath. Had he been almost suffocated, escaped, and been shot after, when he was close to the water, or already in it?

Monk looked back up at McNab. "Interesting," he said with a nod of agreement. "Better find out who he is."

"Yes," McNab agreed. "Not an accident, then, eh? Murder's your job. I'd help you if I could, of course. Cooperation, right? But I've no idea." He gave a very slight shrug. "It's all yours." He turned and walked away.

Hooper had secured the boat in which he and Monk had come, and he stood near the edge of the dock, waiting until McNab was gone. Now he came forward, his gaze still on the retreating figures until they disappeared round the side of the warehouse and he and Monk were alone on the quay. There was noise all around them of men unloading in the nearby docks. They shouted to one another. Mooring chains clanked. There were thumps and the creak of bales landing, the sharper sound of wooden kegs hitting the stone, and from below them the slurp of water.

"I don't trust that bastard as far as I could throw him," Hooper said. Then he looked down at the corpse.

Hooper had taken over as Monk's right-hand man since Orme's death. He was in many ways a contrast. Orme had been white-haired, quiet, a compact man always in a pea coat except in the middle of summer. Good-natured, softly spoken, he had known the river better than most men knew their own backyards. He was devoted to his daughter and new grandchild, and had been just about to retire to a house on the riverbank. He meant to spend his last years with them, talking to old friends, sharing a few pints of ale, and watching the wild birds fly over toward the Estuary.

Hooper was tall and loose-limbed, almost gangling, and naturally untidy. He was probably at least thirty years younger than Orme. He too was quiet, most of the time, but he had a quick sense of humor. Orme had protected Monk, knowing his ignorance of the river to begin with, and his need to learn; Hooper was also loyal in a fight—loyal to the death—but he was not uncritical, as Monk had recently learned.

Now Hooper looked at the corpse's hands, turning them over and examining them, especially the fingers. As he did so, Monk noticed a slight stain so deep into the layers of the skin that the water had not removed it.

"Ink?" he said curiously.

"Well, he's not a manual worker," Hooper responded. "And from his clothes he doesn't look like a clerk or a shopkeeper."

"We'd better find whoever pulled him from the water." Monk turned and stared up and down the broad river, crowded with boats. Nearest them were four- and five-masted schooners, riding at anchor, sails furled, waiting to unload their cargoes. A string of barges moved slowly upstream. Ferries wove their way across from bank to bank.

"I suppose McNab didn't bother to tell us that," Hooper said darkly. He spoke of it rarely, but he, too, held McNab responsible for the gunfight and therefore for Orme's death. He had not given up hope that one day they would be able to prove it. He did not want private vengeance any more than Monk did, but he did want justice. Orme had been not only a good man; he had been in the River Police almost all his adult life. There was a loyalty to be kept, for the sake of the future as well as the past.

"No," Monk said wryly. "But he sent for the police surgeon, at least. That looks like him coming along the dockside now." He inclined his head in a slight gesture toward the figure approaching. "I'll talk to him. Go and see what you can find out from the watermen along at the next steps."

"Yes, sir." Hooper set off, walking surprisingly fast. He had caught up with a group of stevedores and lightermen before Monk greeted the police surgeon.

"What've you got?" the surgeon asked, regarding the corpse without interest. He was a man in his sixties named Hyde, stocky in build with fair hair thinning at the front, and a keen face. Monk had worked with him several times before and liked his dark sense of humor.

"A man with soft hands, suffocated and shot in the back," Monk replied with a twisted smile.

Hyde stared at him with very slightly raised eyebrows. He nodded slowly. "In a nutshell," he replied. "Know who he is?"

"No idea. He was fished out of the water when he came up with the flood tide. If any of the watermen knew, they're not saying. Hooper's gone to see if he can find someone prepared to be a bit more exact."

Hyde kneeled down beside the body and examined it gently and very carefully. He looked at the head, the neck, the hands and feet, the wrists, then turned him over to see the wound in his back, exactly as Monk had.

"It was McNab from Customs who called me," Hyde said at last, straightening his knees to stand up and giving a little wince as his arthritis reminded him to be more careful. "I don't suppose he told you anything useful, Mr. Monk?"

So Hyde knew of the dislike between himself and McNab.

"Maybe he didn't know anything," Monk replied noncommittally.

Hyde gave him a sharp, knowing look. "Maybe. And maybe we'll get three tides today instead of two."

Evidently Hyde didn't like McNab, either.

"One thing," Hyde went on. "Customs doesn't know him, or McNab wouldn't have called you. And he's not a waterman or he wouldn't have hands like an artist. But I'd stake a bottle of the best single-malt whisky that whatever his art is, it's illegal."

"Was he shot first, or after he went into the water?" Monk asked.

"No idea. I'll tell you what I've found, after I've found it," Hyde replied cheerfully. He walked over to the top of the steps and signaled for his men to come up and bring the stretcher on which to carry the body. The morgue was on the other side of the river, and by boat was the easiest way to reach it.

Monk waited until they were gone, and then went after Hooper to see what he had learned. The wind was rising and he felt colder.

It took them several hours to glean all they could, but it was not a complicated story. A lighterman moving out of his moorings early and making his way upriver had found the body tangled in a mass of rope and rotten wood wreckage near one of the many flights of steps going up from the water to the dockside. The steps were used for loading occasionally. Very often, the many ferries crossing from one bank to the other picked up fares there, or dropped them off.

The lighterman had waited for the next ferry, which arrived in a matter of a few minutes. Not able to leave his string of barges, he had told the ferry operator to call the authorities. In this case they turned out to be a couple of customs men checking an early load coming off a schooner moored nearby. At this time of the year, no daylight was to be wasted. McNab had been sent for, as someone of sufficient rank to deal with the matter.

Further inquiry turned up no one who knew the corpse. Apparently he was not a bargee, a ferryman, or a docker of any other sort. None of this information surprised Monk. He had deduced that much from the man's appearance.

He and Hooper were both back at their headquarters in the Wapping Police Station, when at about half past four, almost dusk, they received news that a boat had been reported stolen earlier from the south bank, a mile or two farther down. According to the local police, it was a small rowboat, easily managed by one man. They were linking this to another incident: A prisoner from Plaistow Reformatory had escaped custody while being questioned by customs officers. He was a master forger by the name of Blount, and he answered perfectly the description of the dead man.

"Oh, yes?" Hooper said sarcastically. "And McNab didn't know of that?"

"I imagine that's what he'll say," Monk replied. "Got away yesterday, they said."

Hooper turned toward him, but his expression was near invisible with his back to the gas lamp. "I wouldn't believe McNab if he told me what day it was today, never mind yesterday."

"I'll go to the prison in the morning, see what I can learn about this Blount," Monk said.

"Do you want me to talk to the customs men that allowed him to escape?" Hooper offered.

Monk considered for a very brief moment. "No. I'll do that. Easier once I know something about the man. I wonder who shot him. . . ."

Hooper grunted, and made no reply.

Over a hot cup of tea, laced with a spoonful of whisky, Monk wrote up his notes on the day's work, not only the account of the corpse found by McNab's men, but some small thefts and one case of smuggling. It was the part of the job he liked least, but he had learned that the longer he left it, the harder it was to recall details that might matter later on. Sloppy notes and illegible handwriting had ruined more than one case.

It was two hours later when he said good night to the man on duty and went across the dark, windy dock and down the steps to get the ferry home to Hester, who would cheerfully exchange her news with him. The sweetest part of the day was yet to come.

Plaistow Reformatory, on the outskirts of the city, was almost due north of Albert Dock. The prison was close to the railway line and it took Monk less than an hour to get there. The governor of the prison, Elias Stockwell, was in a foul mood over the escape, but he had already heard that Blount's body had been found and identified, which had alleviated his anger to some small degree.

"Glad the blighter's dead," he said frankly when Monk faced him in his small, very tidy office. "He was here only a matter of weeks. Damn good forger, but a nasty piece of work. Too clever by half."

Monk forced himself to relax in the chair offered him, implying that he intended to remain there for as long as it took to get the answers he wanted.

"At forging, or in general?" he asked. The possibilities as to who had shot Blount were many. It could have been personal, very possibly revenge, or it might have been a falling-out over a planned crime, or the spoils of one already committed. It might have to do with Customs, the giving of information, or any other quarrel past or present.

Stockwell sighed. "Both. He was one of the best forgers I've seen, and not just with documents. He could make a five-pound note that would pass most people's close look."

"Well, most people aren't that familiar with what a genuine five-pound note looks like," Monk replied. It was more than a month's wages for the average man.

"Good point," Stockwell granted. "But he was good with bills of lading, customs forms, and cargo manifests, too, which was why Customs were looking at him so hard."

"Accomplices?" Monk hoped that would lead to someone who was keen to keep him silent.

"Certainly," Stockwell agreed. "But they were never caught. Knew how to keep his mouth shut." He raised his eyebrows slightly. "Are you thinking one of them killed him, to make sure it stayed shut permanently? Sounds likely to me."

"What was he convicted for?" Monk pressed.

Stockwell recounted Blount's crime of fraud with false details of shipments, and therefore false customs duties to be paid.

Monk listened with interest.

"So the ship's captain was almost certainly involved?" he concluded.

"No doubt," Stockwell agreed. "But he was long gone by the time they caught up with Blount. And he was foreign of some sort, Spanish or Corsican, or something like that."

"And the importer?" Monk asked.

"Disclaimed all knowledge of alteration of the papers," Stockwell replied. "Made it seem that Blount himself was making the profit on the difference. Lying bastard. But they couldn't get him on it. He'd covered himself very tidily."

"But Blount knew that he'd been part of the fraud, and could have given him up?"

"Had to have known, but he stayed silent. I daresay there'd have been a nice reward for his silence in the future. He only had five years to go."

"When was he convicted?"

"September."

"Name of the importer?"

"Haskell and Sons. It was Haskell they were trying to get Blount to inform on," Stockwell said. "Been after him for years."

"Customs have?"

"Yes." Stockwell looked interested. "But they said they didn't get anything out of Blount."

"While I'm here, tell me all you can about Blount. Do you know his friends, enemies, anyone who might prefer him dead? Or be afraid of him alive?" Monk asked.

"He was clever," Stockwell repeated, clearly giving the matter deeper thought. "Word around the prison is that he did quite a few favors for people. Not that he didn't collect on them, mind you. But if someone wanted a letter written, a permission forged, a document made up and passed out through a lawyer, or a warder—for a consideration . . ." His expression was bitter. "All Blount needed was the paper, and he could do a good enough job to fool most people. He built up quite a network that way: people who owed him favors, or who might need him again one day. Sly, he was. Never did much without weighing up what he could get out of it."

Monk thought of the heavy face and the soft hands, and found it unpleasantly easy to believe. "Mostly to do with smuggling?" he asked.

"That I heard about, yes. But there could have been all sorts of other things as well—bills of sale, affidavits, anything."

"Who took him to the place where he met with the customs people where he got away? Why didn't they come to question him here? Less risk of his escaping."

"We didn't think there was a risk!" Stockwell snapped back. "He was manacled all the way and had two guards with him."

"But why travel at all? Why didn't the customs men come here? No risk at all, then."

"Because they had papers and other things in a big trunk that they couldn't carry," Stockwell replied. "Machinery he could identify."

"I see. Names of the guards accompanying him?"

"Clerk and Chapman. Both got injured in the escape. Clerk not too badly. Mostly bruises, that's all. Chapman'll be off for a while. Man with a broken arm not much use here."

"Well, they won't be getting much thanks from Blount," Monk said drily. "Shot and drowned. Any ideas about that?"

Stockwell's expression was one of weary disgust. "Somebody wanted to make sure!"

"How long beforehand was this trip arranged?" Monk asked.

"Just the day before," Stockwell answered, but he sat up a little straighter. "Interesting. You're thinking someone saw a chance and took it?"

"That, or someone knew it was going to be asked for, and arranged it," Monk pointed out.

"You're thinking of Customs? Or Haskell himself? You want to see if anyone here had a connection?"

"I do. And I'll certainly go and see the customs officers involved; find out exactly what happened, who sent for Blount, and who knew about it."

"Right. I'll get you all we have." Stockwell rose to his feet. "Wretched fellow, Blount, but we can't have prisoners done away with. And I don't like it when they escape, either."

"It wasn't from here."

Stockwell stared at him indignantly. "It was from my damned men, sir!"

Monk agreed as tactfully as he could.

It was after four and the sun set low on the horizon, sending shadows across the water, when Monk left Wapping again and decided to walk the relatively short distance to the Customs House on Thames Street. It was little more than a mile and he wanted the air, cold as it was, and the solitude to order in his mind exactly what he would say. How he approached the customs men from whom Blount had escaped would determine what he would learn.

Monk wanted information from them. It was not his place to discipline them, were they at fault, and that was not certain.

The walk took him a little longer than he expected; traffic was heavy and the sidewalks crowded. But by the time he reached the magnificent customs buildings facing the river, completely restored since the fire of 1825, he was ready to deal with the men patiently and win what he could not command.

He was received guardedly and shown to a small private room someone had obligingly made available to him. It was not one of those with
a view over the river.

A young man was brought in within moments and introduced as
Edward Worth. The other customs officer who had interviewed Blount,
Logan, had been badly injured in Blount's escape and was recovering in
the hospital.

"Sit down, Worth." Monk gestured to the chair on the other side of
the desk. "Blount's dead, and it's not much loss, except if he was going
to testify against Haskell. Was he?" Monk said.

Worth sat down on the edge of the chair. He looked no more than
twenty-five, and considerably embarrassed by the fact that he and his
colleague had somehow managed to let a prisoner escape, and worse
than that, be killed. He still looked shocked.

Monk could not remember being so young. That age was part of his
lost years. Had he ever looked so vulnerable to his seniors? The impressions he had gathered had been that he had always seemed a little arrogant, perhaps appearing more sure of himself than he was.

"No, sir, not that I could see," Worth answered. "The whole thing was
a waste of time, actually." Then he colored uncomfortably. "Sorry, sir."

"Who told you to question him?" Monk asked.

"Orders, sir."

"I don't doubt that, Worth. From whom?"

"Mr. Gillies, sir. I answer to him but he must have had his orders
from higher up." Worth looked unhappy, like a schoolboy who has been
forced to snitch on one of his fellows.

"I see. Expressly to get Blount to tell you about Haskell, or on a
general fishing expedition?"

"As to who paid him, sir. And there was a whole box of forging
equipment, and special papers as he could identify, if he would."

"And did he? Identify them, I mean."

"No, sir, not really . . . Just said it was the right sort for bills of trad-
ing, some from foreign parts, like."

Monk knew that if he embarrassed Worth too deeply, or seemed to be finding fault with the Customs service in general, he would get nothing from the young man. It would be harsh, but above and beyond that, it would also be pointless. If Worth had made errors, or done less than his best, he would be keener than anyone to make amends. Good leadership would allow him to. Monk was learning these lessons slowly. But as he did so, he pitied more and more the officers who had had to deal with him as a young, clever, and smart-mouthed man. Such young men were the bane of a commander's existence, in part because they were the ones most likely to be of use, if taught well, and if their respect were earned. They would also be the most badly broken, and then the most dangerous if they became the victims of their commanding officers' own weaknesses.

"Describe to me exactly what happened, as far as you can recall it," he directed.

Worth obediently told him about Blount's arrival, and the two prison guards with him.

"Did they come into the interrogation room with Blount?" Monk interrupted.

"No, sir. They waited outside. There was only the one door, sir, and there was just the two of us, as well as them waiting in the next room."

"Sounds safe enough," Monk agreed. "Was Blount manacled during this time?"

"Left wrist to the chair, sir. Rather cold day. Got him a hot cup of tea." Worth looked embarrassed, as if his small act of kindness were a fault in him.

"And then you questioned him?"

"Yes, sir."

"Tell me," Monk began, choosing his words carefully, "did you form the impression that Blount was expecting these questions? Was he prepared for them?"

Worth considered it for a moment. "No, sir," he said, looking straight at Monk. "I don't think he knew rightly why he was here. He acted all surprised. I took it as putting it all on when he was here, but now I think maybe he did have no idea."

"Interesting. Go on."

"We were going about half an hour, getting nothing we hadn't worked out anyway, when we were interrupted. A man had said he was a lawyer for Mr. Blount, and we weren't to go on without him being there. There was nothing we could do about that, so we had the lawyer in . . . if he was a lawyer . . ."

"Why do you doubt it?"

Worth's face reflected his embarrassment. "Because that's when it all started. There was a whole ruckus outside. Two more men came in and attacked the prison guard who was waiting in the next room. . . ."

"Only one?" Monk leaned forward. "You said there were two."

"One of them had gone to relieve himself, sir." Worth looked unhappy.

"And these other two took advantage of that?" It was easy to imagine. And interesting. It sounded like a mixture of planning and opportunism.

"Yes, sir," Worth agreed. "They did."

"Were they armed?"

"Yes, sir, with big, heavy cudgels. Broke the guard's arm."

"The two of them?"

"Yes, sir. Hit me over the head, and must have hit Logan, too, as when I come to myself again, Logan was lying on the floor and the chair Blount'd been manacled to was smashed, like someone'd been at it with an ax."

"And Blount was gone?"

"Yes, sir."

"Did anyone else see any part of this? Either the two men coming in, or leaving with Blount?"

"Yes, sir. Blount was seen going off with one of them. But they was about the same height and build as the prison officers, and in the rain, all huddled up, they just thought it was them gone again. The second man obviously just made himself scarce." He moved uncomfortably in his seat.

"And the man who said he was a lawyer?" Monk asked.

"He said he'd been struck, too, sir."

"Said? You doubted him?"

"Thinking about it, yes, sir. I knew how I felt, an' he didn't look anything like it."

Monk nodded. "I would like you to think hard. I'm only asking for your impressions. Do you think Blount was expecting to be rescued? Did he play for time with you? Seem nervous, as if he were expecting to be interrupted? Was he in the least afraid?"

Worth blinked, struggling to give Monk the answer he wanted.

"He was in prison already," Monk pointed out. "Did you threaten him with anything? I need the exact truth, Mr. Worth. Was he agitated at all?"

"No, he wasn't. In fact he was rather insolent," Worth answered carefully. "As if he knew there weren't nothing we could do to him. Actually, sir, I thought it was a waste of time, myself. He was a real fly one, Blount. I never thought we'd get anything out of him."

"Not fly enough to avoid getting both drowned and shot!" Monk said bleakly. "Thank you, Mr. Worth. You have been of considerable help. I don't suppose you have any idea which of your superiors thought Blount would give Mr. Haskell away? Or whoever it was that paid him?"

"No, sir. I'm sorry, sir."

"I didn't think you would." Monk rose to his feet. "That's all. Thank you."

"Yes, sir." Worth was on his feet, standing to attention. "Thank you, sir."

A good officer, Monk thought. Maybe one day he would take him away from McNab. He would make a good river policeman. They needed recruits.

All the way home through the darkening streets he weighed what Worth had told him. By the time he reached the Greenwich ferry steps and climbed out to walk up the lamplit hill to Paradise Place, he had come to several tentative conclusions. Blount was dangerous to someone: presumably to whoever had employed him, probably Haskell. Blount was a man who always put his own well-being first, and he had known too much.

His murder had been arranged with some skill, and good use made of the customs officers and the lawyer. Someone there was helping— possibly had been paid by Haskell for one favor or another for some time, even years.

It was McNab who had brought Monk on to the case. Was he responsible for Blount's escape, maybe even his death, and was covering himself? That was the one thing Monk wanted to know. McNab was dangerous. Monk had seen the look in his eyes in the odd, unguarded moment. It was more than professional rivalry, more than personal dislike. It was hate, deep and poisonous hate.

The only thing was to face McNab, which he would do the following day. He did not want to, partly because he knew McNab would be aggressive. It was a pattern they had fallen into. But mostly Monk was reluctant because he was always at the disadvantage of not knowing what the origin was of what lay between them. He was perfectly certain that McNab did know, which placed him always a step ahead. McNab acted, and Monk reacted. He hated that.

And yet if he did not go to him with what he had learned from Worth, he would tacitly still have given McNab the advantage, and shown that he dared not face him. That would be intolerable.

As it was, when he returned to the Customs House the next day, he had to wait for McNab to finish a matter of business at one of the docks, but it was half an hour Monk used to advantage. He read several notes about Haskell & Sons, and added to his own knowledge the size of their business, and some of its history.

He was in a small, bare waiting room when McNab strode in. He was clearly annoyed to see Monk there, and the tide of emotion rushed up his face. He stood there for a moment, mastering his feelings before managing to speak with almost indifference.

"What is it now, Monk?" he asked, eyebrows raised. "You can't give us the case back, simply because it's messy! Or have you come as a courtesy, to tell us that you know what happened? Who killed Blount, then?"

Monk concealed his surprise at McNab's forthrightness, if that was what it was. He did not rise to his feet, and McNab sat down in the chair opposite him, hitching his trousers at the knees to be more comfortable. His eyes did not move from Monk's face.

Monk completely changed his mind as to what he would say.

"Probably not Haskell himself," he replied. "But very likely someone in his employ." He was grateful to see a momentary look of surprise on McNab's face, albeit masked almost immediately.

"You could be right," McNab conceded. "We've never caught him in anything provable, and he has friends." He allowed his meaning to hang heavy in the air.

"Patrons, perhaps," Monk corrected him. "Allies certainly, and employees. Different from friends."

"Oh, loyalty bought and paid for is the most reliable of all," McNab agreed. He held out his hand, closed into a fist. "You know who has the reins."

"Haskell?" Monk asked.

McNab raised his eyebrows. "Your case, Monk. Blount was shot, murdered. No way was that suicide, and you'd have to prove it was an accident. Who shoots a man in the back by accident, eh?" He kept his expression serious, but there was a gleam of satisfaction in his eyes.

"Someone who wants him silenced," Monk replied. "Possibly needs it, for his own safety."

"Possibly," McNab nodded.

"So how close were you to getting Haskell?" Monk asked.

"For killing Blount?" McNab's voice rose in amazement. "Not at all. Like I said, it's your case, Commander!"

"I'm sure you wouldn't trespass into my case, Mr. McNab," Monk said sarcastically. "I meant for smuggling, or forged documents. That is what you're after him for, isn't it?"

McNab weighed his reply for a few moments in silence.

Monk realized that McNab did not know what Worth had told him yesterday evening. But the irony went both ways; Monk would not get Worth into trouble by repeating it. He looked at McNab and waited patiently.

"A bit further off now that Blount's dead," McNab answered at last.

"Unless, of course, you can pin this on to one of Haskell's men, and they'll talk . . . which isn't likely." He smiled very slightly, leaving it in the air as to whether he meant Monk's success in catching whoever killed Blount, or the man being willing to testify. He drew in his breath and met Monk's eyes. "I think such a man would give you a good chase, Monk. He'd be caught between Haskell killing him, or you torturing him slowly, poor devil."

Monk stood up, straightening his back. "Pity you let Blount escape, then. Might have been a lot easier to let your man get it out of him. Still, too late for that now." He smiled back, very slightly. Then, satisfied with the anger in McNab's face, he went out of the door, closing it behind him, even though McNab had also risen to his feet.

2

Beata York thanked her maid, and then regarded herself gravely in the glass. She saw a woman in her fifties who had been beautiful in her youth, and had grown more complex and full of character as time had dealt unkindly with her. She had had to search for and find an inner peace to combat the outer turmoil.

Of course no one else knew that of her, and it must always be so. They perceived her as serene, always in control of her emotions. Her porcelain-fair skin was without blemish. The silver in her hair was invisible in its pale shining gold, the heavy waves swept up smoothly.

She wore a somber shade of green, untrimmed by fur or ornament. She was making a visit that duty compelled, and she dreaded it. It was foolish of her. There had never been any possibility of avoiding it, and putting it off always made it worse. However, this time she had actually been sent for.

She turned away from the looking glass, thanked her maid again, and went out of the dressing room and across the landing to the elegant mahogany stairs. The footman was waiting in the hall, standing very straight, respectfully. She could see the shine on his polished boots. The carriage would be at the door, ready. She would not have to give any directions.

She had informed the butler that she would be going to see her husband. Ingram York was residing in a hospital for the insane. He might know her when she went into his room, but, on the other hand, he might not. Apparently his doctors felt that he was becoming weaker, and she should visit him before he lapsed into more frequent coma, where he would not know her at all.

Last time, two weeks ago, he had not known her to begin with, and then had suddenly remembered. It had been dreadful, and acutely embarrassing. As she crossed the hall her cheeks flamed with the memory of it.

Ingram had lain on the bed, propped up on the pillows, when the vacant look on his fleshy face had suddenly vanished, to be filled with hatred.

"Whore!" he had said viciously. "Come here to gloat, have you? Well, I'm not dead yet . . . for all your trying!" He had looked ashen pale, his skin hanging from his jowls, his eyes sunken into the hollows of the sockets, his white hair still ridiculously luxuriant above the terrible face.

Then, just as suddenly, the moment of recognition had gone again. The doctor who had shown Beata in, and stayed with her to offer her what information he could, had been embarrassed for her.

"He doesn't mean it!" he had said hastily. "He's . . . delusional. I assure you, Lady York . . ."

But she had not been listening. Ingram meant it. She had been married to him for more than twenty years. This attack was not the wild break from his usual behavior that the doctor imagined.

Remembering, she shivered as the footman opened the front door for her and she stepped outside, but it was not from the bitter day with its promise of ice before nightfall; it was dread of what lay ahead.

Even now she thought of some way of evading her duty, but it was only an idea, something to play with in her mind. A walk in the park? A visit to a friend, to sit by the fire with tea and crumpets, and a little laughter in exchange for thoughts? Of course she wouldn't! She had stayed with Ingram all these years; she would not fail on these final days. It was a duty she would not fall short in.

The footman opened the carriage door. She accepted his hand to assist her up and help make her comfortable.

She wondered how many of the servants were quite aware of Mr. Justice York's temper tantrums, the vile names he called her at times. Perhaps they had even seen blood on the sheets, and sometimes on the towels as well. There were things that, if she thought of them, overwhelmed her. How could she calmly sit at the dining room table while the butler served her soup if she were to imagine for an instant that he knew how York had used her sexually, when the bedroom doors were locked?

It had begun within weeks of their wedding, at first only a matter of insistence, a certain roughness that had caused her pain. Gradually it had become grosser, more humiliating, and the verbal abuse coarser, the violence more unpredictable.

It had gone on, to one degree or another, for years. There had been times when for months there had been nothing, and she had dared hope her ordeal was over, even if it meant that he never touched her at all.

That was foolish, but in those times of respite he would be witty, so intelligent, and, in public at least, treat her with respect, as if the cruelty were an aberration. Then the darkness was all the greater when it returned.

Oliver Rathbone had been a guest the day it had finally ended. Ingram had completely lost all control and lashed out at Oliver with his cane. If he had struck him with it, it would have been a fearful blow. He could have even killed him, had it caught him on the temple. Thank heaven at that instant of rage Ingram had taken a fit of some kind and fallen insensible to the floor, quite literally foaming at the mouth.

He had still been deeply unconscious when the ambulance had

come for him and taken him to the hospital for diseases of the nervous system. It would have been merciful if he had sunk deeper into the coma and died. Unfortunately that had not happened. He had hovered on the edge of consciousness, with brief moments of lucidity, in the long months since then. It was over a year ago now.

Beata had been a widow in all senses but that of being free to marry again. She still bore his name, lived in his house, and dutifully forced herself to visit him when conscience drove her to it, or the doctor sent for her.

She stared out the window at the other carriages, ladies with fur collars and capes inside.

It was not a long journey but the route passed close to Regent's Park, and the bare trees were like tangled black lace. It would have been a good day for walking.

She looked away in time to see a carriage passing on the other side of the street. She met the woman passenger's eyes for an instant, and saw the warmth, and the familiar gesture with her hand. She just had time to smile back and nod agreement. Yes, she accepted the invitation. It would be something simple, and fun.

The journey passed all too quickly. She was already at the hospital. The footman climbed down with easy grace and held the door open for her. The cold air made her wish momentarily that she had brought furs, too. Then she remembered Ingram giving them to her one Christmas, and she thought she would rather be cold as she walked across the pavement and up the wide steps into the hospital entrance.

She was expected, and the doctor in charge was standing waiting for her. She had developed a reputation for promptness, and he stepped forward, smiling gravely, inclining his head in a slight bow. She was accustomed to it. She was the wife of one of the High Court's most respected judges. It was the convention that none of them acknowledged his altered state as irreversible.

"Good afternoon, Lady York," he said soberly. "I'm afraid the weather has turned much colder."

"Indeed," she replied, as if it mattered in the slightest to either of them. It was just easier to stick to the ritual than to have to think of something different to say.

"How is my husband?" She always said that also.

"I am afraid there has been a slight change," the doctor answered, turning to lead the way to the now-familiar room that, as far as she knew, Ingram had not left since he had first been carried there. "I'm very sorry . . . perhaps he will be in less distress." He forced a lift into his voice, as if it were of some cheer.

He could have no idea at all how deeply she wished Ingram dead. Not only for her sake, but for his own. She had never loved him, although once, years ago, she had imagined she did. But he had had a certain dignity, and such high intelligence then. She would not have wished on anybody what he suffered now, plunging from sanity to confusion, and climbing desperately back again. It was awful to watch. No hunger for revenge could make him deserve this.

They had reached his room, mercifully without any more meaningless conversation. The doctor opened the door for her and held it.

She took a deep breath, steadying herself, and went in.

As always, the smell was the first thing she noticed. It was a mixture of human body odors and the sharp, artificial cleanliness of lye and antiseptic. Everything was too white, too utilitarian.

Ingram was propped up on the pillows. At first glance nothing seemed any different, as if she had been here only yesterday, when in fact it was weeks ago.

Then as she came closer to the bed, she saw his eyes. They were hollower around the sockets than before, and cloudy, as if he could not see through them.

"Hello, Ingram," she said gently. "How are you?"

He did not reply. Had he not heard her? Looking at him, she was almost certain he was conscious. Could he see her?

She touched the thick-fingered white hand on the covers. She half expected it to be cold, but it was warmer than her own.

"How are you?" she repeated a little more loudly.

Suddenly his hand closed on hers, gripping her. She gasped, and for

an instant thought of pulling away. Then with immense effort she relaxed her arm and let it be.

"You look a little better," she lied. He looked terrible, as if something inside him had perished.

He was still staring at her with cloudy eyes. It was as if there were a
window between them, of frosted glass that neither of them could see
through.

"Come again, have you, Beata?" His voice was no more than a whisper, but the anger was there in it, almost a gloating. "Got to, haven't
you, as long as I'm still alive? And I am! You're not free yet. . . ."

"I know that, Ingram," she answered, staring at him. "And neither
are you." The moment the words were across her lips she regretted them.
It was her fault as well as his. How could she have been blind enough to
have married him all those years ago? No one had forced her. She had
been married before, for several years, and her first husband had died. It
had been time she chose again. She had seen what she wished to see, as
perhaps he had also. They were neither of them very young anymore.
Except that she had cared for him. He had never cared for her, or perhaps for anyone. It was advisable for his career that he be married. And
she brought with her a dowry, gathered for her by her friends, after her
father's disgrace. San Francisco was far enough away for word of that
not to have traveled here.

Ingram's face twisted very slightly. Was it an attempt at a smile, a
moment of warmth, even regret? Or was it a sneer because she was as
imprisoned as he was, at least for the moment? Perhaps that was why he
hung on to life, even like this—to keep her trapped as well.

She had something to make up for. She would give him the benefit
of the doubt, however small it was. She smiled back at him, and very
slightly increased the pressure of her fingers around his.

His hand closed tight, hurting her.

"Bitch!" he said distinctly, then seemed to choke on his own breath.
He gasped and the air rattled and caught in his throat. Then the grip
slackened a little on her hand, but not enough to let her go.

She turned to pull away, but she was not strong enough, and she was very aware of the doctor watching her, no doubt imagining some kind of devotion and grief. She must behave with decorum. She let her hand rest easily.

Ingram's nails bit into her hand. He was still strong enough to hurt her.

He opened his eyes again and stared at her, suddenly lucid.

"You liked it, didn't you?" he hissed. "I know you did, for all your sniveling. Whore! Cheap, dirty whore!"

She wanted to reply, to curse him back, but she would not do it with the doctor present. His pity was terrible, but his disgust would be worse. She kept her back to him as much as possible and forced herself to smile at Ingram.

She measured each word. "It seems it was all you could manage," she said deliberately. She could say it now, at last. He was helpless to beat her.

He understood—perfectly. His face suffused with rage and he tried to reach for her. His eyes bulged and he choked, gasped, and choked again, more deeply. His arms tried to thrash; his body went rigid and shook even more violently. He bit his tongue and his mouth drooled foam and blood.

Then just as suddenly it was over. He lay perfectly still and his hand slipped off hers at last.

She let out a sigh of relief and pulled away, gently, forcing herself not to flinch.

The doctor moved forward beside her. He put out his fingers and touched York's neck.

Beata looked at the cloudy eyes and knew that he saw nothing, not her, not the room. They were completely blind.

"Lady York," the doctor said quietly, "he is gone. I'm . . . I'm so sorry."

"Thank you," she said quietly. "You've been . . . very good."

"I'm so sorry," he said again. "It must be terrible for you. He was such a fine man."

The doctor stared at her, afraid she was going to become hysterical. She could have. He was so wildly wrong she wanted to laugh, long, crazily, on and on. Ingram was dead! She was free!

She must take hold of herself. This was disgraceful. She could not stand here beside a dead man . . . laughing.

She put her hands up over her face. The doctor must be made to think she was shocked, distraught, anything but desperately relieved. She covered her eyes with her fingers, and smelled the scent of his hands on her own. The antiseptic, medical smell made her stomach clench and for an instant she thought she was going to be sick.

She put her hands down again and forced herself to breathe deeply.

"Thank you, Doctor," she said calmly, her voice wavering only very slightly. "I am . . . I am quite well, thank you. If there is nothing that you require of me, I would like to go home. Of course I shall be at your disposal, should you . . ." She did not know how to finish. She had been preparing for this day for months, and now that it was here all the things she had thought to say flew out of her mind.

"Of course," he said gently. "No matter how one is prepared, it is always a great shock. Would you like to sit down in my office for a little while? I can send a nurse to be—"

"No, thank you," she said, cutting him off. "I will have a great many people to inform . . . and . . . I think a memorial service to consider. There will be . . . I must inform the lawyer . . . the Bar . . . his colleagues."

"Of course," he agreed. She heard the note of relief in his voice. He had many things to attend to himself. There was nothing more he could do for Ingram York. He must turn his mind to other patients.

She walked alone out of the hospital and found the footman waiting at the curb beside her carriage.

She did not meet his eyes; she did not want him to see her expression when she told him. Perhaps it was cowardly, but her own emotions were so mixed between relief and pity. He had been pitiful in the end, in spite of his last words. It was pitiful for the last thing that you say on earth to be dirty and degrading. There was also anger for all the years, and great relief, as if finally she had been able to take off a heavy garment that had weighed her down, at times almost frozen her movement altogether.

There was also a new freedom, wide, beautiful . . . frightening!

What would she do with it, now that she no longer had an excuse not to try for . . . anything she wanted? There was no one to stop her. No excuses . . . all mistakes would be her own fault. Ingram was gone.

The footman was waiting for her, still holding the door open.

"Sir Ingram has passed away," she told him. "Quite peacefully." That was a lie. She could still hear the hate in his voice.

There was a moment's silence.

She had not meant to look at the footman's face but she did so, and, the second before appropriate pity overtook it, she saw relief.

"I'm very sorry, my lady. Is there anything I can do for you?" There was concern for her in his voice.

"No, thank you, John," she said with a very slight smile. "There will be people to inform, letters and so on. I must begin to do so."

"Yes, my lady." He offered her his hand to steady her as she stepped up into the carriage.

She spent the time of the journey home thinking about what sort of service she should request for him. It was her decision. He had died in circumstances it would be preferable were not made public. She had told those who asked that he was in the hospital. She had allowed it to be presumed that he had had some kind of apoplectic fit, a stroke. No one she knew about had referred to the fact that he had lost his mind. Certainly Oliver Rathbone had told no one that York had attacked him, except possibly Monk.

Did people lie about the cause of a noted person's death? Or simply allow people to draw mistaken conclusions? Some people did die in embarrassing circumstances, such as in the wrong person's bed! This was at least in a hospital.

If he did not have a formal funeral it would raise speculation as to why not. He had been a very public man, a High Court judge of note. Everyone would expect it. She had no choice.

No one else knew what he was really like in his own home, when the doors were closed and the servants retired for the night. How could they? Did any decent person's thoughts even stretch to imagine such things? Certainly hers had not.

Beata wondered how many other women might have experienced the same fear, humiliation, and pain that she had—and told no one.

She imagined being gowned in black, modest and beautiful with her pale, gleaming hair, the perfect widow, exchanging quiet, sad condolences, and looking into the eyes of someone who knew exactly what he had done to her—and she had not fought back!

For a moment as the carriage swung around a corner and slid a little on the ice, she thought again that she was going to be sick.

EVENTUALLY IT WAS A very formal funeral, very somber, and within the shortest time that could be managed. Ingram had grown up on the south side of the Thames and had requested in his will to have his funeral held at St. Margaret's in Lee, on the outskirts of Blackheath. Edmond Halley, after whom a comet had been named, lay in the same graveyard. Ingram had mentioned that often. She would arrange that for him; it was the honorable thing to do. It was a relief to have it over as soon as possible, as it turned out, barely more than a week.

She had, of course, informed the few members of Ingram's family still alive, including his two sons from his previous marriage. It was a courtesy. He had not kept in touch with his relatives, nor they with him, and his sons had grown distant over the years. Still, she expected to see one or two, as a mark of respect if nothing else. Their neighbors would know.

The weather on the day of the funeral was pleasant and Beata arrived early at the splendid old church, built in the Gothic Revival style, with soaring towers reaching upward in solemn glory, and an ornate towering steeple. A few ancient trees softened the outlines and added to the beauty.

She was greeted by the minister and led to her seat inside. In other circumstances she would have taken more notice of the vaulted ceilings, great stone arches over the doors, and a rich array of stained-glass windows. The church smelled of age and reverence, as if the odor of prayer could be a tangible thing, like that of flowers long since dead. It should have been a comfort, and yet she struggled to find it so.

She was greeted coolly by Ingram's sons and his only other relative present, a brother-in-law, a widower himself. They said only what good manners required.

Of course, most of Ingram's colleagues, from his many years in the law, either came in person or sent handsome wreaths. Welcoming people, exchanging grave and courteous words of appreciation, Beata felt as if the long months since his collapse had disappeared. His complete loss of control had been very private. Most of the people who came appeared to have no idea that his breakdown had been anything other than physical. They remembered him from his days presiding over the court. It could have been yesterday.

She offered her black-gloved hand to one dignified couple after another, lords justices from the High Court, from Chancery, from all the legal establishments to which Ingram had belonged. She had met them at formal dinners, exchanged polite conversation, mostly listened.

"An excellent man. Such a loss to the justice system," Sir James Farquhar said quietly.

"Thank you," Beata acknowledged.

"My deepest condolences on your loss. A fine man. An ornament to the bench." Another senior judge gripped her hand for a moment before letting go.

"Thank you," she repeated. "You are very kind."

She noticed that the lord chancellor was not present, nor were one or two others she had liked.

She nodded each time as if she agreed, smiled gravely as though her grief held her from doing more than acknowledging their tributes. Her mind was racing, however, afraid to search their faces for honesty. They were saying all the right things, polite things, as they were expected to do, before they walked silently off to find their peers. How many of them believed any of it?

Did they believe what they wanted to? It was a lot easier than looking for the truth. They accepted that Ingram York was exactly what he appeared to be: a clever, articulate, occasionally irascible judge whose private life was unquestioned. Of course it was. His wife was above reproach. What on earth would make anyone wonder if there were more?

"Thank you," Beata continued to murmur politely. No one attempted conversation. She was supposed to be shocked, grieved. Surely everyone saw what they expected?

They gave generous tributes when they spoke of him from the pulpit. He was a good man, a pillar of society, a scholar, a gentleman, a fighter for justice for all.

Beata looked up from the congregation and listened to their solemn words, and wondered what they would have said if they were free to. Did any of them know him better?

After the service, the exquisite, soaring music, the words of comfort long familiar to everyone, even those who attended church only to be seen, Beata stood in the elaborate carved stone-arched doorway and accepted more tributes and condolences. Some of them were from men who were older than Ingram had been, struggling to stand upright. She was touched that they had made the effort to come. She wondered if their grief was for the fact of death itself, and perhaps for the family or friends they had lost. Their kindness was the one thing that made the tears prick her eyes.

It was then that she noticed for the first time a man and woman together, obviously husband and wife, who were startlingly familiar. She was amazed that she could possibly have overlooked them before. He was well above average height and one of the handsomest men she knew. He had always been so, even twenty years ago when they had first met thousands of miles away in San Francisco, in the early days of the gold rush. It had been another world: raw, violent, exciting, and set on the most beautiful of coastlines.

Aaron Clive, with his fine aquiline features and dark eyes, had drawn every woman's glance then, and he looked to have changed little. There was perhaps a hint of gray at his temples, and the softness of youth had been replaced with a greater strength. He had owned some of the richest of the goldfields on the entire coast, virtually a small empire.

And Miriam was beside him, as always. She was still beautiful in a way few women would ever be. The high cheekbones were the same, the rich mouth, the passion and the turbulence that arrested the eye. Her hair beneath her hat was the same shadowed chestnut with the gleaming lights in it as it had been then.

As far as Beata knew, they had not known Ingram, and yet they came forward now to offer comfort in her supposed grief, as if the years between had telescoped into as many weeks.

"Beata," Miriam said warmly. "I'm so sorry. You must miss him dreadfully." She met Beata's eyes more directly than anyone else had done, but that had always been her way. Her eyes were dark gray, so dark some people mistook them for brown.

"How kind of you to come," Beata replied with an answering smile. "It's wonderful to see you. It really is such a pleasure. I knew you were in London and had hoped to see you at some happier time."

That was true, not merely a politeness. When the three of them had first known one another, in what now seemed like another life, Miriam had been married to Piers Astley, her first husband. He had died tragically in the far reaches of one of Aaron Clive's goldfields. He had managed much of the vast empire for Aaron. They were wild days. Gold fever gripped a raw, adventurous town. Good men and bad came from every corner of the earth, drawn by the magic of instant, dreamlike wealth.

Beata had not known Piers Astley except to speak to on a few occasions, and regrettably death was far too common at sea, or up on the hills where life was hard and fortunes made and lost in days. But Miriam knew what it was to lose a husband, and her memories could only be painful.

The moment passed and Beata turned to Aaron. Here he was one of many, not unique in his looks and stature as he had been in San Francisco, but she was still startled by the magnetism he seemed to exercise. She was aware of others looking at him also, some perhaps trying to place him, to estimate what his power or position might be. They would try in vain.

Of course the women who were looking at him did so for different reasons: ones that had never needed explaining, and were as old as mankind.

Beata smiled at Aaron, remembering to keep her expression suitable for a woman receiving condolences at her husband's funeral. She must not forget that there would always be someone watching her.

"It is nice to see you again after so many years, even on such an occasion," she said graciously. "I very much appreciate your coming. I think Ingram would have been surprised at how many colleagues have come to speak well of him." That was also a total fiction. He would have expected everyone. Not Aaron Clive, of course, because he did not know him. Ingram had never been to San Francisco, or any other part of America. In fact, as far as she knew he had not traveled beyond the coast of Britain. He liked to be where he was known, and had earned his place, his respect, and where those in power recognized him. And, of course, where those without power were suitably afraid of him.

"I hope he would have been pleased," Aaron said in reply to her. He did not bother to gaze around. Did he already know most of these people? Probably not. He was simply too sophisticated to display his interest, or perhaps even to entertain it in the first place.

"And I'm sure quite touched," Beata replied with what she knew was the right sentiment. Perhaps Ingram would have been. She realized with sadness that she had very little idea of what he believed, or felt, behind the barrier of anger and self-defense. It had become habit, and over the last few years she had gradually ceased to care. It was a matter of keeping the bitterness to a minimum: overcivilized conversations with barbarity just below the surface.

Aaron was smiling at her. He had one hand very gently on Miriam's arm. It was a gesture of warmth, almost of protection. For a brief instant Beata envied Miriam. How could Miriam Clive, of all people, have the faintest idea what it was like to be married to a man you were frightened of, and yet whom you both pitied and were revolted by? She would be imagining Beata deep in grief, as she would have been for Aaron, almost stunned by loss. Whereas Beata was suddenly free, even if freedom was also daunting. No, challenging was the word.

"I hope that we shall see you again," Aaron was saying. "After your mourning, of course. We have been too long out of touch. Our fault, I'm afraid . . ."

"Perhaps something suitable before then?" Miriam suggested. "A walk in the park? An art gallery, or photographic exhibition? To be alone too much is . . . hard." There was warmth in her eyes, extraordinarily direct, as she had always been. Memories of other times and places flooded Beata's mind: a sharper sunlight, dry heat burning the skin, the sounds of horses, and wheels rattling over rougher, unpaved roads, salt in the wind.

Then it was gone again. She was standing at the church door, alone. Aaron and Miriam had moved on, speaking to other people. They were all drifting slowly toward the graveside. Some of the women chose not to go. The burial would be brief, and in a desperate, physical sense, final. Odd. Women gave birth, nursed the sick, and washed the dead and prepared them for burial; yet often it was not considered suitable that they should be at a graveside, as if they would be too emotionally fragile to behave with decorum.

Beata decided to wait here, at the church door, rather than pick her way through the somber beauty of the graveyard with its crosses and memorials.

Several other people passed her, the women going toward their carriages where they could wait seated, and in some warmth. Beata envied them, but it was right that she should wait here and speak to all those who came.

Then she saw Oliver Rathbone about thirty feet away. It was the late autumn light on his hair that she noticed first, and as he turned she recognized his face. She had thought he would come, but she had not searched for him. Now, as he took his leave of the man he had been talking with, and started to walk toward her, she found herself suddenly short of breath. They knew each other so well—at least in some ways. It was Ingram who had been responsible for giving Rathbone the case that had brought him down, so soon after he had been made a judge himself. Had Ingram known that the circumstances would tempt

Oliver to take the law into his own hands, and so bring about his disbarment?

She remembered flashes of conversation, but above all the look in Ingram's eyes. Yes . . . yes, he knew, and had intended it to happen exactly as it had.

Rathbone had been perhaps the most brilliant lawyer in London, even in England. He was articulate, witty, and unconventional. He dared to take cases others might have avoided. He won even when it had seemed impossible. He was elevated to the bench. And he was in love with Ingram York's wife. Nothing had ever been said, but she knew it.

And Ingram knew it! It was probably that which had provoked his complete loss of control, and the apoplectic fit that had resulted in his being taken to the hospital, paralyzed, and half out of his wits. Beata had been in limbo since then. But now that Ingram was dead, after a suitable period of mourning, she and Rathbone would be free to . . . what? Marry? Of course! He would ask her. Obliquely he had said as much. At least she thought he had.

But now that they were both free, the reality of the situation might make their feelings different. When things were only dreams, they were so very much safer.

Rathbone had had an unhappy marriage. Ingram had at least created the situation that had ended it—unintentionally, of course. Margaret Rathbone had left Oliver before then, when he had earlier on defended her father the best he could, but failed to save him from conviction for murder. Margaret believed her father innocent, in spite of damning evidence, and blamed Rathbone for his death. Rathbone's open disgrace and disbarment had given Margaret the social excuse to sue him for divorce, which he had not contested.

He was in front of Beata now, slender, elegantly dressed as always, and suitably in black for the funeral of an eminent judge. He was possibly the only person who knew how Ingram had really died, isolated in the horror of his own mind.

"Please accept my sympathies, Lady York," Rathbone said gravely.

His eyes met hers, searching to know how she was, to give her support and a warmth he could not show. "It must be a very difficult day for you."

"Thank you, Sir Oliver," she replied. "Everyone has been very generous. It is something to be grateful for." She had imagined this meeting, when Ingram was gone and it was the beginning of the future. She had thought it would be easier. She was a very accomplished woman, gracious with everyone, able to wear a mask of dignity—and, more than that, charm—no matter how she felt inside. In fact, she was certain that her composure had never slipped. If it had, someone would have commented, and sooner or later it would have come back to her.

With Rathbone, she had always been in control, beautiful in her own way, unattainable to him. Why on earth was she stumbling inside now, and so afraid? Please heaven, people would put it down to the occasion. Ingram's death had been expected for more than a year, yet the reality of it was different. There was no surprise, but still there was shock, a kind of numbness.

"He was greatly respected," Rathbone was saying.

Was he respected? Or did at least some of his colleagues know what he was really like? Did he tell stories about what he had done to her? Men did—some men. She was not completely naïve.

Rathbone was looking at her, waiting for her to answer, however meaninglessly. Had *he* heard stories? The blood flamed up her face, as hot as fire.

"I . . . I believe so," she said abruptly. "But people are generous at such times. . . ."

Now Rathbone smiled. "Of course they are," he agreed wryly. "Either they thought well of him, or they are secretly highly relieved that he has gone." He gave the slightest shrug. "Or else, of course, they have the deepest respect for you, and would go to considerable lengths to offer you whatever comfort or support they can. Why would any of us speak ill of him now? It cannot harm him, and it would be an unforgivable rudeness to you."

"Is that why you are here, Oliver? To offer support for . . ." She had been going to say "a man you despise," but that would be appalling . . .

and pathetic! Tears stung her eyes. She was behaving like a fool. Was she in love with Oliver Rathbone? Yes. Yes, she was. This waiting, this pretense was ridiculous, and yet now that the time was here, or almost here, her heart was pounding and her mouth was dry. She should be quiet, or she would end up embarrassing them both. She had so much to conceal, at least for now.

"Of course," he answered. "This must be very hard for you. You look so perfectly composed, but you cannot be finding it easy."

She made a very slight gesture with her black-gloved hands. "It's necessary."

Lord Justice Savidge approached. He was alone, and she remembered that he was a widower of a few years.

"Please accept my condolences, Lady York," he said gravely. "Good morning, Sir Oliver." He glanced at Rathbone with mild interest. He had to be aware of at least some of the history between Rathbone and York, but if he was curious, he kept it from his expression.

"Thank you, my lord," she replied. "I am grateful that he is not suffering anymore." Perhaps she should have said that she missed him, but it was a lie she could not speak.

A flicker of acute perception crossed Savidge's face and she knew that Rathbone saw it as well. Did they know what Ingram had been like? Had they swapped stories over brandy at one of their clubs? The thought was unbearable. She lifted her chin a little.

"Were I in his place, it is what I would wish," she added.

"You would never be in his place," Rathbone said instantly. He seldom spoke without thinking, but in this occasion he had, and the knowledge of it was in his eyes immediately.

Savidge looked at him, then at Beata, his brows just a fraction higher.

"I think we would all prefer to go quickly," she said, filling in the silence, glancing from one to the other of them.

"I hope it will not be for many years, Lady York," Savidge responded. "But we shall miss Ingram, both personally and professionally."

"Thank you, my lord." She allowed her tone to suggest that the conversation could come to a close.

"I'm sorry," Rathbone said as soon as Savidge was out of earshot. "I get so tired of polite nothings I forget who knows anything close to the truth, and who does not."

"As far as Lord Justice Savidge is concerned, I look straight into his face, and I still have no idea," she told him. "Do you think anyone . . . ?" Then she changed her mind. It was unfair to ask him. What would he say if in fact Ingram had spoken of her disparagingly? But surely he would not wish his colleagues to hear him use the kind of language he had used to her, at his worst times? The explicit vulgarity of it made her cringe. Why had she never found the courage to fight back, to threaten to expose him, or even to leave him?

But then who would believe it of him? That is what he had said to her. He had taunted her with it. Such filthy language, such ideas! Who would have thought a beautiful woman, so calm and dignified on the outside, would ever have submitted herself to such bordello practices?

"Beata?" Rathbone said anxiously. He put out his hand and took her arm, holding her strongly. "Are you all right? You look very pale. Perhaps you have done enough, and it would now be perfectly acceptable for you to go home. It must have been a great strain. . . ."

Not in the way he imagined. "No, thank you, Oliver," she said gently, but not pulling away from his grip. She liked the warmth of it, the strength. "It is my duty, and I will feel better if I complete it. It won't be more than another few minutes." She glanced to where she could just see, beyond the trees, the group of solemn figures beside the grave, heads bowed, men with hats in their hands, wind ruffling their hair. "I think they are very nearly finished."

"Then you have done all you need to," he reassured. "I'll take you as far as your carriage. Come." He put his other hand over hers and she had little courteous choice but to go with him. She was actually pleased to be looked after, and she realized just how cold she had grown standing still.

"Are you all right alone?" he asked with some concern. "Is there someone who can be with you for a while? A relative, or a friend?"

"Thank you, but I will be quite happy alone. The hardest thing was listening to all those tributes, and wondering what they would have said if they were honest," she admitted. She avoided meeting his eyes.

"They're mostly lawyers, my dear," he replied, turning the corner on the path. "They are used to putting up a convincing argument for whoever they represent."

She wanted to laugh, but if she did someone might see her, and no decent woman laughed at her husband's funeral, no matter what she felt. And it would be too easy to end up sounding a trifle hysterical.

They passed Aaron and Miriam Clive, walking along a path almost parallel to theirs. They were close together; he was leaning toward her, listening to what she was saying. Again, for a moment Beata envied her. She had not really known Miriam's first husband, and Miriam had spent almost all her adult life with Aaron. He was clearly still as much in love with her as he had been in the beginning. What was it like to be so loved, so admired? So—so safe!

She wanted to be safe with Oliver Rathbone. But did he see her as a calmer woman than Margaret had been, gentler with him, even loyal? Had he even the faintest idea of the turbulence inside her, the woman she was, and the woman she wanted to be? Would he despise her, if he knew what she had permitted Ingram York to do to her, without fighting tooth and nail to stop him? Was she wise, obedient, loyal . . . or just a coward? Perhaps Oliver would understand and sympathize, but still be revolted by the picture the words would paint in his imagination. The thought that it would stain her forever in his mind—even in reality—was unbearable.

Rathbone had both prosecuted and defended some vile cases. He must be familiar with the dregs of life, the ugliest and the most brutal. But words about cases, professional matters, were nothing like the actuality, and letting it into your own home.

Many men were outraged that a woman should be raped. They had fury for the perpetrator and pity for the victim. Yet when their own women were assaulted, they felt them to be soiled, even ruined. It was a strange, complex, and yet bone-deep passion.

Of course, as Ingram had reminded her many times, you could not rape your wife. She was yours to do with as you pleased. You could kill her spirit, as long as you left her body breathing. The injuries he had left her with had no visible marks.

But Oliver never needed to know. She was being foolish even to remember it now. Ingram was dead. He was lying in a nailed-up coffin under the earth, a couple of hundred yards away, beyond the yew trees.

"Thank you," she said gently to Rathbone. "But it would not be taken kindly by everyone, even if those we care about know that you are merely being courteous. I am quite able to ride home, and my maid will look after me. The fires will be burning and all will be warm. I think no one will disturb me with any more condolences for several days." She smiled at him, and meant it. She was in control of herself again, at least for now.

"Are you certain?" They were standing at the roadside by her carriage. The footman held the door for her.

"Yes, thank you. I hope you will feel free to call at a later date, when there will be no shadow on your reputation."

"Of course," he agreed. "I mean to do this well." He looked at her for a moment longer, and she saw the warmth in his eyes, and knew exactly what he meant.

She swallowed hard. "Thank you, Oliver." She wanted to think of something else to say, but there was nothing that could not be misread.

Another carriage passed them, and through the window she saw Miriam Clive. For a moment their glances met, then the Clives' carriage passed, and Beata accepted the footman's hand and climbed into her own, leaving Rathbone on the path, watching her until she was out of sight.

3

Mᴏɴᴋ ᴀɴᴅ Hᴏᴏᴘᴇʀ ᴡᴇʀᴇ on the river on one of those unusual November days when the sky was almost cloudless and there were moments when it seemed as if the river were made of gray glass. Not a breath of wind stirred the surface. The only movement was the occasional wash of a boat going up or downstream, all but silently. The voices of lightermen calling to one another echoed, and the splash of an oar could be heard.

Now and then a water bird dived for a fish. It broke the smooth surface almost without sound, and then came up victorious. It was an hour short of high tide. Soon the river would brim its banks. An hour after that it would turn.

They rowed randan, that is, holding only one oar each, on two separate seats, one slightly in front of the other. It was swift, maneuverable, and when rowers were well matched they could keep up the pace for hours.

Hooper was a good partner and now that his injuries from the battle on the gun smugglers' ship were almost healed, he was extremely strong. It was a challenge to keep up with him, but one that Monk enjoyed. They were returning from the successful solution to a robbery.

"Hear any more about the drowned man?" Hooper asked curiously. "The one that was shot."

"No. I've got Laker on it," Monk replied. "But whatever happened to Blount, it's probably to do with smuggling, or even someone he rubbed the wrong way before he was caught. I daresay it was to keep him quiet, in case he talked to Customs." He smiled bleakly. "Anyone with knowledge of smuggling is McNab's problem, not mine."

"Right," Hooper agreed. Monk could not see his face because they both rowed facing the stern so all he could see was Hooper's back. But he heard the pleasure in his voice, and he shared it.

Five minutes later they pulled in at the steps up to the Wapping Police Station and saw Laker standing on the dockside, clearly waiting for them. He came down the steps easily, the sun gleaming on his fair hair. He was in his late twenties, overly sure of himself, graceful, quick-witted, and definitely a touch arrogant. Monk had seen the more vulnerable side of him only once, during the gun battle on the smugglers' ship. But it was a part of the man he had not forgotten, and it was the reason he had not disciplined him harder.

"Sir!" Laker said as Monk shipped his oar and stood up.

"What is it?"

"Another escaped prisoner, sir." Laker's handsome face lit with a smile of pure pleasure. "Customs again. This one had just been convicted. Sentence came down this morning. He escaped when he was being transferred into the wagon to go back to prison."

"What's it got to do with Customs?" Monk stepped out of the boat onto the flight of stone steps up to the dockside. Hooper came on the other side and tied the boat.

"One of their convictions, sir. Bad bastard, by the name of Silas Owen."

"Owen?" The name caught Monk's attention immediately. "Isn't he an explosives man? Got caught with gelignite?"

They reached the top of the steps and stood in the sun.

"Yes, sir. They were pretty lucky to convict him," Laker replied. "He's a demolition expert and has done a lot of regular professional work: tunnels, bringing down old buildings, and the like. But he's skipped it this time."

"Any reason to think he's coming our way?" Monk felt a spark of interest, but it was far more likely that the regular police would catch him. He would go inland or maybe across the flat stretches around the Estuary, and hope to get a lift on some sort of barge or collier going north.

Laker looked pleased with himself. "Well, yes, there is, sir. Sort of. Bit of information I got from a snitch downriver from here. Said he thought Owen might make for France, but not the way you'd expect, which would be the first boat down to the Estuary that he could get, then something going across the Channel from there. That's where everybody else'll be looking for him, I reckon. But apparently there's a schooner moored well upriver, sir. Fast two-master. Clean cut, oceangoing. We haven't got much that could keep up with something like that, especially not in the hands of a good sailor."

"And where is this schooner moored, then?" Monk asked.

"Thought you might want to know that." Laker smiled with satisfaction. "Just beyond Millbank, sir. He'll have to go a roundabout way to get there. South bank, just about under the Vauxhall Bridge."

"Skelmer's Wharf." Monk jumped to the conclusion. He knew the place. For a small fee, an oceangoing two-master could well lie there without causing comment. And nobody would be looking for it. Clever. "Any reason to think it's that one, Laker?" he asked.

Laker bit his lip. "Informant of mine. Thing is, the customs men know it, too. It's not for sure, but if we get to Skelmer's Wharf now, we could be there before them. They don't know that stretch of the river. Too far up for them to be there regularly. You could cross over on London Bridge, sir. . . ."

"Right! Then get us a fast, light hansom, and—"

"Got one, sir. Just waiting . . ." Laker increased his pace as they followed him across the open stretch of the dock. Instead of going into the police station, they kept on with even longer strides toward where a hansom was waiting at the curb, the horse sensing the excitement and moving restlessly.

Hooper was on their heels and swung up into the cab, making room for Monk.

"Thank you, Laker. Good job," Monk said, then gave the driver instructions to find the fastest way, generously offering him an extra couple of shillings if he got there within thirty minutes.

"Forty, if the traffic's right," the cabbie agreed. "Over London Bridge should be right at this hour. 'Ang on, gents!"

They leaned back and Monk settled in for a long and fast drive. It was their only chance of catching Owen, even if Laker was right, and if they really had as good a start on Owen as they thought. But Skelmer's Wharf was a good guess. It was a sheltered mooring where even a large oceangoing schooner would not be remarked on. At this hour there would be few people about: mostly workmen, shipwrights and carpenters, possibly a few dockers, but all well involved in their own labor.

A man coming or going, perhaps with a fishing rod and a few sandwiches for lunch, would not seem strange to anyone. His having a friend who turned up in a rowboat was to be expected. It would be a good day on the river, even if they caught nothing. Fishing, the odd pleasant conversation, a couple of pasties and a few bottles of ale, well wrapped up, a fine day, even if cold. Nothing unusual about that.

They had arrested men there before, not fugitives from the law so much as from being asked a few very inconvenient questions.

Neither Monk nor Hooper spoke. Monk was thinking that it would be a nice score against McNab if they managed to catch his man for him. That was two escapees in the space of a week. He would not forget the malice in McNab's face as he had stood over the body of Blount watching Monk turn him over to reveal the bullet wound in the man's back.

They crossed the river at London Bridge and the cab picked up speed along a stretch where the traffic was light. The driver was really taking Monk at his word. He was going to have to pay the extra fare he had promised. They cut inland then joined the river again along the Albert Embankment.

Another few minutes and they crossed the Vauxhall Bridge and swung in beside the dock and the open stretch of water. There was an old man sitting on the wharf with a fishing line dangling over the edge. It was a bright, windless morning and there was barely a ripple on the flat surface of the river. The grim mass of Millbank Prison towered above like a fortress, casting its shadow. Nothing on the river moved.

The two-masted schooner anchored in the lee was reflected on the river as if in a mirror. It looked fast and sleek, perfectly balanced, ocean-going. A flash of admiration crossed Monk's mind, before he alighted and paid the driver, including the extra he had promised.

The driver glanced at the money, estimated it, and put it in his pocket.

"Want me ter wait for yer, sir?" he asked hopefully.

"No, thanks," Monk replied, fearing that he might regret the decision. However, if he had guessed correctly from what Laker had been told, then this was where Owen would be making for. Perhaps it was something as inconspicuous as a string of barges, heavy laden and covered in canvas tarpaulins under which he could hide. He could disappear in some dock unloading the cargo farther downriver. A change of clothes, and he would look like any other docker or waterman. But more likely it was the beautiful schooner he was making for, and the open sea. Either way, the presence of a waiting hansom would give away the possibility of the police, or anyone else, watching.

"Sure?" the driver asked.

"Quite sure," Monk replied. "There could be trouble. That's a good horse. Get her out of here before it starts."

The cabbie's face changed. "Right y'are, sir." Without another word he urged the horse on and within minutes they were out of sight.

Monk looked around. It was pretty open: just the wharf itself, a couple of old bollards for mooring, and some rickety steps down to the water, which were half-submerged now with a high tide just about to turn.

On the bank there were deserted boat sheds. The nearest one had a workshop attached, the door hanging by a broken padlock. Farther along were two benches, the warehouses, and slipways for taking boats down to the water's edge. A hundred yards farther the huge bulk of the brewery and more workshops. This was the only wharf for half a mile or more.

Monk looked at Hooper. At a glance he appeared like any other workingman along the river. His trousers were well worn, his heavy pea jacket like anyone else's, and he had an old blue waterman's cap on his head. It was Monk himself who stood out. His trousers were well cut, his pea jacket new. He was bareheaded, and his hair barbered with some skill.

He could not take his coat off; a man in crisp white shirtsleeves would attract attention on a November morning.

"You stay here," he ordered. "I'll get in that workshop; the door won't take any effort to break. Just keep down." No explanation was necessary.

Hooper nodded, then walked slowly over to the river's edge, as if he was contemplating something.

Monk went to the broken door and gave the lock a sharp blow. It fell off and he was able to go just inside but stop where he could observe, without being seen from the path.

The fisherman took no notice of either of them. Possibly he was asleep.

Ten minutes went by in which two barges went upriver with no sound except the splash of their wash against the uprights of the wharf, and then a tiny ripple on the bank. A rowboat passed the other way, a young man pulling hard on the oars, looking as if he were enjoying the speed and the sense of power. It was slack water, but the tide would turn any minute.

The fisherman stood up and walked away.

The minutes dragged on.

Monk moved restlessly from one foot to the other. Hooper had gone out of sight down the bank.

Then suddenly a man appeared, small and slight, running from the direction of the road, straight toward the wharf in a purposeful fashion.

Just as Monk came out of the work shed, a second man appeared. He was taller, bearded, and heavyset, coming from the left.

Hooper rose up from the bank just as the two men collided hard and staggered to keep their balance.

A single barge came from the west, heavy laden, low in the water, its cargo masked by a tarpaulin.

The smaller man lashed out at the larger, striking him a quick, hard blow on the jaw as if he knew how to fight. The big man staggered, but regained his balance, swinging wildly and missing altogether.

Hooper moved toward them as the smaller man struck again. This time, he connected only with a shoulder, and they both lurched sideways, kicking and punching.

The barge was closer, the lighterman with the oar standing motionless.

Monk reached the fighting men and made a grab for the larger one as he swayed closer to him. He caught one arm, and swung the man round, off balance.

Hooper reached the smaller man and held him back, pinning his arms behind him.

The larger man let out a bellow of rage and kicked hard. Monk moved just enough to avoid being struck, and allowed the man's impetus to carry him further off balance.

They both swayed back and forth, striking and evading. Monk caught one or two blows, but mostly they glanced off his arms or shoulders. He would have bruises. He landed a few of his own, but the man seemed to be built of rock.

The other man caught Hooper where he had been wounded, and he staggered back. The man slithered away like an eel, Hooper after him, but holding his wounded arm slack, as if the pain had robbed him of its use.

Monk's inattention cost him a hard blow to the chest, momentarily knocking the wind out of him. If he were not more careful the man would escape. It was only a few yards to the barge in the river.

Except that, as he turned to lash out at the big man, he saw the barge begin to move away again, the lighterman leaning on the oar and turning it with the customary grace of his kind.

There was a loud splash as the small man fell into the water. Monk stared. Hooper had also disappeared.

The big man roared a string of abuse at Monk and broke away to charge over to the far side of the wharf.

Monk lunged after him, throwing himself at the man's back and bringing them both down hard, sprawling across the wooden planks of the wharf, rolling and kicking, each trying to punch the other, and avoid being hit.

Even above the breathlessness and the curses, Monk could hear Hooper and the other man thrashing about in the water. He concentrated on what he was doing. Hooper could swim, but with the weakened arm he would be at a disadvantage.

Monk feinted at the big man, then altered his aim, half-turned, and struck him hard on the side of the head with his elbow.

For an instant the big man went slack, allowing Monk the chance to scramble to his feet and regain his balance. He rushed to the side of the wharf where Hooper was floundering and the small man came to the surface, momentarily dazed, gasping for air.

Then the big man was on his feet. He gave a roar of fury, put his head down, and charged at Monk, bellowing all the way.

Monk waited until the last possible moment, then sidestepped. He felt the turbulence of air as the man passed him, missed his step, and went crashing over the side and down into the water.

The wave of his wash caught Hooper in the face and went right over the smaller man's head.

The barge was now more than a hundred yards away, and increasing the distance.

The big man came to the surface, arms thrashing, sending water all over the place. He clearly had no idea how to swim, and the river was far too deep for him to reach the bottom with his feet. Even if he could have, it would be only soft, sucking river mud.

Hooper moved slowly toward the small man, who also seemed to be in trouble. He was coughing and spluttering as if he could not fill his lungs. Judging from the way he had attacked the other man, he was the policeman, and the big man the fugitive.

"Help him!" Monk shouted to Hooper, waving his arm at the small man. He could not leave him to drown. More important to Monk, he could not send the vulnerable Hooper after the big man, who was now going under the water for a second time, his mouth open, his face distorted with terror.

Monk took off his pea coat and leaped into the river. The water hit him like a wall of ice and, with a shock of fear, he felt it close over him momentarily, almost paralyzing him.

He came to the surface gasping, and struck out toward the big man, now struggling desperately about seven or eight feet away from him. By the time Monk reached the spot, the man was below the surface. Monk dived down after him and managed to catch hold of his arm. He came up for air, heaving the man as much as he could, but he was heavy, a leaden weight.

He gasped, saw Hooper a few yards away, and then the big man came to the surface behind him and the next moment he was held tight and hard in an arm grip. For an instant he thought the man was trying to strangle him, then he realized it was the panic of someone who knew he was drowning.

"Let go!" Monk shouted at him. "Let go, you fool! And I'll help you!"

The man's grip eased for a moment as he gulped for air and took in water. He choked and his arm closed like a vise around Monk's neck. Another moment and he would take Monk down with him.

Monk used his elbow again, then as the grip eased, he turned round and hit the man on the side of the head, as hard as he could.

The man went limp, and at last Monk was able to get hold of him and keep his head above the water as he struggled to make his way back to the wharf steps, where he could drag him up onto the boards.

But the man was deadweight, and he kept slipping. Monk was freezing cold and losing his strength to keep them both afloat. He was dimly aware of other voices now. He thought they came from the wharf, but he was still six or seven yards from it, and making no headway.

Then Hooper was there, helping, holding the man up by the other arm.

It still took them several more minutes to get the big man's inert body to the steps and feel more hands reach forward and help to haul them up.

Monk clambered out of the water and the cold air hit him like a blow, making him stagger before regaining his balance. Hooper came right after him, white-faced and shaking.

Monk stared at the workman who had helped him. He looked like a docker or laborer of some sort, as did the other man beside him, giving Hooper a hand up the last step. Where on earth had they come from? And where was the smaller man Hooper had gone in to save? Surely not drowned!

"How . . . ?"

The first man smiled and shook his head. "Lighterman told us," he replied. "Good thing, too. Better get you wrapped up." He signaled to his companion. "Bert, pass us that coat, eh?"

Bert obliged, handing over Monk's own pea coat, and a rough jacket for Hooper, whose coat was soaking. He had had no opportunity to take it off before he went in after the small man.

Monk turned to look for him properly now.

Hooper must have thought of it at the same moment, because he swiveled round and went to the top step again.

Then they both saw him, sixty yards away and swimming toward the schooner moored at the far side. They could see quite clearly a figure on the deck, letting down a knotted rope for him to climb.

The man reached the schooner, no doubt exhausted and half numb with cold, but alive. Had it not been slack tide with barely any current, he would have had no chance.

Monk breathed a sigh of relief as he saw the swimmer clasp on to the rope and the man on the deck begin to haul him up. He did not wait to see the rest.

Hooper also went back to the big man lying on the wharf, barely moving. One of the dockers, Bert, was doing what they could for him, but to little effect. His friend had disappeared.

"There's a doctor not far from 'ere," Bert told Monk, explaining his workmate's absence. "Good feller, won't ask no money if yer in't got it. This feller 'ere looks real bad. Reckon 'e must 'ave swallowed 'alf the river. Stupid sod." He said it with disgust, but also some pity.

Monk's sense of pity was for the whole wasted life of a man who turned to smuggling, was convicted, and escaped from custody only to die of his own panic in the water. He was powerfully built. Monk had felt some of his strength when he had tried to rescue him. If he had not succeeded in knocking him out, the man would have drowned both of them. Oddly enough, very few men who worked on the water, either the river or at sea, could swim. Sailors who spent their whole lives on the oceans could not swim, nor could dockers, ferrymen, bargees, or for that matter, most of the River Police. The water was both life and death.

Was it courage that sustained them, or ignorance, or the blind belief in their own immortality?

Monk went over to the man still lying motionless on the wooden planks of the wharf. What was visible of his skin was white.

"Is he breathing?" he asked Bert.

Bert shook his head minutely. "Think so. 'Ard ter tell. Could be foxing, like. Any moment 'e'll get up, 'it someone, an' be off again."

Monk kneeled down and touched the cold, wet skin. "I don't think so," he answered grimly. He moved his hand to the man's neck. He felt what he thought was a faint pulse. "Hope that doctor comes soon . . ."

He looked up as a shadow crossed him and he was aware of another presence.

"Can I help?" the new man asked quietly. He was tall, remarkably handsome with a refined, aquiline face and dark eyes. "My name's Aaron Clive. That's my warehouse just behind you down the river." He looked at the docker. "Bert, did you send for a doctor for this man?"

"Yes, Mr. Clive, sir. Local one, pretty close."

Clive nodded, then turned back to Monk, waiting for him to introduce himself. There was a calm in him, an air of authority he held without effort.

Monk stood up. He was still horribly cold under his dry pea coat. "Monk," he responded. "Commander of the Thames River Police. How do you do, Mr. Clive?"

"Who is he?" Clive asked, looking at the man at their feet.

"Escaped custody on his way to prison," Monk replied. "The customs or policeman chasing him made it as far as the schooner over there." He inclined his head without looking at the ship still at anchor.

"Stupid devil," Clive responded. "Still, I suppose we'd better do what we can for him." He turned to look downriver toward his own warehouse and saw a man and a lanky boy of fifteen or sixteen now running along the water's edge toward them. The man carried a black bag. There was no need to comment; it was obviously the doctor Bert had had his colleague send for.

Monk followed his gaze and recognized the boy immediately. He would have known him anywhere. It was Scuff, the riverside orphan who had adopted him and Hester several years ago when he was thin, undersize, hungry, and streetwise, guessing himself to be eleven, which was probably an overestimate. Which meant that the lean, black-haired, and long-legged man wearing black was Crow, to whom Scuff had, at his own insistence, become apprenticed. The name Crow was both the slang term for doctor, and a reasonably accurate description of his appearance.

They arrived, breathless, and Crow instantly kneeled down beside the big man on the wharf. He acknowledged the others only with a brief look to make sure they were not hurt. With expert hands he felt for a pulse in the man's neck, then under his nose to sense for any breath at all.

Then, with Scuff's assistance, which was more practiced than Monk would have expected, they turned the man over on his face, with his head to one side, and began with considerable pressure to try to force the water out of his lungs. The strokes were even and rhythmic. A little water dribbled from his mouth. Crow stopped for a moment and looked at him hopefully. The eyelids fluttered. Crow began again, moving easily, putting his weight behind it. He was a tall man, Monk's height, and his face reflected his emotions like a glass.

Scuff crouched beside him, watching intently, ready to help the moment he was asked.

No one spoke.

Finally Crow gave up and sat back on his haunches.

"Sorry," he said quietly. "He's gone. The cold and too much water. What happened?" He looked at Monk, not Clive.

Monk should not have been surprised, and yet the fact that he had struggled to save the man and felt the violent, surging life in him, made his death shocking, even though he was a fugitive from the law.

Monk cleared his throat. "He is an escaped prisoner. The policeman or customs officer chasing him caught up with him here on the dockside. The policeman tried to take him down. Hooper and I attempted to separate them but there was a struggle between us and each of them and they both went into the water. Hooper went in with the policeman, and I went in after this man. Hooper kept the policeman up long enough, but it looked as if he could swim pretty well. Slack tide, so the current didn't carry him down. This one panicked. Thrashing around all over the place. I tried to get him out." Monk realized only now how hard the man had hit back. His head was still ringing from the blows.

"Did you have to strike him?" Crow asked, as if it were the most ordinary question. Perhaps it was.

"Yes . . . a couple of times. Or he'd have drowned us both."

"Happens quite often," Crow said bleakly. "Our own worst enemy. There isn't anything I can do to help him. He drowned, but it was his panic that killed him." He climbed to his feet and looked at Monk with some pity. They had known each other for many years, and more than once faced desperate situations together. "Sorry," he added. Then he turned to Scuff and put one arm around his shoulder. He did not say anything. Scuff wanted to be a doctor. He would have to get used to death, and Crow would not embarrass him by treating him as a child.

Scuff stood a little straighter, his chin up, and stared for a long moment at Monk, then gave a half smile.

"Sorry, sir," he said with barely a tremor in his voice. "There in't nothing more as we can do for 'im." His grammar slipped back to his old mudlark days in moments of tension and all Hester's schooling of him vanished.

Monk wished he could protect Scuff from this, but he knew better. "Had to try," he said gravely. "Thank you for coming."

Crow seemed to be on the edge of a smile, but kept it from showing. "And the other man, the policeman?" he asked.

"He made it to the schooner over there," Monk answered. "He got out up the rope, so I daresay the skipper, if that's who it was on deck, will give him a stiff tot of rum and some dry clothes, then set him off somewhere."

"What schooner?" Crow looked puzzled.

Monk turned round to point it out, and saw only an empty stretch of water where the tide had turned and was beginning to ebb. The ship's leaving had been fast, and silent. Or perhaps on the wharf they had been so absorbed in trying to save the big man that they had heard nothing anyway.

"Maybe he took him downriver to the nearest doctor," Clive suggested. "Or if he was all right, to anywhere that he could go ashore and make it back to his station. He'll be spitting fire at having lost his man. You'll have to tell the police that he's dead. That'll be some comfort." He smiled and offered Monk his hand. There was a warmth to the gesture, even in this miserable circumstance.

Monk took it and held it hard for a moment before thanking him and letting go.

He and Hooper walked back toward the road. They would have to inform whoever was pursuing the prisoner that he was dead. Presumably they would want the corpse just the same. Somebody had to bury him. It was certainly not Crow's responsibility, or Clive's.

As they reached the street they saw a hansom coming toward them at a brisk pace. As it pulled up, two uniformed police got out and started across the pavement toward them. On seeing that Monk and Hooper were sodden wet, apart from Monk's coat, they stopped abruptly. The elder of the two looked Monk up and down.

"You seen two men come this way? One big, bearded fellow following an older, smaller one?"

"You're after the escaped prisoner," Monk concluded. "River Police. We were here when they appeared. The prisoner's dead. I'm sorry. The two of them were fighting and eventually went into the water. We tried to get them out, but the prisoner panicked. We couldn't save him. Your man got away. He's one hell of a survivor. It was slack tide so there was no current to battle. He made it to the far side and was helped up onto a schooner moored there." Monk gestured toward the now-empty mooring. "It pulled up anchor and went. Tide was just past the turn, so I expect they went downstream. No doubt he'll have got off at the first wharf where he could get dry clothes, and medical help if he needed it."

The older man stared at him, his face white.

"God damn it! Pettifer couldn't swim to save his soul! Terrified of the water, for all he was Customs."

Monk felt his stomach churn. "Pettifer? A small, thin man, but strong?"

"Hell, no! A big bloke, built like an ox, and a beard . . ." The man closed his eyes. "Don't say he's dead, and that bastard Owen got away. Please don't say that!"

The other man behind him blasphemed. "McNab'll kill us! Pettifer was one of his!"

"Never mind that!" the elder retorted, glaring at him. "Owen got clean away. He'll no more stop now than fly in the air! He'll get another ship and be in France by tomorrow. That's the second one they've lost in a week. First Blount, and now Owen. He's not going to take the blame for both of them!"

"If I know 'im," his companion retorted, "he won't take the blame for either!" He looked at Monk. "The first one evaded us with an elaborate escape plan, though someone got 'im in the end—this one'll be down to you!"

4

Monk felt totally wretched about the whole affair. He had set out with the hope of catching Owen before McNab got to him, although perhaps not for the best of reasons. He had thought he might learn something about the escape, or a whole series of events that might be connected. First there was the escape of Blount, and what seemed to be his murder, and then the escape of Owen, within a few days of each other. Perhaps they were part of some organized plan. At a glance the events looked fortuitous, but were they? They were both connected to Customs. Monk was still certain that the gunrunners who had brought about the battle on the decks of their ship, which had cost Orme his life, had been tipped off about Monk's raid by McNab. Whether it was for money, prestige, or simply enmity he did not know. Nor did he know what that enmity was about. But he wanted to find out, and then prove it, all of it. He had already waited too long.

Monk wondered if he had fallen neatly into a trap McNab had set

up for him. That was a scalding thought. McNab, of all people! Had
Monk allowed a certain arrogance to flaw his judgment, and land him
in this disaster?

He remembered with a sudden lurch of his stomach the moment he
had seen that McNab knew he was vulnerable. It was a couple of weeks
ago. They had been sitting in McNab's office talking about some trivial
matter of business they had in common—something to do with a few
missing kegs of brandy, probably a miscount.

McNab had stopped in the middle of a sentence and looked very
directly at Monk, meeting his eyes.

"You remember Rob Nairn?" He pronounced the name very carefully.

Monk had no idea who Rob Nairn was. The silence in the office
had been intense as McNab watched him. He was trying to keep the
emotions out of his face, and failing. Clearly it was something of intense
importance, and that Monk had to have known, which meant it was in
the past, before the accident.

"He has nothing to do with this." Monk had spoken because he
had to.

But he realized now that it was too late. McNab had seen the moment of blankness in his eyes, and he knew.

Now, as he and Hooper walked away from the wharf to face the
long journey back to the city, Monk knew that he would have to think
of an explanation for McNab as to how one of his men had been
drowned in an incident that should have had nothing to do with Monk.

He had no doubt now that McNab seemed to know him far better
than he knew McNab. At the beginning that had seemed reasonable.
McNab was colorless. One met him, and the next day, or week, one
could barely remember his features. He was apparently thorough at his
job, but not dashing, not spectacular, like Monk. He had not solved any
cases that stayed in the mind.

Monk, on the other hand, had carved a considerable legend for
himself, not all of it good. He was clever, and brave. Evidence also
proved that in the past he had been ruthless. That horror, the terrible

fear, that he had been the one who had beaten Joscelyn Gray to death, had changed him. He had not been guilty of that. The relief still drenched him, in occasional dreams when the past intruded again to darken the present.

He was a different man now. Certainly he was still clever, still dressed rather better than a man of even his new superior rank usually did. But he had seen his own image in other people's eyes, and hated it.

He was also happy now in a completeness he had never tasted before, and that made all the difference. But a man who could only aspire to some element of compassion, even when he was happy, was not worth much. The achievement would have been to be spontaneously generous when he had so little that really mattered to him. It was too late for that now. He had Hester—and Scuff. And he had friends: Rathbone, Crow, Hooper, even Runcorn from the past, who was now so different from the man he used to despise.

And of course there had been Orme. If McNab was responsible for Orme's death, was it because of Monk, and something that he could not remember?

Certainly there was nothing from the last thirteen years to account for the look he had seen in McNab's face, briefly, and then deliberately hidden again.

As they rode back through the wet, gray streets to the heart of London, he went over and over the incident on the wharf, and in the river. He was wretchedly cold, his wet trousers stuck to him, and his feet were numb in his boots. Hooper must feel the same.

He tried to recall exactly what had happened. They had been waiting for the escaped prisoner to appear, followed by the police or one of McNab's men. The two had appeared from different sides of the row of buildings. Owen, smaller and faster, had been ahead, racing toward the wharf, when the big man, Pettifer, had come from the other side. They had collided, but had Owen attacked Pettifer, or was it the other way around?

Certainly they had fought, striking out at each other, getting closer and closer to the water. Looking back, Monk saw it could indeed have been Pettifer who was the pursuer and the small man he now knew to be Owen, the fugitive.

God, what a mess!

When Pettifer had panicked he had all but drowned Monk along with himself. If he had done so, Owen would still have escaped. Who the devil could have expected him to swim like that?

The schooner captain, maybe? He had been on deck. Was that chance? Or by design? Had the shouts brought him up from below, to see what was going on? How many men would there be on a boat that size? Not necessarily more than two or three, not for a two-master.

How did he know that? Had he at some time in the past learned more about sail than he recalled? He had grown up on the coast of Northumberland. Old letters he had kept from his sister had told him that. He knew the sea, the smell of it was familiar, the swing and balance of standing in a small boat on the water, the rhythm of the oars. He had taken easily to being on the swift-flowing, tidal Thames.

Where was the schooner now? Did anybody know its name? He should have asked the local police at the wharf. Or perhaps Aaron Clive had noticed it. It was a beautiful ship, and had lain at anchor near his warehouses. It must have passed them on the way up, and down again.

Any seaman at all helps a man in the water. They would have to find the ship, and pursue the issue, for whatever it was worth. Everyone, on water or on land, would be searching for Owen, the explosives expert, the wanted man.

But Pettifer's death was not Monk's fault, except in the most indirect way. It was Monk who had struck Pettifer, to save them both. Had he hit him so hard that the blow had killed him? He had not thought he had the strength or the weight, especially in the water with no purchase on the ground. Surely he had only temporarily stunned him, as had been his intention. But then he had drowned—which had not been Monk's intention at all!

They would not know that until the autopsy, although Crow had implied it was not the blow that had killed him.

He should go to the police surgeon and ask him to be very precise. It was imperative that they be certain.

McNab would have a field day with it if Monk were directly responsible for Pettifer's death. He would believe it was revenge for Orme. Monk could still feel the weight of Orme's body in his arms, the blood everywhere, dark red and sticky as it congealed, bright and wet where it was still pumping, and nothing they could do would stop it.

He remembered his own heart beating with panic as they set Orme ashore, men in the water up to their chests, all the helping hands, faces, wretched with pity. Then the long wait in the hospital. Monk had sat with Orme all day and most of the night, hoping, praying. He was exhausted and numb when Orme died. McNab would say Monk was beside himself after the battle and keen to blame anyone else for the fiasco on the gunrunning ship.

But that would still invite people to wonder if McNab had betrayed them to the pirates.

When the cab stopped and they paid the driver, Hooper took the omnibus to the station. Monk went straight to the morgue, and found Hyde just coming out of the room where he performed autopsies. He was drying his hands on a rough, white towel and he looked cold.

"Ha! Was just going to send for you," he said with satisfaction. "This fellow of yours—Blount? What the devil's going on with him?"

"Not much," Monk replied. He was far more concerned with asking Hyde to attend to Pettifer immediately, and if possible give Monk some warning as to what he had found. He needed to know the cause of death was drowning, not an immediate result of the blow Monk had dealt him. Surely it could not have been hard enough to have damaged his skull. Had Monk himself panicked enough to do that?

He had lost the thread of Hyde's comment.

"What? What did you say?" he asked.

Hyde looked more closely at Monk. "God, man! You look awful. And your trousers and boots are sodden. Where the hell have you been? It's not that wet outside." He led the way toward his office and opened the door for Monk to go in. As always, every shelf was crammed with books and there were piles of papers stacked on every surface. But there was a brisk fire burning in the hearth and the air was blessedly warm.

"Sit down," Hyde ordered. "You look worse than some of my corpses. What's happened?"

"Just had an escaped prisoner and the customs man chasing him fall into the river," Monk said miserably, moving some papers and sitting down.

"So of course you naturally jumped in after them," Hyde concluded with a bleak, twisted smile. "I hope they're suitably appreciative." He walked over to a small wall cupboard and opened it with a key on his watch chain. He took out two glasses and a bottle of excellent brandy. He poured a generous helping into each glass and handed one across to Monk.

Monk was glad of it; he was beginning to feel a little queasy. He took a large mouthful and swallowed it. Its fire burned into his stomach immediately, and then seemed to leak into his blood.

"Grateful?" Monk examined the word. "Well, the prisoner damn well is. He got clean away. The customs man rather less so. I'm afraid he's dead. He's your problem for the time being."

Hyde took a deep breath. "Really? What happened? Prisoner kill him?"

"No. Either the river did, or I did."

Hyde took a long, luxurious mouthful of the brandy, rolled it around his mouth, then swallowed it.

"Stop being so cryptic and explain yourself," he ordered.

"He fell into the river and panicked. I had to hit him fairly hard to stop him drowning us both. We got him out onto the wharf, but he died. You know Crow?"

Hyde's eyebrows rose. "Of course I know Crow. Lunatic, but he's actually a more than half-decent doctor. Your lad's with him, isn't he?"

"Yes . . ."

"Good decision. Why? Did Crow see this panicky customs man?"

"Yes. Came just after we got him out of the water."

"What did he say?"

"Not much. Just that he couldn't save him."

"Was he dead when you got him out?"

"I don't think so. I saw his eyelids flutter, and it looked as if he coughed up a bit of water. Could be I just wanted him to live."

"Got useful information for you?" Hyde asked curiously.

"No! I just didn't bloody well want to be responsible for his death!" Monk took another mouthful of the brandy and swallowed it, steadying himself. "I'm sorry. I thought he was the prisoner, but I still did everything I could to save him."

"And he turned out to be the customs officer?" Hyde shook his head. "Not your day, was it? I'll look at him carefully when he gets here. One of McNab's men, was he?"

"Of course . . ."

"Not doing well, is he, our McNab?" Hyde said it with relish. "His men who lost Blount, wasn't it? Well, I've got more news for you on that. Poor sod was well dead by the time he was shot. An hour or two at the very least. Now why would anyone shoot in the back some poor devil who was already thoroughly dead? A little exercise for you, Monk."

Monk realized that Hyde was watching him with far more interest than his casual air would suggest. What was he looking for?

"You're sure? He couldn't have been unconscious in the water, from the shot, but still breathing, so he drowned?"

"How the hell long do you think it takes an unconscious man to drown, Monk? Minutes. Three or four at most. He was shot long after that."

"How do you know?" Monk persisted.

"If he'd been in the water, shot but alive, he'd have struggled and bled like a stuck pig from a wound like that," Hyde answered impatiently. "It tore major blood vessels. He's lost very little blood. I don't mind you second-guessing me, Monk, but however much you don't like the answer, that's it! He was dead when he was shot. No heartbeat, and already sodden with water. In fact, from the state of the wound, I'd say he was in the water three or four hours, pulled out very obviously dead, and then someone shot him in the back. I wouldn't swear on oath that they never put him back in the water afterward, but I'm sure enough I'd bet everything I have on it."

Monk did not answer. His mind was pulling at the tangles of why McNab had sent for him rather than keep to himself the fact that Blount had escaped from their custody, drowned, and then been shot. He would not expose his own men's errors, to Monk of all people, unless he had a powerful reason.

In a flash of highly uncomfortable memory, Monk saw the bright, sharp satisfaction in McNab's eyes as he exposed the wound and said, "Murder's your job. . . . It's all yours," to Monk. He wanted Monk on it. Why?

And now there was the ghastly fact that Pettifer had been McNab's man, and he was dead, very possibly from Monk's attempt to save him. And yet, of course, if Monk had stood on the quayside and let him drown, that would very clearly have been his fault, too.

All accidental? Or somehow designed?

No, that was absurd. It could as easily have been Hooper who had gone in to help Pettifer. But then if Hooper were blamed Monk would still be implicated. Hooper was his man—his best man now, with Orme gone—and one to whom Monk owed a personal loyalty.

Added to which, McNab would hardly have arranged for his own man to be drowned, even if he were able to. Monk was allowing his obsession with McNab to make him lose his balance, and his judgment.

"Thank you," he said to Hyde. "When they bring Pettifer in, which should be anytime now, I'd appreciate if you take extra care to ascertain whether he died from drowning, or if from the blow I dealt him to keep him from breaking my neck and drowning us both. If there's anything uncertain about it, McNab will be on to it and blaming everyone else, starting with me."

Hyde nodded, pursing his lips dubiously. "Watch him," he advised. "He's always digging, poking around, asking questions. I don't know what it's about, but he has a long and deep grudge against you. But I imagine you know that?"

"Yes . . ." Monk let the word hang, the idea unfinished. He knew the fact, but he had very little idea what the reason was. To begin with he had assumed general interservice rivalry: the River Police versus

Customs. But lately he had been obliged to accept that it was deeper than that, and a good deal more personal. Did it go back further than his memory? Before 1856, and the accident? Should the name Rob Nairn mean anything to him?

Then why had McNab waited so long to have his revenge? It made no sense—unless he had been afraid of Monk before he knew Monk's loss of memory? Suddenly he was vulnerable . . . and a man with no memory of a past that could be anything was not fit to lead the River Police. He could be manipulated, used too easily.

He thanked Hyde and walked out of the morgue, with its over-cleanliness and the smells that masked the odor of death but somehow made it so much worse.

The street was bitterly cold. The scents of carbolic and lye were replaced by soot and horse manure, and now and then a whiff of drains.

Then he crossed the road, dodging a brewer's dray and a hansom. With perhaps a little careful inquiry into a few events in past history, around the time of the accident, McNab had slowly pieced enough of it together to realize how much Monk had forgotten. Like a shark scenting blood, knowing his prey was wounded, McNab was circling closer.

Was Monk being ridiculous, allowing his own imagination to betray him? Or was it at last warning him of the truth?

He had no choice but to face McNab over Pettifer's death and to learn more about Owen. The sooner it was done the better. He would like to know from Hyde the exact cause of Pettifer's death, but he might not get that for a day or two, and finding Owen could not wait. Or finding the schooner captain, for that matter. Unless, of course, they were both well out into the Atlantic by now.

McNab was at his desk in the customs offices when Monk arrived the following day. There were always administrative matters to deal with. Papers multiplied like rats if they were not attended to.

McNab looked up from his desk. He had a very pleasant office, with a view over the Pool of London. Even at this time of the year, the light was bright off the water and the black masts of a hundred ships swayed and jostled against the skyline with a constant movement.

McNab remained seated, something he would not have done six months ago. His square, heavy face was devoid of expression as much as he could make it, but there was still a brightness in his eyes.

He put down his pen, carefully, so as not to mark his high-quality desk set with ink. The leather looked new.

"Come to apologize, have you?" he asked, looking up at Monk. He did not invite him to sit.

Monk pulled out the leather-padded chair opposite the desk and sat anyway, making himself at least outwardly comfortable.

"Not apologize," he replied with perfect control of his temper. "The man panicked. He'd have drowned us both. Not uncommon, unfortunately. But my condolences. It's hard to lose a man."

"Am I supposed to be grateful?" McNab asked, raising his sparse eyebrows slightly.

"You're supposed to be civil," Monk replied. "As am I. Is there any word about Owen yet? I assume you are doing all you can to find him? He must have been of some value to you, or you wouldn't have been questioning him. Had he any connection with Blount?"

"Thanks to you drowning poor Pettifer," McNab replied, "Owen got clean away. That damn schooner captain took him downriver. We questioned him, but he said he put Owen off at the next wharf. There's no proof whether he did or not."

"You questioned him?" Monk seized on the one point that mattered, and that betrayed at least part of what McNab implied.

"Of course I did!" McNab snapped. He seemed about to add something more, then bit it back.

Monk smiled. "Then he isn't halfway across the Atlantic. Or in France, either. And you will have searched the schooner?"

"Of course!"

"Then it sounds as if he did put Owen off somewhere," Monk concluded. "Of course, Owen could still be in France by now. What do you know about him?"

There was the faintest gleam of satisfaction in McNab's eyes, as if he were savoring something in his mind. "Forgotten, have you?"

Monk felt a stab of fear, as if suddenly he had been thrown back into the days just after the accident, when he felt dislike around him, tension in people he could not place, and had no idea why. He dismissed it. McNab was playing games, perhaps in revenge for Pettifer's death, reminding Monk that he knew his weakness. Pettifer might have been a good man, when he wasn't terrified. Perhaps he had had a particular fear of drowning. Some people had.

He looked McNab directly in the eye and saw the gleam fade again.

"I know his record," he lied, referring back to Owen. "I want to know what you observed of him. Surely you know more than the list of convictions?" He leaned forward a little. "Is he clever, or lucky? An opportunist or a planner? Does he have friends or is he a loner? What are his weaknesses? Carelessness? Disloyalty, so too many enemies? Is he greedy and doesn't know when to stop and take his gains and quit? Has he got something he's afraid of, like Pettifer and the water, for example?"

Fury lit McNab's face, making it momentarily ugly rather than merely plain.

"How like you to ask," he said very softly. "He's not afraid of heights, or falling, if that's what you mean." He watched Monk with extraordinary intensity, as if daring Monk to look away from him. There was an emotion inside him that was impossible to read, except that it was filled with pain. That much burned through everything else.

Monk was put off an instant answer.

McNab waited.

What could Monk say that would not show he had been disturbed by the sudden moment of savage reality, whatever it had meant? One thing he was now sure of: Whatever lay between himself and McNab, McNab remembered it very clearly, and he did not. He was losing his balance on the edge of the unknown.

"I want to catch the man," Monk said calmly. "The more I know of him, the better chance I have. Who is this schooner captain? What do you know of him?"

"Fin Gillander," McNab responded. His voice still had a rough edge to it, as if it cost him an effort to reply to such an ordinary question. "American, I think, or sounds like it. Good-looking man, arrogant. Thinks that because he's got a fast ship he owns the seas. Damn fool, if you ask me. Owen told him he was the police and Pettifer the criminal. At least so he claims. I think he's a bit of a chancer. I daresay Owen slipped him a few guineas to take him downriver."

"Really?" Monk could not help being sarcastic. "And where did Owen get a few guineas from, seeing as he'd just been convicted in court and escaped on the way to prison? Or is that not true, either?"

McNab hesitated. He had been caught out, and they both knew it. For an instant it was there in his eyes, and Monk had the sudden cold feeling that he had overplayed his hand. He must fill the silence.

"You don't trust Gillander? Perhaps he did put him ashore, whether by arrangement or not. Did Owen have help in his escape?" he suggested.

McNab smiled slowly and the tension eased out of the moment.

"Thought you'd never get to it. Looks as if he did. Has no friends that we know of, but hires out to the highest payer, so there are allies." He took a deep breath, hesitated a moment, then spoke again, this time even more carefully. "He did quite a lot of work for Aaron Clive at one time. You know him? Big import and export business. Has warehouses along the stretch of river Owen was making for. And where Gillander was moored. Now that you've got a reason to, you could ask Clive—nicely, of course—what he can tell you about Owen. He might know more about him than just his skills. Very powerful man—indeed, very, very rich. I should think he doesn't know people without finding out what he's dealing with. Him having made his fortune in a single place, like." The smile was back in his eyes. "But you'll know that . . . better than I do."

Monk had no idea what he was talking about. "I've heard of him," he said slowly. "Met him when Owen escaped . . ."

McNab's eyes widened. He was smiling. "That the first time? Really?"

It was a trap, and yet Monk had no idea how. He could hardly say that he had met him before. Aaron Clive was not a man one forgot.

"He never crosses the police path," Monk answered.

"Oh . . . on the river." McNab was now smiling even more widely. "No, I imagine not. I was thinking of long ago. Years."

"I thought he'd only been here a couple of years." Monk knew he was right about that. He knew of the major businesses and landowners along both banks of the river. It was his job.

"Oh . . . he has," McNab agreed. "I was thinking of . . . the past. California, perhaps? I heard San Francisco was a pretty small town, just a few hundred people, before the gold rush."

Now Monk was as chilled through as if he had just been pulled out of the river again. McNab was playing some absurd game with him. It was there in his face, the gloating, and yet the same crazy courage as lights a man's eyes when he places a bet on the table that he knows he cannot cover, should he lose. Monk had seen that look before.

How could he reply? What could he say that would not betray his vulnerability? The gold rush in California had begun in 1848, but it was common knowledge that the big rush was 1849. Was he supposed to know more? It was before his accident.

McNab was watching him. He had to respond.

"What on earth does Owen have to do with the gold rush?" he said with as much disbelief as he could manage. "They panned for gold mostly. They certainly didn't use explosives." He said that as if he were certain of it, but did he know that, or was he guessing?

McNab looked slightly surprised. "Really?"

"Anyway," Monk went on, "you dig mines, you don't blow them up. You're thinking of quarries."

McNab was not in the least perturbed. "Ah," he said, sitting back in his chair, easing his shoulders, "and explosives are also used in salvage. Sometimes. I suppose that's what Clive employed him for. Anyway, you could go and see him. He might be able to tell you something about Owen."

"Thank you," Monk said as he stood up. "Perhaps I'll be able to get him back for you."

"Perhaps," McNab agreed, his smile not fading at all.

————

MONK WENT THAT EVENING to see Aaron Clive at his home in Mayfair, a magnificent house on a corner site just off Berkeley Square. He presented himself early, before the dinner hour, and asked to speak to Mr. Clive about the unfortunate episode the day before. He would ask for his assistance, as well as, of course, expressing his thanks.

He was obliged to wait half an hour, but did so in a very agreeable morning room. The fire had clearly been alight most of the day and it was thoroughly warm. He was even offered a choice of drink, which he would have liked to have accepted, but he was on duty, and it would be inadvisable, in spite of the informality of the hour. He spent the time studying the books on the shelves beside the polished marble fireplace, and the ornaments on the mantel and in the alcoves. The books were the eclectic variety he would have expected, but several of the ornaments were of native origin: carvings of bears and some kind of dog. These disturbed him not only in their beauty, but in wakening thoughts of brighter sunlight, heat in the air, and great distances he could not place. Imagination or memory?

The butler came in after a discreet knock on the door and invited Monk to follow him to Clive's study.

Clive was standing in front of a large bookcase filled with more books, many leather-bound, and placed according to subject rather than size. That indicated immediately to Monk that they were there for use, not ornament. Clive loved them, and did not care what others thought. Monk warmed to the man straightaway. Pretense was a cold, unlikable thing; there was a certain honesty in this. Here the ornaments were a nugget of gold, and more small carvings of animals in turquoise, malachite, and rock crystal.

"Sorry to keep you waiting, Commander Monk," Clive said, stepping forward and offering his hand.

Monk took it briefly. It was a light, strong shake.

"I appreciate you seeing me without notice," he replied. "The last couple of days have been a bit . . . unfortunate."

Clive smiled widely. "A bit," he agreed, inviting Monk to sit down. "I hope you took no harm from your dip in the river. It must have been appallingly cold."

"To the bone," Monk said with feeling. "But I don't think I've come to any harm. Unlike poor Pettifer."

"Pettifer?" Clive's eyes widened for a moment. "The name of the man who drowned? Very sad. Many people panic in water . . . or with fire. It is the most dangerous aspect of many disasters. But natural, I suppose. How ironic, to engineer a brilliant escape from prison, only to drown more or less by your own hand."

"That's what I thought," Monk admitted wryly. "But contrary to how we read the appearances, Pettifer was the customs man."

Clive groaned. "How damned awful. I'm so sorry. So the man who swam all the way across to the schooner was the escapee?"

"Yes. His name was Silas Owen. He was an explosives expert that Customs had caught in a serious plot. I don't know the details."

Clive looked surprised. "Owen? What was he doing here? I haven't used him for . . . oh . . . a year or more. It was just one salvage job, down on the Estuary. Explosives were the only way we could burst open the hold of a sunken ship. Needed an expert for it. Very dangerous thing to do, blow up half a ship underwater. He was good . . . very good indeed. But how can I help you?" He indicated the decanter of sherry on the bookshelf and a row of cut-crystal glasses. "I have brandy, if you prefer?"

"No, thank you."

"Come on, man! It's a filthy evening out and you've no doubt had a long day. I know I have."

Monk convinced himself refusal would be ungracious, and accepted.

Clive poured two glasses of sherry and passed one over.

Monk sipped it. It was the smoothest he could ever recall. Taste was an odd thing. It brought back memories few other things could evoke. Combined with the rich aroma of the heavy wine, it was as if he were momentarily back in time, but he had no idea where.

"You might remember something about Owen that would help," he said in reply to Clive's original question. "For example, do you know who owns the schooner that was moored opposite? How long was it there? Is it possible it was there by arrangement? You've already told me Owen was expert in his field. Did he usually work aboveboard, or was he always available for other things? Did he ever mention connections he might have? May I have your permission to speak to any of your men who worked with him?"

Clive smiled, amusement lighting his face and softening the lines of it.

"Where do you wish me to start? I doubt it was anything but chance as far as the schooner was concerned. It's called the *Summer Wind*, and it belongs to a bit of an adventurer named Fin Gillander. I've known of him for some years. I doubt he arranged to pick up an escaped prisoner, unless he believed him innocent. And knowing what I do of Owen, and of English law, that is highly unlikely."

"For money?" Monk questioned.

"Doubt it. Did Owen have money? I thought he'd just escaped from the wagon taking him from the court to prison. That's what the papers said, for whatever that's worth?" His expression was slightly quizzical.

"If Gillander helped Owen for money, then someone other than Owen paid him," Monk agreed. "It's possible, but not likely. Looks as if it's just the devil's own luck. His escape, Pettifer's drowning, Gillander being at exactly the right place at the right time . . ."

Clive bit his lip. "You don't believe in so much coincidence and neither do I. I don't know what the connection is, but there must be one."

"McNab at Customs lost another prisoner he was questioning. A convicted man taken out of prison to the customs offices, to identify something, I believe. His name was Blount, and that was just over a week ago," Monk told him.

Clive looked startled. "Did he get away, too?"

"Yes . . . and no," Monk said with dark amusement. "McNab didn't catch up with him until someone pulled him out of the water, and called McNab. Blount had been drowned, and then shot." He wanted to see the expression on Clive's face.

Clive blinked. "Drowned and then shot? Is that not . . . excessive? And now Owen has escaped." The gentleness of his voice robbed it of malice.

"While some might agree with you, I don't believe in this much coincidence, either. Blount was a master forger, Owen an explosives expert. Both were in the custody of Customs, at least at the time of their original escape. Although in neither case were customs officers apparently responsible for their deaths. We have no idea who drowned Blount, or who shot him, either. As far as the business with Owen is concerned, it's Pettifer who's dead, and Owen's . . . God knows where. But the question arises, was Owen meant to be killed? You've told me about Owen, thank you. What do you know about the schooner, or Gillander? How long has he moored there almost opposite you?"

Clive smiled. "I've known Gillander on and off for years, something like twenty." He took another sip from his drink and leaned back in his chair. "He's in his thirties, or perhaps forty. Something of an adventurer. Never told anybody exactly where he came from, just turned up in San Francisco, around about the time of the gold rush in '49. He was little more than a deckhand then, picking up an odd job wherever he could find it. Cheeky bastard. All the nerve in the world. Hard player, hard drinker, and easy with women. Mind you, he was extraordinarily handsome, and he knew it, and used it. But he was a good seaman, especially in the smaller boats, two or three masts. Never bothered with the clippers, but then he didn't much like taking orders." His eyes narrowed a little. "Don't you know all this already?"

Monk felt a chill inside him. There was no answer he could afford to make.

"He worked up and down the coast." He made the observation as if indeed he did know.

"Or across the oceans," Clive answered. "Went across the Pacific to the China Seas, at least once that I heard of. Round the Horn to Britain several times, and that's a damn long voyage. You think the Bay of Biscay's rough, try rounding Cape Horn." He smiled. It was a warm, charming expression, and seemed utterly natural.

"I was just thinking of it," Monk said quickly, bringing himself back to the present and the warm room. "Trying to," he amended. His sense of it had been violent, consuming. It made him wonder if he had ever been in a storm at sea, off the coast of Northumberland, in that part of his life that had disappeared. Perhaps such seas were the same anywhere on earth.

He went back to Gillander and the conversation with Clive.

"So he's a man who might walk on either side of the law?"

Clive laughed abruptly, but with genuine humor. "San Francisco in the gold rush didn't have much law, Mr. Monk. A lot of the tall stories you hear are probably just that, but they have roots in truth. At the time gold was discovered, in 1848, California was part of the Mexican territory of Alta California, although it had been occupied by the United States. The area was annexed by us at the beginning of February '48, a matter of days after they found gold. It became a state as part of the Compromise of 1850. For a while we were literally lawless. The town of San Francisco grew from about two hundred people in '46 to thirty-six thousand in '52. Nobody could control that."

Monk's imagination stirred with efforts to visualize the settlement smaller than an English village, suddenly overwhelmed with people of all sorts: adventurers, traders, prospectors, and builders, fortune seekers, drifters, all the human flotsam of any ocean port. There would be both the making and losing of fortunes. Gold could be picked up off the shallow riverbanks, in panning the sand and shale. There would be gunfights, drunken brawls, gambling, theft, itinerant preachers, suppliers of every kind of food and equipment, quack doctors and real ones. And banks would spring up to deal with all the new money, assay officials to weigh gold, and tell the fool's gold apart.

He could almost see it in his mind's eye, the bright light, the huge bays and inlets with the blue water in all directions. Of course it would be lawless for a while. And that was what Gillander had been as a very young man. Monk might have done the same himself, had he been given the opportunity. Californian gold rush, instead of . . . what? As far as he knew, fishing off the coast of Northumberland. A beautiful coast, but a different light, different tides and currents, and certainly not a land of violence, adventure, and gold.

"What is Gillander doing here?" Monk asked.

Clive shrugged. "No idea. Probably scraping a living as he can. If that schooner is his, then he'll have a good business with it. I started out with one ship. But I had a fortune in gold behind me by then."

"You're American?"

"My parents were French and British, but yes, I'm American." Clive said it with some pride, which Monk found pleasing. A man should be proud of his heritage—not arrogant, as if it made him superior, but happy to own it and live up to the best in its promise.

Monk rose to his feet. "Thank you. I'll find out what else I can. In some ways, the river is a small place. I'll see what other inquiries can turn up. I'll see Gillander himself, but if he took Owen on purpose rather than simply rescuing a man from the water, I doubt he'll tell me."

"Good luck," Clive said wryly, standing also and giving Monk his hand again. "Let me know if I can be of any further help."

ANOTHER TWO DAYS OF searching and questioning turned up various scraps of information about Gillander, but none of it added much to what Aaron Clive had said.

No trace whatever was found of Owen, nor any connection with Blount, except what the customs men had said regarding their questioning of both men. McNab raised that again when he came to the Wapping Police Station and found Monk working late, about half-past seven in the evening and long after dark. There were still papers on his desk, reports from his men, and various complaints and affidavits regarding cases. He used an empty mug as a paperweight.

McNab walked in casually, nodding to the constable at the door and walking past Hooper with no more than a glance. It was Laker who stopped him outside Monk's office.

"Got some news for us, Mr. McNab?" he said boldly.

Monk put down the papers he was reading and waited.

"No, I haven't," McNab answered with a touch of irritation in his voice. "You were the ones who lost Owen. If you hadn't interfered we'd have him safely in prison now. I wondered who tipped you off that he was going that way? We should have a bit closer look at them." He looked intently at Laker. "I don't suppose you'd know that, would you? Been poking around a bit, I hear."

"We never had him, *sir*." Laker made the emphasis very slightly harder than necessary. "If your man hadn't attacked him, and so both ended up in the water, I daresay he wouldn't have drowned, letting Owen get away. I can't imagine that's what he meant to do. Just a bad accident. Or perhaps he meant to chuck Owen in, but didn't know the man could swim like a fish."

Monk rose to his feet, sending a pile of papers onto the floor. He went to the door and opened it sharply.

McNab was standing, pale-faced, staring at Laker, who appeared to be enjoying himself. But that was Laker, gracefully insolent. One day he wouldn't get away with it.

"Haven't got much control of your men, have you?" McNab said angrily, walking round Monk and going into his office. He sat down without being invited.

Monk went in behind him and closed the door. He ignored the question, partly because McNab was right. Monk had earned both fear and respect, but not yet obedience, at least not from Laker. But they were closer since Orme's death. Tragedy had created a bond that duty could not. There was an irony to the situation now, since Monk was still certain it was McNab who had betrayed them to the gunrunners, and possibly to the pirates that terrible day.

"Do you know anything?" Monk asked, remaining standing himself.

McNab tilted his chair a little and folded his hands across his stomach. He looked up at Monk. "A little. Pettifer was my right-hand man, you know. Hardworking. Loyal. The other men had a high respect for him. Hard to lose him, especially that way." His face was unreadable. His words suggested grief, yet there was a hard light in his eye, as when a hunting animal scents its prey. "But I expect you understand that, don't you? Tell you for nothing, that young man with the fair hair's going to give you trouble. You'll never keep him in control the way your man Orme would have. He'll always be setting himself up against you, trying you, seeing who wins, looking for weakness. If he scents it, he'll be on to it, like a weasel." Now he was smiling and there was a bright, cold pleasure in it.

There was an element of truth in his words, enough to hurt. The word McNab had left out was *love*. In their own silent way, the men had loved Orme, even seen in him something of a father. They would never see Monk like that.

"How thoughtful of you to come all the way from the Pool of London to tell me," Monk said sarcastically. "If you find a replacement for Pettifer, you'd better teach him to swim!" The moment the words were out of his mouth, he regretted it. To lash back like that was a sure sign that McNab had hurt him. He saw knowledge of it in McNab's face.

"I'll have a few things to teach him," McNab agreed softly. "But I came up here to tell you that we're almost sure Blount was headed for the sea, and probably France when he fell into the water. And shot afterward, it seems. I'd hazard a fair guess Owen's in France by now. Some pretty heavy smuggling going on. Not sure how reliable, but word has it that it could involve gold. Stolen, of course."

Monk did not reply. What was McNab looking for? Was this why he had come, to tell Monk about the stolen gold? Why? In the hope Monk would go chasing after it, and McNab could take the credit? Over the last few weeks he had changed. He used to be very careful of Monk, as if he were too wary of him, even fearful, to let his hatred show. But since he had realized the extent of Monk's gaps in his memory he had probed, like a surgeon looking for the bullet in a wound. Except he did not wish to remove it! He wanted to push it farther in, deeper to the bone.

"I was talking with Aaron Clive," Monk said finally. "He mentioned the gold rush in California, twenty years ago. He said gold made people a little crazy."

McNab smiled as if filled with sudden, deep joy. "He said that, did he? Well, well. He would know. Made his fortune in the gold rush of '49, he did. But of course you'll know all that." He moved over to the door. "See if you can track down that Gillander fellow with the schooner. He might be able to tell you something. Never know what you'll uncover . . ." And with another smile he went out and walked all the way to the outer door into the wind-rattled night without looking to either side of him.

THE NEXT MORNING MONK went to the schooner *Summer Wind*. This time it was moored close in to the south bank and accessible from the shore. It was beautiful, all clean lines, with polished teak decks and immaculate brass work. Everything was lashed in its place, safe, clean, and well tended.

"Permission to come aboard?" Monk called out. He waited a few moments, then called again. A man came up the steps and through the open hatch. Monk introduced himself.

The man gave a casual salute. From the description it had to be Fin Gillander. He was graceful, agile, perhaps an inch or so taller than Monk, and as Aaron Clive had said, remarkably handsome.

"Wondered when you'd come," he said with a lopsided smile as he offered his hand to Monk. His grip was quick and firm. Then he led the way down the stairs and into the main cabin, small, as is everything on a ship, but clean and all in its place.

"Sorry about lifting your fellow out of the water," Gillander went on. "He told me he was the police and he had to get downriver and report that the big fellow with the beard had been drowned."

"So I heard," Monk replied with a slight grimace. "And who did he say we were? I assume he didn't mention that we were River Police?"

Gillander shrugged. "Hardly. He said you were rival smugglers who'd killed the big fellow with the beard, and he was lucky to have escaped with his life."

Monk imagined it for a moment. He could find no fault with the story. It could easily enough have been true.

"Was he hurt?" he asked eventually.

"Said his shoulder was painful and he thought it needed a doctor. I took him down to the next steps along and put him ashore," Gillander replied.

"And then?"

Gillander smiled. "You checking up on me, Commander Monk?"

"Yes."

Gillander laughed. There was nothing forced in it. The whole concept amused him. "Fair enough. I suppose I would, in your place. Needed some supplies. Went to the chandler, and got some more candles, linseed oil, and a little turpentine. Can I offer you a tot of whisky? That wind off the water's as cold as a witch's heart."

It sounded like a good idea. Monk wanted to make a better judgment of the man than a few minutes afforded him. And he would like to look a little more closely at the ship. She was beautiful, swift, built to take even the seas around the Horn. He could see how perfectly she was kept. Obviously Gillander did more than take pride in her: He loved her as if she had been a living thing, like a great tree.

Gillander watched him with a spark of curiosity in his eyes. He led the way to the galley and then the cabin beyond where his chart table was, and his maps. The movement of the river was so slight there was barely enough surge to be aware of, more like a gentle breathing.

There was a bookcase in the cabin, glass-fronted so it closed and locked, in case a rough sea should throw everything around. Monk would like to have seen what the books were, but to look would have been too openly inquisitive.

He did look around at the fittings, which were all in old and rich-colored teak, obviously oiled and polished over the years. The brass was bright here, too, not a patch or streak of tarnish on it anywhere. It gave him pleasure to see, and oddly, it made him comfortable, even familiar. Perhaps a well-loved ship was the same the world over?

Gillander unlocked a tantalus, holding the whisky decanter and glasses, and poured one for himself and the other for Monk. He passed it over.

Monk took it and smelled the aroma, then tasted it. Single malt. Excellent. Gillander did not stint himself. He would like to learn more about the man.

Gillander held up his glass, tipped it a fraction toward Monk in a salute, then drank.

Something heavy must have passed them because the wake of it made the schooner rock very gently. Monk adjusted his balance without thinking.

"Do much sailing now?" Gillander asked with interest.

Monk hesitated for an instant. What was the answer that would not trip him up?

"A little. But that was a long time ago."

Gillander was watching him, waiting.

"Oceangoing, like this?" He smiled. "Been round the Horn in her." He looked at the cabin with intense pleasure. "She can handle anything: Pacific, Atlantic, China Seas, Caribbean." He waited for Monk to respond.

Monk looked at the handsome face and saw nothing but vitality and interest in it. The man was asking him a simple question he could not answer. He lied.

"Mostly the North Sea," he said. "And that has a score of moods."

"They'll all love you, or kill you. If you give it long enough, probably both," Gillander responded. "But by God, while you're alive, you'll be really alive! Tell me the most beautiful thing you ever saw—women apart!"

Monk racked his mind for something honest enough that this man would not sense the lie, and yet a thing that would not reveal more than he wanted.

"Summer dawn over Holy Island," he said. "Sea was like glass, and the light seemed to fill everything."

"You're right," Gillander agreed softly. "It's always the light, isn't it? Like everything worth having, close your hand over it and it's gone. Have another whisky?"

"No, thank you. I have to go and look for Owen. Not that I think there's a cat in hell's chance I'll find him."

5

Beata had put the invitation on the mantelpiece in her boudoir and considered it for a whole day before she replied. She did not use the withdrawing room anymore. It was very formal, designed for entertaining, and it had all been done to Ingram's wishes—in other words, to impress. Also it required a constant fire burning to keep it warm enough to be comfortable. Perhaps she would sell the house, and its memories, before she was out of mourning. She had no wish to live here.

Her boudoir, like that of many other women of means, was her own sitting room on the same floor and wing as her bedroom, and furnished entirely to her own taste. The colors were soft and simple, the chairs comfortable to sit in. The bookcases were filled with books she actually read, such as novels by Jane Austen and the Brontë sisters, some adventure stories, and a great deal of poetry. The pictures on the walls were few, and represented memories she cherished, or dreams she had yet to fulfill. Others were merely beautiful—soft light on water, flights of wild

birds across the sky, reeds spearing a mountain pool—and they gave her
pleasure to look at.

She must answer the invitation today, or she would effectively
have ignored it. It was silly to put it off, because she knew the answer.
She should accept. She would have to be very unwell to decline, and
she would not descend to such a lie. It was not how she intended to
live her life now that she was at last free to choose. What a travesty
that would be!

Aaron and Miriam Clive had invited her to dinner. It was not a
party, which would have been unsuitable for her to attend while she was
in mourning, and if she did, word would spread and everyone would
know. She must not appear to be enjoying herself. Widows were expected, even required, to mourn their husbands for a noticeable period.
The only way to escape it would be to go abroad, and she was not prepared to do that—not yet, anyway. No, the invitation was to a very
quiet dinner over which to discuss the offer Aaron Clive had made to
endow a university chair for the study of law, in Ingram York's name and
his memory.

It was a gracious and generous offer. Aaron was an enormously
wealthy man, but it was still a notable thing to do, and far from inex-
pensive. And since he had not known Ingram personally, it was totally
unexpected. Beata could not help wondering if it were actually for her
that he did so, at least in part. Of course it would also be socially, and—if
he wished it—politically a good move. But Aaron did not need such
public acts. He was highly respected anyway. His wealth was unmea-
sured, his influence discreet, but wide. And his personal charm seemed
to touch everyone. Publicly at least, he had never made a mistake. But
then neither had Ingram, publicly.

What was there for Beata to debate? She had no reason to refuse.
Her reluctance was simply her own feelings about Ingram. The thought
of young men studying law holding him in admiration was offensive,
like throwing human waste into the pool from which all must drink.

No, she must stop such thoughts, and teach herself to think of only
the public man, who had been remarkable, at times harsh, but brilliant

in the law, tireless in the pursuit and conduct of a case. Until the very end, he had been a force for the cause of justice, at least as he saw it. He did occasionally temper it with mercy, but she wished it had been more often.

She went to her desk and composed a letter in reply, accepting the offer both for the endowment of a chair in her late husband's name, and to discuss the nature of such a gift over dinner the following evening. When she had written it to her satisfaction, she rang for the footman to take her reply to the post. They would have it by this evening. Surely they would have known that she would accept?

THE FOLLOWING EVENING BEATA dressed very carefully. She disliked black. She hardly ever wore it from choice. Her coloring was delicately fair, serene. Her skin was still flawless and the odd wisps of white in her hair were lost in the natural pale gold. Lilacs and soft grays, the other accepted colors of later mourning, looked marvelous on her. Black was such a harsh color, or more correctly, lack of color, but it was still too soon to discard it.

And of course she must be modest, everything should be high to the throat, and with little in the way of ornament to relieve it. Ingram would be amused, if he could see her. He had taken pride in her beauty, even if he seldom commented on it without some barb. There was always a worm in the apple.

What did beauty matter anyway? It was the mind and the soul that were the real person.

She had had her dressmaker create two or three black dresses. They had been prepared a few months ago, when Ingram was first taken to the hospital. Now she selected the least unflattering, and her maid assisted her to fasten it. It was right up almost to the chin—as if she were smitten with grief! What did it say? That she was a hypocrite.

The waist was tight and the skirt full. It was going to be uncomfortable. Still, what did that matter? She must stand up straight, walk with her head high, or that neck would choke her.

She should wear jet earrings. Everybody did for mourning. Diamonds would look frivolous.

She thanked the maid, stood up from the dressing table stool, and walked across the room toward the door. Then she stopped in amazement. The reflection she saw in the mirror was startling. She looked fierce and lonely, but quite beautiful . . . all moonlight and shadow. The perfect widow. How absurd!

She never played games with arrivals. To be early inconvenienced people; to be late was rude. To arrive fashionably late in order to make a spectacular entrance with as many as possible of the other guests already there to notice was supremely arrogant, an affectation she deplored.

She arrived a few minutes after the hour, and was welcomed in the hall by Miriam. If Beata were winter, Miriam was blazing late autumn. Her hair was the color of the last leaves, her gown russet, mahogany, and black. But of course it was far lower cut, displaying the warmth of her skin and the fire in her topaz necklace. Her face had the same beauty and passion Beata remembered from long ago. Time had refined it, but left no visible blemish.

"Thank you," she said to Beata immediately. "I don't imagine you feel like going anywhere, but believe me, I really am happy to see you." She turned to lead the way into the withdrawing room. Beata scarcely had time to notice the magnificence of the hall with its glorious chandelier blazing with light. The floor was not black and white as many marble floors were, but a delicate mixture of creams and soft earth colors that accentuated the deeper tones of the pilasters that framed the fireplace and the recesses on the walls to the side. The staircase, which occupied most of the central wall, was not dark wood but carved and rounded marble also.

"We have invited very few other guests," Miriam went on. "Actually only Giles Finch from the university, and Lord Justice Walbrook, whom you must already know."

"Only slightly," Beata replied, trying to bring his face to mind.

"He is recently a widower." Miriam opened the door to the withdrawing room. It was huge, with fireplaces at both ends and sufficient space to house two complete sets of furniture of the utmost comfort. The shades of autumn warmth and polished wood were complemented by the most startling touches of a bright color between blue and green, such as one might find in the tail of a peacock or in tropical seas. They glowed in velvet or satin cushions and in ornaments of glass in exquisite shapes—globes and spires and painted dishes.

It jolted in Beata's mind memories of more than twenty years ago, before she had ever met Ingram. She had spent her earlier years in California, in San Francisco before there was gold discovered in the sand and pebble shores of the American River, before fever had gripped the minds of investors, adventurers, and exploiters from half the world.

She had been born in England, but when her mother died, her father had decided to follow his love of adventure and take her with him out to the west coast of America and the lands that then belonged to Mexico. Since returning to England, marrying Ingram, and settling down, she had almost forgotten some of the wilder things she had done in the past. Some she had forgotten by choice, and only with long and deliberate effort, things she spoke of to no one.

She remembered the early mission posts set up by the Franciscan monks after the first Spanish explorers landed on the coast. How Spanish the buildings were, full of columns or arcades. Even the names of them rolled off the tongue like the words of a song.

The current priests were Franciscan as well, and worked among the people of the nearby settlements. At nineteen she had fallen in love with one of them. She remembered his dark brown robes with the rope around his waist, and his gentle smile. Perhaps she was absurd, but his dedication had filled her with longing to feel just as deeply about something herself, anything.

Of course nothing had happened between them, but the ardent melancholy of her dreams lingered. She remembered standing in the hot sun talking to him, trying to think of something to say that he would think wise. She so badly wanted to impress him. If she closed her eyes now she could smell the dust and the water on the stone and the sharp astringent aroma of crushed herbs. At times when Ingram was hurting her, she had done so deliberately, trying to bring back the innocence she had felt then, the ritual words of forgiveness.

Then she and her father had gone north to San Francisco, to the cooler, bright light on the sea. That was just after the first gold had been found in the river. Her father had set up trade. The wealth, the new people had arrived so fast, he had worked every day and half the night just to keep up with it. He became rich. At that time it was still all good.

She had married—not well, but adequately. It didn't do to be a single woman in those days, unless you were a schoolteacher, or something of the sort. She had had no wish for that, although looking back, she thought it would have been a fine calling. She wanted to taste life far more deeply than any children's classroom could offer. How naïve! But marriage then was an unexplored land for her, full of hope. There had been good times and bad, probably like the marriages of most of the young women she had known.

Then her husband had been killed in a stupid gunfight over a gold claim. She became a respectable widow, and had no desire to marry again. Her father had been too busy to force the issue, but that was a subject she still would not ever revisit willingly.

She still had vivid memories of San Francisco as it grew almost overnight, like a mushroom in a rich meadow. She could remember walking down the street where her father's emporium was and hearing the shouts of building workers, carpenters, roofers, men hauling timbers in horse-drawn wagons. New houses went up every day, and still it was nothing like enough, because more and more ships kept arriving.

Every morning she had drawn back the curtains to look out of her bedroom window with eager anticipation. Her father had always given her some luxuries, like curtains, a proper tin bath with feet, soft leather boots. Her memory was mixed with pleasure and pain, gratitude for all those small things that had mattered so much then. And then there had been the pain of how he changed, how he died.

People were a little mad with gold fever. There were always new ships in the bay, so many she could hardly see the bright water for their hulls jammed together and the forest of masts. They had crews from all over the earth bringing gold prospectors, gamblers, adventurers, profiteers, and men and women desperate for a new life.

She had befriended a few. She remembered Holly, plump and bright-eyed when she arrived. Months later she was thin, gaunt-faced, her skirts tucked up as she stood in the river endlessly digging and shifting through the pebbles, panning for gold. She and her husband lived on the riverbank, cooked on an open fire, slept on the ground. Beata never knew if they found anything.

More ships came into the bay. Too often their crews caught the gold fever as well and abandoned ship to go prospecting. The captains had to remain; they had no men to work the sails, or anything else. They came ashore, too, bringing with them anything they could use or sell. Some of the ships were even taken apart to use the precious timbers for building houses.

This was where Beata's father had made his money, lots of it. She had tried to put it from her memory, but it came back now like an incoming tide. For Aaron and Miriam it was a far shorter time ago. For the guests, Finch and Walbrook, it was a land only of the imagination.

Beata spoke to Miriam now, in this gorgeous room, as if the time between had melted like snow, leaving only the small traces of one winter behind.

She began by admiring the room, which was easy to do. Then she noticed one of the paintings, and recognized the place.

"San Juan Capistrano!" she said with pleasure. She felt the color coming to her cheeks. That was where she had fallen in love with the priest. It seemed like a hundred years ago. Had she ever really been so young?

Miriam laughed and walked over to stand beside her.

"Long time ago, wasn't it?" she said quietly. "Do you think back on those times?"

Beata looked sideways at her for an instant, and saw tears in her eyes.

Then the moment of pain vanished, and they spoke a little too brightly of other things, until they were joined by Aaron, Lord Justice Walbrook, and Dr. Giles Finch and moved to the dining room for dinner. All the formalities were observed, the condolences, the polite remarks about Ingram York and how he would be missed, what an ornament he had been to the judiciary. It was all very gracious, and predictable. Beata made the right replies and hoped she did it with dignity.

Did anybody believe it?

Dr. Finch had also noticed the painting of Mission San Juan Capistrano, and asked, once they were seated, if the mission was near San Francisco.

Aaron explained that it was also on the Californian coast, but many hundreds of miles south, much farther toward Mexico. The conversation turned to the gold rush, to the fortunes made and the changes that had occurred so very swiftly. Buildings came down overnight. Yesterday's paupers had become today's giants of wealth, of industry, of land and ultimately of government. It was contrasted with England, where most wealth and privilege passed from generation to generation.

"We've had our changes," Dr. Finch remarked. "But they were a long time ago."

Aaron smiled. "The Norman Conquest?" he said wryly.

"Oh, since then," Finch answered him with a shrug. "The Reformation. Catholic first and Protestant martyrs, then the other way round, back and forth between Henry the Eighth, Bloody Mary, then Elizabeth. And of course later the Civil War. Charles the First, and the ship money, taxes, divine right of kings, and so forth. And after him, Oliver Cromwell and the Puritans. Rather grim for my taste. No sense of humor. I don't know how anyone has the courage to survive without that. And then the Restoration, Charles the Second, all at the other extreme."

"Maybe we're due for another upheaval," Lord Justice Walbrook suggested with a very slight smile. "Unfortunately, I doubt it will be from the discovery of gold."

"The discovery of gold has its disadvantages," Miriam said quietly.

"A lot of sudden fortunes made, but a lot of deaths as well, violent deaths of men still young. And poverty alongside the wealth."

Beata looked at her curiously. She caught the moment's pain in her voice, the huskiness in it as she hurriedly controlled it again.

Finch was regarding her with interest. Had he caught the emotion as well, or did he just look at her as most men looked at a beautiful woman, and feel an edge of passion?

Miriam looked down at something on the table and smiled very slightly, almost in apology. "Aaron lost his cousin Zachary before the gold rush really began. They were more like brothers. Zack was one of the best men I ever knew." Her voice dropped a little lower. "He died defending an old man from a beating by a crowd of drunkards. They lynched the drunkards, but that didn't bring Zachary back. Actually I don't think they even tried them. Just . . . strung them up in a tree. Not that there was any doubt that they were guilty . . ."

Everyone else was looking at Miriam, but Beata turned and looked at Aaron. Then instantly she regretted it. She saw a sudden, overwhelming sense of loss in his face, as if the grief were still new even now. She felt intrusive to be there, never mind to have observed it.

Why on earth had Miriam mentioned it? And in front of other people they barely knew? How could she be so insensitive?

"And I lost my first husband," Miriam went on. Now her voice was tight with her own pain. "He was . . . killed also . . ."

"I'm so sorry," Finch and Walbrook said almost together.

Again Beata looked at Aaron, and this time his expression was unreadable to her. She remembered hearing the news of her own first husband's death, and the sense of shock and sudden emptiness it brought. It had happened up in the foothills somewhere where the gold claims had no security, where there was no law and very little in the way of community. Miriam's first husband, Piers Astley, had been Aaron's most trusted lieutenant, a man with almost everyone's respect. Maybe that was what got him killed.

But who knew what he was like when the doors were closed and there was no one watching except his wife? They were all sitting here around this rich and elegant table in London, exquisitely dressed, dining on the best food in the land. They ate with silver cutlery from porcelain plates, and drank the best wine from cut-crystal glasses. They discussed the endowment of a university chair in memory of Ingram York—High Court judge, wife beater, and a man of violent and twisted sexual appetites.

For a moment Beata felt her gorge rise as if she were going to be sick. Then she controlled it, sipped her wine, and looked down at her plate so no one could meet her eyes.

They were talking about Zachary Clive and what a fine man he had been. Aaron's voice was warm with the emotion of the memory of Zack's integrity, his generosity of spirit, the things he loved and made him laugh.

Beata looked at Miriam, and saw tears in her eyes. What had happened? And why did any of it matter so passionately now?

It was not until the last course was served that the subject returned again to Ingram York.

Finch turned to Beata. "It must be extremely difficult for you to think of such a thing so soon, Lady York," he said gently. "But there are many arrangements to be made, if it is to be effected within the next year. All we wish from you is your permission to endow a chair in your late husband's name. We feel it would be a most fitting tribute to his memory, and of far more use to society than a marble bust, or some other tangible memorial or engraving. We are very fortunate that Mr. Clive has offered the sort of financial backing that makes it possible."

"Indeed," she said in agreement. "We have more than enough statues and plaques. I have no idea why Mr. Clive should be so generous, but I am most grateful." She looked at Aaron, smiling to rob the words of any implied criticism. "I was not aware that you even knew my husband."

Aaron smiled back at her. It was candid, genuine, and disarming. "I didn't, Lady York. I read some of his judgments, going back several years. I want to endow a chair because I believe in the wisdom of the law, and the lucidity of it. When mixed with mercy it has the power to defend us all from anarchy, industrial or civil. I have no influence on the law myself. I deal in land and international trade. Far better I do this in the name of an eminent judge whose name is held in wide respect, and who unfortunately had recently died."

He glanced at Miriam, then back again at Beata. "I wish two professors to be appointed who will treat the law as a high ideal, with the strength of a great sword that has been hammered out of white-hot metal, and annealed in the pure ice water of logic and impartiality. I hope that you will think that a worthy thing to do for the future and a fitting tribute to your husband, so his memory may last and bear fruit in future years."

Miriam moved very slightly in her seat, as if she had cramped a muscle.

Beata wanted to look at her, and dared not.

"No one could have a more excellent memorial," she replied. What else could she say? That Ingram was totally unworthy of it? That perhaps he had once been a good jurist? The last thing on earth she wanted to do was make his private obscenities public! The lie would have to be lived to perfection if she were to keep any dignity at all. She had a right to privacy; indeed she needed it if she were to survive.

She forced herself to meet Aaron Clive's gaze and make herself smile at him. "It is a wonderful thing to do. Forgive me if I am overwhelmed."

"Of course," he said gently, moving his hand onto the white linen of the tablecloth to touch her. "I'm sorry it is so hasty. I should have left you time to mourn, and then asked you, but I want to do it as soon as possible. Perhaps even for the new academic year, if that is within reach?" He turned to Finch.

"I see no reason why not," Finch replied. "With Lady York's approval?"

"You have it, and my gratitude," she replied.

Miriam rose to her feet, looking at Beata. "Then shall we leave the gentlemen to their port? We could take tea in the withdrawing room, and perhaps a few chocolates? Do you still care for chocolates? Truffles? I have some from Belgium. I always think they are the best, don't you?"

Twenty years vanished and Beata recalled perfectly sitting with

Miriam in the home she had lived in in San Francisco, watching the wind ruffle the bay and seeing the shadows chase one another over the water. They had had a box of chocolates between them. In between laughing and talking, and sharing secrets, they had eaten all but a few of them. It brought those wild and yet oddly innocent days back as if they had been last week.

Beata rose also, steadying herself for a moment against the table, and then turned to Miriam. "I still love them just as much."

The withdrawing room was warm, and extremely pleasant because there were only the two of them. Had there been others, Beata would not have felt it suitable to come this soon after Ingram's death. Mourning was not really a choice, and as such it was a miserable time. The last thing some people wish is continuing to wear drab clothes so you look as wretched as you feel, and sit about in a house with mirrors turned to the wall. There was nothing whatever to do but contemplate your aloneness, and write a few unnecessary letters. She would much rather have been busy, even if it were only with some manual tasks such as arranging flowers or mending the finer linens where embroidery needed restoring.

Oliver Rathbone had often spoken to her of Hester Monk's clinic in Portpool Lane, and now when Miriam asked her how she meant to fill her days, she answered honestly.

"I would rather scrub floors than do nothing at all. Perhaps I shall find something worthy to do." She used the word with self-mockery, and yet she actually meant it. What was anyone, without purpose?

Miriam's eyes widened with interest. "Really? You can hardly scrub your own floors! Where did you have in mind?" There was laughter in her eyes, which she was trying to conceal. Had she already read Beata so well? They had known each other twenty years ago, but that had been in another world, thousands of miles away, and in another age.

"A woman I don't know personally, but about whom I have heard much, keeps a clinic for women off the street, who are injured or ill. . . ."

Miriam shrugged and shook her head. "She sounds frightful! Does she stop for prayers every hour, and preach to them of virtue?"

"Good heavens!" Beata nearly laughed. "I don't think so. She used to be an army nurse in the Crimea, and I have heard that she is highly opinionated. I would doubt that virtue, to her, means abstinence. It is far more likely to mean courage, compassion, and the integrity to be brutally honest, first with yourself and then with others, and never to run away just because you are exhausted or afraid."

"Then I deserve to be fed a large portion of humble pie," Miriam said, reaching for another chocolate and pushing the box toward Beata.

Beata also took another. They really were very good.

The conversation continued pleasantly, a mixture of memories and current interest. Without being aware of exactly how it happened, Beata found herself telling Miriam about Oliver Rathbone, and about William Monk. In answer to Miriam's questions, she described what she knew of him, which was mostly what Oliver had said.

Miriam listened with great interest as if it were important to her, not simply a subject of courtesy. Or possibly it was merely to take Beata's mind off her recent loss. It was a relief to be able to speak of someone else, of interesting things that had not emotionally involved her. She described Monk as vividly as she could, painting a picture in words for Miriam, based mostly on Oliver's description of Monk's nature, his persistence, and his skill in deduction.

"He sounds formidable," Miriam said with pleasure. "There was a chase of an escaped prisoner near Aaron's warehouse on the river a few days ago. Four of them ended up in the water, one fugitive, one customs officer, and two Thames River Police. From what Aaron told me, it was a fearful event, a disaster. The fugitive escaped, the customs man drowned, and the two policemen were left to do the explaining. But Aaron told me one of the police was the commander. I think he said his name was Monk. Could that be he? Apparently he was the one who jumped in and pulled the customs man out of the water, but couldn't save him even so."

"That sounds like him," Beata agreed.

Miriam shook her head, smiling. "Not everyone would jump into the Thames in November to save anyone from drowning. He sounds most interesting—in fact a little like a young man I remember in San Francisco, years ago. Lean and very strong, dark hair and a clever face, all bones, and a sense of humor that was quick and very dry. I liked him, although he frightened me a little." She looked at the rich folds of the curtains, as if into another world. "I had the feeling that when he made up his mind to do something, nothing on earth would stop him. He left after a year or so, and I never knew what happened to him. It couldn't be the same man, could it?" She looked back suddenly at Beata.

"I don't think so," Beata replied. "That would probably describe a fair number of adventurers at that time. Did he seem to you like someone who would make a good policeman?"

Miriam laughed. "Not in the slightest! I just found him interesting. I always liked dangerous men."

"Well, as I recall, San Francisco was full of them then!"

They were both laughing when the butler came to tell Miriam that a Mr. McNab had called to see her, and could she spare him a few minutes.

She looked surprised and somewhat taken aback.

"Are you sure it is not Mr. Clive he wishes to see?"

"Yes, ma'am. He seemed quite clear," the butler replied. "Shall I show him to the morning room, ma'am? I am afraid the fire has rather died in there and it is a little chill."

Miriam hesitated, turning it over in her mind.

Beata stood up. "Please excuse me for a few minutes, and see Mr. McNab in here. I'm afraid we seem to have eaten most of the chocolate! I shall return when he has left." She moved toward the door without waiting for Miriam to answer.

The butler opened it for her and she went out into the hall. She was not quite sure what she was going to do after visiting the cloakroom, but the hall was pleasant, and the pictures and artifacts were full of memories for her.

She passed the man she took to be McNab with no more than an inclination of her head in acknowledgment.

A few moments later, she returned to the hall and was admiring some intricate silver in a niche. Then she moved to another, close to the withdrawing room door, which was very slightly ajar. She heard the voices inside and stopped, motionless. It was the name of Monk that arrested her attention and made her listen shamelessly.

"I need more information!" McNab said clearly. It had to be McNab. Beata had never heard his voice, but she knew he was the only man in there with Miriam. He sounded both angry and urgent.

"Why?" Miriam asked. Her tone was calm but there was an edge of impatience in it. Beata knew even from that short word that Miriam did not like the man. There was politeness in her, but no warmth. And she was a woman who could charm with a glance, and, if she wished to, melt hearts with laughter. "Surely that is enough for your purposes?"

"Just answer me what I ask," McNab said levelly.

"I don't know what else you want," she replied. "I already told you, above average height, lean as a whip, straight, dark hair, and gray eyes so dark they looked black at times."

"His name, woman!" McNab said sharply. "That description could fit a score of men, half the Spaniards or Italians in the world!"

"I already told you," she replied with thinly held patience. "I think the name was Monk, but I'm not sure. It could have been something else like it. I didn't know him. For heaven's sake, he was a sailor, one of the small schooner captains, a chancer out to make his fortune."

"But you saw him with your first husband, Astley?" McNab insisted.

"Yes, briefly, and at a distance," she replied.

"How many times?"

"You exceed your manners, Mr. McNab!" Now her voice was tight and hard. If he had thought she would be intimidated he was no judge of character. Beata had seen Miriam face down bigger men than this McNab.

"Are you not forgetting your own needs, Mrs. Clive?" McNab retorted, but there was less menace in his voice, as if he had taken a step back both literally and also metaphorically. "If he was there, then he serves your needs as well as mine."

"And was he?" she asked instantly. "Are you certain?"

"Not yet," he admitted. "But I will be. Believe me, Mrs. Clive, I will be. Who is the woman in mourning? What part has she in this?"

"Lady York is a friend of mine who has just lost her husband," Miriam answered. "She has no part in this at all. And if you have any sense, you will pass her politely and make no remark beyond wishing her a pleasant evening, and beg her pardon for interrupting. I have already told you what she said. If I learn more, I will tell you. Now leave!"

There was a moment's silence. Beata moved quickly and, she hoped, silently as far away from the withdrawing room door as she could. When she heard his footsteps on the hall floor, she was several yards away, staring at a painting of a woman carrying a basket of flowers, bright blossoms lying casually on the woven straw.

She turned as she heard his footsteps, as one naturally would.

He stopped, and then walked over toward her.

She gulped, waiting. He must not catch even a breath of the notion that she had been listening.

"Good evening, Lady York," he said a little stiffly. "My name is McNab. I apologize for interrupting your evening. It was a matter of some urgency, or I would not have done so."

She smiled at him as if she had overheard nothing.

"Of course," she agreed. "It is of no consequence. I assure you."

"May I offer you my condolences on the death of your husband," he added quietly. "There is nothing harder in life than the loss of someone you love." Now there was emotion in his voice and pain in his face. It robbed her of the chill with which she would have replied to him.

"Indeed there isn't, Mr. McNab," she said gently. "I can see that your sympathy is genuine, and I thank you for it."

He bowed his head just enough to be courteous. "Ma'am." Then he walked toward the door where the butler was waiting to usher him out.

Beata returned very slowly to the withdrawing room.

THE FOLLOWING DAY BEATA put on a plain black costume with a heavy jacket, partly to be inconspicuous among other pedestrians on Gray's

Inn Road, where she left her carriage and walked the short distance to Portpool Lane. There had been no way to ascertain before going that Hester Monk would be there at this time in the late morning. It was too early to have sent a note and receive a reply but it was as good a time as any to begin. If she had to make more than one journey it did not matter. She had nothing else of importance to do. That was one of the more miserable aspects of mourning, the slow boredom of it.

She turned into the lane, checking the name on the wall to be certain. The pavement was so narrow only one person could use it, and the stones were uneven and covered in ice from the water that dripped from the overhanging eaves above. The odor of wood rot and drains was everywhere.

But she must persist. Meeting Hester was important. If she loved Oliver, and ever dreamed of marrying him one day, if he asked her, then she must learn more of the woman he had once really loved. Margaret Ballinger she was not afraid of. That sadness had brought with it its own ending. Beata was not afraid of comparison with her.

Hester was different. Oliver still spoke of her with not just respect but admiration, and there was a softness in his eyes even at the thought of her. Her beauty was inside, not outside, which meant that it would never fade. In fact, it might in time grow even deeper.

Beata was beautiful on the outside; whatever Ingram had thought, she knew that. It was the inside that betrayed her, the weakness to give in rather than fight to defend herself, risk more violence, more humiliation. It was the degradation she had yielded to because she could see no way of evading it and surviving. Hester had survived the battlefield! Her courage must be insurmountable—supreme. How could any woman compare with her?

Beata hesitated on the pavement for a moment before going on. The brewery loomed huge and grim ahead of her. The row of houses that had once been a brothel and was now a clinic dominated the other side.

She went in through the door and approached the small table straight ahead of her. Would she be taken for a street woman in trouble?

The thought was amusing. She found herself smiling in spite of the situation. Ingram would have a fit if he could see her now.

A plain, middle-aged woman came out of one of the several doors and approached her. Her face was calm and she had a unique dignity in the way she walked.

"Can I help you?" she asked quietly, apparently without any judgment as to whom Beata might be.

"Thank you . . ." Now that the moment was here, Beata found the words catching in her throat. This was absurd. She had come to offer help, not to beg for it. "My name is Beata York. I have come to see Mrs. Monk, to ask her if I might be of assistance in any way. I am newly widowed, and I have a great deal of time on my hands."

The woman smiled with apparent surprise.

"Claudine Burroughs," she replied with more warmth in her smile. "I'm sure Mrs. Monk will be happy to see you. Do you mind coming with me up to the medicine room? We are just checking supplies."

"I should be happy to," Beata answered, following Claudine as she turned and led the way back into the warren of corridors that twisted through the three houses that formed the clinic. They went up and down stairs and around corners until they found the medicine room, which was quite large and had a door that locked.

Hester was checking something on a piece of paper as Claudine came to the door.

"This is Mrs. York," Claudine said, as if it were a sufficient introduction. Perhaps the fact that Beata was wearing entirely black clothes told all the rest that was necessary.

Beata had not known quite what to expect, but not the rather thin woman who stood in front of her, pencil in one hand, paper in the other. Hester was not traditionally beautiful, but even more than the grace in her, there was a burning vitality, an energy of spirit that commanded attention. In spite of the strength in her manner, there was a gentleness in her face, even a vulnerability.

"How do you do, Lady York?" she said warmly, and Claudine gave a nod of acknowledgment at her title. "Sir Oliver has spoken so well of you I feel as if I know you, at least in part."

Beata felt some of the anxiety slip away. Oliver had spoken of her to Hester, and well!

"It is obligatory that I spend the appropriate time in mourning," Beata replied. "But I believe it is not forbidden to be useful. It is surely better than sitting at home doing nothing. I have no skills of nursing, but I have not always lived an idle life. Long ago in California I did all kinds of things. Is there something I can do here?"

As if she understood all the layers of deeper need beneath the words, Hester answered without hesitation. "Oh, certainly! If you don't mind chores like making beds, sweeping floors, carrying meals, and helping some people to eat, we will be grateful for all the help you can offer. If you are still willing after your mourning is over, we always need someone in certain social positions to help us raise funds to purchase medicines, let alone food and coal." She gave a rueful smile. "I am terrible at it. I have a finite temper with hypocrites, and a sarcastic tongue. I've probably lost more sympathy than I've gained."

Beata found herself smiling. "I'm afraid I have learned to be polite whatever I feel, sadly. I'm not at all sure it is a virtue . . ." She was apologizing for things Hester would never know, never even guess.

Hester shook her head a little. "I think it's called good manners. I know compassion, but I don't always have good sense. If you would really like to help, we would be grateful. I'll find you a pinafore to protect your clothes, and I'll introduce you to the people you'll need to know, at least to begin with."

She had committed herself. Beata smiled back, and accepted.

Claudine took over counting the medicines, and Beata followed Hester downstairs again to meet the bookkeeper, Squeaky Robinson. He was an irascible man of more than middle age, lean and black-coated, with a tangle of gray hair that looked as if it had never seen a brush, and wildly uneven teeth that made it impossible to tell if he was smiling or snarling.

He looked her up and down as if she had been presented for his inspection.

"Judge's wife?" he said to Hester.

"Judge's widow," Beata corrected him smartly.

Squeaky glared at her. She held his gaze until he finally nodded and pursed his lips. From his look she deduced that he knew something of Ingram, and for a moment she felt her face flame. What madness had brought her here? This was dreadful!

"Then I guess you know a thing or two," Squeaky said at last. "You won't have your head in the clouds, with a Bible in one hand and a feather duster in the other."

She found herself laughing a little hysterically at the vision. It was uneven laughter, too close to losing control. She stopped abruptly.

"I'm sorry," Hester said. "You can see how much we need someone who can exercise good manners, regardless of their own thoughts and feelings. I can do it now and then but, like Squeaky, I slip up." She held out her hand, as a man would have. "I was an army nurse, and at times my experience of reality shows rather too much."

Her smile and her direct, unjudging gaze eased Beata's self-consciousness away like a warm iron over silk. She smiled back. "I imagine only practicality is any use to the sick," she replied, taking Hester's hand and gripping it warmly. As she did so, she understood what Oliver had loved in this woman, and she was not afraid of it anymore. Hester's virtues were real, hard won, and she would like to emulate them. She could! She had the battles to win and the fields in which to do so. Tomorrow she would not bother with black at the clinic; gray was more practical.

"Drowned," Hyde said with a grimace. He and Monk were standing in his small office in the morgue. "But I can't say how much your blow contributed to it. Sorry. Like to be able to say it didn't, but I couldn't swear to that on the stand. You definitely stunned him. It may have been sufficient to stop him from functioning enough to breathe. All I can say, if it's any comfort to you, is that if you hadn't hit him, I'd most certainly be giving this report to whoever would take over from you."

"Thank you," Monk said bleakly. "I assume that's what you also told McNab?"

"It's the truth," Hyde answered. "He was none too pleased, but there's nothing he can do."

Monk did not reply to that. He left the morgue and went out into the street, much less certain than Hyde that there was nothing McNab could do. He took a cab back toward Wapping, the subject still heavy in his mind. Had he really done all he could to save Pettifer? Or, believing that he was the person they were after, had he been willing enough to let him die, if the rescue would have been a real risk to his own life?

He weighed it in his mind as he rode through the gray, busy streets. Was it an excusable decision any man might have made? Even should have made? Or was it an error of judgment that had cost another man his life?

He had thought Owen was McNab's man, and Pettifer was the prisoner. Was that because of something in the way they had attacked each other? Owen had seemed to be behind Pettifer, when actually he had simply come from the other side. Pettifer was big, heavily bearded, and had used some pretty ripe language, so had Monk simply assumed he was the prisoner through personal prejudice, a judgment based on superficialities?

But then, if he were a customs officer who had just lost a prisoner, the second one in a week, might he not be expected to be in a fury? Anyone judging Monk would point that out.

Anyone? Who, for example?

McNab, of course.

Monk got out of the hansom, paid the driver, and walked along the dockside in the wind. There were gulls circling above him and the incoming tide was choppy, here and there white-crested. It was a day when a water patrol would be hard work. Not only strength would be required but endurance, and seamanship.

He thought of Orme with a recurring emptiness of loss. In spite of the fact that he had been well into his sixties, he could keep going all day, hoarding his strength, using the water's current, the boat's weight, its impetus. Monk had learned to appreciate him at the time, but even more since his death. He realized only now how much he had asked his opinion, relied on his judgment of a situation, his word of warning now and then, his example dealing with men.

It had not been just his knowledge, it was his wisdom, his rare laughter, his love of the wild birds in the sky across the Estuary. He knew them all by their flight patterns. It added to Monk's pleasure to know such things.

And it was his ability to tell a man the harshest truths without making them seem like criticism. He had learned his craft through years—and took pleasure in passing it on. He had had no sons, only a daughter, and it was his legacy that he had taught two generations of River Police what he knew. That very much included Monk.

Now Monk wished intensely that Orme were here to help him make a judgment of McNab. How much was it simply personal dislike that McNab was using on Monk, as a skilled man learns to use his attacker's own weight and impetus against him?

He stopped and stared across the gray water, trying to think of every operation he had carried out that could have had any effect on the customs men, or on McNab in particular. Nothing came to mind. Usually they both benefited. Was there one where McNab felt he had done the work, and Monk had taken the credit? Could it be something as petty as that? It sounded like the sort of thing schoolboys do in the playground.

Or was it interservice rather than personal? Customs against police? Orme would have known. Monk tried to think back if Orme had ever said anything, given any warning, however discreet.

There was none he could think of.

He wondered about asking Hooper but felt reluctant to do so. Maybe he cared more what Hooper thought of him. Or was he more afraid of his judgment because in some way he trusted him less? Hooper was roughly his own age, whereas Orme had been almost a generation older and had known Monk's weaknesses right from the beginning, when Monk was still only temporarily assisting the River Police. He recalled the horror of plague and the nightmare ship going down the river with Devon at the wheel, sailing into oblivion, giving his life to save everyone else.

A man who had shared that with you forged both a bond that was not like any other, and a unique kind of grief at his loss.

Had McNab in effect murdered Orme, by betraying the raid to the gunrunners, or was Monk trying to blame McNab for something that was essentially his own fault?

It was past time he found out for certain whether the battle on deck had been a piece of bad luck, which strikes anyone now and then, or if his suspicions about McNab's betrayal were in any part correct.

Why had he not faced it and pursued it to the end before? It was months since Orme's death now, and yet he had not looked at the evidence regarding the ambush of the gunrunning ship by river pirates at exactly the same hour as the River Police raid.

Monk and his men had come from upriver, just at daylight. They had come out of the west and the darkness, catching the gunrunners completely by surprise. The battle had been raging on deck in the broadening light. This had been very definitely to the police's advantage, when the river pirates had boarded from the downriver side, climbing up onto the deck and very nearly carrying the battle.

It was in that chaos that Monk and his men had won, but at the loss of Orme. He had been so badly injured that in spite of everything they could do, he had bled to death. They had got him ashore, Monk carrying him in his arms. He had seemed so light. Monk's own exhaustion had been nothing. They had done all they could, every one of them, weary, blood spattered, desperate to help. But in the end Monk had sat all night in the hospital, watching the life drain out of Orme's body and leave it a surprisingly small and empty shell.

It was Monk who had had to go and tell Orme's daughter and her husband and child that Orme would not be coming to retire with them in a couple of weeks. He could still see the shock in their faces, the empty eyes. They had not blamed him, at least not openly. But he had blamed himself—and McNab, for giving warning of the raid to the pirates.

It was time he proved this, even if no more than to himself. And it was time he found the truth as to how much it was his fault . . . even if that turned out to be entirely.

He reached the Wapping Police Station and went inside, passing his men with a brief acknowledgment. In his office he started going through all the reports of information before the event. Who had first learned of the shipment of guns coming in? What had they said, exactly? A man in Customs named Makepeace had warned the River Police, specifically

Laker. Who had followed it up? What information had they, from where? After that Laker, then Hooper, had been getting it from McNab himself. How reliable was any of it? It had seemed, at the time, beyond doubt.

What could McNab have known of the planned raid, and when? What had he told Monk? That was less specific. Monk read every paper and wrote down the time sequence, all the information, how they had received it, from whom, and exactly when.

It was when he read the statement from Customs for the third time that he caught the discrepancy. It was very small, just two pieces of information out of order in time. Originally it had been an estimate of tides and therefore of the hour the pirates would attack. It could even be a clerical error, a three misread as a five, and carried that way. He'd done that himself, years ago. He had been lucky that error then had not cost him more. The issue was that he knew it could occur accidentally.

But if this was not an error, then one of McNab's men had known of the smuggling and contacted the river pirates to question them two hours earlier than he had said he did. There was all the difference in the world between five in the morning, and three. If the pirates had been questioned at three, that would have allowed them time to lay the ambush.

The man was Makepeace. But if he were to be trapped, it must be carefully, with all the information in Monk's hand before he acted.

Feeling a little light-headed, Monk folded up the sheet of paper with the statement on it and locked it in the safe. Then he called Hooper.

Hooper came in with his easy, loose-limbed stance, and half smile. "Yes, sir?"

"I think I've found where the information went from McNab's office to the river pirates." Monk passed his notes across to Hooper. "Original's in the safe," he added. "But tell me what you make of that."

Hooper sat down and read the notes in Monk's handwriting. Then he looked up. "If that's right, and we follow it up, we could be certain of it," he said without hesitation. "But what a river pirate's word is worth in court, I don't know."

"I don't want it for court, I just want to know for myself." Monk realized he had been more honest than he intended. "It might get more weight later," he added. "If McNab is the instigator and he'll do that once, he could do it again. Even if it doesn't stand alone, it could be corroborative. He'll know I know. He won't catch us a second time."

A curious expression crossed Hooper's face. "You sure you want to do that, sir? Sometimes it's better not to tip your hand. McNab's . . . dangerous."

It was not fear. Monk stared at Hooper and saw nothing but puzzlement in him, and caution. He had never seen Hooper retreat from confrontation, only from foolishness, from rushing into ill-thought-out attacks. He was a good second in command, better than Monk thought he had ever been himself. Better than he himself had been to Runcorn, at least in the days he could remember. But then he had hated Runcorn, as Runcorn had hated him. Hooper was far less readable. He had an internal composure, a knowledge of himself that Monk was beginning to ascertain only now.

"I need more," he said. "I want to go and meet this man, Makepeace's informant, Torrance. Do you know him?"

Hooper's smile was sour. "River pirate, sir, when it suits him. Mostly takes no risks, sells information. But a good captain's going to take him along, just to keep him honest, like. You don't set somebody up if you're going to be there yourself when it happens. You could too easily be one of the casualties."

"Indeed you don't," Monk agreed. "Where do I look for him? Jacob's Island? Sounds like his sort of place."

"Yes, I think so," Hooper agreed. "I'm coming with you."

Monk had seldom tried arguing with Hooper. Hooper weighed what he said. So far, when he insisted on something, he had been right, except on the one or two occasions they had both been wrong. Neither had referred to them again, just exchanged the odd, wry glance, an acknowledgment of luck and error.

Jacob's Island was not a real island in the sense that the river flowed right around it. It was one of the worst areas in the dockland, separated from the shore by a morass of deep, hungry river mud. It was built up with scores of rotting warehouses and warrens of passages and rooms, all slowly sinking into the ooze beneath. Most of it was dangerous because of the rats, both of the human variety and the literally verminous that infested it. And all of it was dangerous from the rotting wood and collapsing floors, which could drop a heavy man into mud that would never let him go. From the thick slime beneath it, lost bodies did not rise to the surface, to drift up or down river. The tide rose and fell, but it did not run. There was no current. The stench was palpable.

Monk and Hooper walked the last three hundred yards from where they had moored their boat. Both of them carried loaded weapons. It was a kind of no-man's-land.

It was one of those leaden November days when the rain threatened but did not come, and there was what was called "a lazy wind," meaning it would go through you rather than around.

Hooper turned up the collar of his pea coat. "D'you think McNab planned for all this, sir?" he asked quite casually, as if the idea had just occurred to him. He had a dry sense of humor and Monk waited for the follow-up.

"Don't you?" he said at last, when Hooper did not add anything.

"I think he's a chancer, an opportunist," Hooper answered. "He takes other people's work and bends it around. He doesn't make it himself."

Monk considered for a moment, recalling what he could. "Riding on other people's backs," he said at last. "Sounds about right."

Hooper smiled and said nothing.

Monk shivered as they walked across one of the rickety bridges over the mud onto the island. The dank buildings creaked and sagged lower. The air tasted foul. Hooper followed just behind him, looking from left to right for any sign of human movement. The wind fluttered a few discarded rags and bits of old newspaper. The water lapped higher with the rising tide, giving the illusion that the ground was sinking fast enough to see.

As soon as they were inside the first building they saw a bundle of sacking and an old blanket in the corner. It stirred vaguely, enough to show that there was a live person sleeping underneath, and not a corpse.

Monk was profoundly glad not to be alone. One man could not watch in all directions in case he was crept up on. He and Hooper ignored the rats. No one wasted bullets killing them. There were thousands of them, and the shots would be a warning to anyone here.

A hundred feet farther in they found the man they were looking for. Hooper knew him by sight. They were deep inside the warren of passages and interconnected rooms. He actually had a wood-burning stove going and the air was warm. It made the smell worse, more acrid in the throat and lungs.

Torrance was a lean man with a large mouth and a thick black beard and mustache, which made his head look disproportionately huge. He looked up as they came in. There was neither fear nor curiosity in his eyes. Monk had not expected there to be. Jacob's Island had eyes everywhere. Torrance would have been aware of them as soon as they set foot on the bridge.

Monk had a bag with half a dozen fresh ham sandwiches he had bought from a peddler on the quay. "Food," he said, holding the bag so Torrance could see it. Neither of them made any comment. He sat down cross-legged on the floor. Hooper remained standing, looking casual, but with his weight so balanced he could have struck out in an instant, or moved at the sound of a breath.

Torrance said nothing, waiting for Monk to speak.

"I want a little bit of information," Monk began quietly. "Old stuff. The gunrunners we caught about three months ago. Big battle. I'm sure you remember it. . . ."

"Everybody remembers it," Torrance replied guardedly. "Sent 'em all down. Won't see the water, nor the sky again, for years. Hard, that, for a man o' the sea."

"Right," Monk agreed. "Unless they escape, of course. But that's not likely. Won't be getting them out for questioning, or evidence."

Torrance gave a gap-toothed grin. "Not doing too well, Mr. McNab, is 'e? That's two 'e's lost in the last ten days, like. 'E in't no friend o' yours. Everybody knows that."

Monk drew in breath to ask Torrance if he knew why, then stopped himself. It was an admission of ignorance that would give Torrance a leverage he would certainly use.

"I know," he agreed instead. "Who told you in the first place?" He made a guess. "Was it Mad Lammond?" He mentioned a river pirate well known along the waterfront.

Torrance looked slightly taken aback, then he recovered quickly, a gleam of satisfaction in his eyes. "No it weren't. Wouldn't go nowhere near Mad Lammond, even if yer paid me!"

"Then who was it that told you?" Monk resisted the temptation to put the name in his mouth.

"Were McNab's own man. Big feller wi' a beard. Good as mine." He gave the huge, gap-toothed grin again.

Monk had the uneasy feeling that somewhere in this he was being distracted, duped, but he could not see how. "Name?"

"Never asked 'im," Torrance replied. "'Ow about one o' them sandwiches, then?"

Monk passed him one and he ate it, cramming it into his mouth in two bites, and then had trouble swallowing it.

"Name?" Monk repeated.

"Feller wot got drowned," Torrance replied, looking slightly sideways at Monk and holding his hand out for another sandwich. "Reckon you knows all about that. Did us a favor, you did, so I'll let you off light. All them sandwiches'll be enough. Won't ask fer nothing else, not this time, like."

Monk looked at Hooper.

A bubble of gas came up through a stretch of mud, and burst, releasing a foul stench.

Hooper remained where he was, staring around in all directions, then back at Torrance.

Torrance groaned. "That in't nice, Mr. 'Ooper. Yer think I've got someone as'll jump yer? There in't nobody 'ere, ceptin' me. Leastways, not on this part o' the island."

"We've been here long enough," Monk said quietly. He passed the rest of the sandwiches over to Torrance, who snatched them from him.

Hooper took a step toward Torrance, and he shrank back.

"Why?" he said softly. "What was in it for McNab to give the pirates that tip-off, eh?"

Torrance blinked.

Monk glanced around them, then at Torrance. He, too, took a step closer. Was it as simple as money?

Torrance clutched the sandwiches close to his chest. "'Ow in 'ell should I know? Mebbe find out, but it'll cost yer!"

Monk leaned forward. "Leave it alone, if you know what's good for you. You don't want to make an enemy of either of us."

Torrance smiled very slowly, and with soft, insolent sarcasm. "Oh, I know which side me bread's buttered, Mr. Monk, sir. Believe me. I know 'oo's goin' ter last, an' 'oo ain't. Mr. McNab don't like yer, an' that's fer sure. An' I don't wanna be in the middle of yer. What 'appened ter Mr. Orme, an' Mr. Pettifer, I ain't gonna let it 'appen ter me."

Somewhere out of sight something fell into the water. Monk knew it was time they left. Perhaps it was even past time. He was glad of the weight of the gun in his pocket. He signaled to Hooper with his hand.

Without speaking, they turned and went, picking their way out slowly, careful not to return the way they had come in. There seemed to be water dripping everywhere. The ground underneath them was wetter. Was it sinking, or the tide rising? Or were they imagining it out of fear?

The smell of river mud and sewage filled the nose and rested on the tongue.

Another rat fell into the water somewhere.

Outside under the open sky there was a sudden sense of freedom. The rain had stopped and there were clear patches of blue above, even a weak light on the water.

Monk strode forward rapidly; he had to control himself not to run. If Torrance was telling the truth, then it was beginning to make sense. McNab was behind the pirate sabotage of the raid on the gunrunners, as Monk had believed. It might be for money, or some bigger ambition of McNab's. That was something he would still have to find out, if he were to prove it. But he felt freer just from the knowledge. It was McNab, whatever the reason, whether Makepeace had known what he was doing or not. It was not Monk's incompetence in the raid, which had been the source of the dark fear crouching at the back of his mind. Makepeace, acting for McNab, was responsible for the injured men, and for Orme's death.

They reached the place where they had left their boat and got in, glad to heave hard on the oars, stretching their backs on the way upriver toward Wapping. The smell of salt and fish was clean. Even the turgid water was better than the stagnant, clinging odor of mud.

They rowed in silence. Conversation was difficult when they were both facing the same direction, one behind the other.

They were almost at the Wapping Stairs and in the slack water close in to the shore, when Hooper finally spoke. He leaned on the oar, holding the boat still, then turned in his seat and put one leg on each side of the bench so he could face Monk.

"Why's McNab doing this then, sir? If he's that bent on it, we need to know why. Can't bring Mr. Orme back, but might save the next one he has in his sights." He looked at Monk steadily, his dark eyes almost unblinking.

Monk took a deep breath. It was McNab who had been the immediate cause of the ambush, and if it was hatred of Monk that had driven him to it, then Monk had no right to lie to Hooper.

"I don't know," he admitted. "You'll remember I told you about the accident I was in, that I lost my memory—lost my past?"

"Of course. And you thought McNab might have a grudge against you."

"Yes, and now I'm certain of it, though I can still remember nothing from before I came round in hospital after the accident."

"What are your memories from then?" Hooper asked tentatively.

Monk chose his words carefully, and yet they were still awkward.

"When I was well enough to leave the hospital I got my own clothes back. They were better quality than I had expected, more expensive.

And yet they all fitted pretty well. A bit big in places, because I had lost weight lying on my back doing nothing." He recalled it ruefully: a phys- ical memory of discomfort, smooth fabric that did not seem right and yet slipped on easily.

Hooper sat watching him, still holding the oar to keep them steady in the water.

"I found where I lived," Monk went on, wishing Hooper would show some reaction. "Very ordinary rooms, but my landlady knew me. I went back to work because there was no choice. There were bills to pay, largely tailors' bills!" He had thought of it since with amusement, self- mockery, but telling Hooper in his work trousers and old pea coat, it brought back his feeling then of embarrassment.

Hooper conceded a smile, but he did not interrupt.

"They gave me a case still unsolved from before my accident. It was a gentleman officer from the army in the Crimea, and here, who had been beaten to death in his flat."

Hooper nodded, his eyes steady on Monk's face.

"I went over the crime, detail by detail, and eventually I solved it," he said, only just loud enough to be heard over the noises of the river. "But while I was doing it I discovered a lot about myself, and why other men feared me. I also recognized many of the scenes from the crime. I had been there before. At one time I even thought I had killed the man myself. . . ."

Hooper jerked his head up, caught by the moment, looking at him at last. Monk saw pity in his eyes, gentle, without judgment.

He smiled, partly to hide his gratitude. It should not matter so much!

"I didn't, but I came close. He was one of the worst men I ever knew. After the end of that case I went on working in the regular police, get- ting more and more at odds with my commander. I never did tell him I'd lost my memory, except for the very occasional flashes of a scene or two. I managed to fake it. He knows now, and we have become the friends we used to be, in the beginning twenty years ago."

"Who else knows?" Hooper said at last.

"In the police, only Superintendent Runcorn of the Metropolitan Police, my old commander. He's in the Blackheath area now."

He would be highly unlikely to keep his position, if it were known. But Hooper would know that.

Sitting on the bank, rocking slightly, as if the river were breathing beneath them, Monk felt as vulnerable as if a firing squad were standing aiming at him. Only every gun was loaded, not just the one unknown.

"So there could be any reason why McNab hates you?" Hooper said softly.

"Yes," Monk agreed. "It could even be justified. . . ."

"Or not," Hooper argued. "A good man would have faced you with it."

"He may have," Monk pointed out. "Or it could have been so obvious no one could have misunderstood. I don't know."

Hooper took a deep breath, then bit his lip. "Does he know that you can't remember?"

"I think so." Monk swallowed, and then his mouth was dry. "He's made a few oblique remarks and he smiles far too often."

Hooper looked at him steadily. "Then we assume he does."

Monk heard the word *we*, not *you*. Did Hooper mean it? Was he even conscious of having used it? Then he realized that of course Hooper would be thinking of the safety of the whole force, not just the survival of Monk himself, and he felt a loneliness so wide and deep he could drown in it.

"We'd better give away nothing," Hooper went on. "But assume the worst. At least now we know he's after you, so don't trust anything he says or does. Don't believe anything without proof." He stared at the water beyond Monk, all the time gently moving the oar to keep the boat from drifting out into the current again. "I wonder how much he set up, deliberately, and how much was just a damn clever use of circumstances. With your permission, sir, I'd like to look further into these escapes. Were they really as clumsy as they look? Is McNab capable of setting up his own man Pettifer? Maybe we should know more about him."

Monk followed Hooper's idea instantly. "You mean, was Pettifer loyal, or might he have turned on McNab and become a liability? A lieutenant who knew too much?"

Hooper nodded with a tight smile. "Wouldn't do to take McNab for a fool, sir."

Monk looked across at Hooper, intensely grateful for his quiet loyalty, not necessarily to Monk himself, but to the value he placed on mercy.

"Better get on with it," Monk agreed. "I need to know as much about McNab as he does about me."

"Or more," Hooper said, leaning forward to pull on the oar again, as soon as Monk was ready.

BACK IN THE WAPPING Station in the warmth of his office, Monk was still chilled. The hot woodstove could have been an open window.

He searched his mind again to remember anything McNab had said that indicated a previous relationship between them, good or bad. Nothing specific came back to him, except the moment he had seen that flash of knowledge in McNab's eyes, and knew he understood. Everything was about smuggling, arguments over jurisdiction, what information should have been shared, and had not been. Who had said what, and to whom.

But McNab had known him in a past he could not recall. Of course he had. That was inescapable now.

It was a fact that must be faced, because the cost of not doing so could be greater than any unpleasantness now. Yet he must not precipitate the result that he feared, betraying his weakness to McNab by the very act of raising the subject.

He spent the rest of the afternoon going over all he could find on other prison breaks in the past six months, whether involving the river, smuggling, or major thefts with connections either to Blount or to Owen. The results were an unpleasant shock. There were two other major criminals who had gotten away without trace, both possessed of unusual skills. Possibly they were also pieces of the same puzzle at last falling together.

Tomorrow morning, early, he would see McNab.

HE WENT HOME LATE, and he did not tell Hester about it. She was tired after a long day at the Portpool Lane Clinic, overwhelmed by victims of the cold weather and life on the streets. He set his own concerns aside, hoping to have an excuse to forget them, above all to avoid discussing with her the fear that ached deep inside him that the man he used to be had somehow made McNab's belief of him justified.

He wanted to hear news of Scuff. He would like to have heard only that he was doing well, learning medicine from Crow, being of use and enjoying it, and that Crow was pleased with him as a protégé. But if he thought it was less than the truth, he would be either worrying at it, or looking for the pain beyond the words.

They ate quietly, then sat beside the fire in the parlor. It was a room warm in every way: the soft colors of their well-used furniture, the familiar pictures on the walls, the few ornaments of more sentimental value than monetary—a hand-stitched motto, a copper vase he had given her years ago, a painting of trees in water.

He looked across at her and saw the weariness in her face. Perhaps she was not beautiful, at least not in the traditional way. There was a strength in her that many men would have found uncomfortable, even challenging. She was in her early forties now, and maturity suited her well. But he imagined that even as a child, she would have been challenging, eager to learn and never accepting less than what she took to be the truth.

He smiled as he remembered some of their early confrontations. He had thought her aggressive, sharp-tongued, quick-minded, and unfeminine. But then he had been used to agreement from women, or at least some submission that had passed itself off as agreement. She had found that contemptible, in the women who were so lacking in either courage or self-respect, but even more so in a man who wanted something so worthless. He, too, must consider himself worthless if his vanity had to be catered to in such a fashion. And she had said so.

Only when he was in trouble too real and too desperate to be plastered over with vanities had he come to value her lack of compromise and see her courage as the one quality that mattered.

He was frightened, but perfectly well. Should he trouble her with his fear? It would be so much lighter if he shared it, and she might see the way forward more clearly than he did.

Frightened! He had actually framed the word in his mind. That was an admission he seldom made, if ever. And so bluntly. It was to admit the unknown. Everything before waking in the hospital was unknown, and above all, the man he had been. Evidence varied from those who respected him, who said he was extremely clever, even brilliant at times, inexhaustible, apparently fearless, and uncompromising to those who did not like him. A larger number agreed he was clever, but added that he was too arrogant to be afraid, too angry to give in to tiredness, and too judgmental to compromise.

And now? He had made too many mistakes of his own to afford easy judgment. He knew fear very well. Perhaps he had before, but hid it better. Now at least he not only knew he needed others, but found it easy to accept, even comfortable.

"We've got evidence that McNab's men were working with the river pirates, at least as far as telling them about our raid," he said.

"Enough to prove it?" Hester asked with a lift of hope in her voice.

"Not yet," he admitted.

"Did he do it for money?" she asked. "That might be a way of linking up the evidence. You have to be very clever indeed to hide unearned money, once people know it's there, if they look for it." She was watching his face. "Or was that not the reason?"

"The man who drowned at Skelmer's Wharf—Pettifer—seems to have been a part of it. Of course, how much he knew is another question. . . ."

"You mean only McNab knew what was really going on? Why? He's got a good career, William, money and respect, and there's very little danger in his job. Why would he risk that?"

That was the heart of what frightened him. What had he done to McNab that mattered so much to him that he would jeopardize all he had to damage Monk? He had lain awake searching what was left, what he could find and piece together of his memory, but there was nothing.

"William . . . ?" she said gently.

He looked up. "I don't know," he admitted. The words were difficult to say, even to Hester. "I don't have any memory of him at all, not his name, his face, anything."

"Did you ever work on the river before?" she asked. "I don't mean remember, but you must have looked at records. You know where you were in the police."

This was dangerous territory now, too close to the shards of memory that Aaron Clive was stirring up, and Gillander.

"I was in the Metropolitan Police from 1852 onward. The records are clear. I don't know before that, but not on the river. Not anywhere that I can trace." That was what frightened him, that yawning gap of the unknown. Working in the police, yes. But at what? Clever, successful, ruthless . . . and what else?

"And have you looked for McNab's name in the old records?" Hester asked. Her voice was so gentle, her eyes troubled; she knew he was afraid of what he might uncover.

"Not . . . yet . . ." he admitted. "I must, mustn't I?"

"It'll be there waiting for you if you don't." She did not pretend it would be painless. She never had avoided confronting what was painful. Instead she moved forward off her seat and onto her knees and put her arms around him, holding him with all her strength.

"Have you spoken to Crow lately?" he asked at last, letting go of her.

She looked up at him and smiled, lifting the weariness from her face and softening the shadows. "Yes. Scuff makes mistakes, of course. But Crow says he has good instincts, and is so keen to learn. He's also patient, which I admit surprises me."

He asked the question that hovered at the edge of his mind, where anxiety waited.

"Is he actually any use to Crow, other than as an assistant, a messenger? If he's doing us a favor having Scuff, rather than his actually helping, then I must pay him."

She leaned back a little, smiling. "Crow will be gentle, but he won't spare the truth. It wouldn't be a kindness, either now or later. Scuff must become a good doctor, or no doctor at all."

He smiled back at her. "I suppose that's what he wants?"

"Of course it is," she agreed. "I know you would like to spare him the pain of failure. So would I. I have to keep reminding myself that I wouldn't accept comfortable lies, or anyone else protecting me from life."

He winced. "I wouldn't have dared!" he said, only half-jokingly. He had wanted to, and failed. He loved her, and had seen the pain she concealed from other people. She seemed so fierce, so sure of herself. Did anyone else see the capacity for hurt in her, the self-doubt she had to hide from the patients because they needed to believe in her? Without knowing it she was possibly teaching Scuff the exact same qualities.

She was looking at him a little ruefully.

He put his hand on hers for a moment, then sat back in his chair and let the silence of the room settle over him. There was no sound but the whickering of the flames in the hearth, and the patter of rain on the windows beyond the curtains.

"William . . ." Hester said quietly.

He sat up straighter. "Yes?"

"The man Blount. He was drowned, maybe accidentally, maybe not, and then after he was pulled out of the water he was shot."

"Yes."

"Do you know by whom?"

He saw the anxiety in her face. "No. Why?"

"That's what I was thinking . . . why? What is the point of shooting someone who is very obviously already dead?"

"You are thinking it was to bring me into the case? I thought of that, too. McNab sent for me personally."

"He is a problem, isn't he? A slow, careful man, but clever?"

The words chilled him a little. "Yes."

"Then he has something planned," she answered quietly. "Are you sure that Owen's escape was chance? Be careful . . . please . . . You have to go into the records and look, however hard it is. You can't afford not to."

"I know."

IN THE MORNING HE went across the river before dawn, which late in November was around eight in the morning, especially when the day was overcast. All the riding lights on the ships at anchor were still bright, and the streetlamps were lit along the water's edge. If an unpleasant thing had to be done, it was best it were done as soon as possible.

He paid the ferryman and climbed the steps up to the quayside. He called in briefly at the office and spoke to the night watch coming off duty, then went out to the street and caught a hansom cab to the office where police records were kept. He knew he looked grim. He had debated how much he should tell anyone, and hated the necessity of the conclusion he had reached. No more lies, at least not outright ones.

"Good morning," he said to the archivist as pleasantly as he was able, though he heard the edge to his voice. "I have someone in a court case who is causing me trouble. I can't remember dealing with him before, but he seems to have a grudge against me. It would be safer to know."

"Yes, sir. If you'll come this way, sir. Just your own records, you say?"

"Thank you."

He went through all he could find from the time he joined the police force up until his accident. It was a tedious job and stirred many emotions in him: respect for his skill, fear that there was an arrogance in it and a degree of ruthlessness he was not now proud of, but he saw no dishonesty, and no mention of McNab at all. It took him until the early afternoon. His head ached, his neck was stiff, and his eyes were tired by two o'clock. He had spent nearly six hours studying reports. He had learned nothing except that he had been even more efficient than he had been told, and that his path had never officially crossed that of McNab.

He went back to Wapping to check on current cases, dash cold water on his face, and have a hot cup of tea, too strong and too sweet, and a couple of rather good ham sandwiches, then he went to see McNab himself.

He found him sitting at his desk with a large cup of tea so strong it looked like mud. McNab glanced up from the papers he was working on. At first he was startled, tense, then slowly he relaxed and his face eased into a smile.

"Funny you should call. I was going to come to see you tomorrow."

Monk deliberately made himself look relaxed. He was in McNab's territory, and very sharply aware of it. He walked forward, giving the man who had conducted him here a brief nod of thanks.

"I've conclusions, and more questions," he answered.

McNab did not offer him tea. "About what?" he asked curiously, as if he had little idea.

Monk sat down, uninvited.

"Blount, Owen, and a couple of other prisoners who've escaped custody in the last six months," he replied.

"Oh, really?" McNab's expression quickened with interest. "Not from us. Where from, and why do you care? You haven't lost anyone, have you?" His voice lifted with hope, ready to be amused.

Monk had expected that. "No. From a little farther north, not far. Less than a day's journey. Fellow called Seager. Heard of him?"

"No. Why should we care, particularly?"

"Expert safecracker," Monk answered. "Escaped from Lincoln, but he's a Londoner. Thought to be heading this way. Top of his skill, so they say."

"Ah . . . ?" McNab was watching him closely now. "That ties in with what I was going to say to you. No trace of Owen for certain, but a few rumors . . . You haven't heard? Then a good thing you came. Damned good explosives man just turned up in Calais, on the way back here." He looked at Monk unblinkingly. "And then there's Applewood. . . ."

"Applewood?" Monk resented being made to ask.

"Another expert," McNab said with relish. "A chemist. Can mix all sorts of gases, among other things."

Monk waited.

"All known associates," McNab added.

There was a moment's silence. Footsteps in the passage outside were audible, then faded away.

"I see." Monk let out his breath. "Associates in what?"

McNab oozed satisfaction. "A major robbery. Gold bullion. Got caught, but more by mischance than any skill on the part of the police."

"Police. So nothing to do with Customs, or the river, that time," Monk said, his mind racing. McNab was enjoying this, but why? Had that any relevance to its truth?

"What do they need a chemist, an explosives expert, a forger, and a safecracker for?" Monk asked. "Or don't you know?"

"I have some ideas," McNab said slowly, his eyes never leaving Monk's. "But we need to know what they're after. And they have to replace Blount with somebody of equal skill. That would be where we start." He smiled. "Unless Blount had already done the work, and they killed him because they didn't need him anymore?"

"Then we should keep an eye open for any bodies that could be one of the others," Monk added. "How did Pettifer know that Owen was going upriver, instead of down to the Isle of Dogs, and the sea?"

McNab froze.

Monk tried very hard to keep the emotion out of his face. This might be his chance to learn more about Pettifer, and possibly about the plot too big for McNab to deal with without Monk's men. McNab would undoubtedly cooperate until the capture was sure, then turn on Monk at the last moment and, if he could, make a fool of him. It was all in the timing.

McNab relaxed, letting his breath out in a sigh. "Pity we can't ask him," he said with an edge to his voice that was unmistakable in its implication.

"Perhaps he spoke to someone?" Monk said as if he believed it likely. He needed to know more about all of it, but especially about Pettifer.

McNab sat absolutely motionless for several seconds. Then a slow satisfaction seeped through him and he met Monk's eyes with a candor unusual for him.

"Skelmer's Wharf is pretty near Aaron Clive's big warehouses, isn't it." It was not a question, rather a reminder, something for Monk to take hold of. "Big importer and exporter. Lot of very valuable stuff would pass through his hands. Some of it small enough to be stolen relatively easily, wouldn't you say?"

It would be ridiculous to deny it.

"Yes . . ." Monk agreed guardedly.

"And there was the schooner lying inshore on the south bank," McNab went on, still looking at Monk. "Seagoing, do you think?"

"No doubt at all," Monk conceded.

"And Owen swam for it." McNab was enjoying himself now. "And the captain helped him aboard. Told you that he took Owen downriver and put him ashore. Did you believe that?"

Monk hesitated. Either answer tripped him up. If he believed Gillander, then he sounded naïve. If he did not, then he should have questioned him further. Honesty was the only thing that would not catch him later.

"I believed Gillander at the time," he admitted.

McNab pursed his lips, but it was a pretense at regret. His eyes were shining. "Pity. Too late now. The bird has flown. Maybe you should learn a little more about this Aaron Clive, and his business? I can give you copies of what we have about him. Very rich man . . . indeed." His smile widened. "Seems he made a king's ransom of money in the gold-fields in California. Decided to come and taste the good life in London. He's American. Don't know much about him before a couple of years ago." He sat back a little in his chair. "If you find anything interesting, Customs would regard it as a nice piece of cooperation if you would let us know." His eyes met Monk's and they gleamed with satisfaction. It was not an expression that Monk enjoyed.

"Naturally," he agreed. "If you'll send us copies of the most recent cargo manifests of Clive's business, that would be a nice piece of cooperation, too." He stood up. "Good day, Mr. McNab."

"Good day, Commander Monk. So glad you came."

Monk found Clive in his offices on the riverbank, just short of the place where Owen had escaped, and Pettifer had died. It was a beautiful room, more like a gentleman's study than a place of business. The furniture was heavy, polished teak and cherrywood, the chairs covered with leather. The pictures were unobtrusive landscapes, beautifully framed.

"Good morning, Commander," Clive said courteously. He was a man of reserved charm. The warmth was easy, but never did he seem to court favor. Had he been English, Monk would have taken him for an aristocrat of considerable power, the sort of old blood that comes with the centuries of privilege, and obligation, and almost certainly thousands of acres of land somewhere in the Home Counties. It said much for Clive that within one generation of land with gold in it he could assume that power with such grace.

"Good morning, Mr. Clive," Monk replied with equal assurance, although it was far from what he felt. "I am sorry to trouble you again, but the matter is a slightly different one this time. I have been conferring with Mr. McNab, of the Customs service. If you recall, it was one of his men who drowned. . . ."

Clive indicated one of the leather-padded seats by the fire for Monk to sit, and he took the other.

"I remember," he said with interest. "Does this appear to be a smuggling matter? I thought the man who escaped was an explosives expert? Owen?"

Monk chose his words carefully, watching Clive's reaction. "There have been four escapes by prisoners in the last half year or so. The first I knew about was the forger I mentioned to you before—Blount. He had been forging ships' documents when he was caught. Which is why Customs wanted to question him further about a whole lot of things."

"I'm as certain as one can be that none of my cargoes could have been affected," Clive said.

"No, sir. It's not just his past crimes that concern me. It is his death. That's why McNab sent for me," Monk replied.

Clive froze, but it was for so short a time that it could have been an illusion created by the quiet room, the light on the windows, the silence.

"Of course . . . McNab," Clive responded. "I remember now you mentioned a bullet wound, so his man's death is under investigation by the River Police?"

"Yes."

Clive sat still for several moments, clearly turning it over in his mind.

Monk studied him. Since he was waiting for his reply, he could do so without it being in any way unusual. Clive was quite a big man, well built, and yet at the same time elegant. The sense of power in him was not physical but sprang from his deep-seated confidence in himself. Monk wondered if he had ever been truly afraid. If he had, it had left no mark on him.

"A warning to someone?" Clive suggested at last. "'This is what happens to those who betray me'?"

Monk was surprised. Clive looked so much the gentleman, so unacquainted with any kind of violence or brutality. And yet of course he must be. No man would have survived and profited superbly from the gold rush without skill, luck, courage, and a certain steel in his soul.

As if reading his thoughts, Clive smiled. It lit his face, making him seem much younger, as if a layer of responsibility had slipped off his shoulders.

"If you knew the goldfields of '49, you wouldn't imagine me so very civilized, Commander. Our veneer of sophistication was thinner than a coat of varnish, I assure you. San Francisco grew almost overnight."

"Yes," he said quietly. "I apologize."

"Do you think Blount was killed for having betrayed his employees?" Clive asked.

"Possibly," Monk conceded. "But to his rivals, not to the police, or the Customs."

A flash of humor lit Clive's eyes, quick and vivid. "Are you sure? Even if you trust McNab himself, do you equally trust all his men? Or for that matter, all your own men?"

Monk looked straight at Clive and met his gaze boldly. "Yes, I trust all my men. Would you put your life or your career in the hands of men you didn't trust?"

Clive dropped all the pretense of courtesy. "I might use men I didn't trust," he answered. "But I'd make damned sure they couldn't use me."

"Exactly." Monk smiled back at him, quite genuinely. He respected Clive, and could even like him. "I don't know who shot Blount, or who drowned him. I think the drowning could have been an accident. . . ."

"And the shooting?" Clive was openly amused now, even if there was a bitter edge to it.

"I think that might have been to make it a police matter, and take it out of McNab's hands."

"Because you are better equipped to solve it? Or simply for Customs to be rid of it themselves?" Clive asked. "Or to distract you?"

"Very possibly the last," Monk answered. "Or again, to draw me in. There have been two more escapes of interest in the last half year: Seager, who is a first-class safecracker, and Applewood, who is a chemist, working on gases, particularly those that blind or suffocate." He waited a moment, watching Clive's sudden awareness of what more that might involve, the meaning far beyond the words.

"All four escapees worked together before," Monk went on quietly. "On a major gold robbery. There might be something else, but they specialize in highly valuable cargo, heavy but not large. We are afraid that something in your warehouse might be a possible target, once they find someone to replace Blount."

Clive weighed this for quite some time before he answered.

"A specific set of skills," he said finally. "Forgery is easy to understand. All shipping needs papers. A gas to disable is easy, too. Safecracker, less certain of. I don't keep any gold or silver bullion, or gems. No works of art at the moment."

"Papers of ownership, purchase, authentication?" Monk asked.

Clive bit his lip. "Yes . . . most thieves don't bother with such things, but of course if they're taking stolen goods into Europe to sell to collectors, they'd have a much wider choice, and better price, if they don't appear to be stolen. Why the explosives?"

"Take down a wall," Monk replied. "Doesn't have to be a big explosion. With an expert of Owen's skill, it could be very carefully controlled. Just a possibility, Mr. Clive. A forewarning, if you like?"

"And who could be behind this?" Clive asked with sudden intensity. "Do you know that? Or is it part of the 'possibilities' we have yet to learn?"

Monk could see a tension in him now, as if his mind were racing to learn which threads he could disentangle.

"It's just a possibility," Monk replied. "When we find them, I will let you know, sir."

Monk arrived home at Paradise Place well after dark, and barely noticed the carriage drawn up to the curb fifty feet or so behind him. He paid the cabdriver and went to the front door, glad to be out of the cold.

Hester met him in the hall. He went straight to her, even with his coat still on, and took her in his arms. She yielded and kissed him gently.

He was still standing in the hallway when there was a sharp knock on the front door. Hester pulled away from him and turned to answer it, but he caught hold of her wrist.

"I'll go. Whoever it is, I don't want to see them. I'm tired and hungry and looking forward to a long evening at home."

She gave him a brief smile and let him go to the door.

He opened it and for a moment was totally confused. A woman stood alone on the step, outlined against the lamps of her own carriage, which was now drawn up at the curb behind her. In the light from the hallway he could see her face. It was turbulent, filled with conflicting emotions, and by anybody's standards, disturbingly beautiful. He had no idea who she was, or why she should be here. Presumably she was lost, and looking for someone else.

She saw his confusion and gave a tiny, bleak smile.

"I am Miriam Clive," she said. "I'm sorry to call so late, and without warning or permission, but I believe my errand is urgent, and certainly it is private . . . at least from my own family. I need to speak with you, Commander Monk." She made no movement forward, waiting to be invited in. The wind gusted behind her and caught at the heavy cloak she wore, scattering rain from its fur-trimmed hood onto her shoulder.

There was no civilized alternative open to him. He stepped back and invited her inside. As she moved past him he closed the door, then offered to take her wet cloak before he took off his own coat and hung it up also.

"Thank you," she said gravely.

He led her into the parlor, then excused himself to explain to Hester that dinner would have to be delayed. He asked her to make some tea and bring it to the parlor. What else did one offer a lady at this hour, and one who had come alone, and uninvited? How had she even known where to find him? And why had she not gone to the Wapping Police Station?

When he went into the parlor she was not sitting as he had expected, but standing near the fire. Her gown was plain, dark green. It had no ornament to it and her amazing face needed none. She did not ask if she were disturbing his dinner. She had been waiting out in the street in her carriage, so she knew he had only just returned.

She stared directly at him, as a man might have done.

"You came to speak with my husband this morning, Mr. Monk. He told me much of what you have said, and what he had replied to you." She stood very still, her shoulders stiff, her chin lifted a little, even though she was already of more than average height. "What he said to you was perfectly true, but containing such omissions as to make it in effect false."

Monk was surprised. He had thought Clive candid, as far as his information went. "What did he omit?" he asked her.

"Did you ask him if he had enemies, specific ones who might wish him harm?" she countered.

"Indirectly." He tried to recall exactly what he had said. "He told me he had no idea who could be behind any attack such as I warned him may be possible, nor indeed did he know of any merchandise he carried that could be a specific target. Do you think differently, Mrs. Clive?"

"Of the merchandise, I have no idea." She dismissed it with the lightness of her tone. "I know nothing of the business, except occasionally the different countries involved, if we entertain representatives from them. Some have been most interesting, especially those from the Far East. Their culture is different from our own. But I think it far more likely that an attack, if it is indeed aimed at my husband, would be personal, and the actual robbery only a means to an end." She still looked away from him as she spoke, and her voice was filled with emotion, as if she dared not let him see it so naked in her.

"The end being to injure him?" he asked gently.

"Yes," she agreed. "You cannot amass the wealth or the eminence he has without making enemies. I imagine that you are very well aware of that yourself, Mr. Monk?" Now she looked at him. "You are a man of adventure, and decision. You will have succeeded where others have failed." Her eyes were disturbingly frank as she regarded him from a very slight distance, taking in not only his face but his build, his manner, the confidence that masked his weariness and all the doubts inside him. It was as if she already knew him thoroughly, even though they had never met before.

"If you know who the enemies might be, Mrs. Clive, please tell me. As well, you might let me know why you believe that your husband did not tell me all this himself."

She gave a very tiny smile that softened her face completely. She had moved a little and the lamplight caught the fine lines around her eyes and mouth. They did not spoil her beauty, but added passion and vulnerability to it. "I am not entirely sure myself," she admitted. "But I can tell you the facts that I know. The reasons I can only guess, and perhaps this is not the time for opinions I cannot prove."

He wanted to help her, but she was not giving him enough to work with.

"Then the facts, Mrs. Clive. Who is such an enemy that they would go to these lengths merely to settle a score?" He could not help thinking of McNab as he spoke. How far would McNab go to destroy Monk? As far as betraying a customs operation, and creating a situation where it was likely Monk or his man, or both, would be killed? That was what he believed.

The difference was that Aaron Clive would have his full memory, and he would know not only the enemy, but his reasons.

"Mrs. Clive?" he prompted.

She nodded, as if accepting some inevitable challenge long expected.

"I married Aaron nearly twenty years ago, in San Francisco." She spoke very quietly, as though there were someone else just beyond the door who must not hear her. "Before that I was married to Piers Astley. He was . . ." She took a deep breath. She could not hide that this was going to be deeply painful to her, and in her imagination she could feel it already. She began again. "He was brave as well, but quieter than Aaron, less . . . dashing." There was apology in her voice. "He was someone men were loyal to, because he was loyal to them. His word was unbreakable, but you knew that only after some time, after testing." She gritted her teeth, struggling to keep what composure she had.

Monk waited. He wished he could comfort her, but there was nothing he could do. To speak, still more to touch her, would be intrusive beyond excuse.

Hester brought in tea for them both and left it with no more than a smile, merely nodding to Miriam as she murmured her thanks.

Monk waited again.

"There were darker sides to him," Miriam said at last, as if she had made a difficult decision, an irreversible one. "Things I did not know until long after we were married. I believe the Greeks had a word for it.

Hubris. It is a kind of arrogance, a sense that you are entitled to the best you can take for yourself." Now that she had broken the surface of resistance she spoke freely, without having to search for the words. She was drawing on elements she was long familiar with and her words came quickly. Still she did not look at Monk but into something beyond him, in the past.

"He could be charming, very funny at times. I remember laughing so easily, till I had tears on my face. He loved life, adventure, the beauty of the world. All of it, to be relished almost as a duty. He stared up at the great redwood trees and adored them. They were centuries old, you know? Giants with their heads among the stars, he used to say." Her voice was thick with emotion, on the edge of tears.

"Yes," he agreed. He did know that. "They make us seem like tiny earthbound creatures."

"He revered them," she said. "Oddly enough, I'm not sure he ever revered any people. He was a truly good man . . . generous of soul, sweet of nature, like the wind off the sea." She gave a little shiver, and blinked away tears. "But that was a long time ago. It took me until very recently to acknowledge that the dark side of . . . my husband . . . was real. I won't speak of it. I am ashamed, and I have no wish or need to tell you the details . . . the realities. It is enough for you to know that he got into a very serious fight over a gold claim and I was told that he was dead. . . ."

Now he could see the total grief in her face, just for an instant. It was devastating, and so complete that he was afraid for her. Then she mastered it, and assumed an air of calm.

"My dream of what could have been, what at last I believed, was also dead. It was Aaron who came to my assistance in those dark days, and protected me from those who wished me ill. After my first husband was officially declared deceased, and a decent time had passed by, Aaron asked me to marry him, and I accepted."

Monk was waiting for her to get to the point, and he did not want to assume anything yet. What she had said was far from clear.

"Go on," he invited her.

She looked as if her last hope of rescue had vanished. This time she lowered her eyes. Clearly she could not bear to look at him while she said it. "I never saw Piers Astley's body," she whispered. "If he is alive, his enmity of Aaron would be awful. He was not a man who forgave."

Now he understood both her grief and her fear, perhaps even a sense of guilt, as if her beauty were her own fault.

"You think he would look for vengeance against your present husband?" he concluded. "How is he at fault? As far as he was concerned, and everyone else, you were a widow. Why should you not marry again?"

"Some people are very possessive, Commander Monk. Piers would consider that I belonged to him, all my life, whether he were dead or not."

"Are you afraid for yourself?" he asked. Without thinking, he moved a step closer to her.

Suddenly she seemed exhausted. She answered as if it hardly mattered to her. "Not at all. What use am I to him if I am damaged? You do not spoil your own property, Mr. Monk. If someone steals it from you, you steal it back. Perhaps you have to destroy the thief to do so, but not intentionally. Maybe you do it simply to demonstrate to others that you punish those who trespass in such a way. Then you can be sure it won't happen again."

Monk poured the tea and gave her the first cup. She accepted it and seemed grateful, sipping it straightaway, but still she did not sit down. He took the other cup himself.

"Describe Piers Astley for me, Mrs. Clive. You said he was handsome, in a quiet way, but you did not say if he is fair or dark, or anything of his voice or mannerisms, his way of moving, speaking, things that might not have changed over twenty years. And if he is responsible for these crimes and plans more, something of his mind, his way of thinking." She stared at him, considering. "Has he any deep loves, or fears?" he went on. "If I am to find him, I need to know all I can, especially of the things that don't change. One can lose hair, or grow a beard. Gain a limp, acquire a new habit. But a love of nature, perhaps of dogs, a taste for chocolate, a fit of sneezing when near a cat, a phobia about spiders—those stay the same."

"I see." She was clearly weighing what he had said and searching her mind for answers.

He waited, not wanting to hurry her, and with some sense of guilt he saw her eyes fill with tears. She did not seem to be aware of them herself, as if they came from some well within her. Guilt disturbed him for wakening a grief so profound, but if this Piers Astley who had hurt her so much was now planning to destroy her present happiness by robbing Aaron Clive, or otherwise ruining him, Monk had to know everything about him that he could.

"He was English," she said at last. "Don't look for an American. He never lost his accent. He came from a good family, though not aristocratic. They lived in the country, in the north, near the Great Dales; he loved the big, sweeping open lands where the hills seem to touch the sky. You can walk for miles and never see a soul. And of course the city of York, close by, was completely different, teeming with people, narrow, winding streets, and the old walls are still standing. Did you know that York was a city under the Romans, called Eboracum, and is still the sacred place in England for the Church?"

"If he is alive, do you think he will have gone back there?" Monk asked, hearing the remembered tenderness in her voice.

"I don't think so." She shook her head. "He might be afraid someone would recognize him. At the time of his supposed death there was much in his face that had not changed since youth. His cheekbones, his mouth, the way his hair grew. Most of all his voice."

Monk was curious. Would it be so dangerous for him to be recognized?

Her voice was choked with emotion. "He didn't talk about his home much. He grew up on the outskirts of the city. He liked to walk miles out into the country." Her eyes brimmed with tears as if they were her own lost memories. "I'm sorry . . . none of that is useful. He never gambled, but he took wild chances in other ways. He was a good judge of horses, but he drove too fast. Rode too fast as well, if the ground was firm. I don't expect that has changed."

"Any habits of speech?" he asked. "Things I could ask people to listen for?"

"He could read Latin, but I'm not sure if he could have a conversation in it. He knew lots of the words. Said so much of English was based on it, it was always useful to have. And he doesn't mind spiders, but he is afraid of moths. The fluttering upsets him. He hid it, but you could still see they bothered him. You know how if something disturbs you, you keep an eye on it. If there is one in the room, you want to know where it is?" She made herself smile at him. "He always took care of his feet. No matter how sick or poor he was, he wore good boots."

"Did he have a quick temper?" he asked. "Or drink much?"

"Yes, he had a quick temper. But he drank very little. He . . ." Again she took a deep breath. "He could hold a grudge. And he was very clever. He could do those puzzles with words and ideas that I can't even understand."

Monk was aware that she was watching him intently, even as she sipped her tea.

"Do you really think he could be alive, after all these years?" he asked. "Why would he wait so long to come back to England and take revenge? Why not do it straightaway, and while you were all in San Francisco?"

She gave a very slight shrug, almost a gesture of defeat, of loss. "I don't know. You asked Aaron if there was anyone who would hate him. He said there wasn't. I'm afraid for him. Somebody seems to, and Piers is the only person I can think of. They began as equals, when Aaron's cousin Zachary was still alive. That was a long time ago." Her face softened and for a moment she was clearly lost in her memories.

Again Monk waited, beginning to drink his own tea.

"Zachary was one of the best people I ever knew," she said. "Everybody trusted him, Aaron most of all. When Aaron found gold, it was Zack who helped him set everything up legally, and see that all those who helped him were rewarded." She stopped abruptly, as if a new thought had occurred to her.

Was any of this relevant to an attack against Aaron Clive's business? It was beginning to feel more and more remote.

Miriam's eyes filled with tears almost beyond her ability to control. "Aaron grieved for him terribly. He was changed, almost as if he had lost part of himself."

"Mrs. Clive . . . are you all right?" Monk asked anxiously.

She straightened up and raised her eyes to meet his again. "Yes. Thank you. It is all a long time ago now. Zack was killed defending a helpless man from a mob of drunkards. California was a pretty lawless place at that time. It was as if a light went out . . . something of goodness was lost. Without him some of us lost our way. . . ."

Monk tried to think of something to say. He clung to the one thing relevant.

"But it's possible Piers Astley could still be alive? In spite of the fact that he was legally declared to be dead, and you free to marry Aaron Clive?"

"I was told he was dead; he never came home," she said simply. "He had worked for Aaron for some time. In fact he was his right hand, as it were." She gave a little shrug. "You don't understand what it was like, Mr. Monk. It was another world, out there. Gold is magic, as if it had a power within itself to change men, circumstances, anything. Suddenly from worrying about every meal and debts of a few dollars, people think they can buy anything, and sometimes everybody. Some find a few nuggets, and think it will never end. People even gave it away, thinking there would always be more. But there isn't. Except for a few, it's never sufficient, though enough to live on, perhaps. The best thing is to buy land you can farm." She shook her head. "But gold is power, and power sends most people a little mad."

He knew that what she said was true; he had a faint memory of it himself, a kind of lunacy in the air, like having drunk too much.

He became aware that Miriam was watching him, and felt as if his thoughts were wide open to her gaze.

"Men gambled and lost fortunes," she continued. "Many found gold and were gripped by the madness of it, the elation. Some settled, some died poor. Some prospered by creating businesses, schools, churches, stores. A few, like Aaron, struck a rich seam of gold and became little kings of their own realms." She lifted her shoulders very slightly. It was a gesture of helplessness. "Some, like Piers, vanished. People came from all over the world, and went again. And of course there were the native people to whom the land really belonged. Many of them disappeared, too. What was one English adventurer more or less, except to those who loved him?"

"Have you any real reason to think Piers Astley is alive?" Monk asked.

She thought in silence for several moments. He was about to ask her again when at last she replied, looking away into the corner of the room, lost in some vision in her mind.

"Maybe none, but I see him everywhere, perhaps only because I want to. Fleeting glances of his profile, once, in San Francisco, and then again, just a month ago, here in London. I don't know. Perhaps it was my imagination. Then you came and told Aaron that it is possible someone is seeking to harm his business, perhaps commit a huge and clever robbery. How can I not at least tell you of this?"

He conceded, "I shall see if I can find any trace of him, or any connection whatever with any of the men who have escaped."

She seemed to reach a decision within herself. She set down her empty teacup and turned a little to face him.

"Do you think that schooner is moored almost opposite my husband's warehouse totally by chance, Mr. Monk?" she asked.

"I don't know, but I shall assume it is not chance, until I can prove otherwise," he promised. "And tomorrow I shall begin inquiries into Piers Astley's disappearance, and his possible return to England."

Her smile of gratitude was dazzling, and as if someone had turned up the light. He saw the beautiful woman she was when she was happy, safe.

When she was gone, he stood alone in the hall for several minutes, absorbing the new information in his mind. Hester found him there when she came through, having heard the front door close.

Over dinner he told her what Miriam Clive had told him.

"She's very afraid of what you will find," Hester said at last. "But I think she may be even more afraid if you don't find it. It must be terrible to live in fear of someone you once loved, and now don't know if he's alive or dead, or how much he's changed."

Monk looked at her, saw the pity in her face, and knew that no answer was necessary, or even appropriate.

HE SET OUT THE next day to contact all the people he knew in other forces, and could trust to pass on information discreetly. If Piers Astley were in London, somebody somewhere would know.

It was a long and laborious job, because each new person had to have some explanation as to why Monk needed the information, and then as much as he could tell them of Astley's description, and possible activity.

There were people who owed him favors, or who would dearly like Monk to owe them, and he knew they would be certain to collect. This made him a trifle less eager than he might have been otherwise.

One such person he contacted early that evening was a receiver of stolen goods at the upper end of the market. The profession was known as that of an opulent receiver, because he dealt in only the best, small and easily movable works, such as jewelry, gold and silver statues, carved ivory or jade. He was known as "Velvet Boy," perhaps because he had a soft childlike face atop an enormous body.

"English," he said sarcastically. "That should be easy to spot—an Englishman in London! You've come to make fun of us, Mr. Monk. I take exception to that, I do." His china-blue eyes regarded Monk with affront.

"An English gentleman from Yorkshire originally, but who spent at least twenty years of his life in California, from the gold rush until now," Monk amended. "Don't jump to conclusions, Velvet."

Velvet moved one of his huge legs a couple of inches. "I can't jump at all, Mr. Monk. It in't kind o' you to speak about it like that. You're making fun o' my afflictions. I take exception to that, too."

"Conclusions are things of the mind," Monk replied. "And yours is one of the most agile I know. You could jump over the moon, if you'd a mind to."

The look of petulance was ironed out of Velvet Boy's face for a moment or two, then it returned. "Is that what you want me to do, then, Mr. Monk? Jump over the moon for you? What's it worth to me?"

"It's worth my not coming back to bother you for some time," Monk replied levelly.

"You in't bothering me anyway. I'm too far from the river for most o' your business these days."

"You want me to keep it that way?" Monk asked, raising his eyebrows slightly.

Velvet Boy thought for several moments.

Monk waited. The room was oppressively warm. There was far too much furniture in it. Every surface was crammed with ornaments, which were almost all rubbish. There were a few real gems camouflaged among them, but it would take an art expert to recognize them. Monk did not bother to pretend interest. Velvet Boy would not be fooled. He rarely stirred from his seat, but he knew his art and his thieves as a concert violinist knows music, making his own notes with his fingers, with perfect pitch every time. If there was something planned he would have wind of it. He drew knowledge as a magnet draws iron filings.

"Come to think of it," Velvet Boy said at last, "I did hear of someone who might come by a few interesting artifacts in a little while. Very nice bits o' carved turquoise, and bone, even. Said as they were Red Indian things, held by them to be magic." He watched Monk's reaction with his large, unblinking eyes.

Monk found he suddenly knew exactly what he was talking about. He could even picture them, like little roughly sketched animals—bears, fish, frogs, coyotes. He remembered touching them: the smoothness, the limpid quality of the best turquoise, almost without blemish. He was taken aback by the clarity of the images. The art was different from European: more a re-creation of the essence of the creature than seeking to show others its beauty. Its spirit was understood. The carving was a totem, nothing to do with the identity of the carver. There was no vanity in it; it was rather an act of worship. Perhaps that was what gave it its real beauty.

"If it's your totem, the carving carries the spirit of the creature with you, as long as no one else touches it," Monk explained, speaking almost before he knew it, as if the knowledge had just flown into his mind.

Velvet Boy blushed slowly. "An' 'ow do you know that, then, Mr. Monk? You a collector, are you? That what you want? Arrest this feller you're looking for, and take his artworks?"

Monk had an instant of chill. How *had* he known about this? Why could he see the little animals in his mind, rather than remember someone telling him about them? He saw them exactly, made of turquoise, bone, silver, sometimes even gold.

He swallowed and breathed in and out, taking his time. "I want to stop a very large robbery," he replied. "An act of revenge. This man has come all the way from San Francisco in order to destroy another man he envies. If you help me find him, then any of his artifacts that he's sold you, or 'lent' you, I will be willing to forget about it."

"Bent, then, are you, Mr. Monk? Let me help with stolen goods? Not like you, at all. Some reason I should believe you? I think as you're setting a trap for me." Velvet Boy looked straight into Monk's eyes. "I take exception to that, I do!"

"And I take exception to you thinking I'm bent, Velvet," Monk replied. "I was thinking I'm too busy to look through your place. Got bigger fish to go after. But perhaps I'm not, after all. That's a very nice piece of ivory you've got hanging on the wall behind you."

Velvet Boy pursed his lips. "There to remind me not to get taken in by fakes, that is. D'yer think I'd hang a real piece up there for every Tom, Dick, and 'Arry ter see? What do you take me for?" He looked hurt.

"A very clever man," Monk assumed truthfully. "Bluff, double bluff, triple bluff. But if it's fake, then you won't mind if I take it from you . . . ?"

There was an instant of alarm in Velvet Boy's eyes, there, and then gone again. "I take . . ."

"Exception," Monk finished for him. "I know." He pretended to begin rising to his feet, his eyes fixed on the ivory on the wall.

"I did get some more stuff from a feller about a year or so past. Couple o' dozen o' them earrings. Some was real big. 'Andsome feller. But 'e wasn't Yorkshire no more'n I am. American, 'e were, but with a touch now an' then of Irish. Just a touch, mind, like 'e were a long time from the Old Svelde!"

"Describe him," Monk ordered.

"Tall, graceful, very 'andsome, an' 'e knew it."

"Clean-shaven?" Monk asked.

"No . . . mustache." Velvet touched his own upper lip.

"Dark?"

"Not really."

"Name?"

He shook his head. "I don't ask no names. You know better than that, Mr. Monk. They was real. That's all I care about."

Gillander? Not Piers Astley. Monk stayed only a short time further, but as he was leaving, his mind was not on which man it might have been, but on the clarity with which he could remember the carved animals. How did he know?

A SECOND DAY LOOKING, AND he had found nothing definitive about Piers Astley. However, he had definitely learned more about the dead man, Blount, and the other two men who had escaped earlier: the safecracker, Seager, and the chemist, Applewood.

"Worst mistake we ever made," one policeman said ruefully, when Monk visited the station in Bethnal Green where Applewood had been arrested. The man's face colored with embarrassment. "Looked so ordinary, could 'ave been your postman or a bank clerk behind the counter. Sort of . . . shortsighted, harmless. Kind o' man who could trip over 'is own bootlaces. But clever. 'E were like a weasel, always thinking. Knew what everything was made of. Even knew what smells they were. Wore them dark glasses, an' when 'e took them off, 'is eyes were enough ter give yer nightmares."

According to the sergeant in nearby Hoxton, where Seager had lived, he was a different matter altogether. He seemed merely a quiet man who was obsessive about his fingers. He always wore gloves to protect them, even in the summer, and would never shake hands with anyone. Curiously, he liked to play the piano, and did it well.

Blount, it seemed from the customs man Worth, was less individual, but nevertheless highly thought of in his profession, if you could call it such. He would be hard to replace. Was that what was holding up the robbery of Aaron Clive? Or was the victim someone else, and perhaps it was already begun? It was time, Monk thought, that he reported to McNab, before McNab came to him.

Should he be honest? He could not afford to be seen as dishonest. He might well have to justify himself if the robbery, whatever it was, succeeded.

McNab looked up when Monk went up the stairs from Worth's room to McNab's. Monk was not used to such easy access. McNab was almost civil.

"Ah! Morning, Monk," McNab said with something like cordiality. He nodded his thanks to the man who had shown Monk in, and gave him permission to leave them.

Monk sat down in the chair opposite the tidy, polished desk and gave McNab an edited version of Miriam Clive's assertions about Piers Astley. "If he's alive and he's here, then he's keeping well low," he finished. "But I found an opulent receiver who bought some American Indian art from a man answering Gillander's description, over a year ago."

"Not our gold baron, Mr. Clive?"

"No. Besides, I don't see Aaron Clive importing bits and pieces and selling them through a receiver, opulent or not. No, this was someone who wished to make a nice sum of money, but quickly, without drawing any attention to himself."

"Interesting," McNab agreed, nodding his head slowly. Then his face grew more earnest. "Fits with what I learned. Looks more and more like Clive is the target. Can't wonder at that. He's a very rich man indeed. Daresay he got himself a few enemies out there in San Francisco. Can't get that rich without treading on people now and then. Might be as honest as the day now, but was he always that way?"

"I don't think we can find out in time for it to be any use to us," Monk replied. "It can take months to get to California, and the same back. Otherwise one can either sail to New York, or Panama, and then go overland, but that's both hard and dangerous. Or sail round the Horn and up the other side of the country all the way north again to San Francisco. And that's long and dangerous, too."

McNab looked doubtful. "Too long," he agreed. "But safer. Stay on your ship, just wait . . ."

"Ever been around the Horn?" Monk said sharply. McNab's ignorance and contempt angered him. "The South Atlantic has seas a hundred feet high, and more, in bad weather."

McNab looked at him with fascination, his eyes wide, suddenly the color in them clear hazel. "Really?" His voice lifted with interest.

"Yes!" Monk replied with the force of memory.

"Been there, have you?" McNab showed his teeth in a rare, wide smile.

Monk felt the coldness run through him again. He was looking straight into the face of the wolf. His slightest tremor would be seen. That hesitation would be like the smell of fear that a predator gets, a shark at sea smelling blood half a mile away.

"Long time ago," Monk replied. "All I can remember is the fear, and the cold. But if you really want to know about it, you should listen to some of the seamen you deal with who have brought cargoes from the West, and the Pacific beyond."

"Oh, I do listen, Monk. Hear all kinds of things I don't expect to. You'd be surprised." He nodded several times. "But you're right. It's another world out there, and we know very little about it. We've no time to find out any more. We'd better assume that this Piers Astley could be here, and keep an eye on Clive's warehouse. Wish we could find Owen, but I've asked the Metropolitan Police to keep an eye out for him, or for any other first-rate forger they might get hold of instead. Perhaps I'd better go and have another word with Mr. Clive? What do you think? He seems to have a remarkable memory. . . ."

Monk waited, watching McNab.

McNab looked back at him, studying him slowly, quite openly.

"Find anything about the other escapees?" McNab said at last, an edge to his voice now.

"Only what you already know," Monk replied. "The best at their jobs. Dangerous, clever."

McNab pursed his lips thoughtfully. "Hope we didn't get caught out," he said, staring at Monk. "Clive wouldn't be a good man to cross. He knows about the threat. Pity about that . . ." He let the implication hang in the air.

Monk wanted to think of a retort, but nothing came to mind. He was always aware that McNab knew him better than he knew himself. He was fighting with one hand tied behind his back.

He stood up. "Pity you didn't get anything useful out of Blount," he said. "Or Owen, for that matter."

McNab's eyes narrowed. "Might have, if Pettifer'd lived," he said between his teeth.

Monk went back to Wapping to find out what Hooper had learned about the raid on the gun smugglers that had gone so disastrously wrong. McNab's face haunted him in the short cab ride from the customs office to his own station. Was he imagining the jubilation in McNab's eyes, the knowledge that he was playing with Monk as a cat does with a mouse? The hunger was for the game, not the prize at the end. Well-fed domestic cats did just the same. Eating it was merely tidying up afterward.

He had slipped up over his reference to Cape Horn. His own fears were causing him to make mistakes. He was vulnerable, and McNab knew it, with his senses if not his brain.

It must stop. Monk must take the offensive, move McNab's attention to something else. He found Hooper waiting for him when he went in. He looked pleased with himself. It was discreet, but there was an energy in him as he stood up and walked over to meet Monk.

Monk looked at him expectantly.

"Found a lot more about Pettifer," Hooper said quietly. "He's been working for Customs most of his life. Taken down a lot of smugglers of all kinds of things, particularly guns. I can't prove that he set us up on the gunrunners' raid, but I certainly can confirm that he knew enough to sell us out completely. Did very nicely for himself, did Mr. Pettifer. He drank at the Dog and Duck, down by Shadwell way. Found out he owned it, on the quiet, like. You get all sorts drinking there and Pettifer liked to keep his customers happy. Don't think I could prove it, but I'm satisfied Pettifer set up both sides against the middle on that one."

"Thank you," Monk said slowly. "Thank you very much."

"Nothing to tie in McNab," Hooper went on a little ruefully. "But quite a lot to add into these escapes. It seems Pettifer was the one who actually found Blount, but gave the credit to someone else."

"Really? That's interesting." Monk told Hooper what he had learned about someone selling Californian artifacts to Velvet Boy. He repeated the description Velvet had given.

"It sounds like Gillander," Hooper said with quiet conviction. "That means he's part of it."

"I know," Monk conceded reluctantly. He had liked the man, but personal regard had nothing to do with innocence or guilt. There had been outwardly good men, virtuous and upright, whom he had disliked for their speed and relish to judge others, even at times for their total lack of humor. And there had been villains who had made him laugh, whom still he had admired, whose love of life he had enjoyed.

"I'm going to see him now," he added.

"I'll come with you," Hooper stated, straightening up.

"That's not—" Monk began.

"I'm coming with you," Hooper repeated, squaring his shoulders and turning toward the door.

THEY FOUND GILLANDER ON board the *Summer Wind,* anchored opposite Aaron Clive's warehouses again, and he welcomed them with the same easy grace as when Monk had met him before.

"What can I do now? Still looking for Owen?" He led the way across the deck and down the steep wooden stairs to the main cabin. It was surprisingly warm, as before, and there was a pleasant odor coming from the galley. Everything was still impressively tidy, brass fixtures polished.

"Got no tea," Gillander said with a smile. "Got some very good soup. Won't tell you what's in it. Like a mugful? It's a devil of a day."

Monk was inclined to agree with him. The water was choppy and the wind scythed in over its rough surface like the edge of a blade.

"Thanks," he accepted.

Hooper was staring around the cabin with appreciation. He tended to make a first judgment of a man by the way he cared for his boat, and his tools. He accepted also that perhaps he would judge a man by how he cooked.

Gillander disappeared into the galley, and a few moments later returned with three tin mugs of soup, clearly hot from the steam that rose from them.

Monk thanked him and waited a moment before he took a sip. It was almost too hot to drink, but it was delicious: a beef broth of some sort, with a generous dash of brandy in it.

"Good," Hooper said appreciatively.

Monk nodded his agreement. He had already decided how he was going to approach the subject of their visit with Gillander.

"No sign of Owen," he observed. "We think he might have been involved in a pretty big plan, which could have included the other man that escaped: Blount."

Gillander looked puzzled, but Monk had not expected him to reveal himself, even if he knew all about it. Monk was by no means certain that Gillander was the mastermind, just the one who could be present without causing suspicion. He still thought it could be Piers Astley behind any planned raid on Clive's premises.

"Blount was a forger," he continued. "There've been a couple of other escapees in the last half year or so. Altogether four men who worked together on a major robbery before."

"Interesting," Gillander agreed. "Robin Hood and his merry men . . . or not so merry. Who killed Blount, then? Was he going to betray them to Customs?"

"It's a thought," Monk said.

There was a silence. Gillander looked from Monk to Hooper, and back again.

"About what? Another big robbery?" Then he laughed loudly. "From Aaron Clive! Of course. That's why Owen came here. And you think I have something to do with it? Because I fished Owen out of the water?"

"It's one possibility." Monk nodded, keeping the smile on his face also. "You're perfectly placed. Why do you anchor here, anyway? It's a long way up the river, and there are few conveniences."

"Which is why it's cheap." Gillander shrugged. "Surely you understand that, Mr. Monk? You've run your own boat. You save money where you can, but never save on equipment, right, Mr. Hooper?"

Hooper nodded his agreement, but did not take his eyes off Gillander. He was sitting sideways to the small table, always keeping the way open across the floor if Gillander moved suddenly. Nothing would be in the way to stop Hooper going for him.

"Right," Hooper said.

Monk nodded also, as naturally as if there were complete understanding between them, but he could feel his muscles aching from the tension of what Gillander had just said about him running his own boat.

Hooper was picking up the thread. "Where'd you come from?" he asked Gillander. "And if you're not waiting for Owen and his friends, who are you waiting for?"

For the first time Gillander hesitated.

Monk was surprised. He would have expected him to have a smooth, easy answer ready. Now he looked even a little uncomfortable.

"I have a service to perform for Mrs. Clive," he said after a moment. "As soon as I've done that, I'll . . . consider moving on. Maybe the China Seas. Ever been that far east, Mr. Monk?"

Monk had no idea and he was distracted by Gillander's mention of Miriam Clive. He couldn't be looking for Piers Astley as well, could he? "No," he said with conviction. "It's the West that used to interest me. Now I'm happy here on the Thames. Sooner or later all the world comes here."

Gillander smiled widely. It was a charming gesture, full of humor.

"I love the arrogance of the English; it's so totally unconscious. You are not even trying to impress. You are too secure in your pride to care what the rest of the world think of you. I've been watching, and trying to copy it."

"I would say you're doing rather well," Monk answered just a fraction too quickly. "Is that Irish I hear in your voice?"

"Ah! You caught it. Sure, and it is. But not for a long time. I've been in California—but you know that. . . ."

Now Monk was aware that Gillander was watching him far more closely than his casual air would suggest. He was leaning back in his seat, the mug of soup on the galley table at his elbow, but his neck was stiff and his eyes were searching Monk's face.

"You must know Aaron Clive pretty well," Monk remarked, just a little late to be a reply. "Especially back in '49."

"I was young then," Gillander said ruefully. "Used to work on smaller boats as a deckhand, sailing up and down the coast. Across the Atlantic now and then and way out east. I first got to know him in San Francisco when I was finding work where I could. He made one of the biggest gold strikes of all. Created a kind of empire, over the past few years. Never gambled it away, like some people. Built himself a nice place, but invested some of his fortune in things that paid, and went on paying. Gold, trade for the things people need, more money, more trade—gold again." There was no hard edge to Gillander's voice, no envy.

"But you went for freedom and adventure on the open seas," Monk observed. He understood that far more. He had never wanted power other than that which gave him safety for work and let him owe no one. The rest of what was worth having was health, skill, courage, being answerable to nobody. Great wealth tied you to its service, whether it was land, trade, or gold.

He had a sudden memory of a coastline of pale hills in the sunlight, wild rocks, seas that leaped high and white where they crashed onto the shore, a haze of amber light as the day was dying, luminous over the water.

Gillander was watching him curiously. Did he see the memory in Monk's face, and the momentary loss of time and place?

Monk brought the subject back to the suspected robbery, moving his position to face Gillander more completely. "This robbery we think is planned . . . against Clive—he's the wealthiest, and maybe most vulnerable along this stretch of the river."

"And you obviously think I know something about it?" Gillander was direct again, staring at Monk almost challengingly.

"I think there's another mind at the back of it," Monk answered. He was playing his hand far more openly than he had intended, but he did not want to be caught trying to be devious, and failing. The more he spoke to this man, the more he feared that Gillander actually knew more about him than he did himself, at least for a short space of time in the gold rush, twenty years ago. Had he known Clive as well? He thought back to his interview with the man. Clive had given no sign of knowing Monk at all. Had he forgotten him? Or never known him? Or the whole matter was simply of no importance to him?

"Do you know who?" Gillander asked.

"There have been some suggestions made," Monk replied. "Why? Do you?"

Gillander gave a slight shrug. "Well, Clive has many enemies. Anyone that rich has to have. But most of them are from the early days. Why would anyone wait so long?"

"Opportunity," Monk said immediately. "Clive's been here in England only a couple of years. Things like this take planning. Maybe he was too powerful in California for anyone to dare."

"So you're looking for a Californian?" Gillander looked amused.

"Or an Englishman," Monk said with an answering smile. "Or a European of any other sort. There was every nationality under the sun in San Francisco in '49. Take your pick."

"So there was," Gillander agreed. "Then you're looking for anyone who feels that the uncrowned king of San Francisco twenty years ago would be a good person to rob here on the Thames—now."

Monk decided to tell Gillander the exact truth, as Miriam had suggested it. "I think it might be revenge," he said, watching Gillander closely.

Gillander was unnaturally motionless, but for so short a time Monk considered he might have imagined it.

"Again, why wait so long?" Gillander said then, moving his shoulders a little as if suddenly uncomfortable on his seat.

Monk felt the prickle of excitement, like scenting the prey, seeing movement where something was hiding, waiting, breathing in the darkness.

"So long?" he asked. "Not so long when you think of the journey, the planning necessary."

Gillander said nothing.

Monk smiled back at him. "Or were you assuming that the revenge had to be for something that happened long ago? Say in '48 or '49?"

Gillander was too agile-minded to lie. He must see the pitfalls ahead. What was it he imagined Monk knew?

"Those were the wildest years, the biggest claims," he said carefully, still watching Monk. He seemed to discount Hooper in the exchange. Was that because Monk had been there, and Hooper had not?

Monk actually knew nothing, but Gillander did not know that.

"You're implying revenge for something lost?" Monk said with a lift of surprise in his voice. "I was thinking of something personal . . . perhaps an attempted murder, the seduction or ravishing of a woman. Something closer to a man's heart than money."

Gillander did all he could to keep absolute composure, but tiny things betrayed him: a second's holding of the breath, a tightness across the shoulders, a pallor to the skin of his handsome face. "And Aaron Clive is to be the victim?" He forced a lift of disbelief into his question. "Mrs. Clive is well, and unseduced or ravished. No one attempted to kill her, or Clive." He realized his error. "That I know of . . . of course. . . ."

"You know them both well?" Monk said innocently.

There was color now in Gillander's cheeks. "I was a young man, very young, twenty, of no account, when I knew them in '49. I ran errands." He indicated the ship with a wave of his hand. "I got all this since then. Sorry, but from what little I do know of Aaron and Mrs. Clive now, I don't think your idea makes any sense."

"What about Piers Astley?" Monk suggested almost casually, but never taking his eyes off Gillander's face.

"Piers Astley?" Monk knew Gillander was repeating the name to give himself time to think.

"Miriam Clive's first husband. Attacked, disappeared, and later declared dead. And she married Mr. Clive," Monk explained. "Don't you think he might bear Clive some grudge? Miriam Clive is one of the most beautiful women I've ever seen, and if he is alive, he would clearly still be in love with her."

Gillander's eyebrows shot up. "Piers Astley . . . behind a plot now to ruin Clive?" His face was filled with disbelief, and laughter.

"One of the oldest motives in the world," Monk explained, but there was unease rippling through him like a fast-rising tide.

"Piers Astley's dead!" Gillander told him.

"Presumed dead," Monk corrected. "There's a big difference, a crucial one."

Gillander sighed and suddenly looked stricken, as if the joke had evaporated as he watched. "He's dead," he said quietly. "I saw his body, riddled with bullets. Actually I was one of the two who buried him. If we were in California I could take you to the grave. It's unmarked, but he's there, God help him."

Monk was stunned. "Then why was he only presumed dead, and his widow not told?"

Gillander rose to his feet—stiffly for a man so young, barely forty. "She was carrying a child." His voice cracked as he said it. "With the shock, she lost it. That was when Aaron Clive slipped in to look after her. She was ill, vulnerable, in a very bad way. Piers Astley isn't planning a revenge against anyone." He looked across at Monk. "Perhaps she was too grieved to remember clearly exactly what she was told about Astley's death. Perhaps a part of her was unconsciously living in a vain hope so that she then confused it with reality. I don't know. But it's not your jurisdiction. Stick to the Thames, Monk! This is deep water of a different sort. It doesn't belong to you."

Monk stood up also. Gillander was right. It was not his jurisdiction. If what Gillander said was true, and Astley was really dead, then he needed to begin again searching for whoever meant to harm Aaron Clive. If he was even right about that!

As he and Hooper got back into their own boat and set off down-river again it was Miriam Clive's face he could not get out of his mind. She was beautiful, troubled, so filled with emotion she moved like a storm with her own energy. But was she speaking the truth? Did she even know it?

Or had her grief, and her lost child, turned her mind from reality to a nightmare that never resolved itself?

8

Since Beata was in mourning, there were few places she could go alone in public. Too often she walked in the park along the smooth gravel paths under the bare trees as she was doing now. The beauty of their stark branches against the sky pleased her. Their nakedness was not masked by leaves, and there was a unique grace to it.

She moved slowly, more because she was loath to return home than for any other reason. And yet dressed entirely in black, walking with a measured pace and not stopping to speak to anyone, she must have appeared to be the perfect, traditional mourning widow, solitary under a leaden sky. People did not approach her, treating her supposed grief with respect.

She felt no grief, except for the wasted years she had spent, hating Ingram and yet doing nothing about it. She had allowed him to convince her that there was nothing she could do. But was that true?

Had imprisonment been freedom of another kind? She could not make her own decisions, which meant she had not had to think, or consider, take any responsibility for the results. The excuse was perfect. "I had no choice. I couldn't fail because I was not allowed to try!" If no success were possible, then equally, neither was any failure. As an errant wife if she had left him then the law would have brought her back, if he had wished it. Perhaps he would not have. She had not tried.

How childlike, in the ugliest way. It was not innocence; it was the abdication of responsibility.

She walked down the slight incline, past the shrubbery—now only the evergreens in leaf—and went over the bridge.

But she had a little longer to decide what she would do, and how. Ingram had left her very well provided for financially, so she had no need even to consider how she would live. Which meant equally that she had no need to marry again. But she wanted to marry Oliver Rathbone . . . didn't she? It had been only Ingram's stubborn survival that had kept them apart.

And the fear of another involvement in emotions, and in intimacy. Had she the courage to put all the pain and humiliation of the past behind her, and try again?

She stopped and gazed at the dark brown water.

She must stop this. It was ridiculous. Courage! Nothing worth having was gained without courage. Or if it were, then it was lost again the first time a hard wind blew. She despised cowardice, and yet here she was on the brink of it herself.

She turned and walked briskly back the way she had come.

THAT EVENING SHE WENT again to Aaron and Miriam Clive's house to dine. The excuse for it was a further discussion on the chair that was to be endowed in Ingram's name. That was if anyone should inquire—or worse, offer a criticism of her for leaving her home for a frivolous reason such as merely dining out.

It would be so much easier to boast a little about the endowment, rather than give them a freezing reply as to the impertinence of such a remark.

She dressed in black, of course, but in a different gown from the previous time. This one was more feminine, the silk softer and more becoming. She wore the traditional jet jewelry. Whitby, where the best jet was mined, must make a fortune out of bereavement!

She would rather have worn pearls; they were so much more flattering to the face than the jagged black facets of jet. But she was not in a mood for weathering the comments, spoken or imagined.

Actually it was only admiration she saw in Aaron Clive's face as she was shown into the withdrawing room where he and Miriam were standing beside the fire, waiting for her to arrive.

Aaron bowed, smiling, and complimented her on the gown. Miriam, in deep burgundy herself, took both Beata's hands warmly and bade her welcome.

"We are waiting for Dr. Finch?" Beata asked, glancing around. "I am so glad I did not cause you to delay dinner. I was afraid I would be early, and then left a fraction late." It was the truth. She had dithered in her decision over the jet . . . as if it mattered to anyone!

"Dr. Finch is not coming," Aaron replied. "We really don't need to inconvenience him this evening. We can easily inform him of any decision we reach."

Miriam shrugged her beautiful shoulders and smiled. "We never intended to ask him. This is simply an excuse to have a pleasant dinner together. He's nice enough, but if he were here then we would have to talk about the chair, the subjects, or the requirements of students permitted to study, and so on." She regarded Beata critically. "You look awfully tired, my dear. You must be bored to weeping. London is very nice, but don't you long for the wild days in San Francisco sometimes? I don't remember anyone mourning there; there were no tears." She smiled suddenly, her whole amazing face lighting. "Wouldn't you love to go out in the sun, in a pair of whaddayoucallums, and ride a bicycle over one of the hills?"

That was not true. People lost many they loved, but they mourned inwardly, as Miriam herself had done. But Beata chose not to say so. She laughed in spite of herself, in her memory feeling the wind in her face, and the freedom of wearing "bloomers," big like a skirt, but divided like trousers. One of the best of inventions. "Not quite like riding sidesaddle in Rotten Row," she agreed.

"But we would do that, too," Miriam said quickly. "All dressed in black, of course," she added. "Perhaps even with a half veil. I always think ladies' top hats with a half veil one of the most seductive head-wear imaginable. Far more than the most glittering tiara."

"You will invite comment," Aaron pointed out. Beata could not tell from his voice whether that was a criticism, or merely an observation, but she thought it the latter, as there was laughter in his eyes.

"Good," Miriam said, smiling at him for an instant before turning back to Beata. "I should hate to go to so much trouble, and then not be noticed."

Beata had no idea whether she meant it or not. From the look on Aaron's face, neither had he. Could she not know that she was always noticed?

They spoke of current events and people in the news, until it was time to go through to the dining room and take their places. All three of them sat at one end of the magnificent gleaming cherrywood table.

The food was excellent. A delicate clear soup was followed by a white fish in sauce, then a rack of lamb with lightly cooked vegetables. But Beata was too engaged in conversation to care very much. They moved from one subject to another, observations on common memories of the past. Sometimes it was of people they had all known. They were far too well-mannered to speak of what was openly controversial, yet they managed to differ quite often.

"He was always very agreeable," Aaron remarked of one gentleman they mentioned.

"Of course he was," Miriam agreed ruefully. "He was a banker. He would have been considerably damaged if you had removed from his keeping the money you had with him."

Aaron was startled. His dark eyes widened. "You really thought him such an opportunist?" There was disappointment in his face, though whether at her, or at the possibility that she could be right, Beata could not tell. She recalled the banker clearly enough. He had three quite comely daughters to see married well, and the responsibility of their making successful matches never seemed to leave him.

"Not so different from London," she observed with a smile. "One does what one has to, to care for one's own."

"He was charming," Miriam agreed. "Although charm is skin deep . . ." She glanced at Beata, then back at Aaron. "It's a practice, not a quality. Fame, fortune, and friendship can be won or lost on charm."

Beata saw a flicker of irritation in Aaron's face. "What is charm?" she asked quickly, to forestall any sharpness between them. "Can you tell, beyond that it is there in people you like?"

"Or who take you in, until it is too late," Miriam added. "You realize that what you had believed was warmth is actually cold, and completely empty." There was a momentary edge to her voice that sounded like pain, but she was still smiling.

"I don't always like charming people," Aaron said with a slight downturning of the corners of his mouth, but rueful, not angry.

"It is the quality that makes you believe that they like you, whether you initially feel that about them," Miriam replied with complete certainty. She did not look at either of them.

"Believe that they like you?" Beata caught the precise wording.

"Yes . . . correctly or not," Miriam agreed. She seemed to avoid Aaron's eyes deliberately. "They might not actually like you at all. In fact, quite the opposite. But you may not ever know that. Some people are beguiled by charm all their lives. They never see it, probably because they know better than to look."

"How foolish." Aaron shrugged. "And perhaps essentially vain. Just because someone smiles at you doesn't mean more than that they have good manners."

"I'm surprised that you should say that." This time Miriam did look at him. "I would need all my fingers and toes to count the people who believed you liked them because you treated them with such warmth. It was always one of the qualities for which you were known."

"Perhaps I did like them," he said, then glanced at Beata, and she knew that beneath the surface lightness he was studying her intently. Why? What had changed without her realizing it?

"I always had the impression that you were far too wise, and too gracious, to allow any other belief," Beata said quite honestly. Then she turned to Miriam. "And that warmth and inner vitality lifted your beauty above that of any other woman in California."

Aaron put his hand out and touched Miriam's arm. It was gentle, affectionate, but quite unmistakably a gesture of possession.

They finished the meal and all three of them returned to the withdrawing room. They spoke easily of many other memories. Aaron was very relaxed and he was surprisingly funny, when he chose. Beata did not stay late, but she left with laughter still ringing in her ears, and a startling feeling of being alive again.

MIRIAM KEPT HER WORD about riding with Beata in Rotten Row, that lovely long earthen and gravel path beside Hyde Park where ladies and gentlemen of the aristocracy and of high fashion took their daily ride on horseback, frequently regardless of the weather.

This day was dry, but there was a hard, cutting wind whining a little in the bare branches above them. It was not a morning to dawdle in conversation as the horses walked sedately. It was definitely an occasion on which to move to the front of those getting ready, then take a brisk canter along the open stretch ahead. Had it been twice the length, they would both have chosen to urge their horses into a gallop.

They came back breathless but with their hearts pounding and the blood drumming in their ears. They gave their horses to the grooms and took the waiting carriage back to Beata's home, not far away.

"Thank you, that was marvelous," Beata said cheerfully as they took their riding boots off in the hall and went in stocking feet into the morning room, where the fire was burning nicely. A few minutes later one of the footmen brought slippers, including a pair for Miriam, and two silver-handled mugs and a jug of steaming hot chocolate.

"Do I have to pretend solemnity?" Beata asked with a smile as the footman closed the door behind him, leaving them alone.

Miriam smiled back. "I should be disappointed," she admitted. "I was hoping you would feel something good—relief, exhilaration, at the very least—the chance to forget propriety and do as you wished."

"I did," Beata said frankly. She looked across at Miriam sitting comfortably a little sideways in the chair. She did not have the smooth perfection of youth anymore, but the laughter and the passion in her face would always capture the attention, and perhaps it would always disturb.

Memories came back to her of gold rush days . . . not just of the town or the bay with its jungle of ships of every kind, mostly abandoned by their crews who had left them, with all they could carry, to go to the goldfields.

The hot chocolate was finished but Beata had not bothered to ring the bell for anyone to take the tray away.

Miriam sat opposite her, her hands folded on her knees, not comfortable anymore. "Do you remember Walt Taylor? A big man but very gentle."

Beata tried to recall, but nothing came to her: no face, no voice.

"I'm sorry," Miriam said quickly. "I think that was before we really knew each other. Piers was still alive. . . ." She tailed off as if the words had evaporated into the warm, fire-lit room but the name of Piers Astley drove out all other recollections and for a moment Beata saw her expression, the lost look.

"I'm sorry," Miriam said again, leaning forward compulsively, gathering herself. "That was clumsy of me. Here you are mourning the death of your husband only a couple of weeks ago, and I am talking of twenty years in the past. But . . . something of the edge remains, the sudden cut where you thought it was all healed." Indeed she looked as if the pain were raw inside her and time had done nothing to heal the wound. "I really am sorry, Beata. I did not mean to be so thoughtless."

"Please don't apologize." Beata did not find it hard to say. "It was not sudden, like Piers's death. Ingram was ill for over a year, and he was not a young man."

"But you're young," Miriam said warmly.

Beata smiled with a quite natural ease. "Thank you, my dear. I admit that under the black weeds, I feel it. Most of the time, I look forward to the future." That was only partly true. She also dreaded it. The hold of the past was very strong, as if Ingram's last grip on her had not loosened with his death.

"Most of it? You have times of grief. It's natural. I didn't know Ingram, but you must have memories that linger, fill your mind with sorrow."

Oh, yes! She could see Ingram's face in her dreams. She could feel the touch of him, smell his skin as if he had only just let go of her.

Should she give Miriam the answer she expected? The hypocrisy of it almost suffocated her.

"Yes, I do," she agreed. "You might have found Ingram interesting, but you would not have liked him." Was that too much truth? She longed to be able to tell someone, to talk to Miriam as they had years ago, sharing young women's secrets, as if they had been sisters.

Miriam stared at her, the beginning of understanding in her eyes. The softness of her expression almost evoked their old intimacy. Was it conceivable that Piers Astley had abused Miriam the way Ingram York had abused her? Was that the understanding in Miriam's eyes?

She should change the subject, if she could—or take the chance to speak.

"It is a . . . relief." She chose the word intentionally. It left her room to interpret it differently if she changed her mind and wished to retreat instead. She was afraid, on the brink of not being alone with her secret wrapped up inside her, eating away at her like a disease. Would Miriam have the faintest idea what she meant? Has she ever been possessed, owned but not loved?

"Was he in pain?" Miriam, too, was guarding her meaning.

"I have no idea," Beata said more sharply than she had intended. Now that the possibility of real honesty was so close she was irritated at the hesitation in reaching it.

Miriam's face clouded. The tenderness in her eyes was so deep it seemed to be her own pain she was feeling.

"What was he like? Really?" Her voice was no more than a whisper.

Now it was either the truth, or lie. Either way, it was irreversible. She was soul-weary of lies.

"For the first couple of years he was all right." Beata chose her words with as much precision as she could. "Then little things changed. At first it was only the occasional roughness, a deliberate hurting at moments of intimacy. But they grew more frequent until it was every time." She was going to say it all now. She did not look at Miriam's face because she knew she would not stop. This was a test. If Miriam was disgusted, disbelieving, then Beata would know she could never risk telling Oliver.

"He began to exercise other tastes," she continued. "Revolting things that were humiliating, and terribly painful. I should have had the courage to stop him. I tried two or three times, but he hurt me more. Of course it was in places no one else would ever see. I couldn't go to a specialist doctor, another man, and tell him my husband had done that to me."

She felt Miriam's hand on her arm, very gently, and at last she looked up at her.

Miriam had tears in her eyes and her face was pale with anger.

"I'm so sorry."

Beata sat motionless, hardly breathing. All she could feel was her heart thundering in her chest. Miriam understood. She did not know how or why, but she understood!

"Thank you," she said very quietly. "Actually, justice caught up with him eventually, but it was not my doing. Less than a year ago, he had a seizure and was paralyzed, in and out of coma and, I think, nightmare. He couldn't move, and could only speak a little. He suffered a great deal. It would have been more merciful if the first seizure could have taken him."

"How hard for you . . . waiting," Miriam said softly. Then the anger was gone from her eyes and there was only a tenderness. "Piers died very quickly, I was told. He was shot in some stupid kind of brawl, in a saloon up in the gold country to the north, where he was looking after Aaron's affairs. That was what he did. He was trying to stop a fight, and got in the way." She stopped, her voice gravelly in her throat.

"And you were just . . . told about it?" Beata tried to picture hearing such news about a man you had truly loved, not one whose death was your release.

"It must have been like a stab in the back from an assassin you did not even know was following you," Beata whispered. "I can't imagine it."

Tears filled Miriam's eyes. "They buried him out there. I rode out a few days after. The hills are beautiful, spring flowers everywhere. People in dusty clothes on the sides of every river and stream, panning for gold. You can see it in your mind. Women scraping at the earth to dig it up enough to plant greens and vegetables. Shacks with nothing over their beds and a stove of some sort, or even an open fire outside." She gave a short, jerky laugh. "They don't call it gold fever for nothing. But those wild days had their advantages, too."

Beata knew that very well. Her own father had been one of the wise ones, who did not look for gold themselves but made their way by providing for those who did. They lost a little on the failures, but made enormously on the successes, until he started to gamble. But she would not speak of that now; she had torn open enough wounds for the day.

"You didn't go alone?" she asked, really just to show her attention to Miriam's story.

"Yes I did, except for one of the men from Aaron's homestead. I don't even remember who he was. A friend of Zack's, I think." Miriam smiled ruefully. "A nice man. He was very kind to me, patient. I feel guilty that I can't even think what he was called, or even exactly what he looked like. I was . . . stunned. The whole world changed for me in a few days." She was looking into the past herself now, in turn acknowledging pain that would never entirely leave her.

"It wasn't Zack himself?" Beata asked it for something to say, not because it mattered. It was all so many years ago.

Miriam shook her head. "No, poor Zack was dead by then. Over a year before. That was a bit before you and I really knew each other.

"Zachary was the most totally honest man I ever knew. He and

Aaron were closer than brothers. He was the only person whose opinion of him Aaron even cared about. Zachary's father took a huge area of
land over from the Indians and that's where Aaron's success began. He
was better at defending it than Zachary." Her words were perfectly plain,
but there were conflicting emotions in her face, respect and doubt
mixed.

Beata knew something of the history of the West. This would not
have been a purchase; it was plainly land-grabbing.

"Zack didn't agree with what his father had done," Miriam went on.
"He felt he shouldn't have taken it, gold or not. His father gave Aaron
command of it, and when the old man was killed, Aaron inherited it."

Beata was startled. "Not Zack?"

"No. But Zack didn't mind. He would have given it back; we all
knew that. And the big gold stakes made it certain. There'd have been
an Indian war, which the Indians would have lost, if they'd fought."

"And Zack?" Beata asked.

"He yielded to the inevitable," Miriam replied. "But he spent more
and more time up in the Indian parts, trying to see they got something
out of it. When he was killed, Aaron grieved for him terribly. That's
how he understood my grief over Piers, I think. The world changed for
him when Zack died. He lost something of himself that day, something
good inside him." She remained silent for several minutes, seemingly
imprisoned in memory.

That was all about Aaron and Zachary. What of her first husband?

Had Piers Astley not been anything like the man Miriam had allowed people to suppose? Beata thought that if Miriam meant her to
know she would have told her now. Beata herself had led people to
think that Ingram was a clever, subtle, cultivated man, interesting in
public and quietly decent at home. Why should Miriam be any different? She was a beautiful woman fighting for acceptance within her own
society. London, just as much as the frontier town of San Francisco, was
a place where to be outcast was a kind of death. Perhaps it was the same
everywhere.

Had Aaron, who was clearly still in love with her, rescued her from a man who had abused her, and she dared not admit it? Why was a woman afraid to acknowledge that she had been beaten, or intimately used by a man who, at least in part, hated her?

Aaron obviously still found Miriam beautiful, whole, and lovely, even after nearly twenty years of marriage. Would Oliver Rathbone ever see Beata in such a way? Perhaps, if she never let him know the truth! Could he possibly understand as Miriam seemed to? There was the gulf between empathy and pity that Beata could not bear that he should cross.

But if she did tell him, wouldn't he always have the question in his mind, whether he gave it words or not—"Why did you let him?"

"You are very fortunate to have met Aaron," she said quietly.

Miriam looked at her for a long, steady moment, then turned her head away and stared out of the window.

"It was a marvelous ride today," she said softly. "Almost a gallop. Who would have thought you could do that in the middle of London, and all dressed up as if to meet the cream of the aristocracy . . . ?"

"We did meet some of them," Beata said, allowing herself to embrace the complete change of subject. "We spoke to at least one marchioness, a duchess, and two viscounts."

"And with the horse you lent me, I felt the equal of any of them," Miriam said, suddenly cheerful again, as if she could dismiss the past with a flick of her hand. "I am envious and grateful. With such a veil as you had, I doubt anyone recognized you. We must ride again. Please . . ."

Beata had no hesitation in agreeing. A weight had gone from her, not far perhaps, but gone nevertheless.

"Oh, certainly. I would like that very much."

ACTUALLY, THE NEXT OCCASION on which Beata had any social contact at all was a brief visit to Dr. Finch's chambers in Belgravia, regarding the university chair in Ingram's name. She found the subject awkward because she did not really like Finch, and it was difficult to keep up the pretense that Ingram was an admirable man. She was relieved when

Aaron Clive came into the room, interrupting a rather awkward conversation.

As soon as Aaron saw Beata he came over to her, smiling, taking both her hands in his and searching her face.

"How are you? You look wonderful, but you always do."

She knew she looked tired. She saw her own face in the glass enough to understand what she should wear, whether a dash of color was needed.

"It gets easier every day." It was a gracious answer that was also the truth.

She saw his candid smile and knew that he understood. How utterly different he was from Ingram!

"Are we progressing?" he asked Finch, turning to him with a smile of optimism.

"Most certainly," Finch agreed. He was polite and kept a very slight distance, yet Beata had the powerful impression that his respect for Aaron came somewhere close to awe. Was it no more than Aaron's money, and therefore his power to endow the university with the funds it needed to obtain the very best from its teaching? Or was it the aura of power, and even romance that surrounded a man who had traveled, observed, created, and sustained an estate the size of a small country, as Aaron had? And yet still kept his grace, and always his temper?

They concluded the business quickly. Beata had come in a hansom. It was not worth getting her own carriage out for such a comparatively short journey. Aaron offered to take her home, since he had his carriage, ready for a considerably longer journey back toward his offices down by the river. It was a pleasant afternoon for late November. Unusually, there was no wind.

"Thank you," she said, accepting with pleasure.

As it was, it took longer than either of them had expected. There was no way to hurry traffic where a dray had turned too abruptly and lost some of its load. They were obliged to wait, since they could move neither back nor forward.

"Miriam told me how much she had enjoyed your ride in the park," Aaron said conversationally. "I hope you feel free to go again."

From his tone of voice she was not certain if he was being a little ironic. Had he any idea what Ingram had been like? Could Miriam have told him? Surely not! That thought was unbearable! Or possibly Ingram's reputation was a good deal more accurate than he would have liked to think? She turned toward him, but there was no criticism in Aaron's face, only a slight humor, as if he could see the joke, but thought it unkind to let her know that. Many wounds can be borne simply because we believe no one else knows.

"I enjoyed it myself," she replied. "I find the enforced silence and lack of any theater, opera, concert, even exhibition of anything that might be considered beautiful or frivolous, to be an addition to grief rather than a respite from it."

He raised his eyebrows. "Are you sure that is not what it is meant to be? This is London, you know? Ancient, and magnificent, the complicated heart of empire where manners and conventions are like an enamel on the surface of power. So elegant, but crack it, and you see the raw steel beneath. Your husband was a judge, my dear, one of the arbiters of judgment."

She looked straight at him, meeting his eyes. "I notice you say 'of judgment,' not 'of justice.'"

"I did," he agreed. "Do you fault me for it?" He had been smiling; now suddenly he was totally serious.

"Not at all; I am only surprised you are so candid," she replied.

As if changing the subject, he looked out at the passing street. "I like London. It surely is the heart of things. One might turn a corner and bump into a man from anywhere on earth, and it would all seem perfectly natural." He hesitated only a second. "Take this policeman, Monk, who is investigating the wretched escape of the man from Customs, and the drowning of their own man, practically on my doorstep. He would be equally at home in San Francisco. Many of the conditions are similar, and the rules. He seems to know cargoes and seamen, as well as thieves and opportunists, and he is able to measure them up pretty quickly. At least that is my estimate of him. Is it correct, do you think?"

"He is a very good policeman," she said with care. She did not know

Monk personally, but she knew he was Oliver's closest friend. He had been loyal when Oliver was in trouble. Nothing had been too arduous or too dangerous for him to risk in helping him. And Oliver held a higher regard for Hester Monk than for anyone else she had heard him speak of. That was a subject she used to find painful, if she allowed herself to think of it too closely. At least it was so until she had gone to the clinic and met her. Now Hester seemed remarkably human. But still from what Oliver had said of her, Hester would never have been weak enough to allow any man to ill-use her, let alone do some of the things that Ingram had done to Beata.

Now as Aaron Clive looked at her, she could feel the hot flush burn up her face at the memory.

"I don't doubt it," he agreed. "Was he a seaman before he joined the police?"

She had no idea. Oliver had never mentioned Monk's youth or his upbringing in any way, let alone what other professions he might have followed. "I don't know. It seems not impossible as he is in the River Police. Why do you ask?"

He smiled widely and leaned back a little. "Just curious. The man will hold part of my fate in his hands, if his suspicions are correct. I am wondering if there really is a plot to rob me, as he believes, and if so, if he is equal to catching those involved. If they are land-based thieves, then I am not concerned. But if they are operating from the river, then their escape would be straight down into the open sea, and I would probably never get any part of my goods back again, if Monk is basically a landsman."

"Ask him," she said with a smile in return, to rob the remark of any sting.

"He reminds me of a seaman I knew very slightly in San Francisco, about twenty years ago," Aaron said lightly. His words were well chosen, but he made them with a casual air. "Young man then, something of an adventurer; a chancer, one way or another. He had a bit of a lilt to his voice. Piers told me he must be from the north of England, Northumberland, perhaps."

"Oh, really? I didn't detect that in Mr. Monk," she answered. "But then I have seen him only a few times, and that mostly in court."

"In court?"

"Testifying," she explained. "In his role as commander of the Thames River Police. He has dealt with some very big cases."

"Of course. I don't think of someone of his rank doing the ground-work where he could testify to anything."

"Oh, he does." That she knew both from his testimony in court, and from Rathbone. "He doesn't sit in an office and direct other people."

"An interesting man," Aaron observed, completely without emo-tion. Was he merely making polite conversation during their stop in traffic? His comments now suggested it, and yet the tension in his body, still turned toward her, and the stiffness in his face, said that the subject stirred some kind of feeling in him.

"You think the seaman you knew in San Francisco was Monk?" she asked bluntly.

"I hope not." This time his emotion was quite open. "He answers exactly the description of the man who murdered Piers Astley."

Beata barely even noticed the jolt as, without warning, the han-som started moving again, throwing her back in the seat. Thank heaven there was now enough noise of traffic outside that she could be excused from giving any answer. Had Monk been in San Francisco? Was that what Aaron was suggesting? Did he believe that? Did Oliver know?

Or was Aaron Clive, for some reason or other, just making trouble?

It was not until she was nearly at her own door that she finally spoke again.

"Did you tell Miriam this?"

He had been staring forward. Now he turned to her again. "I'm sorry, my attention was elsewhere. I beg your pardon?"

"Did you tell Miriam that Monk might be the man who killed Piers? Or at least he might know who did?"

"No," he said, smiling gently. "There is nothing that could be done about it now. It was nearly twenty years ago, and thousands of miles away in another country. From here it seems almost like another world. There is nothing she could do, and it would only disturb her."

"Yes . . ." she said slowly, not meaning it, but what else was there that she could say? "I see."

BEATA KEPT UP HER habit of walking alone in the park, regardless of the weather. In fact a windy or wet day gave her the excuse to wrap a shawl around her shoulders and keep it high under her chin. A suitable hat for such weather also made her hard to recognize, and thereby made polite and meaningless commiserations easily avoidable. Everyone had the best of excuses—"I'm so sorry, I did not realize it was you!"—and so was free to pass by without discourtesy.

She was glad of it. It became harder and harder to think of something polite to say, and to repeat pleasant and artificial remarks about Ingram. Did she miss him? Yes! And the feeling was like breathing clean air again after the filth of fog and smoke, and the smells of the street.

She had wanted to see Oliver so much she had several times considered writing him a letter asking him to call. Then she thought how precipitate that would be, and he could so easily misunderstand her. She had taken it for granted that the feeling between them was mutual, and not spoken in words for decency's sake. As long as Ingram was alive, it could never be acted upon.

He could not yet decently call on her alone, unless he had legal business and she were too unwell to visit his office. And since he was a trial lawyer, not conversant with wills and property, she had no call for his skills.

Instead she purposely walked the same route, at the same hour, aware that if he were free to do so, he might take a brief walk that would cross her path.

One morning she was pleased to hear, with a flutter of excitement, a lifting of the spirits, his footsteps behind her. She admitted to herself she had been hoping very much that he would come.

"Good morning, Lady York. I hope you are well," he said just as two men passed them walking in the opposite direction, too busy in their own conversation to notice others. They were dressed in black frock coats and striped trousers, each carrying a rolled umbrella and using it as if it were a walking stick.

She smiled at the typical sight, then met Rathbone's glance. "I am quite well, thank you. And you?"

"Are we really reduced to such a level?" he asked bluntly.

She felt herself coloring. Had she imagined it, all the teeming words that lay unspoken in the imagination? How unseemly it would be for her to speak first. And if she were wrong, how ridiculous! And mortifying . . .

She must really collect her wits and tell him what she needed to, for Monk's sake. She must share with Oliver what Aaron Clive had said.

"I have been meeting with Aaron Clive once or twice regarding the endowment of a chair at the university, in Ingram's name," she began. She saw the look of distaste in Oliver's highly expressive face, and understood it totally. "I know," she murmured with a twisted smile. "But I cannot say anything to the contrary."

"But it troubles you?" he asked. "Don't deny it: It is in your voice, and your eyes."

She knew that he was looking at her intently and was very conscious of it. And yet she wanted him to. She must control her voice and sound normal. She made a small gesture of dismissal with her hand. "That is not what concerns me at the moment. I was speaking with him in the carriage on the way home. He mentioned the death of Miriam's first husband, Piers Astley. . . ."

"What of it? Was it not years ago?" He was puzzled. They stopped and stood facing each other on the path. The wind gusted and blew her skirts. He held his hat in his hand, in case it blew away. There is little more comical than an otherwise dignified man chasing his hat across the grass.

"Nearly twenty," she agreed. "And over five thousand miles away . . ." Why was she reluctant now to tell him? Would he think she was asking him to become involved? But of course she was.

"Beata? What is it?" There was concern in his voice.

She met his eyes and saw fear in them. Why? Was he afraid she was going to expect something of him more than he wanted to give?

"What is it?" he repeated, more urgently.

She could feel the heat in her face. "He said there was a man who looked very much as Mr. Monk must have, twenty years ago, in San Francisco. He was a seaman, an adventurer."

"Oh . . . ?"

Why did he look so worried?

"It probably wasn't him," she added. "This man had a slight northern accent. Aaron thought Northumberland, or somewhere like that."

"Monk is Northumbrian," Rathbone said quietly.

She shook her head. "I didn't hear it in his voice."

"He's ambitious, and will have lost it deliberately." He smiled very slightly as he said it, but there was a furrow between his brows. She knew the expression.

Now she was cold. "You think it could have been him?"

"I don't know. What did Clive say of him?"

Now she had to say it. "That he fits the description of the man who killed Piers Astley."

"Killed him accidentally . . . or murdered him?"

"Murdered . . ."

Suddenly she wanted to put it to the test, the outcome of which she feared more than any other. She began to walk, very slowly. The wind was edged with ice and the path curved down to pass into the shelter of trees.

He caught up with her, taking her arm as they came to some steps.

"This is absurd. Monk would not murder anyone," he said so decisively that she wondered if it was himself he was trying to convince.

She took a breath, steadying herself. "Not even if perhaps the man concerned were abusing his wife?"

"Was he? Then Miriam would have said so," he pointed out.

She faced straight ahead. She must say it, otherwise it would be a tacit lie. "I don't mean beating her . . . I mean the sort of abuse one practices only ever in private." Now she could never take it back. She could not look at him. She imagined the revulsion in his eyes.

"She told you that happened?" he asked levelly.

She tried to read the emotion in his voice and failed.

"You don't tell anyone such things. . . ." she replied.

He said nothing. They walked a few paces farther on. They were on the level now and he let go of her arm. The wind scythed across the grass, cutting through scarves and veils, even through the woolen fabric of coats.

"No," Rathbone said at last, "I suppose one doesn't." There was intense gentleness in his voice, and perhaps even remembered pain. He felt that for Miriam, perhaps because she was beautiful, and he hardly knew her. What would he feel for Beata? She did not wish pity. Thank God she had tested him only with the thought of someone else!

"And the shame!" she added fiercely, and instantly wished she had not.

He took her arm again and she did not move away.

"It is not her shame," he replied. "It is his."

Now she was fighting tears. Thank heaven the wind was harsh enough to explain them. "And hers, too," she said huskily. "For not having seen what he was . . ."

"Beata, no one wears such a thing on his shirt front!"

"And having put up with it," she added. She must say it now. She would never ever speak of this again.

"We do," he said gently. "We put up with all kinds of things, hoping it will get better, that it won't happen again, or that there will be something we can do." He was chiding her, as if she were judging someone else too harshly.

"Do you think so? How do you know?" Then she blinked. That was a question she should not have asked. "I'm sorry, Oliver! That was . . ." She had no word for it.

He smiled. "Honest? I'm a criminal lawyer, Beata. I've defended a few people who were driven to kill, in self-defense. And I've prosecuted a few who richly deserved it. Although their stories also would make you weep. Most of us at one time or another, are guilty of 'passing by on the other side,' at the very least. We all have times when we are willing to see only what we can bear."

"And you don't despise them for tolerating it?" It was the last question, the last fear.

"That's how fear works," he answered. "Pain, humiliation, until you believe you deserve it, and it is inevitable. In the end the victim accepts that there is nowhere to which they could escape."

They walked a few more paces in silence. Finally she had to speak.

"You must have seen some terrible things . . . you haven't looked away. Pity hurts, too. . . ."

"Very much," he agreed. "But sometimes you win. Fighting helps, it really does."

"And if you lose?"

"I don't lose very often."

"I know that. But when you do?" she insisted, turning to face him.

"Then it hurts terribly," he said frankly, and she saw the fear in his eyes. "But please heaven, I learn from it."

She wanted to tell him that Ingram York had never learned, but it would break the moment, and it was intensely important that she did not. Tentatively she slipped her arm through his.

He put his other hand over hers for a moment, then let it go again. It would not be wise to have others observe such a moment. But she glanced at him, and saw that he was smiling. Slowly they began to walk again.

Monk walked slowly up the hill toward his home. The night was intensely dark. The lights along the shore seemed hemmed in by wreaths of mist, and clouds blocked the moon.

But he knew the way so well that even the gaps in the cobbles seemed familiar.

So Piers Astley was dead, and had been for nearly twenty years. He had been murdered in the time Monk could no longer remember. In fact, it was even possible that Monk himself had been in San Francisco when it had occurred.

Astley had apparently been Aaron Clive's chief lieutenant, if a military term were appropriate. Perhaps it was, in such a hectic age when power was extreme. Gold made fortunes in a week, a day, and violence was easy, and there was no law except whatever you provided in agreement with others, and such decency as was not tainted with gold.

What sort of man had Aaron Clive been then? Had his ease and apparent sophistication come with power? Or had he always possessed it? What Monk had heard suggested the latter. If anything, the extraordinary preeminence he had had in the gold rush seemed to have tarnished a little of it, overlaid the original modesty with a certain sense of entitlement. But was any man free from hubris, if circumstances gilded everything he touched? The great landed aristocracy of England certainly was not. Some saw their position as a call to duty. For others it was a birthright, to be used as they chose.

Monk turned the last corner and continued to climb. In a few minutes he would see the lighted windows of his home. Hester would be waiting for him. He would ask about her day at the clinic, and for a while he would put off his own decisions about McNab, the question of a plot to rob Clive, and the fact that Astley could have had no part in it.

Tired as he was, he increased his stride.

Hester opened the door before he had time to take out his own key. He stepped inside, finding himself smiling with the pleasure of seeing her. He pushed the door closed behind him and then took her in his arms, holding her so closely she gasped and pushed him away a couple of inches so she could breathe.

Then after tightening her arms about him just as fiercely, she stepped back and looked at him with her clear, unwavering gaze. She had been skirting around the issue for some time. Now she was characteristically blunt.

"What is it, William?" She bit her lip so slightly the movement was almost invisible. "What are you afraid is going to happen?"

That was it . . . fear of what was going to happen? Now it was either lie to her, or tell her the whole truth. As long as he had known her she had trusted him, even when it seemed impossible that he could be either honest, or completely right about the facts. That trust was perhaps the most precious thing in his life. Certainly it seemed so now. And one lie would break it. Then what would he have left?

"I can't remember twenty years ago. . . ." Why was he beginning here? She knew that. "It looks as if I could have been in San Francisco in the gold rush, even if only for a short time, a year, or less. Not for gold! As a seaman. I don't know if I'm imagining the things I hear about, or if I remember them. Just a flash here and there. The way the light hits the water, bright flowers that don't grow in England, places I've seen pictures of, but haven't been to. Like a harbor crammed with ships, where thousands of people live on them."

"Is San Francisco like that?" she asked, always practical. Nurses dealt only in the real. First establish with the physical!

"It was twenty years ago," he answered. "I expect it's changed a lot now. Even London changes in twenty years."

"Not much," she said with a flash of wry humor. "Why does it matter so much?"

"Because I can't remember . . ." He had not meant his voice to sound desperate, but it did. They were still standing in the hall, close together. "But I'm afraid that Aaron Clive can . . . and maybe Fin Gillander, the schooner captain, can as well."

"Oh . . ." Her eyes were clouded now. She understood. She had lived through all this dark uncertainty before.

He had still avoided the most dangerous part. He should say it, before somehow he evaded it. "I looked at all my old records that there are, and I still don't know why McNab hates me so. It's more than just professional rivalry. I can see it in his face. I can almost smell it on him. And I'm afraid . . ." There, he had said the word, the weakest, ugliest one. "I'm afraid he knows that I can't remember why. If he really does know that everything's gone from my memory before '56, he'll use it when it's worst for me, when it will ruin me." Had he meant to say so much? He could hear the edge of despair in his voice.

"Then we must find out why," Hester said gently. "You may learn that it is no more to his credit than to yours. William, you can't fight without knowing! It would be throwing away all your weapons."

He looked at her, studying her face in the soft yellow of the gaslight on the wall. Her eyes were steady, shadowed with anxiety, but if she was afraid, he could not see it. She was angry, ready to defend him. She would not have been if she didn't understand that the threat was real.

"Come and have something to eat," she said, half-turning to lead the way back to the kitchen.

"I'm not hungry. . . ." he began.

"Of course not," she agreed, walking away from him. "Hot tea, and a cold roast beef sandwich. You can't fight on an empty stomach."

He was so tired his body ached, and he could feel a ridiculous prickle of emotion as his eyes stung. They had faced great voids before, determined to win. But this was the darkness of the past racing forward to engulf them. And he did not know what it was!

She walked on toward the kitchen. She was not beautiful in any traditional sense, too thin for fashion, comfort, the sweetness some men expected from women. But her head was high, and she moved with a grace he had never seen in anyone else on earth.

He followed her, as if she held the light.

The kitchen was warm, and the kettle was simmering on the stove. She made tea and he sipped it while she sliced the bread and carved the beef. Perhaps he was hungry after all.

"So what are you going to do next?" she asked as she put the plate down in front of him. "There must be a whole lot that isn't in the police records." She sat down opposite him and poured tea for herself as well. "You wrote them up yourself?"

"Yes . . ." For a moment he did not grasp her meaning, then he understood. "You mean if there were something I was ashamed of, or embarrassed about, then I wouldn't have put it in?"

She winced, but she did not look away from meeting his eyes. "Would you?"

"Probably not," he agreed. "But I was just looking for mention of his name at all. It wasn't there."

She thought for a long moment before speaking again, as if she knew that what she was going to say was delicate.

"The only person who has known you all that time, and worked with you, is Runcorn. William, you have to know. It's too dangerous not to . . . whatever the truth is. Not knowing won't change it; it will just give McNab more weapons to hurt you."

She was right. Of course she was right.

"I know," he admitted at last. "I'll ask him. I have avoided all discussion of my past for too long; trying to get away with not confronting it, maybe. Or just hoping that it didn't matter, that I could actually leave it in the past."

Hester smiled and put her hand over his. She did not need to say anything.

THE NEXT MORNING MONK went early to see Superintendent Runcorn. He was stationed at Blackheath, which was not far away. Monk arrived well before nine o'clock, and found Runcorn sitting in his office with a large cup of tea and a pile of reports on his desk, less neatly stacked than he used to have them. He had relaxed a little at last. Happiness had bound his old demons.

When they had both served, as younger men, in the Metropolitan Police, they had begun as friends, and gradually become enemies. Runcorn had been stiff, an obsessive rule follower, unsure of himself, only feeling safe with orders. Monk had capitalized on it, taunting him, probing his weaknesses.

Monk himself was intelligent, quick-witted, able to improvise, a natural rebel. In the end it was Monk who had been dismissed for insubordination, and Runcorn who had been promoted. Now it was Monk who held the higher rank.

After the accident, Monk had been forced to look a great deal harder at the man he discovered himself to be. He had not liked what he saw in himself, and he was not proud of his taunting of Runcorn.

Later Runcorn had fallen hopelessly in love with a witness in a case they had worked on together. In spite of every difference in background, education, and social class, Melisande had seen the gentleness in Runcorn, the deep, sincere love he had for her, and had found to everyone's surprise that she returned it. Runcorn was happier than he had dreamed possible. He was a changed man. Enough so that Monk judged him to be the one person he could trust with the question he must now pursue.

Monk closed the office door behind him as Runcorn looked up, surprised to see Monk, and then, studying his face, concerned. He waved at the other chair for Monk to sit down.

"Tea?" he asked.

Monk shook his head. "Not yet . . . thank you. I've got a lot of questions to ask, and I don't know anyone else. . . ."

Runcorn leaned back in his chair and looked steadily at Monk as he recounted his latest case. It turned out that, stationed as he was near the river, Runcorn already knew some of the facts and the people involved.

"If I knew anything useful I'd have told you," he said quietly when Monk had finished. "I'd barely heard of Aaron Clive until this episode of McNab's man drowning. And I have no idea what Blount was doing, or Owen. I've asked around, but I haven't heard anything back."

"What do you know about McNab?" Monk's nerves were tight and he came straight to the point. "Why does he hate me?"

Runcorn stared at him. He sat totally still, as if something long forgotten had suddenly flooded his mind.

"Oh God!" he said very quietly. "I never put it together. . . ."

Monk was cold inside, as if the blood in him had stopped flowing. "What together? What did I do to him?"

Runcorn pushed his hands through his thick, wiry hair. "It wasn't really your fault, but of course that isn't the way we look at things. . . ."

Monk wanted to scream at him, "What things? For the love of God—tell me!" He controlled himself with an intense effort. This was not the way to behave. He could not afford to antagonize Runcorn, who was one of the few friends he had. And he was still a friend, even though he knew so much of the truth.

"What things?" he asked almost levelly.

"Do you remember Robbie Nairn?" Runcorn asked, watching Monk closely, his long face very grave.

Monk searched his mind and could think of nothing at all, yet the name was vaguely familiar. He had no idea if he was another policeman, a friend, an enemy, yet he had surely heard the name recently. "No. Who is he?"

Runcorn sighed. "Almost sixteen years ago, a young man in his early twenties. Very violent. Also charming, in his own way. Handsome, too. Looked a bit like McNab, I suppose, though you might not see it, if you didn't put them side by side."

"So who was he?" Monk did not want to know, but he had to. "McNab's son?"

"No . . . no. McNab was only thirty then, Nairn about six or seven years younger." Runcorn looked very directly at him. There was no pleasure in his eyes or in his face. "Nairn got into a bad fight with another young man. It ended with Nairn injured and the young man dead, his throat cut."

"A fight? Who started it?"

"No one knows. Nairn had some bad injuries, too, and he said the other man started it. For a while we were inclined to believe him. It was you who discovered the evidence the other way. . . ."

"Was I wrong?"

"I don't think so. Nothing ever indicated it. The jury believed you."

"Did you?" Monk pressed.

Runcorn nodded. "Yes. I had no doubt. Still haven't. Nairn was a bad one."

"What are you not telling me?"

"You pushed pretty hard to get the evidence."

Monk winced. "Did I beat it out of him? Keep him up all night? Shame him, threaten him? What?" He did not want to think of it, but he knew he had been capable of all that.

"I don't know," Runcorn admitted. "Lots of things were suggested. You questioned him alone, which was foolish, especially with your reputation."

"There must have been proof. Not just my word. If it was a fight gone too far . . ."

"It was more than that, Monk. There was a girl. That's what the fight was about. She was dead. Her throat was cut, too. It was pretty horrible. Nairn said the other man did it. It was your evidence that tipped the balance."

"But was I wrong?" Monk asked, leaning forward, his body clenched tight. "Was there any doubt in the facts? Why would I lie?" Had he really changed so much? The thought of lying to convict a man was repellent, and worse, it was an offense against the law, and against everything that honor stood for. It was too easy to come to the wrong conclusion. All the evidence had said that Monk had killed Joscelyn Gray. He had even thought so himself! It was only Hester and John Evan, his new assistant after the accident, who had believed in him. And yet they were right. He had never harmed Joscelyn Gray, in spite of all that he had done.

But that was after the accident. After the terror and confusion of losing all he knew of himself. What about before?

"What did I do to Nairn?" he asked again. "And what was it to McNab?"

"Nairn was his half brother," Runcorn answered quietly. "Same mother. Grew up together. McNab went the right way, Nairn the wrong."

"And he holds me responsible?" Monk said incredulously. "Did Nairn kill the woman, too? Was that what it was about?"

"It was never proved, but the jury took it that way."

"Did I claim that he did?" Monk insisted.

"No. You didn't say one way or the other. Nairn denied it, and McNab believed him. He begged you to ask for mercy for Nairn. You wouldn't."

"What happened?" Monk had to ask, although from the misery in Runcorn's face, he already knew the answer.

"They hanged him," Runcorn said. "After the usual three Sundays. McNab did everything he could, begged and pleaded everywhere, but to no effect."

"So I wasn't the only one who didn't—"

"You were the officer on the case." Runcorn cut across him. "The judge might have listened to you, and given him life in prison instead. I'm sorry, but that's the truth."

"Would that have been better?" Monk thought he might have preferred to be hanged than spend the rest of his life in one of the vast, wretched prisons around England. It was a slow death, inch by inch.

Runcorn stared at Monk, deliberately meeting his eye.

"McNab always believed that in time he would have been proved innocent. Not much point in an appeal if you're dead. Added to which, if they've hanged someone, Her Majesty's judiciary are a lot less willing to consider that they might have made a mistake."

There was no argument to that. Monk sat in aching silence.

"He wasn't innocent," Runcorn said at last. "There were other charges we couldn't bring against him, but we knew he was guilty. He had a bad reputation with women. Beaten a few, and got away with it. McNab didn't know, and didn't want to. Couldn't use any of it in the trial, but we knew."

"I knew?" Monk grasped at the straw.

"Of course."

Monk had to test the last possibility. If he left it, it would haunt him.

"Did I judge him on the past cases? I mean . . . could I have tilted the evidence a bit, to make sure he paid this time?" He said it with loathing. It was an arrogant, despicable thing to do. But could the man he had been have excused it to himself? He was not stupid—he had never been that—but he was arrogant enough, convinced of his own rightness.

"No," Runcorn said with a twisted smile. "You were important, but not enough for a jury to have taken your word without proof. And if you'd been stupid enough to try, the judge at least would have slapped you down. In fact, the defense lawyer would have made mincemeat of you."

"Are you sure?"

Runcorn nodded slightly. "Certain. Nairn was convicted on the evidence."

"But I could have asked for mercy? Why? He killed the woman and then the other man. What could I have said on his behalf?"

"It could have been the other man who killed the woman, and Nairn killed him for it," Runcorn said.

"But it wasn't," Monk insisted.

"Probably not."

"Probably!" Monk's voice rose sharply. "Hell! You can't hang a man on a 'probably'!"

"The jury believed you on the evidence. Actually so did I."

"Is there any possibility I was wrong?"

Runcorn sat absolutely still. "Possibility, I suppose so. Reasonable doubt, no, not a reasonable one."

"But McNab thought so!"

"Only because he didn't know about the other cases."

"Neither did the jury," Monk pointed out. "Why did the jury convict?"

"Possibly because they believed you and they didn't believe him. He was an arrogant son of a bitch!"

"So was I, by all accounts!"

Runcorn smiled, a flash of humor in his eyes. "Indeed. But you were the law." He let it hang in the air with all its responsibility, its power for good or evil. Then he added, "But you were right, he was guilty. McNab just didn't want to believe it. And I daresay he didn't want to admit to himself that he hadn't liked the boy all that much, either. But it's blood, I suppose. And remembering how things had been when they were children. People always do that, when it's too late: remember the child as they used to be."

Monk considered that before saying anything more. He believed Runcorn, but he had absolutely no recollection of any part of it. But it did sound like the man that all the evidence showed he had been. What had he felt? Anything? Had it all been judgment, and a degree of self-righteousness, exactness of the law? Or had he known far more than the main facts that Runcorn had spoken of? Were there other circumstances, details? Who had the girl been, other than a name? Had he known something about her? Parents, friends, even a child of her own? And the dead young man?

"Who was the girl?" he asked. "Was she a prostitute?"

"Just a girl with no home," Runcorn replied. "Mother married again and threw her out. She probably did whatever she could to survive." His voice was edged with pity as he said it, and Monk felt the same emotion engulf him.

Then he was drawn back into the present. What did McNab want now? It was years too late for Nairn. Damaging Monk would not clear his name, if that mattered anyway. Was it simply revenge? Was that why Orme had died?

Or had McNab intended it to be Monk himself? Maybe all he had deliberately brought about was a fiasco, instead of a simple operation to arrest gun smugglers and retrieve the actual guns.

Then there was the whole other issue of Piers Astley's death. That couldn't have anything to do with McNab. He might be using it, even if Monk couldn't see why or how. McNab knew Aaron Clive, at the very least, professionally.

Which raised the question to which he had to find the answer—had he been in San Francisco during the gold rush of '49, even briefly? Could he have known Piers Astley?

He was moving in the dark, tripping over things, possibly even going in circles. He could go on doing this until he fell over and could not get up again. He was being what McNab wanted . . . passive, too afraid to act. The next thing he would know would be when it was already too late.

He stood up.

"Thank you," he said quietly, his feelings too deep to find extra and unnecessary words.

"Where are you going?" Runcorn asked anxiously.

Monk gave him a bleak smile. "Not to tackle McNab, don't worry. I'm going to see Fin Gillander. He might know something about the past in San Francisco that will help with Astley's death."

"And he might make it worse," Runcorn added. "If he's worked out that you can't remember. And he could have, if you were in San Francisco."

"If he knows the truth already? Then if he's against me, for whatever reason, he'll do that anyway."

"Who else knows?"

"For certain? Hester, Oliver Rathbone, and now Hooper."

"What is Gillander's interest in this? Seems quite a coincidence that his boat was moored so conveniently for Silas Owen's escape."

"That's something I would like to find out. Along with who killed Blount, and why, what happened to Owen, and exactly how much Pettifer knew about any of it. I have to know if this is a master plan to bring off a big robbery, or if it's all coincidence, and to do with something else entirely . . . or nothing."

"Could that be what McNab wants you to do, make a fool of yourself over nothing?" There was a note of real fear in Runcorn's voice.

"Possibly. I'm still not going to let him dictate the action. I'm going to take a chance on Gillander."

"Be careful!" Runcorn warned.

"I will." Monk turned at the door. "Thank you."

MONK STAYED ON THE south side of the river and took a hansom all the way up to the bank where Gillander's schooner was moored. If he were somewhere else, Monk would have to wait for him. He had no way of tracking him down. He spent the considerable time of the journey through the wet, jostling streets putting together all the facts he knew for certain regarding the affair, starting with McNab calling for him to take over the inquiry into Blount's death.

The shooting did not amount to murder, since Blount was already dead, but what on earth was the purpose of it? And for that matter, was his death by drowning accidental, or was that actually the real murder? Blount had been a master forger, available for hire. McNab said his men had been questioning him about who had hired him most recently, and achieved nothing by it, except a chance for him to escape. Or to be rescued by possibly whoever had killed him.

Had Blount been ready to betray his employer? Or had he actually done so, and McNab had declined to tell Monk? That was a possibility.

And there was the whole episode with Owen and Pettifer. Hooper had found out a little more, but it was mostly to do with Pettifer's reputation as McNab's right-hand man. The association seemed to go back several years. Monk had seen Pettifer only when he was in panic and drowning. It was impossible to form any opinion of a man in those circumstances. Hooper said that in his job obviously he had been efficient, decisive, even ruthless, and certainly he had been clever.

It seemed to be only the most extraordinary mischance that Owen had escaped, and Pettifer drowned. It was the whole case that McNab was pursuing that was Monk's excuse for finding Gillander now. But the truth about Monk's past in San Francisco was the real reason, and that was what made him tense as he stood on the shore and hailed the *Summer Wind*, moored a few yards out where the river was deep enough.

He had to call three times before Gillander showed up on deck. His face lit with a smile as soon as he recognized Monk. He came down the steps and loosed the rowing boat immediately. In a dozen long, easy strokes at the oar, he was up against the steps.

"Want to come aboard?" he asked cheerfully. "Hot cup of tea, strong enough to bend the spoon? Sugar? Rum?"

Monk accepted and climbed down to take his place in the stern. He had been planning all during the ride in the hansom what he was going to say, and now the words sounded artificial in his mind. He could not afford that. He waited until they were on board, the rowing boat lashed tight and both of them in the cabin with the hatch barely open. Gillander stood in the tiny galley with the kettle boiling and made strong tea with sugar and rum, then brought Monk his mug before sitting down opposite him.

"Did you sail her all the way from California?" he asked.

"Yes. Pretty good weather most of the time," Gillander replied.

"How many crew?"

"Three of us," Gillander told him. "Needs two, but always good to have a man spare, in case you hit a really bad patch, or someone gets hurt."

"I imagine it's never hard to find a man willing to work his passage," Monk observed. There was a memory just beyond his reach: bright sun, heavy seas, white water curling on the wave tops. And wind, always wind, sometimes hard and heavy, making the canvas of the sails above crack as they came round. It was a sound like no other.

Where did he remember it from? The North Sea?

Gillander was looking at him, waiting.

"You told me you've known Aaron Clive since the gold rush days. Did you go looking for gold, too?" Monk asked.

"Me? Can you see me up to my knees in the river, shaking a pan around to see what landed up in it?" Gillander laughed. "I prefer the sea, most of the time. It was a good chance for adventure, see new places, get out of the Mediterranean, where I'd made a few friends, and a few enemies. I thought if I were lucky I'd own my own ship one day. And I did." He was watching Monk steadily. "Why? What does it have to do with a plan to rob Clive?" He took a long swig of his tea and rum. "Anyone would be a fool to try! A few tried it. Nobody did twice."

Was that a warning?

"Are they in jail?" Monk asked. "Or dead?"

Gillander let out his breath slowly. "Mostly dead," he replied. "They were hard times . . . but you know that. It was twenty years ago, but you can't have forgotten."

Monk froze. The seconds ticked by. He had to say something. "A lot of water under the bridge since then."

Gillander smiled. "But I like secrets," he said with some amusement. "I didn't think so at the time, but they draw me in. Like war, for some men, or exploring Africa, looking for the source of the White Nile. But Africa holds no love for me. Nor would I want to go looking for the North Pole. I like the contest with people . . . and I suppose the sea." He seemed about to add something, then changed his mind.

They looked at each other for several seconds. Monk knew that if he were not to lose the chance, this was the moment he must be honest. Ignored now, it would be compromised forever.

"So do I," he agreed. "London is its own jungle." He took a deep breath and let it out slowly. He could feel his heart pounding. "Did you know me there . . . in San Francisco?"

Gillander's gaze was completely steady. There was not a flicker in his hazel eyes. "A little. Enough to know your mettle, sail with you now and then, more often in competition for a cargo. You haven't changed all that much. Not until you look carefully."

So that was it, beyond question now. He had been there.

"And then?" He left it hanging in the air. It was as if he had been struck by a wave, lifted right up out of the water, and then slammed back again, bruised and shocked, the breath knocked out of his lungs, but still alive.

"Then?" Gillander smiled. "Then I can see that you are still dangerous, but in quite a different way. You aren't hunting anymore, not the way you used to."

It was time to come to the point. "I'm hunting whoever is planning to rob Aaron Clive. I don't want it to happen on my piece of river."

Gillander laughed outright, a sound of pure pleasure. "Perhaps you haven't changed all that much! Don't give a damn if it happens somewhere else, eh?"

Monk evaded that question. "*Do* you know anything about it? Do you work for Clive, or against him?"

Gillander hesitated. Several expressions flickered across his face: deep emotion, unreadable, and then self-mockery. "Both," he said finally. "I work mostly for Mrs. Clive."

Monk grasped at an idea, part of a memory: Gillander staring at Miriam, a youth seeing the most beautiful woman in his life. "Does he know that?"

Gillander winced and color burned up his face in spite of himself. "You were always quick."

Monk was seeing flashes, or inventing them, grasping for signs and clues as he went. "Was I?" he said thoughtfully. "I rather thought I had improved."

"Oh, yes." Gillander smiled again, it was an expression of peculiar charm. "I wouldn't have trusted you half as far as I could have thrown you. But then I wouldn't have trusted myself, either."

Monk looked at Gillander carefully, at his handsome face, his easy manner. Had Monk really been like that, twenty years ago, from when he could remember nothing? He doubted he had ever had Gillander's charm. It seemed far more than skin deep. There was wit in it, self-mockery, and perhaps a genuine emotion.

Did Monk have to know the man he used to be? He did not want to. And yet it would always be there in the shadows behind him.

"Did Clive dislike me?" he asked impulsively. He offered no explanation as to why he did not know for himself.

Gillander looked puzzled. "I'm not sure he liked or disliked anyone, after Zachary died. He changed then. It wasn't obvious at first, but some light inside him went out." He seemed to be searching for words. "He trusted Astley, but he was never close to him in the same way. Honestly, I didn't see any reason to think he cared about you, one way or the other. What does it matter now?"

"Maybe it doesn't." Monk wished to change the subject. He was not yet desperate enough to ask any more. He liked Gillander, but he would be a fool to trust him with any more than he had to. "Tell me again exactly what Owen said to you when you pulled him out of the water. Anything he let slip could help us piece together who is behind all this."

"First off, he said his name was Pettifer, and that he was a customs officer," Gillander said with a rueful smile.

Monk nodded, but allowed the skepticism to show in his face. "And what reason did he give for swimming across the river to you, rather than helping us capture the fugitive and take him in? I assume you did ask him?"

"Of course I asked him!" Gillander said a trifle tartly. "He never looked back even to see what was happening to you."

"And what did he say? It must have been good, if you believed it."

"It was good." Gillander's voice had an edge of irritation. "He said Owen was a lot bigger than he was, and stronger, and during questioning he, Pettifer, had realized that Owen had killed Blount, murdered him in cold blood, drowning him in the river, because he had betrayed the master plan they had, but he didn't say what the plan was. Owen turned on him, and at the point you intercepted them, Owen was about to kill Pettifer as well. Considering the relative size of them, that was very believable."

Monk pictured it, and realized that it made sense, if you believed that Owen was actually Pettifer. He was clearly a strong swimmer, but in any physical struggle between them, he would have lost to the bigger man, who was not only half his weight again, but also could have had at least six inches' advantage of reach.

"Did he say where 'Owen' was supposed to have killed Blount?" he asked. "Or anything about this master plan he had?"

"He said he killed Blount down Deptford way, opposite the Isle of Dogs."

"Drowned him?"

"Yes. Why?"

"Did he say who shot him?"

Gillander looked surprised. "Shot him? He was drowned . . . wasn't he?"

"Yes. And then after he was dead, someone shot him in the back."

"What the hell for?"

"I'm beginning to think it was to make it look like a crime, rather than possibly an accident, in order to bring me into the case," Monk replied. "But very interesting that Owen should not know that."

"Do you think the real Pettifer did?" Gillander said curiously.

Monk thought for a moment. "Well, if Owen risked his neck swimming across the river to get away from Pettifer, then perhaps it was because he knew Pettifer was going to kill him, too. Maybe he came on this far up the river to find a good place to drown him, and claim that was an accident, too?"

"Makes sense of what happened, but why?"

"That means the real Pettifer killed Blount, and would have killed Owen," Monk said, thinking aloud. "Obviously Owen didn't go back to McNab, or any other part of Customs. He may be in France by now. On the other hand, if there really is a master plan, he could still be here somewhere down the river."

"Question I would ask is who else knows about this plan," Gillander replied.

"The question I'd like to answer is who put Pettifer up to killing Blount, and then Owen," Monk argued. "Is it McNab, or somebody else? And does Aaron Clive have anything to do with it at all?"

"I know where Blount was killed," Gillander said. "At least, I know where Owen said it was. Might find someone down there who saw something. Would make a defense to blaming you for Pettifer's death."

It was a risk. Should he trust Gillander? He might be led into a trap. But he was in a trap already, and he could feel the teeth of it closing on him. He thought of the steel gin traps poachers used. They tore flesh, even the bones.

"Good idea," he agreed.

Gillander stood up. "Right! This is my ship. You obey orders. Understood?"

Monk did not hesitate. It was the rule of the sea. Any man who argued with the skipper was a fool.

They weighed anchor and Monk lashed the ropes without even thinking about it. Only when he turned to do the next task of hoisting the foresail did he realize that his fingers had tied the complicated knots without hesitation. If he stopped now to weigh his decisions, the instinct faltered. He must not struggle for it, searching his mind, but simply allow the instinctive movements of the body to take over.

They reached Deptford more than two hours later. It was not so very far, but there was plenty of traffic on the water, and they had to maneuver in and out of it under sail, and then find a place to moor for the three or four hours that they might be there.

Monk enjoyed the time. He began by worrying how he would manage the seamanship part of it. He trusted Gillander to be clear with his orders. He was surprised to find how easily it came to him. He must have sailed a two-master like this before and, like the police skills, some part of him never forgot. His balance was easy, his knowledge complete of handling ropes and not standing in the wrong place, especially on rope ends—desperately dangerous in case it pulled suddenly and took you with it. His care never to risk being struck by a swinging boom, or sailing too close to the wind and having a sail luff, all came instinctively. He was tense, and yet exhilarated at the same time.

Ashore, Gillander led the way across the dockside and down a winding alley, around a corner into another alley barely five feet wide.

Monk could have put his arms out and easily touched both sides at once. It was cold. The stone sides of the buildings were wet, and funneled the wind until it found every way in through his pea coat in spite of its thickness, and made him wish he had thought to wear a heavier sweater and thicker scarf.

Gillander took Monk to a very small public house called the Triple Plea, one of the few tavern names he did not understand. Inside it was warm and the air so filled with fumes Monk took a moment or two to catch his breath.

Gillander seemed to be known, and the one-eyed bartender motioned him over to a small table against the far wall.

"Don't call him Patch," Gillander warned Monk. "He answers to Pye, and will appreciate a little respect."

"Understood," Monk acknowledged, sitting down on a polished wooden stool and finding it less uncomfortable than he had expected.

"I'll do the talking," Gillander added. "Just drink your ale and listen."

Monk bit back the rejoinder on his tongue, and obeyed.

They sat and drank ale for more than half an hour. Monk barely tasted it, which might have been just as well, although the crusty bread and slab of cheese were good.

Finally a very ordinary-looking man came over and joined them, taking his place on the third stool. He had thin hair and a wispy beard. Only his eyes marked him as unusual. They were very light silvery gray, half-hidden by the heavy lids.

Gillander did not introduce Monk more than to say, "He's all right," and then, moving on, "Seen Owen?"

The man, who remained nameless, pulled his face into an expression of disgust and denial. "Long gone," he said hoarsely. "In France by now."

"Pettifer's dead," Gillander told him.

"You think I don't know that?" the man asked sarcastically. "He'll be replaced."

Monk was aching to ask not who would replace him, but who

needed him replaced. The man who masterminded whatever the plot was? Or someone who meant to foil it, perhaps Clive? Or McNab? But a sharp kick under the table reminded him to keep silent.

"And Owen?" Gillander asked. "Replace him, too?"

"For what?" The man's expression filled with disgust. "He scarpered to France to get out of Pettifer's way. He's a sly little sod, Owen, but he was scared witless."

"Of Pettifer?" Gillander managed to look amused.

"O' McNab, you great fool!" the man snarled, almost under his breath. "Pettifer was his man. He'll find someone else. God knows who'll be alive or dead by the end of this one."

"Was he behind the plan?" Gillander now looked dubious.

"Why do you care?"

"If Clive is going to be taken down, I want to know about it," Gillander replied. "Might be something in it for me."

"Best thing in it for you is to get the hell out of here, and keep yer mouth shut," the man said almost under his breath. He looked at Monk, then back at Gillander. "And take this one with yer. Smells like River Police to me. And not many o' them's crooked, but watch yer back!" He emptied his ale tankard and left, lurching from side to side as he made his way to the door.

The thoughts raced around Monk's head. So Pettifer had killed Blount, and tried to kill Owen. For McNab? Or for some reason Monk had not even thought of yet? Was the great plot a mirage?

Gillander was looking at him, waiting for a response.

"Thank you," Monk said quietly. "I think we should get out of here."

"You believe him?" Gillander asked as they moved through the crowd to the door, and into the cramped street. The rain was coming down hard and the gutters were now overflowing.

"It all fits," Monk answered. "McNab's plans, whatever they were, have been stalled because Pettifer was killed instead of Owen. Maybe it doesn't really have anything to do with Clive, except incidentally. And maybe Piers Astley doesn't have anything to do with it, either . . . at least not if he really is dead."

They came out of the alley onto the riverbank. The *Summer Wind* was riding easily. It was almost slack tide.

"He is," Gillander said softly. "I told you. Poor devil . . ."

"Did Clive keep the details from Mrs. Clive to save her feelings?"

"Astley was murdered," Gillander said with a sudden savagery. "I suppose Clive might have kept the details from her. . . ." His face was quite suddenly filled with pain, and an intense pity. "Piers was a good man. One of the best. In some ways he was out of his element there . . . straightest man I ever knew, and loyal to a fault."

"They never found who killed him?" Monk asked, feeling as if he were intruding on a private grief.

Gillander stared out over the water, the light catching his eyes and an expression on them that was unreadable.

"Not yet . . . but she will."

Monk sat close to the fire and saw the steam rise from his wet trouser legs. He did not bother to change because he was tired out. He had told Hester what he had drawn from the revelations about his past in San Francisco, what he knew and what he guessed. Now all he wanted was to eat his supper and go to bed. He had swallowed the last of his baked apples and cream, and was trying not to fall asleep.

"They say Owen is almost certainly in France," he said, moving to a different subject.

"And Blount is dead," Hester replied. "So I suppose Owen did rather better. Do you think Pettifer meant to kill him, as Gillander said?"

"I think there's a lot about Pettifer that I don't know, and I need to find out," he replied.

"What about the other experts McNab told you about? Are you sure they're real?"

"Yes, of course I am! Did you think I wouldn't check? I don't trust

McNab to tell the truth on anything, if a lie would serve him better." He had not told her the whole story of Nairn, but enough of it for her to have some idea. He was ashamed of it, but more than that, if she understood the depth of McNab's hatred, with the reason for it, she would be more afraid for him.

"And where are they now?" she asked very quietly.

He had not checked on that. He had inquired, but not followed up. "I don't know," he said. "There's no word of them."

She did not answer, but the anxiety deepened in her face. She was silent for several minutes, then she changed the subject completely.

"Beata York has come to help at the clinic in the last few days. I like her very much. There's far more depth to her than I realized. I suppose I never thought about her. I just hated her husband for what he did to Oliver. She hasn't said anything specific, but I have a feeling that she probably had far more reason to loathe him than I do."

Monk was startled. "What?" he said abruptly.

"She has said nothing, but I saw the look in her eyes if she had occasion to mention him. When he took his fit, he was attacking Oliver with his cane, you know? He was going to strike his face, his head."

"She told you that?"

"No, of course not. Oliver did."

"What made you think of it now?"

"Hatred," Hester replied. "York hated Oliver because he was all the things York was not. Inner things, I mean, the things that matter."

He looked at her, still not understanding.

"McNab hates you for some reason," she explained swiftly. "You can never win because you will always be better than he is."

The warmth spread inside him, as if he had drunk a sweet flame. "Do you think so?"

"Yes, I do." She smiled. "But don't let it go to your head! I'm saying it because I don't think McNab will let it go. I don't think he can. It has him by the neck. He has to keep trying to destroy you, and probably not only you, but the River Police as well." She was watching him to see if he had grasped the enormity of what she was saying. "You've got to fight him, William. Find out if this plot is real, or if it is his invention in order to trip you up."

"It won't damage the River Police," he told her.

"It might, if you make the wrong judgment. If the plot is real and you know about it and did nothing, then Aaron Clive won't forgive you. Just as he won't if it is all invented, and he takes massive precautions, and nothing happens, or was ever going to. He won't accept being made a fool of."

"How do you know so much about him? Don't tell me your street people know him. He's been in England only a couple of years, and his reputation is perfect."

"Of course it is," Hester agreed impatiently. "And it probably always will be. Even should rumors exist, he has the power to squash them, and those who spread them."

"How do you know this?" He smiled slightly, sinking a little deeper into the enveloping comfort of the chair. "You've never even met him."

"Beata lived in San Francisco for years," she replied. "She is very far from a stupid woman, William. She saw his rise to power, and she knows Miriam Clive very well, too. Please . . . tread softly. Be sure of everything. . . ."

NEXT MORNING MONK AND Hooper stood together on the dockside watching the light rise over the water, gray and wind-dappled, dark silhouettes of the ships riding easily at anchor. Ferries pulled across from the south side, oars rising and dropping rhythmically. They were back again trying to separate the truth and lies about the escaped prisoners, and whether there was any link between them, or not.

"Already looked into Applewood," Hooper said, squinting a little into the rising sun. "He's back in prison, up north. Can't find any trace of Seager. Looks as if he's gone to ground. But he's a Liverpool man, so he could be up there."

"Interesting," Monk said thoughtfully. "Does that mean there's no plot, or just that McNab gave us the wrong names, intentionally or not?"

"Bluff or double bluff?" Hooper smiled with wry humor. "Maybe we can make him bite his own tail, d'you think?" He sounded hopeful.

"He'll use our strengths against us, if we let him." Monk believed that. His loathing of McNab had deepened, but so had his respect. He had been guilty of underestimating him before and he did not intend to do it again. "I wish I knew exactly how clever he is."

"Better to set them against each other, and then step well back." Hooper was smiling now.

"Them?" Monk asked.

"Him and Clive," Hooper said.

"You don't like Clive, do you?" Monk was surprised how much he regarded Hooper's opinion of people. He was not used to accepting anyone else's judgment, even Orme's. Was that a strength or a weakness? Or both?

"He got rich by luck." Hooper was still looking out at the water. "He stayed rich by cleverness. Right friends, right enemies. And don't forget, he probably knows more about you than you do yourself. He'll be as sweet as honey until you cross him, but he'll be like biting on a wasp if you become a threat. Or if he thinks you will."

"I'll remember," Monk promised. It was a warning he took seriously. Nevertheless Hooper's suggestion of turning Clive and McNab against each other was a good one.

MONK WENT STRAIGHT UPRIVER by hansom and then ferry, and was at Clive's office a little after nine. He asked to see Clive, and had to wait no more than twenty minutes, during which time he was offered tea and given a comfortable place to wait.

Clive came in cheerfully and closed the door behind him.

Monk rose to his feet. "Good morning, Mr. Clive. I apologize for taking more of your time."

Clive took his hand in a firm grip and then let go quickly. He sat opposite Monk, crossing his legs easily. "Not this robbery plot again? I assure you, I am always aware of such possibilities, and I made a few inquiries of my own. McNab, from Customs, has been here on several occasions, you know."

"Yes, I did know," Monk answered. "I gather you were very civil to him."

"A necessary evil," Clive said drily. "Better to have them on your side. They can be a damn nuisance against you. But I imagine you know the river as well as they do, if not better."

Monk was aware of Clive watching him more closely than he pretended to. Was he remembering him from twenty years ago, as Hooper had warned?

"The *Summer Wind* seems to be moored opposite you a great deal of the time." Monk threw this observation into the conversation to see where Clive would take it. His answer was surprising.

Clive smiled widely, showing beautiful teeth. "When you have a wife as beautiful as mine, you get used to living with other men in love with her, perhaps all their lives. I first met Gillander when he was a raw youth of about nineteen, and Miriam was thirty. He saw her and fell in love with her then, and I don't think he'll ever entirely grow out of it. Some men are prisoners of their dreams. She is quite aware of it, and is kind to him, but no more."

Monk did not argue. As far as he knew, Clive could be right. Certainly he was as far as Gillander was concerned. What Miriam felt he had no idea. It was a responsibility she might grow tired of. On the other hand, perhaps she was tempted to use him in the search for who killed Piers Astley. Gillander did say he was performing some service for her.

Was Beata right about Clive having a core of steel? Or was that only her perception, also dictated by her own past?

"Lady York speaks very well of her," he said, to see what Clive's response would be. He must know that, even if Monk had no memory of the past, Beata certainly had, and had known all of them far better than Monk had.

Clive smiled, but this time there was a slightly sharper edge to it. "Ah, yes, Beata. Poor woman. Her first husband was more a convenience than a love match, I think. York I have little idea about. He was certainly professionally respected, but not a nice man, from what I hear. She has been unfortunate. Not that her father was her fault, of course. We none of us choose our parents."

Did Clive mean him to ask? Yes, of course he did. He was dangling the suggestion in the hope of his taking the bait like a fish.

"I didn't know her father," Monk responded.

"Possibly not . . ." Clive pursed his lips. "He was well known enough in San Francisco. But you were always up and down the coast, and I daresay you had little enough money to bank."

He was dribbling out the information bit by bit. His smile was still there, but the warmth was gone from the room. This was like parrying before the real battle. The lunge would come without warning.

It would be childish for Monk to say he was not there for the money, like an excuse for not having made much.

"Didn't need a banker," he said casually.

"But you must remember his death." Clive watched him intently now. Even a change in his breathing, the light in his eye would be noticed.

A lie would be a greater sign of weakness than an admission. There was nothing in his mind to search. He could not even remember the man's name.

"No. Perhaps I was up the coast."

"He played cards a lot toward the end. He was accused of cheating, and shot in the resulting brawl. Created quite a scandal. Poor Beata . . . Of course she never mentions it. I doubt even York knew." He let the suggestion of deceit hang in the air.

Monk felt a wave of resentment rise inside him. It was the first thing Clive had said that showed an uglier side of him. It was a warning, whether he intended it to be or not. Monk would be wise not to show his distaste.

"Unfortunate," he said with a slight show of regret. "I can see why she chose to return to England."

"People came for many reasons," Clive said mildly. "I often wondered why you returned. You seemed to be doing rather well for your-

self." It was not a question, yet unanswered it would become one, a sign
of weakness.

Monk felt himself like a butterfly pinned to a board, struggling. It
was all very civilized, nothing but polite conversation around whether
there were any danger to Clive's wealth or his security from some inde-
terminate theft that was looking increasingly like a mirage.

But if it were real, and Monk had not acted, he would look a complete incompetent. Who was playing him? McNab? Or Clive? Or both
of them, each for his own reason? Clive's most visibly prized possession
was his wife, and Monk was quite sure he had never trespassed there.
Whatever his memory loss, it would have been in Miriam's face when
she came to visit him.

"Got an interesting offer," he lied. "The California coast is marvelous, but this one has its charms, too."

"The river?" Clive's eyes widened. He sat back a little in his chair.
"The Thames, as opposed to the Barbary Coast? For a man like you?"

Monk met his eyes unflinchingly. "I'm English, blood and bone.
This is my heritage. Go down the Thames, slowly, and you pass through
history, from the Roman legions of Julius Caesar to the Greenwich Ob-
servatory, where the world's time is set, from zero longitude."

"Is that what you love?" Clive said curiously. "The heart of empire?
How very English."

"No," Monk said with sudden realization. "It's dawn farther east, the
huge skies over the Estuary with the wild birds flying over with such
purpose and certainty, as if they know something we don't."

For once Clive was silent.

"It's worth caring for," Monk added. "All its teeming life, good and
bad, it's something to care about."

Clive did not answer. He returned instead to the subject of the possible robbery, and remained with it until it was exhausted and Monk
excused himself. He had done all he could to forewarn Clive of an event
neither of them believed in.

As he was walking away toward the road he saw Miriam Clive coming toward him. She was wearing a deep burgundy-colored morning

dress and a jacket trimmed with black fur. Again he was startled by her appearance. Her beauty was fierce, almost exotic, with high cheekbones and wide, dark eyes, but it was the passion in the mouth that most caught the attention. It was a face to reflect storms of the soul.

"Good morning, Mrs. Clive," he said politely.

She stopped, as if pleased to see him. "Good morning, Commander Monk. I hope it is not business that brings you here?"

"Only precaution," he replied. "Mr. McNab still seems to think it is possible, if unlikely, that someone may attempt a robbery."

She concealed all emotion in her expression. "Mr. McNab? Really."

"I believe you know him, at least slightly?"

She moved one slender shoulder in what was almost a shrug.

"I am acquainted with him. I think he is something of an opportunist. I would take what he says with a degree of skepticism. But I'm sure you already know that."

He was aware that she was watching him closely. Did she care what he thought of McNab?

"Of what he says to me, yes," he agreed. "But to you?"

Miriam drew in a deep breath and let it out slowly, her decision made. He had placed her in a position where she had to answer, or deliberately evade it.

"Yes," she said with a charming smile. "I wanted to find out more about you from McNab. I knew Piers was dead but I need to know who killed him. McNab told me you are the best detective in London, and of course you were in San Francisco at the time of Piers's death. I knew that if anybody could succeed in finding the truth, it would be you, and I had to convince you to help me."

"But what difference would it make to you now?"

She smiled still. "In knowing who did kill Piers, Mr. Monk, then I also know who did not. That is sometimes even more important, don't you think?"

She was lying. He was absolutely certain of it, yet what she said was absolutely true; it was just not what she meant. Did she want the truth in order to hide it forever? Or to manipulate someone? What could McNab have to do with it, other than as a means of contacting Monk?

"I'm sorry I've been of no help to you," he said as courteously as he could.

Her face was completely unreadable. "Not at all, Commander. You have helped me understand a great many things. My old friend Beata speaks of you most highly, and I am sure she is right." She glanced beyond him, across the river to where the *Summer Wind* lay at anchor. "And of course, Mr. Gillander," she added. She turned back to Monk. "Good day."

"Good day, Mrs. Clive," he replied. In spite of himself, he watched her until she turned the corner toward Clive's office and disappeared.

WHEN HE ARRIVED BACK at the Wapping Station, Hooper was pacing the floor waiting for him. He swiveled around on his heel and grasped Monk by the arm, half-dragging him outside again onto the dockside.

"I've got it," he said urgently. "Laker found for certain that it was Pettifer that shot Blount, possibly on McNab's orders. But we've got McNab. It'll never stand up in court, but we know what happened with the gunrunners and the raid, and that McNab's directly responsible for it. We can finish it our own way." His face was alight with the certainty of it, and in spite of himself Monk felt a surge of exhilaration.

"How? If you can't prove it . . ." he asked. Questions filled his mind. Could he afford to challenge McNab? McNab would fight for his freedom, his life. If he went down, he had the means and the will to take Monk with him.

Hooper's smile was wolfish. "Mad Lammond," he replied.

Monk was stunned. "Mad Lammond? The bloody river pirate?" Of course he would not stand up in court. The man's name was an obscenity from London Bridge to the English Channel.

Hooper colored very faintly. "You'll know the truth," he said a little less jubilantly. "Knowledge is power, even if you can use it only limitedly. Come with me; he'll tell you himself."

Monk stood his ground. "Why the devil should he? Why wouldn't he just slit our throats?"

"My enemy's enemy is my friend," Hooper quoted. "At least sometimes. By Mad Lammond's reckoning, McNab owes him money, which he isn't going to pay."

"Explain yourself," Monk requested. "What kind of business could McNab and Lammond have together?" He would like to believe it, but he couldn't.

"Guns," Hooper answered, as if it should have been obvious.

Monk began to see the glimmer of light. "The pirates that attacked us on the gunrunner's ship were Mad Lammond and his men?"

"Right!"

"McNab told them of the raid? Why?" Monk was so overwhelmed by the memory of it he had to clear his throat to speak. "So Mad Lammond killed Orme? Why the hell did McNab want that? It's only me he hates. Was he really prepared to kill anyone to get to me?"

"No," Hooper said quietly. "It was you they were supposed to kill. The rest of us were incidental. Only they got Orme, and we won the battle. They got no guns, and McNab wouldn't pay the second half of what he owes Mad Lammond because you were still alive."

Monk blasphemed, something he rarely did. It was terrible, worse even than he had thought. The guilt was suffocating. Orme had not only died because of the battle; he had died in Monk's place.

"All over Robbie Nairn . . ." Monk said quietly. "Revenge is a hideous thing, a kind of madness that rots the heart."

"Yes," Hooper said quietly.

"And you believe this? It was Pettifer, acting for McNab? Giving Mad Lammond the information, and money to kill me?"

"And disgrace the River Police in general," Hooper added. "But we can't prove it . . . not yet, anyway."

"God help us," Monk said softly, and he meant it.

11

M ONK WAS WOKEN EARLY the following morning, before daylight. It was still pitch-dark outside, and it took a moment before he realized where he was. He had been dreaming of bright sunlight and heavy seas roaring into a rocky coast, crashing in white water.

Hester turned over and sat up, pushing her hair out of her eyes. She was immediately wide awake. Her voice came out of the darkness beside him.

"What is it? What's happened?"

He climbed out of bed and went to the window, pulling the curtains aside. In the dim glow from streetlights twenty feet away he could see two uniformed police standing on the pavement just outside his front door.

"Police," he told her. "I'll turn up the gas on the landing and go down. Something must have happened. I'll dress first." There was no time to shave. He dashed cold water over his face and pulled his clothes on. Running his fingers through his hair, he went down the stairs to the front hall. He pulled the bolts back and opened the door.

There were two police in uniform standing on the step, so close to the door now that it was as if they were trying to hide from the street. In the light from the hall they both looked uncomfortable.

"What's happened?" Monk demanded, thoughts of a fatality filling his mind, some appalling incident, even something like the sinking of the *Princess Mary* a year ago.

"I'm sorry, sir," the taller one said quietly. "We've come to arrest you for the murder of James Pettifer, off Skelmer's Wharf. Yer'd be wise to come quietly, sir. We don't want to waken all the neighbors, do we?"

Monk was absolutely stunned, as if he needed to grasp the doorframe to make the world stay still. It made no sense. It was totally absurd. And yet, staring at the men, he could see they *were* police. Their uniforms were plainly visible, along with the numbers that identified them. The shorter of the two actually held a warrant in his hand, awkwardly, as if he were not sure what he was supposed to do with it.

And they were right. The last thing Monk wanted was to have the neighbors wakened to come out to see what was happening.

He stepped back a pace or two, still dizzy.

The taller policeman looked nervous, and took the same size step to keep the distance between them, as if he were afraid Monk might slam the door on him.

"I'm going to tell my wife," Monk meant to snap at him, but his voice was hoarse and the words came out lamely, even a little mumbled.

The policeman looked past him up the stairs to where Hester was coming down slowly, her gown held tightly around her. With her hair loose and falling over her shoulders she looked younger, and more vulnerable.

"I'm sorry, ma'am," the policeman said unhappily. "But we've got to do this. Don't make it worse than it is."

"Do what?" She looked bewildered.

"Arrest Mr. Monk for 'aving drowned Mr. Pettifer, ma'am."

"Drowned him?" she said incredulously. "Pettifer jumped in the water himself! Commander Monk was trying to rescue him!"

"Was you there, then, ma'am?" he asked politely, but his knowledge that she was not was clear in his face.

She drew in her breath to argue, and then realized the futility of it. It was not this man's decision, and he had not the power to disobey.

She came down the rest of the stairs and took Monk's heavy overcoat off the peg in the hall.

"I'll get dressed and then I'll go straight to see Oliver," she said quite calmly.

That was Hester! She would always be calm in the crisis, and then lie awake, reliving it when it was all over, trying to think what she could have done differently.

If this would ever be all over!

Monk put the coat on. "Thank you," he answered, hoping she understood that it was "thank you" for everything, all the past, and the future.

She smiled at him, meeting his eyes for one intense moment, then turned away.

He followed the policemen out onto the step, then into the road. They did not look at him. Was it decency, to allow him this dreadful moment in some privacy? Or were they embarrassed?

It was bitterly cold with the wind coming up off the water, and the roadway was slick with ice. A carriage was waiting for them. It was much like an ordinary hansom cab, not a Black Maria, the usual closed-sided vehicle for carrying prisoners.

Monk climbed in, one policeman on each side of him, and they moved off, turning west, away from the beginning of the dawn paling in the east. The wide, flat surface of the river was already dotted with ships.

Where were they taking him? This had to be some idiotic mistake! It was perfectly obvious he had tried to save Pettifer. Even thinking at the time that he was Owen, the escaped prisoner, he had still done all he could to get the man out of the water. If he hadn't clipped him over the side of the head, he could not have saved him. It would simply have meant they both drowned. Everyone who works near the water knows that a drowning man can panic, and take you both down.

Among his own men, who was going to take over at Wapping while he was gone? Hooper? No, of course not—Monk was only going to be away a day or two at the most. This whole thing was farcical! Some young man looking for fame must have jumped to a wrong conclusion and acted without reference to anyone senior. It would probably all be over tomorrow—maybe later today.

He wouldn't even have to disturb Rathbone with it.

"Why am I supposed to have drowned Pettifer?" he asked.

"I wouldn't know that, sir," the taller man answered. "We're just the arresting officers."

"I'd never met him, never even heard of him," Monk went on. "We didn't know which man was the fugitive and which the officer. In fact, we got it wrong."

"Maybe that's why you killed him," the policeman suggested. "You thought he was the escaping prisoner?"

"Or looking at it the other way," the shorter man added, "maybe you knew right enough that Pettifer were the customs man, and the one who got away were the fugitive?"

"Why on earth would I do that?" Monk asked angrily.

"Most likely money," the man answered. "That's why most people do things they shouldn't."

Monk drew in breath to argue, and then knew it was pointless. They were only making noises. Nobody's mind was going to change. This was a waste of time he could not afford. They were ordinary police who had arrested him, but who was behind it? McNab . . . surely? Pettifer had been his man, and Owen the second prisoner to escape from his custody. There was no one else involved.

There was no great conspiracy to rob Clive, or anyone else. But he had been sure of that yesterday. It was all to do with Robbie Nairn, and the past.

Monk had been in San Francisco; that now seemed unarguable. God only knew how many other places he had been, how many other enemies he had made who could remember his acts, good or bad, and he did not even know their names, their faces, anything about them at all. He was stumbling around like a blind man, falling over things everyone else could see.

He must stop this! Panic would take away any chance he had to save himself. The truth was that Pettifer had effectively drowned himself, because he had panicked! Monk had done all he could to save him. That was an irony. Was he now going to drown—in the law—because he panicked? Pettifer's revenge!

If McNab were behind it, it was because of Nairn, whom Monk had not spared. It was irrelevant now as to whether he should have or not. Perhaps he should have tried. There had been a lack of pity in him then that he did not admire now. But there was no going back. The only way anyone could move was forward. He couldn't change the past, only learn from it.

Or did Clive have something to do with it also? Clive and McNab together? Why? What could he have done to Clive?

Or Miriam . . . Astley, as she was then? Had Monk had some part in Astley's death that he could not remember? Was that why it seemed that everyone's hand was against him? If he had killed Astley, then maybe he deserved it.

He had lacked pity, wisdom, patience, humility . . . but surely he had never been a gun for hire? To murder people, for someone else? There was no money on earth that could make that of him!

Damn, damn, damn that carriage accident that had robbed him of all his past . . . not the living of it, but the recall! How could you repent of or make good what you did not know about?

He straightened up. This was pointless self-pity and would gain him nothing except perhaps other people's contempt—and his own. Wiping out the past was not all loss. It had given him a chance to begin again, to weigh and judge who he had been and to see more clearly, from the evidence, what was ugly in him and must be changed. How many people got an opportunity to do that? Habits locked them in, but he was free.

Hester believed in him. So did Scuff, rightly or not. And others. No matter what he owed himself, he owed it to them to fight to the very last breath.

If McNab were behind this accusation, there must still have been an element of collusion with someone else, or betrayal. Gillander, after all? Why? In justice for Piers Astley? Or did McNab have some hold on him, perhaps for a crime committed along the river? Smuggling? Maybe not a crime, just a carelessness? Or to protect Miriam Clive? He would probably do almost anything for her. Getting rid of Monk, if he were somehow in her way, would be a small thing.

Or of course to revenge herself on him if he had killed Astley. She said he had helped her to know who it was!

And she had said she didn't care if the law could touch him or not. She did not need the law. She was going to find her own vengeance—intimate, not impersonal, like the gallows. So did this all have to do with San Francisco, and Astley's death?

He did not ask them any further questions. They knew nothing, and it would only make him look more vulnerable. He sat in silence the rest of the way, and when they arrived at the police station, he said nothing more than to acknowledge his identity. In due course he was put into one of the cells.

He was familiar with such places. Even with more than half his life lost to amnesia, he had still worked enough years on ordinary police duties that he had seen a score of such cells. One wall was iron bars from floor to ceiling; the other three were whitewashed stone. One window, too high to see out of, gave the only daylight there was. There was one bunk bed with a straw mattress, and stale, sour-smelling blankets, like the odor of rancid butter. The sanitary facilities were of the most basic.

This, of course, was for a man still presumed innocent! What would follow for those found guilty was a different matter altogether.

But he was not guilty! Not of this, at least.

It must have been midmorning by the time Rathbone came. It seemed to Monk as if he had waited an eternity, but when he tried to be rational about it, he realized that Rathbone would find out at least the basics of the charge, the evidence and the reason for it, before he came.

Would he believe Monk was innocent? Yes, of course he would! This was nothing to do with the past, or the parts of it he did not know. This was totally in the present. And it was absurd. He had tried to rescue Pettifer, not drown him. He didn't even know the man!

It was all McNab trying to take his obsessed revenge.

Monk turned from pacing the floor, five steps, back again, five steps . . . and there was Rathbone standing in front of the duty sergeant, the lamplight gleaming on the pale sweep of his hair. He looked slender, elegant as always, his clothes immaculate. But he knew what this was like. He too had been accused, robbed of his own clothes, his dignity, his right to decide anything at all, even when he would eat or sleep.

He walked over to the cell just a step ahead of the sergeant.

"If you please?" he said, indicating the lock.

The sergeant hesitated a moment. He glanced at Rathbone, and decided that any further delay would be extremely inadvisable. He turned the lock and motioned Monk out.

Monk stepped through the door. It gave an illusion of freedom. For a wild moment he wanted to run. But that was what guilty men did. He stood motionless, waiting. Or maybe that was really what guilty men did, knowing they were already beaten?

The sergeant led the way across the passage to the interview room, and showed them into the small room where lawyers could consult with their clients in something like privacy. As soon as Rathbone was inside, the guard slammed the door shut. Both Rathbone and Monk heard the teeth of the lock fall into place.

"Right." Rathbone indicated one of the two chairs for Monk to sit down, and then sat in the other himself. The rickety wooden table between them was scarred with initials of long-dead prisoners written in ink, or carved with anything sharp enough to make a mark. It was stupid, damage just for the sake of stating your identity, your separateness from the anonymity of the system.

Suddenly Monk was lost for words. He shouldn't waste the short time they had in such thoughts.

As it was, Rathbone did not wait for him to speak, but began immediately. "The charge is that you murdered Pettifer by striking him over the side of the head and neck so that he was too stunned to save himself from drowning. The evidence for this charge is the words you yourself spoke to two men who came on to the scene and helped you out of the water, and also Pettifer. The marks of your blow were on Pettifer's head, and you told them that was what had happened."

"It was," Monk said, the fear solidifying inside him. "But Pettifer was a big man, and powerful. He panicked in the water and when I tried to get him to turn so I could pull him ashore, he started fighting with me. The only way I could get either of us out was to stun him enough that he didn't drown both of us." He could hear the edge of fear rising in his voice.

"I believe you," Rathbone said. "It happens often that when people panic in the water they lash out. Unfortunately the only witness to that is Hooper, who is your own man. . . ."

"He's not a liar," Monk said sharply. "And there are no witnesses that can say differently. The other police officers arrived far too late to have seen anything."

"I know that, too," Rathbone said calmly, his face very pale. "The only other witness, who might or might not have seen anything, is Owen, the person who escaped. And he's long gone, probably across the Channel. Or Fin Gillander, the man on the schooner across the river. But unless he was looking through a telescope at the whole thing, he was much too far away to see what happened. There was a man in a boat of some sort who called for help, but he claims he saw nothing."

"Pettifer and Owen were fighting each other, then when Hooper and I tried to separate them they started fighting us," Monk said, struggling to keep his voice in control and stop the fear that was rising inside him. "Hooper and Owen fell into the river first, then Pettifer charged at me, missed and went in, and I went in after him. Owen escaped and fled across the river. If it had been anything but slack tide he would have been swept away. I tried to save Pettifer. Actually I thought he was the prisoner, just as Hooper did. Which was why he turned to help me, rather than go after Owen."

Rathbone was quiet, his voice grim. "I believe you, Monk, but you can't prove it," he said.

"I'd never seen Pettifer before, or even heard of him. Why should I wish him any harm?" Monk said angrily. "I don't like McNab, whose man he was, but I've never done him any harm. At least . . . at least not since his brother was hanged."

Rathbone stared at him.

Monk realized he had not told Rathbone the story, and neither had Hester. She had kept his secret for him to tell it in whatever terms he wished. He did so now in bare facts, including that it was Runcorn who had told him.

"So that's why McNab hates you," Rathbone said thoughtfully. Then he looked very directly at Monk. "And is that why he rigged the gunrunning arrests and you ended up with a battle in which Orme was killed?"

"Yes. And he did rig it. He even paid Mad Lammond to kill me, but the shot went wide and got Orme. I know it, but I can't prove it. Mad Lammond isn't exactly the ideal witness. And if you think I hate McNab for that, you're right. I do. I want to get him for it, but legally. Had I deliberately killed Pettifer it wouldn't solve anything. And, as I said, I thought the big man was the fugitive, and that McNab's man got away. In the light of that, my killing Pettifer makes even less sense."

Monk searched Rathbone's face, his steady eyes. There was no relief in them at all. He felt himself go cold.

"You showed less mercy to McNab's brother than he thought you should have, for which he hates you," Rathbone said slowly. "You know that because Runcorn told you, but you can't argue it yourself, or explain why no mercy was due. In fact you can't remember it at all. I think we would be better not to refer to it. But, on the other hand, McNab may give that to the prosecution, if he knows you have no memory. Best to steer clear of it altogether."

Monk wanted to argue, but he could see the reasoning. He was fighting the whole battle for his survival with his hands tied behind his back.

Rathbone continued: "McNab started taking his revenge with the gun battle on the river, but can you prove that?"

"I might be able to. . . . Hooper's working on getting some kind of proof." He sounded desperate, a rope made of straw.

"Then the question arises, why did McNab wait so long to have his revenge? His brother was hanged almost sixteen years ago."

"I . . . don't know . . ."

"Yes, you do, Monk." Rathbone's face was filled with an extraordinary grief. "He realized you had no memory. Something happened that stopped him being afraid of you, and suddenly he knew you were vulnerable . . . and exactly how. He began his plan for a perfect and complete revenge."

Monk felt a dense, heavy wave of despair close over him. For a moment he could barely breathe. McNab would see him hanged for having killed Pettifer. It had an exquisite symmetry to it.

"But it makes no sense. Why would I kill Pettifer? I didn't even know who he was!" He could hear the hysteria rising in his voice now.

"I know you didn't," Rathbone said. "But can you prove that? They will say that you did. And the only witness that you have is Hooper, who is your right-hand man now, and far more than that, your friend. The very most he can say is that he doesn't believe that you knew Pettifer. It takes only one witness, lying or not, to convince a jury that you did."

Monk felt the cold deepen inside himself. Rathbone was right. He struggled to find any argument against what he said, and there was none.

"And there's more than that," Rathbone continued. "If McNab's man really was responsible for the gun smugglers' arrest going wrong, and you can prove it—"

"We must!" Monk interrupted.

"What if it proves that Pettifer was one of the main actors in that?" Rathbone asked. "And he's not alive to deny it, or to say that it was McNab's idea. Or even that McNab ordered him to do it."

Monk did not need to hear the rest of the thought. It was obvious. McNab would hang all the blame on Pettifer, and the rest of his men would either not know the truth, or if they were implicated, would be only too glad to use Pettifer as a scapegoat.

"I see," he said. "I killed Pettifer in revenge for Orme. Unless I can prove somehow that it was McNab himself who paid Mad Lammond."

"Even if you can, you can't prove that you didn't know it before you killed Pettifer," Rathbone pointed out.

"I didn't kill him! He drowned because he panicked!"

"That's academic to the court, Monk. You clipped him over the side of the head."

Monk swallowed. "Did the police surgeon say that the blow killed him? I thought he said Pettifer drowned."

"He did drown." Rathbone's face was pale. "But he drowned almost certainly because he lost consciousness."

"So what should I have done? Let him drown by himself? I was trying to rescue him, but he was too hysterical to let me."

"I know that. But we have to be prepared for the prosecution to say that you believed McNab's man, specifically Pettifer, to be responsible for the fiasco of the gunrunning arrest, and therefore, obliquely, for Orme's death. You wanted revenge, and this was your chance to take it. If they're clever, they may even provide a chain of evidence to link Pettifer to the betrayal, and in one stroke, acquit McNab of it, and give you an overwhelming motive to kill Pettifer. Some people would even understand it. But however morally or emotionally justified it seems, it is still murder."

"I meant to rescue him," Monk said again, but his voice was hollow.

"I know that," Rathbone agreed. "But I have to find a way to prove it."

"Pettifer killed Blount." Monk was searching frantically for anything at all that would add weight to what he was saying.

"Who is Blount?" Rathbone asked.

"The first prisoner to escape McNab's custody, a week or two before Owen. He was drowned, then shot in the back afterward. I don't know why, but it looks now as if it were to draw me into the case."

"Proof? A witness?"

"No one you'd believe. Although I have a corroborating witness: Fin Gillander."

Rathbone's eyes widened slightly. "I'm not sure how much that's going to help. What was he doing assisting you in the case?"

"He pulled Owen out of the water. Owen told him he was McNab's man, and Gillander believed him."

"So Gillander took you down the river to find evidence?"

"Yes . . ." Another pitfall was looming up: the fact that Gillander could remember Monk from the gold rush, and Monk could remember nothing. "I'm . . . I'm not sure if you want to put him on the stand."

"I've thought of that," Rathbone said in agreement. "And I daresay McNab has also."

Monk felt as if the walls were closing in on him, not only metaphorically but physically. There was less air. The fear of it almost stopped him breathing. Of course. If Rathbone called Gillander, then it would be child's play for the prosecution to get from him that he had known Monk in San Francisco, and that Monk could not remember anything about it. He could say anything he wanted about Monk's character, temper, his abilities, how he earned a living, honest or not. Monk couldn't rebut any of it. It could be true, for all he knew. He was as trapped as if his ankles were manacled to the floor.

"What are you going to say?" he asked Rathbone.

"I don't know yet," Rathbone said. "I need more evidence. We're handicapped because your enemies know so much more than you do."

"I don't even know who they are! I'm . . . lost!"

Rathbone put his hand on Monk's arm. "Well, you know who your friends are. And you have friends, Monk. Never forget that."

"Perhaps I don't deserve them. I really don't know if I am involved in Piers Astley's death or not. This could be justice finally catching up with me."

Rathbone sighed. "Well, you'd better tell me all you know, or have deduced."

As briefly as he could, Monk did so, including Hooper's encounter with Mad Lammond, for whatever that was worth.

Rathbone did not interrupt him until he was finished.

"And you don't remember Astley at all?" He looked bewildered. He was putting as good a face on it as he could, but he was overwhelmed.

"I might have killed him," Monk said miserably.

"It's not this court's jurisdiction," Rathbone pointed out, but his voice was flat. "They have no proof, and even if they had, California is five thousand miles away, and Astley died nearly twenty years ago."

"But if I had killed him, then it might be the real motive for all of this," Monk pointed out. "A long-delayed revenge. McNab's brother's death is almost as long ago."

For several moments Rathbone did not answer. He looked thin and pale.

"If I killed Astley, it could have been over almost anything," Monk said. "A debt one of us owed, and didn't pay, a gold claim, a woman, a perceived insult. I had a quick temper, Gillander told me. And I was something of a chancer. The more I learn about myself, the less I like the man I was then."

"There's nothing you can do from here," Rathbone told him. "Except remember, if possible. Anything, any detail at all, and how it tied up with other things." He stood up. "Don't give up, Monk. We've been in some hard places before, and come out of them."

How easy to say. How trite!

And yet looking up at Rathbone's face, Monk saw in him a compassion he had not seen before. His own experiences had softened him, and at the same time put a steel into his soul. If it was humanly possible, he would win.

THE REST OF THE day passed in total misery for Monk. He tried to assemble the facts he knew for certain, and make sense of them. But there were just too few. Almost everything was capable of more than one interpretation. And all the time he grew colder. Food was brought to him but he could barely force himself to eat it, although he knew he needed to keep up not only his physical strength but his mental concentration as well. His stomach seemed to be clenched in a knot. The only thing he could take easily was the strong, stewed black tea, far too sweet. It was disgusting, but it warmed him and kept him reasonably alert.

He was not yet tried and convicted of anything, so the law allowed him one visitor, apart from Rathbone. Well after dark, at last Hester came. She was treated with bare civility, no more. She was warned that she could not have long.

Monk was too pleased to see her to allow his anger at the police's attitude to darken the moment. Just the sight of her face was like light in the darkness.

She knew there were only minutes, and she wasted none of them. Whatever her emotions, no matter what she suffered, Hester was always practical. Her nursing training never left her. It was woven into her nature. She gave him the quickest kiss, on the cheek. That instance's warmth brought the smell of her skin, and the tickle of a stray hair. Then she sat down in the chair Rathbone had occupied what seemed like an age ago. She looked extremely pale, but she spoke steadily. Her voice was perfectly level, as though she were reassuring a patient who was mortally wounded.

"I have told Scuff, who will tell Crow. Also I have told them at the clinic," she said calmly. "We will all look into everything we can. We need to gather all possible information on McNab, Pettifer, and any other of the customs men who might be involved. If we can discredit McNab it might help, but we cannot rely on it. It was very much a double-edged sword and the worse he is, the more motive you have for wanting to attack him, possibly through Pettifer."

"I hit Pettifer; maybe I did kill him," he said grimly.

"Pettifer behaved like a fool, and brought about his own death," she replied, almost as if he had not spoken. "He may well have panicked before. Someone will know of it. He was a bully. He'll have enemies."

"But it was not they that killed him, Hester. . . ."

She touched his hand gently. "I know that. It would be only to show that he was violent, and given to losing his self-control. It was obvious that you had no choice but to hit him. It becomes no more than an accident, brought on by his own loss of self-control."

"I'm not sure that this is about Pettifer," Monk said grimly, trying to pitch his voice so that she could hear him and the guard at the door could not.

"McNab," she replied. "I know that. And perhaps Miriam Clive as well. I could hate her for it but then I realized how I might feel if you were killed and I never knew who had done it. My grief might make me lose my balance, too."

He looked at her and saw self-mockery in her face. It was too hideously true. She might very well be about to lose him, only she did know exactly who was doing it. She was watching it happen. There were tears in her eyes, but she refused to weep. There was work to do first.

"Yes, of course McNab," he agreed. "Gillander knows me from San Francisco. At least he says he does. I can't argue because I don't know. I keep getting flashes of memory, here and then gone again. Light on the water, brighter than England, sharper-edged. I can visualize going around Cape Horn. I can see the great rocks looming up out of the fog, and hear the roar of breaking waves and the wind through the rigging. I can feel the pitch of the deck under my feet. Can that all be imagination? Isn't it the obvious thing to assume I was really there?"

"Yes," she said. "And you were in Joscelyn Gray's apartment. But you did not kill him. That is proved beyond doubt, reasonable or not."

"No one hated me in the Gray case," he replied. "And Gray was a swine! From what Gillander has told me, Piers Astley was an unusually decent man."

"Maybe he was," she conceded. "And maybe not." She leaned forward a little. "William, we cannot afford to take anybody's word for anything at all that can't be proved. We need to count up exactly what we know, what seems to be a sensible assumption from it, and then see what answers are left."

Her voice was steady; she was being reasonable. But he could see the fear in her eyes, and he noticed how often she swallowed hard and had to steady her breathing before she continued. She was doing it for his sake. He knew that. When she went home she would keep that same composure as long as Scuff was there, and Hester had told him Scuff had returned to his old home as soon as he heard that Monk had been arrested. She would not give in, or cry, until she was alone.

He wanted to reach across the battered wooden table and hold her in his arms, cling on to her. But he knew the guard would come and separate them as soon as he did. He would probably take her away, by force, if necessary. Even hurt her.

"Who was Astley?" she asked. "Why would anyone kill him? All the reasons . . ."

"Miriam Clive's first husband," he started to explain. As he did, he realized how little he knew about Astley's death, and yet how important it seemed to be, as if it overshadowed everything else.

Hester listened gravely and without interrupting.

"So it was never solved?" she said when he finished at last. "And everybody seems to be lying about it, one way or another."

"Apparently. Miriam wondered if he was even dead, though according to Gillander, Astley is unquestionably dead. Also he was a good man, unusually so, and loyal to Clive through thick and thin."

"And then Clive married his widow soon after. Do you like Aaron Clive?"

"What does that matter?" Monk was puzzled.

"I just wondered. He seems, from what you have said of him, a remarkable man, not only talented, but with a grace and intelligence that hold most people's attention, even regard."

"Yes, that's true. And I suppose I do like him. There is something about him that attracts . . . although I did see a brief glimpse of the steel beneath last time we spoke. There's a quiet arrogance in him."

She smiled bleakly. "And Miriam?"

"I'm not sure." He was being completely honest. There was a passion in Miriam that disturbed him, a complexity. "I think she's lying about something. I have a feeling that she is manipulative, but I have no idea how, or over what. She feels very deeply about something, and I believe that I am involved in it. I wish I knew what it is."

She gave a tiny nod, barely a movement. "I know you do."

"It all goes back to the gold rush," he said grimly. "It has to do with Astley's death, but there may be something else."

"Who was there, that you know, and is here now?"

"Miriam and Aaron Clive, Fin Gillander, and me," he answered. "That's all I know about."

"Not McNab?"

"No. I thought of that, and I checked his history. It was not difficult. His professional record is clear. He has never left England except for a couple of visits to France."

"Then there's another extraordinary coincidence, or a connection we don't know about," Hester said. "We'll find out."

That was the last thing she had a chance to say. The guard came too close to her to allow further talk, and very firmly told her that her time was up.

She rose to her feet, gave the guard an odd, barely civil stare, and walked out with her head high and her back ramrod straight. It was as if she took all the light and warmth away with her, and yet her posture was like a candle flame in the enclosing darkness.

12

Beata heard from Oliver Rathbone that Monk had been arrested and charged with having killed Pettifer deliberately, a crime for which he would be tried, and if found guilty, hanged, and suddenly her own personal future seemed of very little importance.

She was sitting opposite Rathbone in her own withdrawing room, after he had arrived with no warning and, in the eyes of some, inappropriately. She stared at the misery in his face and, knowing how deep was his friendship with Monk, she ached for him.

"What can we do?" She spoke as if they were as one without even realizing it until the words were out of her mouth. Now it was a slip that hardly mattered.

"I don't know," he said. "The evidence is dreadful, and I can see no way of proving it false."

"But it *is* false!" she insisted.

There was a moment's warmth in his eyes, before he answered. "Yes,

I believe it is, but that is because I know Monk. To anyone else it proves guilt—not as beyond any doubt, but beyond a reasonable one." In a quiet, almost flat voice he told her about the enmity between Monk and McNab, dating back to the hanging of Robert Nairn, and all the cumulative evidence after that.

She listened with growing fear. It was worse than she had imagined. In his face she saw the pain, even fear, of losing not a case or a battle, even a professional standing, but a friend who had proved his own loyalty, at any cost, over many years. If he could not save Monk, Rathbone would lose part of himself. It was in those moments that Beata realized how deeply she loved him. She would protect him from that, even at the cost of all she had herself.

But this required reason, and self-control.

"Was Nairn's trial fair?" she asked, attempting to concentrate on the facts and set all feelings aside, as a lawyer must do.

"Yes," he said without hesitation. "There is no question he was guilty. But Monk could have asked for some clemency, and he didn't."

"Why not?"

She saw the conflict in Rathbone's face.

"Is it a matter of confidentiality, Oliver?" she asked as gently as she could. "My dear, if it's Monk's secrets you are guarding, are you willing to let him die to keep them?"

He looked at her steadily for several moments, appearing to turn it over in his mind, and then he reached a decision.

"He had a carriage accident in '56," he said gravely. "He woke up in hospital with no memory of anything whatever before that. I can't even imagine how difficult it was for him to hide that from everyone, except Hester. He met her then, when he was investigating a crime he actually thought he might have committed himself, a very violent murder of a Crimean war hero. He was working blind, with no idea who his friends or enemies were."

"But his memory came back?" she said, appalled by the thought of the fear and confusion he must have felt. The suffering was beyond her grasp. Many of her memories were hideous, painful, both physically and emotionally, but there was nothing hidden, no darkness unexplored with unknown terrors waiting to strike her.

"No," he replied. "He pieced some of it together from clues, but he never remembered. He thinks he was in San Francisco, maybe even knew Aaron Clive and Piers Astley, but he remembers no facts. He had no idea why McNab hated him until he asked one of very few people who knew him before, and whom he can trust."

"So he doesn't remember Nairn?" She began to perceive the gulf they were in, like being at sea, with no idea even which way the land lay.

"Only what he can read about, or other people can tell him," he agreed.

"And San Francisco? Is that the same?"

"Yes. He has flashes of familiarity, but he doesn't know if it's memory or imagination. He seems to know how to work a schooner, but knowing that means he could have been across the Atlantic, or simply around the coast of Britain. And up into the North Sea. He knows from the evidence of others that he grew up on the coast of Northumberland."

"And Astley, you say?" Beata asked. "Can't he remember him at all?"

"No. But they were wild, rough days in '49. A world away from here. Gillander and Clive both say Monk was there, but they could be lying. So could anyone else, or even all of them."

"Oh . . ." Her mind raced through the chaos of unknown facts, people, possibilities, trying to find something to grasp on to. She would have given anything to be able to remember Monk herself, but she couldn't. "But he didn't intentionally kill Pettifer?"

"I'm certain of that. But it isn't enough."

"No . . . of course it isn't." She wanted to help, to think of something that would spark hope, but false hope was worse than useless; it was also dangerous. "We need the truth, or as much of it as we can find." She was used to the law. She had listened to Ingram going on about it for enough years. Sometimes she could still see it in her dreams: the anger in his face, too close to hers, shouting at her. But that did not matter now. Only saving Monk mattered. "And we need to divide the case into what we can prove, and what we believe because we deduce it, or we trust the people concerned," she finished.

The ghost of a smile touched Rathbone's face. "If I thought I understood the reason people did whatever they did, then I would know where to look for other facts, proof, connections between things. I could make a line of reasoning and find what is missing, or at least enough of it to be believable to a jury. Nobody does things without some reason."

"Oh, I know something that perhaps you don't. . . ."

His eyes widened, but he did not interrupt.

"Miriam and Aaron Clive are about the only people I have spent any time with since Ingram's death, largely for reasons of propriety. One occasion I was there McNab called. It wasn't to see Aaron over some business matter, but to see Miriam."

Rathbone was startled. "How would he even know her?"

"They have some concern together, some interest. I'm trying to remember exactly what I overheard. . . ."

"You were there?" There was surprise in his voice.

"In the hall, just outside the door," she replied, feeling a heat rise in her face. "I excused myself to allow them privacy. But I waited in the hall. There was no one else there and the sound of their voices carried. There was information they wanted from each other. Monk's name was mentioned. But even when I didn't catch the words, I could hear the depth of conviction in their voices. It mattered intensely to Miriam. I think it was to do with San Francisco. So if Monk was there, that would make sense."

"But why did McNab care about Monk and San Francisco? Do you remember anything he said?" he asked with growing interest.

"I can't remember why, but I think it was to do with Piers Astley's death. I remember very clearly wondering if she was relieved. . . ." She felt embarrassed even by the thought, but this was not a time to be concerned with herself. "If perhaps he had been cruel to her and that was why he had been killed."

There was confusion in his face. Did he know anything of what Ingram had done to her, beyond the little she had said? She must not allow it to matter now. It was the truth, and maybe more of it would have to come out: details rather than generalities with carefully blurred edges. Oliver might have to know. Did she want to live her whole life hiding things from him, skirting around the real words, inventing explanations . . . at heart, deceiving him? He would know it, wouldn't he? It was his profession to know other people were lying, half-lying, evading what they could not bear to see.

"So you think Astley's death was to do with his being cruel?" he said very gently. He made no move to touch her, and yet it was almost as if he had. She often thought what sensitive hands he had, and imagined them holding hers.

"I think Miriam has known terrible pain," she murmured, trying very hard to grasp the truth. "And it has to do with Astley."

"Who was responsible for his death?" Rathbone asked.

"They didn't know at the time, and I'm not sure if they do now. But what if she needs to know, and that's what she wanted to find from Monk?"

"But Monk doesn't know anything. He doesn't even know if he was there."

"She doesn't know that."

He bit his lip thoughtfully. "Very interesting, because McNab does know that Monk has no memory."

"Then he is deceiving Miriam if he is telling her that Monk can help. I wonder why? It is somehow to trap Monk, isn't it?"

"Exactly. If that is what they were talking about."

"Is he wanting her somehow to get at Monk?"

"He doesn't need to. In the attempt to rescue Pettifer, and his panicking and accidental drowning, McNab has all he needs to convict Monk. All other plans could be abandoned."

"But why would McNab claim Monk had killed Pettifer on purpose?" She knew from his face, even before she finished speaking, that there was a terrible answer to that.

"Because Monk blamed him for Orme's death," he said. "And from what Monk has now told me, he was right to."

"Was Pettifer to blame for that? Did McNab set it up, but use Pettifer to do it?"

"It looks like it," he said. "I need to know a great deal more before I can present any defense at all, and have proof of it. Monk himself thinks that the key to the whole thing is the death of Astley. He's afraid that somehow they'll make it look as if he killed him. He can't defend himself because he can't remember."

"It's thousands of miles out of the court's jurisdiction," Beata pointed out.

"Of course it is," he said. "But if the evidence can be made to indicate that Monk was responsible, jurisdiction won't matter. They'll introduce it as motive, and it will have marked him as a man who would kill if provoked. All the objections and ruling it out of evidence won't make the jury forget it, or put it out of their consideration. There are words and acts that you cannot take from your mind."

"Then we need to find out whatever anyone knows about who really did kill Astley," she said with absolute certainty. "I will speak to Miriam."

"Beata . . ." He leaned forward as if to take her hands, and stopped.

"Don't try to dissuade me, Oliver," she said quietly. "We don't have any time to waste on pointless arguments. And it is pointless. I can speak to her in ways that you cannot. And don't try to close me out for my sake. It would not be a favor, and I don't need protecting. Close me out only if you think I will do more harm than good." She looked at him steadily, meeting his eyes.

She had not intended to challenge him to anything today, or even in a future close enough to consider, yet here she was doing exactly that. In her own way she was asking him if she was to be part of his future, or not. Now it was too late to be discreet, or take a step back.

This time, almost without thinking about it, he put his hand over hers. "It may be unpleasant," he said. "You may learn things about her you would prefer not to have known."

"Oliver, would you caution Hester Monk in such a way?"

He looked completely taken aback, and for a moment could find no words.

"Then let me answer the question for you," she responded. "No, you would not. You would expect her to fight side by side with you—from what I have heard, maybe even a step in front of you, of all of us. And I believe you once loved her. . . ." That was difficult to say. She had never truly and completely loved anyone but Oliver. She realized that as she spoke now.

"Did I say that?" He looked puzzled and embarrassed.

"You didn't need to, my dear," she replied. "It is in your face when you speak of her."

"We could not have made each other happy," he said frankly. "It is a very good thing we did not try. I think she would always have loved Monk . . . and I will always love you."

She felt the hot tears of relief fill her eyes. But this was no time for more questions and answers. She was ready—fully, heart-deep ready—but saving Monk came first. Afterward there would be time for everything else.

"Then I have all I want," she whispered. "But we must see that Monk does also. I shall call on Miriam and see if I can oblige her to tell me the truth about Piers Astley, and anything she knows about Monk in California."

"Please, be careful!"

"I have weathered and survived a great deal worse than an uncomfortable conversation over the tea cakes, I assure you."

"But—"

"I have cultivated a serene and perhaps fragile look because it has served me well, but it is only skin deep." Then she wondered if she had said too much. She had meant it to be light, but some of the old pain must be visible. He was too clever to have missed it.

He was also too sensitive to acknowledge his understanding now. But the time would come, and perhaps soon.

"I will call on Miriam Clive today," she said decisively. "The hour is a little late, but needs must, and it is certainly the devil who is driving!"

Rathbone did not answer but all the unspoken words were in his look.

WHEN RATHBONE HAD GONE, Beata called her footman and asked for the coach to be made ready to take her immediately to visit Mrs. Clive. She did consider going to see Hester, so that they might compare notes with each other and so work more effectively. But she knew that Hester would be distracted with anxiety, or perhaps think Beata was taking too much upon herself. Maybe she was, but she was beyond worrying about who approved of her, or who did not. She had been in San Francisco and she knew Miriam. It had been a world different from anything a London woman could imagine, even one who had nursed in the Crimea. Better to do this first, and ask forgiveness afterward if she had committed any social gaffes.

She did not bother to change her clothes to a dress suitable for afternoon visiting. Appearance was irrelevant. A hat was sufficient, and of course a coat. The weather was bitterly cold.

When the carriage was brought around to the front door she requested the footman to accompany her, and gave the coachman instructions to make the best speed he could, without jeopardizing the horses.

All the way through the wet, windy streets she weighed what she was going to say to Miriam. Certainly she would ask for privacy. Miriam might be kind enough to instruct that all other callers be invited to leave cards rather than intrude.

She would like to prepare her words, but experience had taught her that hardly any conversation went the way one had anticipated. Well-thought-out responses became irrelevant, even absurd. She had once been very close to Miriam, and in many ways the qualities she had cared for were still there: the quick humor, the love of beauty, the passion for life, the ability to feel others' wounds as well as her own. But people can change. Old virtues could not always be relied on.

Despite the weather it was a pleasant journey and the classic Georgian façades of houses were graceful even under gray skies. The bare trees in the squares had their own beauty. The traffic was light: a closed-in carriage with a coat of arms on the door and a liveried coachman driving. An older couple walked arm in arm along the pavement, heads bent toward each other in conversation.

Beata arrived at the Clives' house in Mayfair and was received by the footman with courtesy and well-concealed surprise. There was a fire in the morning room where she was greeted by Miriam. She looked as beautiful as ever in a deep forest-green gown, the warmth of her own coloring making it seem richer than it was.

"Beata! Are you all right? You look very pale," she said with concern. "Has something happened?"

"Yes, it has." Beata seized the opening without hesitation. "How sensitive of you to notice. May I ask you the favor that should anyone else call, they might be asked merely to leave a card? I need most urgently to beg your assistance."

"Of course," Miriam said immediately. "Would you like tea?"

"Thank you, that would be excellent." She was not in the least thirsty, but she was cold. More important, tea gave the visit a nature of hospitality that would be less easy to break than mere conversation.

Miriam rang the bell. When the footman arrived she told him they were not to be interrupted, except by a tray of tea, which was to be brought, and then the parlor maid should withdraw.

"Yes, ma'am," he said, then left and closed the door behind him.

Beata began immediately. "Commander Monk has been arrested and charged with the murder of the customs man Pettifer," she said. "Of course it is ridiculous. He was trying to save him and the man panicked and more or less drowned himself. But the charge springs from an old enmity, and will be desperately difficult to disprove."

Miriam was startled. "Enmity with Pettifer? Isn't that beneath Monk?"

"Of course it is. He was never even acquainted with Pettifer." Beata tried to control her emotion and speak only with reason. "The enmity is with McNab."

Miriam did not hide her surprise. "Really?"

Beata hesitated only a moment. "You know him. He called upon you when I was here. Do you honestly find it so difficult to believe?"

"I know him only as a professional acquaintance of Aaron's, because of his position in the Customs service. Import and export requires Customs clearance all the time." Miriam's face was almost expressionless. Only the tiniest wavering in her glance betrayed uncertainty or perhaps deceit.

Beata retreated and approached from a different angle. "The enmity is very old. Many years ago, around the early fifties, McNab's half brother committed a very violent and horrible crime. Monk caught him and he was tried and sentenced to death. McNab begged Monk to ask for clemency, and Monk refused. The young man was hanged. McNab has not forgiven Monk for that."

Miriam was looking openly confused, but Beata thought she saw a shadow in her eyes of something else, something quite distinct that showed she understood very well.

This needed a great deal of care. If she mishandled the situation she might lose the chance for Miriam's help. If she insisted at the wrong moment, or with the wrong words, she could make an enemy instead of a friend. Perhaps she should retreat again, show her own vulnerability, painful as that was.

How well did she really know Miriam? It had been twenty years since they had been young women together in gold rush California. Had they been friends by nature, or by circumstance? They had both lost husbands, and that alone had drawn them together. They had both found freedom impossible to women in the older, more rigidly civilized worlds. They had traveled to extraordinary places, of both beauty like the breathtaking Californian coastline, and desolation like the inland deserts where skulls of men and beasts littered the sand.

They had become inventive, creating the things they needed and could not buy. They had mixed with people they would never have spoken to on the east coast of America, let alone in England.

But how different had they been inside, in loneliness or hunger for a place where they belonged, where they did not need to imagine and create simply to survive?

Beata had returned to England, and married Ingram York, and regretted it bitterly. She had still to feel the deep happiness in the soul of knowing that she was truly loved. It was the most profound hunger there was.

Miriam had mourned her first husband, but she had been comforted and protected by the richest and most charismatic man on the entire west coast, and then courted by him. It seemed as if the hand of fate had given her everything she might have dreamed of . . . except children. But was that chance, or choice? Perhaps after losing Astley's child with the shock of his death, she had not been able to have another? But she had love.

Beata would have had children, had she been able to, but not with Ingram. That thought was too horrible to entertain.

So had she anything in common with the woman in front of her, except memories of a unique time and place, twenty years ago? A friendship of sharing, born of necessity.

But they were going to hang Monk if no one managed to find a way out of this tightening noose. Whether she married Rathbone or not, whether she could find a way to be honest with him, and not drown him in her own ocean of pain and humiliation, was swept aside.

"However," she said with sudden urgency, "Monk did not kill Pettifer on purpose. He had no motive, did not even know the man or that he worked for McNab. But there is only his word for it, or that of his own men, and a jury would weigh that with some skepticism."

"But you believe him?" Miriam said curiously. "Why?"

Beata hesitated. What was her own dignity worth? No one's life!

"Because I know Oliver Rathbone well, and he has known Monk for fourteen years through good times and bad, and he believes him absolutely. They have fought some fierce battles side by side, and never failed each other. Monk never gave up on Oliver when he was in terrible trouble and facing ruin."

Miriam smiled with quick, complete understanding. "You know

him well? Sir Oliver Rathbone?" All the light and shadows of meaning were there in the question: pain again, and the sharp, empty feeling of loss.

"Yes," Beata answered.

"And I think perhaps you are fond of him?" Miriam asked. The shadows in her eyes, in her face, showed plainly that it was not an idle question.

Another stripping away of the masks of comfort. Beata felt almost naked. She found herself avoiding Miriam's eyes, not because she was lying, but because she could not bear this poised, beautiful woman, so deeply loved, to see into her feelings. One thing would lead to another until everything was laid bare.

"I find him very agreeable," Beata answered. How empty that sounded, and how artificial. Surely Miriam would see right through it? Would she imagine something far more . . . intimate? She felt the blood hot in her face, as if she had lied already.

She must remember what she was here for. "Miriam . . . I want to help Oliver to defend Monk, and win. McNab has nursed a long revenge, sixteen years long. It was not Monk's fault McNab's half brother committed a crime for which he was hanged. Even if revenge is ever just, which I am not certain it is, this one is not."

Miriam gave a tiny, sad smile. "McNab's revenge is not just, but society's revenge on his brother was?"

"Monk was not guilty of Nairn's crime, and he isn't guilty of killing Pettifer. But he'll hang for it if we don't find the truth, and prove it. Do you remember him from San Francisco? I suspect McNab is going to try to link Monk somehow with Piers's death, in order to show a pattern of violent behavior."

Miriam looked stunned. "But that's . . . that's absurd! Why on earth would Monk have killed Piers?"

"I don't know!" Beata tried not to sound impatient. "Maybe for money. Heaven's sake, Miriam, there were enough adventurers along the Californian coast who would do anything for enough money to get a stake to buy land that might have gold. Life was wild and terrible and exhilarating . . . and deep. Of course Monk would have fit in then, as a young man looking for the chance of adventure and a future."

Miriam seemed to look for words without finding them, unable to comprehend what she was hearing.

Beata dismissed it. "Never mind. What did you want McNab to do, and what does he want from you?"

Miriam remained silent.

The parlor maid came in with tea, put the tray on the table, and left, closing the door behind her.

Miriam poured the tea for each of them. She remembered exactly how Beata liked it, with no milk, and a tiny drop of honey.

"What do you want from McNab?" Beata repeated.

Miriam passed the tea across and Beata took it. "I suppose you will tell Rathbone if I don't explain it to you," she said.

Beata put the cup down. With no milk in it, the tea would be scalding hot. "Yes. I'm not going to let McNab have his revenge."

Miriam smiled, but there was sadness in her eyes. "You always were more straitlaced than you looked. Still, I'm surprised you stayed married to a High Court judge. It must have been like wearing an iron corset. . . ."

"Red-hot iron . . ."

"I'm sorry. You think I don't know, but I do."

"Do you?" Beata doubted it.

"There are different kinds of pain: that the loss of dreams leaves, and the pain of emptiness that gradually starves the soul."

"McNab . . ." Beata reminded her. Only the present mattered now.

"He wanted information about Monk, and the gold rush years," Miriam replied.

It all made sense. "I see. And what did you want from him in return?"

There was no mistaking the color in Miriam's cheeks now.

Beata waited.

"Information about Monk," Miriam replied. "I needed to know Monk's skills and what kind of a man he is now. I remember him from

those days. He was like steel—hard, supple, almost beautiful in his
strength of will—and razor sharp. If he was the same man I knew, I
knew he would not rest if he knew an injustice had been done to Piers
and if anyone could help me get my revenge, it would be him."

Beata was stunned. "Your revenge? For what? Upon whom?"

Miriam was pale now, all the color gone from her face like a vanished tide.

"On the man who killed Piers, of course. He was never caught,
never punished." The look in her eyes was fury, but far deeper than that,
it was pain, utter and devastating loss.

Beata opened her mouth to speak, and found no words adequate for
what she was feeling. The sense of loss emanating from Miriam was so
strong, it was as though something had crawled beneath Beata's own
skin and torn her own heart out.

"I loved him so much—more than I think he ever knew."

Beata had a glimpse of understanding. This turbulent, passionate
beauty who stirred a kind of madness in some men. Was it possible that
Clive could have killed Piers? To have Miriam? No! No, that was . . .
absurd. Aaron and Miriam . . . the great love story? Aaron the beautiful
man, the King of the Barbary Coast?

"I have to know," Miriam said huskily. "I needed Monk to find his
killer."

"Why? There's nothing you can do now." It hurt to say it but it was
true.

"I don't need to. Knowing will be enough. I will show the world that
Piers, the most honest, loyal, and brave man in all those wild days, was
betrayed by his closest friend."

Although Miriam couldn't say his name, Beata's fears about Aaron
were undeniable. "Are you absolutely sure?"

Miriam's eyes blazed with anger. Her voice was choked with it. "As
sure as I can be."

"Then why have you waited so long? Why now?" It made no sense.

"Why has McNab waited so long?" Miriam demanded.

That was a question Beata did not want to answer. It was Monk's
secret to give or keep, not hers.

"Why do you want to know?" she asked instead.

"You expect me to trust you, but you won't trust me!" Miriam said.

"Yours is your secret; mine is Monk's to give or keep."

"How much do you want to save him?" Miriam demanded.

"You'd let him hang for something he didn't do?" Beata challenged her. "That won't get you your . . . your vindication of Piers." Was that all she meant? Or was it really only revenge?

Miriam sat perfectly still. "Why did McNab wait so long? What is it that you are not willing to tell me? If you want my help, then trust me!"

There was no way of evading it now and still trying to save Monk. Beata swallowed hard, and told her.

"Monk had a carriage accident about thirteen years ago. He can't remember anything before that. Nothing of San Francisco at all. And McNab knows that!"

Miriam stared at her. "So he can't help me!" Her body clenched as if she were trapped. "Poor devil, he can't even help himself."

"Stop it," Beata said sharply. "Don't you dare give in! You waited until now—why? Why didn't you do anything about Aaron if you knew he killed Piers? What do you need Monk for anyway?"

"I learned only recently that Aaron killed Piers. Fin Gillander brought me proof."

"Then what else do you need?"

"It is proof to me, not to anyone else."

"What proof?"

"Piers's shirt, soaked in blood, and the deeds to a strip of land along the American River where there was gold, signed over to Fin by Aaron. It's payment for Fin swearing Aaron was somewhere else when Piers was shot."

"Then what do you want from Monk? Surely this is proof enough?"

"It could have been anybody's shirt," Miriam replied. "I knew it was Piers's because I made it for him. I recognized my own stitching, the unevenness here and there, the rhythm of the backstitching, but there is only my word for it. And what would that be against Aaron's?"

"Gillander's word?" Beata asked.

Miriam looked a little embarrassed. "He adores me. People would assume he would say anything to back me up, even about the deed."

Beata was about to ask her if she was sure, but she saw it in her eyes: the pain; the helplessness; the terrible, bitter disillusion; the crumbling of beliefs.

"I see," she said softly. "And you thought Monk might have known the truth, or at least have been able to deduce it. And do what? Ruin Aaron?"

"Along with Fin's testimony, he might have known enough to prove that Piers went there to that place on Aaron's orders, and died doing his job . . . by Aaron's orders."

"You have no doubt?"

"None. I wish I had. God in heaven, Beata! Do you think I want to believe the man I'm married to now killed my first husband, whom I loved beyond words, so he could have me? I feel . . . vile! Used and . . . dirty, like something you buy and sell, because you want to own it. Do you think my flesh doesn't crawl every time he touches me?"

Beata did not need to imagine that; she knew it not only in her mind but in her body's memory, like old pain reawakened.

"McNab knows about Monk's memory loss, which is why he now feels able to take his revenge," she said. "He knows Monk can't defend himself—he daren't even take the stand to testify." She spoke slowly. "And that means Aaron probably has to."

"Yes . . . I suppose he does." Miriam closed her eyes. "I wonder if he has any idea that I know about his part in Piers's death, and he's waiting for me to act. God damn McNab!"

"He was using you," Beata said with an edge of bitterness. "What are you going to do about it?" That was a definite challenge, and it was meant to be. She was desperate, and had no intention of allowing Miriam to escape.

Miriam stared at her, waiting, thinking.

"God may very well damn McNab, eventually," Beata went on. "In the meantime, it is up to us! You know a great deal about McNab, if you think about it. You must tell Oliver, and be prepared to testify to it, if it helps Monk. Think hard what you know, what you remember of every conversation. What did McNab want of you?" She leaned forward. "I know you think you were using him, and perhaps you were, but he came here equally as much to use you!"

A faint flush stained Miriam's cheeks. "You don't need to keep on reminding me. I can see it. He wanted to implicate Monk in something he wouldn't be able to escape from. That's clear now."

"What did you think it was?" That sounded too critical. She might have been no wiser in Miriam's place. She could barely imagine the fury and the grief Miriam must have felt when she realized the truth of Piers's death. "I mean what did he pretend it was? It might help to know."

"I learned from Fin Gillander that Monk had been in San Francisco twenty years ago," Miriam said quietly. "I couldn't recall him at first, but Fin recognized him straightaway and knew what kind of man he was, simply in so much as Fin liked him. He said they did many things together, or at least in the same fashion. Their paths crossed quite often. They've both changed, of course. People do, in twenty years. Fin is forty, and Monk must be fifty. And Monk is certainly different in that the anger inside him is gone. Whatever he was looking for, he's found it."

"And he's about to lose it again!" Beata interrupted sharply.

Miriam looked at her and the pain in her face was temporarily naked. Beata realized with a rush, as if suddenly drowned in the force of a wave, that Miriam had never recovered from Piers's death and that Aaron had never been more than an ease of the loss, and now that, too, had been shattered. Everything gentle or good in him had been wiped out by the knowledge that it was he who had killed Astley, directly or indirectly. The fact that it had been out of desire for Miriam only added guilt to the grief.

"I'm sorry," Beata said quietly. "But we have no time for pain now. We have to find a way of proving that Pettifer's death was an accident, caused by his own panic. Monk doesn't know who killed Piers, or anything else about San Francisco and the gold rush. If he ever did, it's gone from his memory. I'll tell Oliver all you know, including about the land deed on the American River, and the shirt. But first we must prove that Monk did not have any reason to hurt Pettifer."

Miriam frowned. "How? We don't know anything about the enmity between McNab and Monk."

"I know that," Beata said. It felt dark, terribly dark, and heavy inside her as if she could not breathe. "But we must try. I shall go and see Hester. I am only getting to know her now but I think she will accept anyone's help. I would in her place. You will think of everything you can that McNab asked you about Monk."

Miriam swallowed hard. "Yes . . . of course."

13

Hester moved through the days leading up to the trial as in a nightmare. Everything she thought of to prove Monk's innocence seemed to melt into nothing as soon as she grasped hold of it. In her mind McNab grew to almost demonic brilliance.

Rathbone came to Paradise Place one evening and she asked him what she could do, what proof there was.

"There must be something!" she said desperately. Monk had loathed McNab—nobody doubted that—but he had done nothing to him.

They were sitting in the parlor. It seemed dark and peculiarly empty. After his initial arrival to support her, Hester had forbidden Scuff to leave his studies to come home, at least until the trial began. His work and other people's needs were a kind of respite.

Rathbone looked pale and there were lines of tenderness in his face.

"It wouldn't help to prove that McNab was responsible, even if we could prove that William had never heard of Pettifer," he said with as much gentleness as he could manage. He would never care as she did, but Monk was his closest friend, and they had fought many battles side by side. It had been Monk who had finally saved Rathbone when he was exhausted, deeply afraid and facing imprisonment, possibly for years.

"Well, what will help?" She heard her own voice slipping out of control. "If McNab were responsible, then why would William have wanted to harm Pettifer, let alone kill him? If he could have been persuaded to testify against McNab, the last thing William would want would be Pettifer dead!"

"Because our proving it doesn't help," Rathbone said miserably. "If we prove it now, that doesn't show that Monk believed it back when Pettifer died. It isn't really time that counts, it's what he thought was true then."

"We've got witnesses. . . ." She tailed off without finishing the sentence. They were Monk's men, friends, colleagues, other River Police. The prosecution would point that out instantly. Hester herself could have testified, but she knew, before Rathbone said anything at all, that she could never be put up for cross-examination. It would be only minutes before a decent prosecution would draw from her that Monk had no memory! With every new thought, the noose closed tighter.

There were others who would help, if they could think of anything to do. Scuff was knotted up so tightly with fear for Monk that he could not concentrate on the work he loved. Both he and Crow spent more and more time scouring the riverbanks for information that could damn McNab. At the clinic in Portpool Lane, Squeaky Robinson was calling in every favor and making every threat that might work, and a few that had no chance whatever. Even Worm, the nine-year-old orphan whom Scuff had found a home for there, was out at all hours, up and down the riverbank, asking and listening.

MONK SLEPT LITTLE THE night before the opening of the trial. Every noise seemed to intrude on his thoughts. Men coughed, moaned, cursed; one or two even wept. Like him, they were all alone, cold, and above all, afraid. There was probably little any of them could do to affect their fate now. It lay in the hands of others, sometimes others who did not care.

Was it better or worse to have those supporting you whose lives would also be darkened forever if you were found guilty? It hurt almost beyond bearing to think of Hester, or for that matter of Scuff. What of the men he would let down, if they believed him guilty? What of the River Police themselves, Hooper and all the others, stained by his failure?

The thought of McNab winning was enough to make him almost choke for breath. But neither rage nor pity was now any help. They were barriers in the way of thought. It was only intelligence and self-control that could save him. Or a miracle! Did he believe in miracles?

What did he believe in? It was a little late to decide now.

THE TRIAL BEGAN WITH the usual formalities. These they drew out over precise notes, which scraped on Monk's raw nerve edges.

He stood in the dock of the Old Bailey high above the courtroom and looked sideways at the gallery. It was full. He should have expected that, and yet it was disconcerting. How many of those people hated the police and were here to see one of them brought down? How many had been helped by law or police at one time or another, and would rather see him vindicated?

He searched for Hester, and saw the side of her head, the light shining on the fair streak in her hair. Who would love her, if he were hanged? No one, not as he did! She would be the widow of a hanged man. Would she always believe he was innocent? Or would she, in time, give in to the pressure, the sheer weight of everyone else's certainty?

They were beginning at last. Sorley Wingfield was prosecuting. He was a lean, very dark man with a cutting sense of humor. He had probably called in a few favors to get this case. His dislike for Rathbone was deep and long lasting, and he was bound to know that this one was personal to Rathbone. It was Rathbone's first really big case, the first capital case, since his return to the bar after his disgrace.

Monk did not admire Wingfield for taking his revenge for other
losses on such an easy win. Like shooting at a sitting target, a living one
that could face fear and pain.

The judge was Mr. Justice Lyndon, a man he knew very little about,
except that Rathbone had said his reputation was good. But then he
would hardly have said otherwise, when the outlook was more than
dark enough as it was.

The first witness to be called by Wingfield was Hooper. He climbed
the steps up to the witness stand, looking pale-faced and profoundly
uncomfortable. He was dressed in River Police uniform and stood a
trifle awkwardly, as if the shoulders of the coat were too tight on him.
Monk could not remember seeing him in it before. He usually wore an
old seaman's pea coat.

He swore to his name and occupation, facing Wingfield as if he were
flotsam clogging up the waterway. He had a gift for conveying contempt
with barely the movement of an eyelid.

"You work for the Thames River Police, out of the station at Wapping? Is that correct, Mr. Hooper?" Wingfield asked smoothly.

"Yes, sir."

"And you have been recently promoted, to take the senior position
assisting Commander Monk, the accused?"

"Yes, sir." Hooper's dislike of Wingfield was in his tone as well.

"The position until recently was held by a Mr. Orme?"

Hooper was wary. "Yes, sir."

"Would that be the same Mr. Orme who was killed recently in a
skirmish on the river involving a gun smuggler?" Wingfield asked with
an air of innocence.

Rathbone rose to his feet. "My lord, there is no argument as to Mr.
Hooper's identity, or that he has an honorable record of service in the
River Police and was recently promoted upon the death of Mr. Orme,
who had been due to retire. And just in case Mr. Wingfield is disposed
to take up the court's time with the subject, Mr. Hooper has an honorable record in the Merchant Navy. Nothing is known against his character here, or anywhere else, and he has been many times commended
for his courage."

One of the jurors smiled.

Wingfield looked irritated, but he was too confident of ultimate victory to take exception. Monk could see it even from where he sat.

Wingfield shrugged and walked a few steps farther forward.

"If my learned friend has finished . . . ?" he said with slight sarcasm.

Rathbone sat down.

"Now, Mr. Hooper, you were, I believe, at Skelmer's Wharf with the accused on the day Mr. Pettifer was drowned?"

"I was," Hooper agreed.

"Why? What were you doing there?" Wingfield managed to look interested, as if he had no idea what the answer would be.

There was a rustle of anticipation in the crowd.

"Hoping to apprehend an escaped prisoner," Hooper replied.

"A particular one?" Wingfield said sarcastically. "Or just any that might happen to pass that way?"

One of the jurors laughed nervously. A look of very light irony crossed Mr. Justice Lyndon's face as well.

"A second one to escape the customs officers within the last couple of weeks, sir," Hooper said rather loudly. "This one we hoped would be still alive. We were only called in when the first one was already dead."

There was a rustle of movement in the gallery, and this time a quite unmistakable twitch of amusement in Mr. Justice Lyndon's face.

"Drowned also?" Wingfield inquired with his eyebrows high.

"Yes, sir," Hooper replied. "And shot! In the back."

"Seems excessive," Mr. Justice Lyndon observed. "Does this have something to do with Pettifer's death, Mr. Wingfield? Are you accusing Commander Monk of having drowned this man as well?"

"No, my lord. However, it was this man Blount's death that appears to have drawn the River Police into the whole affair," Wingfield replied.

The judge turned to Hooper. "Do I understand it, Mr. Hooper, that you and Monk hoped to find the second escaped prisoner while he was still alive, for some professional purpose?"

Hooper looked as if he were relieved that someone was at last getting the point.

"Yes, my lord. We had been given the case of Blount's death because of the bullet in his back. We believed there might well be a connection between his escape and this second man's escape from the same force, that is the Customs service."

"Proceed, Mr. Wingfield," the judge directed.

"Thank you, my lord." He looked at Hooper. "Why Skelmer's Wharf? Did you have some information that made you believe he would be there?"

"It was a good, secluded place with a landing," Hooper replied. "Tide was right, just on the turn. We thought the escapee would make for France and we'd had a tip-off that a fast boat was moored upriver and was maybe part of his escape plan. Good guess, as it turned out."

"Just a good guess?" Wingfield sneered very slightly. "Is that how you usually apprehend escaped prisoners, Mr. Hooper? On a 'good guess'?"

"We don't usually lose 'em, sir," Hooper answered.

There was a ripple of laughter around the gallery, and one of the jurors took out a large handkerchief to hide his amusement.

"Whose idea was it to go to Skelmer's Wharf? Yours, or the accused?"

"We received the tip-off and immediately went in pursuit together."

"How loyal of you! You are very loyal to your commander, aren't you, Mr. Hooper? Risked your life for him, more than once, if I read your records right?"

"Does the record also say how many times he risked his life for me? Or any of the other men?" Hooper demanded. "Don't suppose your job has room for sticking your neck out for any of the men you work with. More likely have a knife in your hand!"

"Hear, hear!" someone shouted from the gallery, and there were a couple of catcalls and a whistle.

"Mr. Wingfield!" the judge said sharply. "Will you please at least attempt to control your witness?"

"May he be noted as hostile, my lord?" Wingfield said angrily.

"I'm sure we have already observed that he is hostile, Mr. Wingfield. You seem a little late in remarking it," the judge replied.

Wingfield smiled bleakly. "You have made your loyalties and your predispositions in this case more than clear, Mr. Hooper. I warn you to be very careful indeed that you do not allow your emotions, or your obvious personal interests and ambitions, to cloud your veracity. That means your ability to recollect and speak only the truth . . . the exact truth, do you understand?"

Hooper's face tightened in anger that must have been visible to the jury. Monk in the dock could see it quite clearly.

"I've no reason to tell you lies, even if I wasn't under oath," Hooper said quietly. "Speak plain, and I'll speak plain back to you."

Two of the jurors nodded in agreement.

"So you were waiting at Skelmer's Wharf?" Wingfield prompted. "What happened, Mr. Hooper?"

"Two men appeared, one from each side of the row of buildings," Hooper answered. "They saw each other and began to fight. No use asking me which one attacked first 'cos I don't know. They went at each other, hammer an' tongs. All the time they were moving closer to the water's edge—"

"A moment, Mr. Hooper," Wingfield interrupted. "Do I understand it that you and the accused did nothing to stop this battle? Nothing to intervene and apprehend your escaped prisoner? Who did you imagine the other man was?"

"Regular police, or customs man," Hooper replied. "Both Commander Monk and I intervened, but then each man started fighting us. I took on the smaller man and we fell into the water. While I was occupied with that, the big man fell in and started thrashing around. He wasn't much of a fighter, and we thought he was the prisoner."

"Indeed?" Wingfield raised his eyebrows in disbelief. "So you had no idea as to the identity of the prisoner, or his description? A bit lax of you, wasn't it? Might you not very easily have apprehended completely the wrong man?" He smiled. "Oh . . . that is what you are claiming you did—isn't it? Completely the wrong man? Didn't you, in fact, drown the customs officer and allow the prisoner to swim right across the river and escape to . . . God knows where? France, for all any of us can say?"

Hooper's lips closed into a thin line and he swallowed his temper with difficulty.

"The smaller man fought like a polecat, and he swam away from me. Mr. Monk tried to help the big fellow with the beard, but he panicked, thrashing around like a madman. Nearly took Mr. Monk down with him. You have to stop someone like that, or they'll drown the both of you. You can't swim, and save a man that's swinging his arms. But maybe you've never tried that. Doesn't go with your horsehair wig an' the fancy robes. You'd drown in minutes in all o' that."

Again there was a gust of laughter from the gallery, but it was nervous, and then the jury twisted in their seats uncomfortably.

Wingfield kept his temper this time. "I seldom wear this attire when I go swimming, Mr. Hooper. And I have never jumped into the Thames to save a customs officer, or to drown one. Tell me, after the smaller man had struck out to swim across the river, what did you do?"

"I helped Mr. Monk pull the big man out of the water and up onto the wharf. We tried to get the water out of his lungs and bring him round but he was too far gone."

"A sufficiently hard blow to the side of the head will do that, don't you agree?"

"If he hadn't panicked an' tried to drown Mr. Monk, he'd have been all right."

"Maybe he was frightened because he couldn't swim, and he knew Mr. Monk wanted to drown him?" Wingfield suggested mildly.

"If he was as deep into letting the prisoner go, and trying to blame us for it, then he'd be more use to us alive," Hooper pointed out.

"Your loyalty is to be commended," Wingfield responded. "Unless, of course, it amounts to complicity? Could that be the case, Mr. Hooper?"

Rathbone stood up again. "My lord, since that is not the case, the question is hypothetical. Mr. Hooper has not been charged with anything, and the jury should not be misled into thinking he has. My learned friend is accusing him at once of loyalty . . . and of disloyalty."

"Misplaced loyalty," Wingfield corrected him a trifle condescendingly.

"Loyalty to the truth," Rathbone replied.

"That remains to be seen," Wingfield snapped, but he dismissed Hooper, passing him over to Rathbone.

Rathbone hesitated only slightly. Probably Monk, sitting high up in the dock, was the only one who knew him well enough to notice it.

"I reserve the right to call this witness at a later stage, my lord," he said.

Monk felt the sweat break out on his skin. Was it relief, or only a matter of delaying the inevitable? Hooper would have to testify at some time, and be subjected to Wingfield's cross-examination. Monk needed someone to rescue him. He understood exactly the panic Pettifer must have felt when he was drowning. He could not breathe. The water was sucking him down, closing over his head.

And yet Monk did not want to take Hooper down with him. He liked Hooper, and the guilt would be crippling.

Wingfield called Dr. Hyde, the police surgeon. He went through the usual formalities of establishing his qualifications, then played straight into the core of the case.

"Were you called to Skelmer's Wharf to examine the body of the dead man, Pettifer?"

"No," Hyde said with asperity. "They brought him to me. Get your facts straight, man!"

Wingfield flushed. He had left the details to a junior, certain that the evidence was what he wanted. The expression on his face now suggested dire trouble for someone later.

"But you did receive the body of Pettifer, to determine the exact cause of his death, and anything else that might be relevant to it?"

"Yes."

"Then is there some reason why you are so reluctant to tell the court what you found?"

"When you ask me." Hyde stared straight back at him. "Ex-army doctor. You learn—never volunteer."

"What did you think you were here for? I'm asking you, Dr. Hyde."

Hyde smiled, but it was from amusement, not good humor. "The man's lungs were full of water, and there were tiny dots of blood on the whites of his eyes, as one gets with suffocation of any kind. He drowned."

"Had he any other injuries that would account for why he drowned to death?"

"You don't drown except to death!" Hyde rolled his eyes. "And yes, he had a very slight bruise on his skull, and another on his neck."

"Very slight?" Wingfield's sarcasm was back. "How hard does it have to be to command your attention, Dr. Hyde? It knocked the man senseless!"

"Damned senseless to begin with to jump into the river when he can't swim," Hyde retorted. "Perhaps he wanted to take Mr. Monk's attention in order to give Mr. Owen the chance to escape? Had you thought of that?"

"It's irrelevant," Wingfield pointed out with an equally tight smile in reply. "I doubt he intended to give his own life for it!"

"Which would indicate that he trusted Commander Monk to save him," Hyde said. "He obviously didn't think they were enemies."

"Then his drowned corpse, with the bruises on his skull, would indicate the depth of his mistake in that," Wingfield said triumphantly. "Thank you, Dr. Hyde. That is all."

Rathbone rose to his feet.

The court was silent. Every juror was staring at him, waiting.

Monk felt his heart race.

"Dr. Hyde, you said the bruises on Mr. Pettifer's neck and skull were slight. Does that mean he was not struck very hard?"

"No, sir, it means it was very shortly before his death. The bruises had not time to form."

"I see. Whereabouts on his neck was the bruise? Would you indicate on your own neck, so the jury can see?"

Hyde put his hand to the left side of his neck, just a little forward of the ear.

"Not his throat?" Rathbone asked.

"No. Such a blow to his throat might have killed him. Here was where a man trying to rescue him might have intended to stop him long enough to save them both."

Wingfield stood up sharply.

"Yes, yes," the judge agreed. "Dr. Hyde, you know better than that. We must go through the correct . . . rigmarole!"

Rathbone half hid a smile. "Dr. Hyde, what would be the result of the blow you describe, please?"

"To render him dizzy, perhaps cause a momentary lapse of consciousness lasting a minute or so."

"Long enough to get him out of the water, for example?" Rathbone asked with exaggerated innocence.

"Precisely," Hyde agreed.

"Thank you. Oh . . . Dr. Hyde, the defendant was concerned with another prisoner that the Customs service inadvertently lost, a man named Blount. Did you also examine his corpse?"

"Yes," Hyde agreed.

"He also was drowned?"

"Yes."

"Were there any other marks, bruises, et cetera on his body?"

"Gunshot wound on his back," Hyde replied totally without expression.

"I presume Mr. Monk had nothing to do with that?" Rathbone went on.

"Not so far as I know," Hyde agreed.

"Thank you, Doctor."

Wingfield seemed to consider coming back to Hyde, and then decided against it. After the luncheon adjournment he called Fin Gillander to the stand.

Gillander came in with a slight swagger, one perhaps so natural to him he was not even aware of it. He was a handsome man, approaching his prime, and there was a sigh and a rustle of people straightening up, nudging each other and a few whispers as he took the oath.

Wingfield intended to make the most of it. He established Gillander's occupation, his ownership of the *Summer Wind*, what manner of ship she was, and that Gillander had sailed in her all the way from the coast of California, coming around the wild and treacherous Cape Horn. Every man and woman in the court was listening with total attention, although possibly for different reasons. A jury of women might have believed him whatever he said. But of course there were no women on juries. They were not eligible.

"And you were moored by the opposite shore from Skelmer's Wharf?" Wingfield asked.

"Yes," Gillander agreed.

"And you were on deck, in spite of the inclement weather?"

"It wasn't bad."

"Did you observe Mr. Monk and Mr. Hooper waiting on the wharf?"

"I didn't know their names at the time, but I saw two men waiting, and I heard later who they were."

"Just so. And you saw the other two, Mr. Pettifer and Mr. Owen, arrive?"

"Yes. From opposite sides of the buildings. Couldn't say who was chasing whom. They collided and started to fight. I saw Mr. Monk and Mr. Hooper intervene."

"You could see that, right from the other side of the river?" Wingfield was openly skeptical.

Two of the jurors leaned forward.

"Telescope," Gillander exclaimed with a smile.

Wingfield's face lit with understanding. "Of course. What happened next?"

"The smaller man and Mr. Hooper fell into the water, then the big man leaped into the water and started thrashing around," Gillander answered. "Panicked, by the look of it. Damn stupid, but it happens quite often."

"But the smaller man could survive, and instead of rescuing the drowning man, he struck out across the river toward you?"

"That's right."

"And when he reached you, you helped him out of the water into your boat?"

"Yes."

"Why did you do that, Mr. Gillander?"

Gillander's eyes widened. "What did you expect me to do? Leave him there to drown? I wouldn't do that, whoever he'd been."

Wingfield shrugged. "But you didn't take him prisoner and hold him for the police? Why not?"

"He told me his name was Pettifer, and he was from Customs. He'd been after an escaped prisoner, very violent man. Tried to kill him. But it looked like the River Police had him by then, so he asked me if I'd put him off at the next steps down, and he'd get help."

"And you believed him?"

"No reason not to. The other fellow was the one who fought against the River Police. I thought he was going to kill the man who pulled him out. Lashing out at him like he meant to."

Wingfield suppressed his irritation with difficulty. "He was drowning, Mr. Gillander. He panicked. The man you helped out and took down the river, and so obligingly let off at the next steps, was the escaped prisoner—whom no one has ever seen again!"

Gillander struggled to conceal a smile, and almost succeeded. "Yes . . . I learned that afterward."

"Did you see anyone strike the man who drowned, Mr. Gillander?"

"Saw a lot of arms flailing around. No idea who struck whom. Sorry."

Wingfield moved a step forward.

"Did you subsequently become acquainted with Commander Monk?" he asked with an edge to his voice. "In fact, did you become friends with him, after the incident, and before you were called to testify here as to what you saw?"

Gillander hesitated.

Monk knew exactly the trap he was in. They had known each other on the Californian coast, twenty years ago. Was that what Wingfield was trying to force him into saying? His only way to be honest about it was to admit the earlier knowledge openly. Wingfield was clever. One would be a fool to forget that.

"Mr. Gillander?" Wingfield prompted. "It does not seem a very difficult question. Did you become friends with Commander Monk, only after you pulled the escaped prisoner out of the water? Yes or no?"

Gillander gave a slight shrug. "I renewed an acquaintance."

Wingfield's eyes opened wide. He made the most of the dramatic moment.

There was total silence in the room.

"Did you say you 'renewed' it?" Wingfield asked, emphasizing every word.

Now the gallery was so quiet that when one woman moved position slightly, the creak of whalebone could be heard even by the jury. One man gave a nervous cough.

"Yes," Gillander agreed. "I had known him some twenty years earlier."

"Indeed? And where was that?" Wingfield asked.

"On the Barbary Coast," Gillander answered. "California, not North Africa. Gold rush days."

"And yet William Monk is part of the Thames River Police. Their reach hardly extends so far!" Wingfield now had the smile.

Gillander's eyebrows shot up. "Is that a question?"

"No, of course not," Wingfield snapped. "Did you know him well at that time, Mr. Gillander?"

"Moderately. As well as one knew anybody. We were rivals in the same business. Occasionally allies."

"And what business would that be? Not police, I presume?"

"Hardly. There was no law there, except what was easy to keep. In the very early days, California was still not part of the United States."

"How interesting. So what business did you share, Mr. Gillander? Smuggling? Gunrunning? Gambling? Helping wanted men to escape? Guns for hire?"

Rathbone started to rise to his feet to object, but Gillander answered too quickly. "Don't know much about building and settling a new town, do you?"

"Nothing at all," Wingfield agreed. "I'm a Londoner. We were settled here before Julius Caesar landed in 55 BC. Please answer the question. What did you carry up and down the Californian coast, with the accused?"

"Food, furniture, tools and equipment, timber, bolts of cloth, household goods, and of course rations and prospectors. It's a long way from Bristol down the Atlantic, around the Horn, and up the Pacific coast all the way across the Equator again and into San Francisco Bay. You don't do it in a few weeks. Once a year is enough for most people. You don't want to go round the Horn in winter . . . which down there is June, July, and August."

"Thank you, I am aware that Cape Horn is in the Southern Hemisphere, Mr. Gillander. So you and the accused were facing hardship and danger at sea in a part of the world most of us here only dream of?"

"Yes," Gillander agreed reluctantly.

"Is this going somewhere, my lord?" Rathbone asked a little wearily.

"Get to the point, Mr. Wingfield, if there is one," the judge prompted.

"It will become apparent later on, my lord," Wingfield said.

Monk felt himself cold, as if somebody had opened a door to the icy weather outside. Wingfield was going to raise Piers Astley's death later on. He would when the subject could be brought up naturally, somehow or other. And Rathbone would find no defense against it because Monk had none.

"So you were already well acquainted with Mr. Monk when he questioned you about Owen, the escaped prisoner?" Wingfield said.

"It took me a few minutes to recognize him," Gillander answered. "It had been twenty years. But yes, I soon realized who he was."

"And who was he, Mr. Gillander?"

"Commander of the River Police at Wapping," he said. Gillander smiled again. Then before Wingfield could interrupt. "But it was the same man I knew as a damn good sailor in California."

Wingfield let out his breath slowly. "And you were friends, after a manner? You were both soldiers of fortune? Or perhaps sailors of fortune would be more appropriate?"

"If you like."

"Allies at times?"

"And rivals at others," Gillander added.

"Just so. Now, in the matter of getting Mr. Monk, and probably yourself, out of this predicament regarding the rescue of the escaped prisoner, and the violent death of the customs officer, Pettifer—are you rivals or allies in that, Mr. Gillander?"

"Allies, Mr. Wingfield. We would both like to find the truth and prove it, on both counts," Gillander said without hesitation.

"Or at least to blame it all on someone else," Wingfield retorted.

"Wherever it fits!" Gillander snapped back at him. "I don't know where that is yet, and neither do you!"

Wingfield put his head a little to one side. "Yes, I do, Mr. Gillander. It fits with Mr. Monk, and very possibly also with you!" He turned to the judge. "Thank you, my lord. That is all I have for this witness at present, although I reserve the right to recall him if new evidence emerges."

The judge adjourned the court for the day. Those who were free to do so went out into the rapidly darkening afternoon, and the wind and ice.

Monk was taken back to his cell to lie idle through the long evening, and then awake and chilled all night. He tried desperately to think of any way to prove his innocence. He had not killed Pettifer intentionally. That was the one thing he was sure of. Everything else was as impenetrable as the dark of the cell with its closed door, iron lock, and barely a glimmer of light from the one high window into the yard.

AARON CLIVE WAS CALLED in the morning. He was treated with the utmost respect. Even Mr. Justice Lyndon spoke to him with grave politeness.

Monk knew why he was called, even though he could add nothing to the sum of knowledge. Clive impressed the jury. They would believe every word he said, and Rathbone would be a fool to try to trick him or interrogate him in any way. He had warned Monk of that, speaking quietly, levelly, and as if he had some plan, although he did not say what it was.

Monk had seen Rathbone comfort accused men before, trying to give them more hope than there was, but out of compassion, and because a man without hope looks to the jury like a man who knows his own guilt. Would not an innocent man believe in the ultimate justice of his cause, and have faith in it?

Not if he had as much experience of the law as Monk had! Hester was not here today. He had searched for her along every row that he could see and then forced himself to believe she was following some hopeful trail, some clues that would condemn McNab. Any other thought was unbearable. He must not look as if he had lost belief. He must not look guilty!

Clive was handsome, calm, and almost heroic, not reckless like Gillander. He had the kind of charm that both men and women warm to. He spoke with authority, as if he had never in his life wanted or needed to lie.

He recounted accurately exactly what his men had reported to him of the events on Skelmer's Wharf. Even Monk, listening to every word, could see no evasion or addition of unnecessary detail. The account was limited to facts, largely already known, but it gave them the imprimatur of truth.

Rathbone asked him nothing, but reserved the right to recall him, if it should prove necessary. It sounded like an empty, formulaic thing to say, and that knowledge was plain in the faces of the jury.

Then the main prosecution witness was called: McNab. He strode across the open space from the entrance to the witness stand, and climbed up the winding steps to face Wingfield. He swore to his name, official status, and his occupation.

Wingfield was now getting well into his stride. He stood easily, almost gracefully, his dark face calm, oozing confidence.

"Mr. McNab, so far we have heard a great deal about the actual circumstances of Mr. Pettifer's death, but no real reason why the accused so passionately wished for the destruction of a man with whom he had no personal relationship. Why when chance offered itself, even in front of witnesses, could he not control his passion to kill?"

McNab stood silently on the stand and smiled. He reminded Monk of a hungry man at last sitting at the table with knife and fork in hand, and his favorite meal in front of him.

Rathbone sat rigidly, the light catching the silver in his fair hair, his shoulders locked. Did he have any weapons at all with which to fight back?

Wingfield cleared his throat. "Mr. McNab, how long have you known William Monk?"

"On and off, for about sixteen years," McNab answered. He looked comfortable, his hair brushed back hard off his blunt face. He was dressed neatly, but his suit was very plain, that of an ordinary man who worked hard.

"Professionally or personally?" Wingfield asked.

"Professionally."

"And do you know, to your own knowledge, whether Monk was also acquainted with Mr. Pettifer, the dead man?"

"Not as far as I am aware, sir," McNab said politely. "Mr. Pettifer quite recently told me that he knew Mr. Monk only by repute, as a hard and clever man who was exceptionally good at his job, but prone to take it all a little personally."

Rathbone stood up. "My lord, that is hearsay."

"Indeed it is," Mr. Justice Lyndon agreed. "You know better than to ask your question in that way, Mr. Wingfield. Find some other way to establish the relationship, or lack of it, between the accused and the victim."

"I apologize, my lord. Of course you are right."

In that instant Monk knew that Wingfield had done this on purpose. He now had all the latitude he wished to bring in the supposed acquaintance a great deal more obliquely. It was Rathbone's first slip.

"I believe that in the course of your professional duties, you would work with Thames River Police?" Wingfield continued. "As, for example, on the apprehension of dangerous smugglers, such as gunrunners, perhaps?"

"Yes, sir," McNab said, nodding slightly.

"Did Mr. Pettifer ever work with Mr. Monk on such a case, to your certain knowledge?"

"Yes, sir, he did." McNab's face was almost shining with his anticipation.

"Will you tell the court about it, please?" Wingfield directed him.

Rathbone sat still. There was nothing for him to object to. If he tried, he would only draw even more attention to it.

Monk felt as if they were making a certainty of the verdict against him.

Detail by detail McNab described the knowledge gained by the Customs service and the Wapping Station of the River Police concerning the schooner that was coming upriver with the smuggled guns.

Wingfield did not interrupt him except here and there, reluctantly and to clarify an issue, a time, a state of the tide. It was a good tactic. It made McNab seem uninvolved personally, and it emphasized all the points that were most telling.

"And who knew this exact time and place of the gun smuggling, Mr. McNab?" Wingfield asked gravely.

"I heard just before we left, sir," McNab answered. "Mr. Pettifer arranged it. I don't know if he told anyone else. He said to me that he didn't."

"And what happened, Mr. McNab?"

"The river pirates boarded the schooner, from the downriver side of the smugglers, within seconds of the River Police coming up the side and boarding from the west, the darker side."

"One would presume that was the natural side to board?" It was a question for the jury's benefit.

"Yes, sir. No one would be looking for pirates that way, at that time."

"Indeed. And what happened, Mr. McNab?"

Would Rathbone object that McNab had not been there, and could only know from other people's reports? There was no point. It would make Rathbone look to be out of control, grabbing at anything he thought could distract the jury from the increasingly obvious truth.

"There was a very nasty gun battle going three ways, sir," McNab answered. "The schooner crew were locked below deck and breaking their way out through the hatch. The River Police were on the decks, and the pirates were swarming up the east side of the hull and onto the deck. They could then take advantage of the fact the River Police had locked the crew below and spent most of their ammunition, shooting at them as they tried to break out. And effectively they were marooned there because their own boats had gone when the pirates attacked. They were outnumbered and outgunned."

"A desperate situation," Wingfield said gravely. "What happened? How is it that Mr. Monk, and indeed Mr. Hooper, are still alive?"

"They were badly wounded," McNab said, nodding his head slowly. "And one of them, Mr. Orme, Mr. Monk's longtime friend and mentor, the man who brought him into the force, was killed. Very bad business. He bled to death." He spoke with reverence, as if it were a grief to him also. "Mr. Monk did everything he could to save him, but he could not stop the bleeding. Mr. Hooper was injured also. In fact he is not long back on full duty. Mr. Laker, another young man of Mr. Monk's, was badly hurt, too."

"And this was all brought about by Mr. Pettifer's betrayal to the river pirates?" Wingfield said with amazement. "Why was he not hanged for such a heinous act?"

"No, sir, he was not responsible. But for a time, before we could investigate it thoroughly, it did look like it."

"Then whose fault was it?"

McNab bent his head in apparent sadness.

"A series of mischances, sir. The river pirates have men all over the place. Someone was not careful enough. I'm afraid it happens."

"So Mr. Monk, convinced, as you yourself were for a while, that it was Mr. Pettifer, had a very powerful reason to hate him?" Wingfield said in the silence that followed.

Monk sat in the dock with his fists clenched, his teeth clamped so hard his whole head ached. He had never thought it was Pettifer. He knew damned well that it was McNab himself. And he knew why!

"Yes, sir. I'm afraid he did," McNab said. "He also believed that Mr. Pettifer both drowned and shot Blount. Which of course he didn't! But Mr. Monk became obsessive about it. That is why I believe he was determined to catch Owen himself. He thought there was some huge plan to rob one of the warehouses along the river. Blount was a forger, and Owen an expert in explosives. He thought they were planning, with a couple of other men, to rob Mr. Clive's warehouse."

"And were they?"

McNab was perfectly straight-faced. "Not that we are aware of, sir.

Anyway, Blount is dead and we have good evidence that Owen escaped to France, thanks to Mr. Gillander's assistance."

Wingfield pursed his lips. "You said that Mr. Monk became obsessive about Mr. Pettifer, and his part in the fiasco of the battle with the gun smugglers. Can you give us an example of what you mean, so the court understands? *Obsessive* is a powerful word. It conjures up visions of unnatural behavior."

McNab considered for a moment, as if he had been unprepared for this particular question. "Yes, sir," he said at last. "He has gone over the evidence a number of times, at least four, and sent two of his own men, Mr. Hooper and Mr. Laker, to check on my personal movements leading up to the event."

"Perhaps he is checking to see if he made any errors himself?" Wingfield suggested. "Or possibly that his own men did? He must carry a profound sense of guilt for Mr. Orme's death, on top of his natural grief for a man who did so much for him."

"He was looking for my men's errors," McNab said with contempt. "He knew it was Mr. Pettifer who was going after Owen because of the questions he asked my men about Blount. He got it into his head that there was some large conspiracy involving them, with two other people with high skills, and that Mr. Pettifer was the connection between them. It was frankly ridiculous!"

"Are you certain of this, Mr. McNab?"

McNab nodded. "Yes, sir. Mr. Aaron Clive knew about it because Mr. Monk thought it could have been a robbery planned against Mr. Clive's warehouse, very near Skelmer's Wharf. Mr. Gillander was part of it, too, at least in Mr. Monk's mind."

"I see. And who else has any proof of this . . . conspiracy?"

"No one, sir. I think it was all part of Mr. Monk's revenge for Mr. Orme's death. A shifting of the blame, if you like."

"Thank you. And may I offer you my sympathies for the distress all this must have caused you?" Wingfield added.

"Thank you, sir," McNab said humbly.

Monk was furious. He could feel the rage build up inside him, but he was helpless to do anything about it. He had to sit and listen in si-lence.

Rathbone rose to his feet and walked elegantly to the center of the open space in front of the witness stand as if it had been an arena. Every eye in the room was on him. It was the first time he had moved forward to join battle.

There was a sigh of anticipation around the gallery.

A juror coughed.

"Mr. McNab, you told the court that you have known Mr. Monk, on and off, for about sixteen years, is that right?"

"Yes, sir, I have." McNab was totally unperturbed. This elegant law-yer with his smooth hair and calm, slightly smiling face did not bother him in the slightest.

"So you did not know him in his Californian days, which would be more like twenty years ago?"

"That's right," McNab agreed.

"You have never been to California? In fact you have never been off the shores of Britain, other than for a brief trip to France?" Rathbone continued.

McNab moved position very slightly. He did not like the question. It made him look unsophisticated, a man of narrow experience.

"When you first met Mr. Monk you said it was professionally rather than socially?" Rathbone went on.

"It was."

"Your profession, or his?"

McNab swallowed. He looked steadily at Rathbone. "His," he said at last. Rathbone would have checked anyway. McNab had not been in the Customs or the police at the time.

Rathbone nodded. "Just so," he agreed. "A very tragic affair, I be-lieve . . ."

Wingfield half-rose, then changed his mind and subsided again. Ob-jecting would be futile, and he knew it. Better not to try than to be seen to try, and fail.

McNab's face tightened, but he was not going to help.

Rathbone was far too wise to deliberately lose the sympathy of the jury. "A crime in which your younger half brother, Robert Nairn, was involved, and for which he was hanged. You asked Mr. Monk to intercede for him, to plead for mercy. Mr. Monk did not do so. That is a very brief summary, but is it correct?"

McNab's voice was tight as he agreed it was the truth. If he was trying to conceal his emotion, he did not succeed. It was palpable in the air, like a charge of electricity. His blunt, rather lumpy face was white and his shoulders bulged with the knotting of his muscles.

"And you have resented Mr. Monk ever since for that?" Rathbone sighed. "Misguided. Mr. Monk did not sentence Robert Nairn, nor had he the power to prevent the full execution of the law. But it is understandable. Your half brother paid for his crime with his life, and you with that grief, and that stain upon the rest of your life."

McNab's hand tightened on the rail till his knuckles shone white.

"It would be fair to say that you did not like Mr. Monk, would it not?" Rathbone was still calm, as if they were at a dinner table and the court were fellow guests around it.

"I hate him," McNab agreed. He must have known that denying it would be hopeless. "Just like he hated Mr. Pettifer. Difference is, I didn't kill Mr. Monk. Not that I wouldn't be pleased if it had been the other way round, and Mr. Monk the one as drowned."

"Thank you for your honesty, Mr. McNab," Rathbone said politely. "It makes all this so much easier to understand. It must have been trying indeed to have a man of Mr. Monk's skill and tenacity forever on your tail, after the gun battle and the death of Mr. Orme."

McNab gave an exaggerated shrug. "I can live with it. He's not as dangerous as he thinks he is."

"But you did check to see if any of this big conspiracy theory of his was true?"

"Part of my job."

Wingfield stood up. "My lord, we have already established all of this. My learned friend is wasting the court's time."

Rathbone looked at him with a flash of hope. "Then are you willing to agree that Mr. McNab himself, and with the assistance of Mr. Petti-fer, very thoroughly investigated the entire possibility of a clever rob-bery planned against Mr. Aaron Clive and his warehouses and other premises along the riverbank?"

"Of course he investigated it," Wingfield said. "And found nothing! Again, it is his job, and a courtesy to Mr. Clive that he was happy to af-ford."

"Thank you." Rathbone inclined his head in a tiny bow. "That would explain his frequent and private visits to Mr. Clive, and to Mrs. Clive, both at the warehouse and at their home."

There was a hiss of indrawn breath around the room. Every man in the jury stiffened.

"Your point, Mr. Rathbone?" Mr. Justice Lyndon inquired with in-terest clear in his face.

Wingfield smiled. The jury was staring at Rathbone, and Wingfield and McNab relaxed visibly.

Monk felt a wave of fear run through him. Rathbone had no idea of a defense. He was fishing, and desperately.

Rathbone was still facing the judge. "My point, my lord, is that there is very much more to this case than has been apparent so far. It is some-thing like an iceberg, with by far the largest part of it out of our view. I shall call witnesses who will tell us if Mr. McNab's . . . shall we say ex-tremely discreet . . . visits to Mrs. Clive at her home and their discussing events throw a very different light on the affair. I can, if necessary, call Mrs. Clive herself. The whole matter has roots far into the past, not only concerning the hanging of Mr. McNab's unfortunate half brother."

Now the court was electrified. In the witness stand McNab looked first one way, then the other, as if seeking escape. At least half the men and women in the gallery were staring at him.

Wingfield opened his mouth to protest, and then was uncertain as to what he meant to say.

Monk turned to the warden next to him. "I wish to speak to my lawyer. It is urgent." What the hell was Rathbone playing at?

"I'll see he's told," the warden replied. He was a fair man, and his attitude made it clear he had no particular affection for customs officers.

He had said more than once that he liked his tobacco and resented the duty he paid on it.

"My lord!" Wingfield had decided on his action.

Lyndon looked at him.

"I would like to ask for an adjournment to speak to my witnesses, Mr. and Mrs. Clive, regarding this extraordinary claim from Sir Oliver. I believe he is wasting the court's time, but I need to prepare to meet his . . . tactics, all the same."

Rathbone made no objection, and the judge granted the request.

FIFTEEN MINUTES LATER MONK was alone in the room where accused people were permitted to speak privately with their lawyers.

"What the hell are you doing?" he demanded, fear almost choking his words. "If you question Clive, or Miriam, they'll accuse me of having killed Piers Astley! And God help me, I don't even know if I did. I can't deny it." He could hear the hysteria in his own voice, and it was slipping out of control. This was worse than when he had thought himself guilty of killing Joscelyn Gray. Gray had at least deserved it. He had perpetrated one of the most vile and destructive pieces of deception on the grieving families of the dead from the Crimean War. He had been beaten to death, but he had deserved to hang. Piers Astley had been, by all accounts, a particularly honorable man, not only respected but deeply liked by almost everyone who knew him.

And, unlike the time of Gray's death, when Monk had little in his own life he cared for enough to mourn its loss, now he had everything on earth to live for. Above all he had Hester, a woman he loved with every part of himself. He had a home, a family, friends, a job that was worth doing, and people who trusted him. He wanted to live, with a fierce and consuming hunger, a passion! He wanted to be all that they believed of him.

Rathbone was pale, but he seemed more composed than he had any right to be. This was his professional face. Monk wanted to hit him.

"I am beginning to see a shape to this," Rathbone said quietly. "Even the motive makes no sense—"

"I know that!" Monk snapped at him. "McNab couldn't have known Pettifer would drown. . . ."

"Be quiet and listen!" Rathbone ordered. "We haven't time to waste. Of course he couldn't. It was an opportunity he seized . . . brilliantly. Which means he must have had some other plan before that."

Suddenly Monk saw a thread of light, as thin as spider silk. "And changed when he saw a better chance!" he said.

"Exactly," Rathbone agreed. "I need to find that other plan, and trace it back, then show its foundations, how McNab built on it, and when and how he changed. I think Miriam Clive knows about it."

"To do with Piers Astley? She won't tell—"

"I don't intend to give her a choice," Rathbone said, cutting him off. "I believe that first plan was to make a fool of you, send you after this great robbery plot, which never existed. Done well enough, it would have made you look like a laughingstock. But then when Pettifer died, obligingly at your hand, McNab abandoned that and took up the idea of your revenging yourself on Pettifer for Orme's death. It's very neat. I may have to unravel the whole issue of Astley's death and Miriam Clive's plans to have you solve it in order to expose him."

"And get me hanged for Astley's death?" Monk said bitterly.

"You didn't kill Astley," Rathbone assured him. "Miriam knows who did. She hoped you would help her prove it. Now she knows you can't remember, so it has to be done another way."

"If I take the stand I'll have to admit I can't remember!" Monk took a deep breath. "Still . . . I suppose losing my job is better than losing my life . . ."

"Monk, just be quiet and do as you're told!" Rathbone stood up. "Just . . . just believe in me. And in the rest of us . . ."

"Hester . . . ?"

"We're all working: Hester, Scuff, Crow, Squeaky Robinson . . . even Worm."

Rathbone reached the door just as the guard unlocked it from the other side. He turned and looked at Monk for a moment, then went out.

"C'mon," the guard ordered, glaring at Monk where he stood. "They don't want you no more for now."

Bᴇᴀᴛᴀ ʜᴀᴅ ɪɴǫᴜɪʀᴇᴅ ᴀᴛ the clinic in Portpool Lane when they expected Hester, and she had gone there deliberately at that time, first to
help with the work she was able to do, such as checking on supplies and
funds, and generally assisting Claudine Burroughs, but more urgently to
her, to see Hester herself.

Beata could barely imagine the despair she must be feeling, but
perhaps there was practical help she could offer. Providing a carriage
that Hester could use whenever she wished would be swifter and
pleasanter, especially in this weather, than her having to take an omnibus.

More important than that, she could tell Hester of the memories
she had of San Francisco, of Monk, and the truth Miriam had finally
told her about Aaron Clive. Surely that could not be unconnected with
Piers Astley's death? Hester's imagination and understandings might
show her something Beata had not thought of.

They spoke quietly in the huge kitchen in the clinic. Breakfast was over and it was not yet time for lunch. They sat at the main worktable and had a cup of tea.

Hester listened intently, repeating what Beata told her to be sure she had grasped it properly.

"Yes," Beata agreed, looking at Hester and seeing fear in her eyes. "Miriam knows what happened, and that Monk had nothing to do with it."

"And her revenge on Clive?" Hester almost whispered the words, as if the emotion of it overwhelmed her. She was imagining Miriam's pain as if it had been her own. The pain of losing Monk to the hangman was as deep within her so she could barely fail to understand.

"It will have to wait," Beata said without hesitation. She could not tell Hester how she had hated Ingram, how easily she could share the feeling of helpless loathing. The shame of that still burned her for what she had permitted York to do to her. "I hope she gets it," she went on. "But not at the cost of Monk's life, no matter how dearly she deserves it."

Hester had faced dangers and grief Beata could not imagine, physical privation and overwhelming loss in the Crimea, countless men she could not save, and she had survived it. But now she looked so terribly vulnerable, Beata ached for her. She had no faith in the justice of the law now. Perhaps she was right.

Beata finished her tea and Hester poured more, then realized they needed milk. She stood to fetch it, then clearly forgot where she had put the jug. She was confused because she was angry, angry because she was frightened.

She found the jug and picked it up. Her hand slipped and it fell to the floor and smashed. She used language she must have learned in the army, and blushed scarlet when she realized Beata must have been startled.

Beata stood up, forcing herself to smile quite calmly. It was the depth of Hester's distress that shook her, not the words.

"I've heard that, and worse, in the goldfields," she assured her. She bent to pick up the shards of the jug then fetched a cloth from the sink to mop up the milk. Hester stood helpless, for a moment like a lost child, the tears filling her eyes.

Beata threw away the shards, washed out the cloth, and put it down.

She went back to Hester and abandoned all propriety and the issues that might have stood between them, real or imaginary. She put her arms around Hester, very gently, and held her.

"We will win," she promised, to herself as much as to Hester. "We will not let this happen . . . whatever we have to do!"

It was a wild thing to have said, and she was acutely conscious of it when Rathbone called that evening. Of course it was a complete impropriety, but she had asked him to come, sending a note to his chambers. She must tell him all she knew and make certain he understood that she was prepared to testify, if it would help. And he must force Miriam to speak, if she did not do so willingly. She suggested that if the indiscretion worried him, for his own sake or for hers, that he come through the back entrance, like a messenger or a servant.

He did so, and was in the withdrawing room a little after nine o'clock. Outside, the rain lashed the windows and wind rattled branches against the glass.

Rathbone was so tired his skin was shadowed around his eyes and even his hair was untidy, falling forward where he had run his fingers through it over and over.

"Miriam must be persuaded to testify that Aaron killed Piers," Beata said quietly.

"She can't help, my dear. There is a man who swore an affidavit at the time to say that Aaron Clive was with him at the assay office in San Francisco, forty miles from where Astley was shot," he pointed out.

"Roger Belknap," she agreed. "I know. Actually Belknap was charged with another crime, a robbery, and he was found not guilty because Aaron swore they were together at the assay office."

"Does it matter now? Belknap's testimony stood."

"Because Aaron, whom everybody trusted, swore for him," she said. "Of course he did! Because effectively, Belknap was swearing for Aaron."

He stared at her, blinking as if his eyes were too tired to see clearly. "Are you saying Aaron actually killed Piers himself? Why? He had any number of men who would have done it for a few dollars!"

"And have been in their power forever after . . . unless he killed them, too," she pointed out. "And Piers was very well liked. He ran a great deal of Aaron Clive's business. He was a sort of 'first lieutenant.'"

"So Clive lost his closest friend when his cousin died, and his next closest when Astley was killed?" Rathbone asked.

"And gained the most beautiful woman on the Barbary Coast as his wife," Beata added.

He drew in breath to reply, then changed his mind.

She laughed for the first time since the trial began. "You were going to say that that was hardly a good bargain!" Her amusement was quite open. "Very wise you didn't."

"I suppose she is beautiful," he replied, a little too reluctantly. "It wouldn't matter that much to me. I prefer the beauty from inside that shines through any kind of bone structure or coloring." He looked at her more intently. "But you are certain of what you say? Please be absolutely honest. If I base my strategy on that, it will be disastrous if you are mistaken."

"She knows it, Oliver. She told me so herself. What actually happened is a complete change in direction from McNab's original plan. His first idea for revenge on Monk for Nairn's death was quite different. It was based on a hoax robbery of Clive's business, but in the meantime he drew Miriam in to find out what he could about Monk in San Francisco, hoping to discredit him. Then Pettifer drowned and McNab saw a chance to link that with Piers Astley's murder, showing Monk to be an undoubted killer. He and Miriam exchanged information about Astley's death and about Monk, who she thought might help her. She isn't proud of it, but Astley's death had consumed her, and her growing need to find the truth had driven out everything else. Gillander brought her the evidence only relatively recently," Beata explained. "She had hoped Monk could help her discover the truth, but of course if he ever knew anything he's forgotten it now, along with everything else."

"And McNab waited because he didn't dare attack Monk until he knew he was vulnerable," Rathbone said grimly. "It's . . ." He could not find a word that suited his thought.

"Going to be difficult," she finished for him.

"Please God, that's all it is!" he said gravely.

She had already made her decision. Now she must tell him, with whatever decisions followed from it.

"I will testify, if you wish. But I am not sure what weight will be attached to it."

"I understand that you prefer not to—" he began.

"No, Oliver, you don't," she interrupted him. "I am perfectly willing to testify, for Monk, and for Hester's sake. But you know very little of my time in San Francisco. There are things I haven't told you, because I am ashamed of them." She breathed slowly and steadied herself. "Part of the reason I came home again to England was that my father died. I didn't tell you how. For a while he did very well financially. Then he started to gamble. By the time he died he was in great difficulty. He . . . he cheated at cards, and was caught. He was shot in a bar brawl that was started because he was caught palming cards. It was a scandal at the time. I was a widow, so I didn't have the same name, but everyone knew I was his daughter."

She thought she could get through it all in a flat, clear voice, and without crying, but the tears were thick in her throat now.

"I'm sorry," she added. "It's not very pleasant. Perhaps I should have told you before, but I didn't think I would ever have to."

"You don't have to apologize," he said quietly.

"Yes, I do. Aaron Clive knows, and if my evidence is unpleasant to him, you can be certain he will raise it."

"Does that mean you would prefer not to testify?"

She looked up at him. "No, it does not! I shall testify if I can say anything of use. I'm . . . I'm part of this!" It was a statement of belonging, made with anger because she desperately wanted it to be true.

He slid his hand over hers, very gently. "I know you are. And I want you always to be. As soon as you tell me it is decent to do so, I shall ask you to marry me. And I shall continue to argue the case until you accept me."

She wanted to make some charming, graceful reply, even one that was mildly amusing. Instead of which, she could only be totally serious.

"I think when Monk is safe, and free, we must wait a few months before we speak of it to anyone else, but we may be agreed between ourselves," she said gravely, but with a smile so gentle and so filled with hope he could not have mistaken her emotions.

"Then I had better renew my efforts," he said softly. "We must win."

THE TRIAL RESUMED LATER in the morning. The judge warned Rathbone that he would be required to make good in his extraordinary remarks of the day before. The court would take a very serious view of statements given purely for dramatic effect.

"Yes, my lord," Rathbone said with apparent humility. "Perhaps your lordship would allow me to re-call Mr. Aaron Clive directly?"

Wingfield made no objection, although Beata, looking at him, saw him hesitate for a moment. She was certain he was searching for a reason to disturb Rathbone's plan, his sense of timing, but he could not think of anything that would not be transparent. He knew well enough not to show any vulnerability, any doubt whatever in front of the jury. She had sat through many trials, particularly in the early days of her marriage to Ingram. She had watched him when he was a large presence in front of some of the lesser men who had since succeeded him. That may have been part of the reason he had so disliked Oliver—and he had! She recognized that now.

Aaron Clive crossed the open space around the witness stand. He looked grave and sad as he was reminded of his oath. As always, his manners were perfect, his voice filled with charm.

Rathbone walked out into the open space before the witness box as if totally confident. Perhaps Beata was the only one in the room who knew how very far that was from the truth.

"Good morning, Mr. Clive," he began. "You stated previously in your testimony for Mr. Wingfield that you had occasion to be acquainted with Mr. McNab, of the Customs service. Was this a personal acquaintance, or purely professional?"

Clive smiled. "It was professional, but I did not draw a rigid line between the two."

"Do you mean, sir, that you permitted Mr. McNab to visit you at your home, not only at your place of business? Possibly to discuss certain larger or now more valuable shipments, for example?"

"On occasions, yes." Clive looked puzzled.

"So if I tell you that a witness overheard Mr. McNab in a private conversation with your wife, in your home, you would not find that impossible to believe?"

"Unlikely, but not impossible," Clive conceded. "It was probably no more than courtesy, if I were temporarily unavailable. One does not leave people in solitude." He spoke as if perhaps Rathbone did not grasp such a matter of courtesy.

"Did Mr. McNab ever discuss Commander Monk with you, Mr. Clive?"

Clive should have expected such a question, but he managed to look surprised. Or perhaps he was giving himself time to think of the best answer.

Beata stared at him, as did everyone else in the court. But her thoughts were not on his charm, or his extraordinarily handsome face, or even the skill and courage with which he had built up an empire. She was thinking of the passion she had seen in Miriam's face when she spoke of the death of Piers Astley. Oddly enough, Beata had never considered the possibility that he, not Clive, had been the man Miriam had truly loved. She thought back now, with a different perception, searching for different moments of emotions, mourning and grief. Miriam's voice changed when she spoke of Piers Astley. Beata had thought it a kind of guilt for forgetting him and marrying Clive.

But she had seen what she expected to, what Miriam had asked everyone to see. Perhaps her illness, her fragile bewilderment had been not only from the loss of the child, but from the loss of the man she would always love.

Had Clive the faintest idea of the truth? Or even that Miriam knew what he had done?

How much was her passion for revenge also guilt?

Beata brought her mind back to the present. Clive was testifying. He looked sad, as was appropriate, but totally composed. Would Oliver really have the skill to break him, even to make any mark at all on the perfect surface of his manner? He would be a bad enemy to make. Did Oliver know that? Did he appreciate his extraordinary power? Was he brave, or merely ignorant? She had tried to explain to him.

Clive was talking about the few times McNab had mentioned Monk, not actually to malign him, but certainly to warn of his unreliability.

"Did that surprise you, sir?" Rathbone inquired blandly.

Clive was prepared for that.

"No. It appeared that Mr. Monk had not changed much from the adventurer he used to be when I knew him in San Francisco, twenty years ago," Clive replied with a slight smile. "A man, like many others at that time, always with an eye to his own advantage."

"Oh, yes. You knew Mr. Monk then." Rathbone smiled. "And I believe Mr. Gillander also?"

"Slightly. He ran certain shipping errands for me," Clive said. For a moment he sounded overwhelmingly condescending, and then the tone was gone again, like a shadow over water.

"Did you tell Mr. McNab that Gillander had worked for you?" Rathbone asked.

Clive seemed unconcerned. "Probably. It was of no importance."

"To you, perhaps not. But to Mr. McNab, with his hatred of Mr. Monk, surely it was of great value?" Rathbone asked.

Clive let out his breath. He had made a slight error, very slight, but the fact that he had made it at all was indicative that he was being very careful. There were pitfalls for him that did not wait for an innocent man. Beata saw it, and she knew that Rathbone had.

Wingfield looked impatient. Either he was a very good actor, or he had not seen the shadow. Beata thought it was the latter. There was hope! Frail as early April sunshine, but it was there.

"I did not know of his . . . enmity for Commander Monk," Clive answered slowly.

"I imagine you would have no way of knowing, unless he told you," Rathbone agreed. "And it is not the sort of thing that slips into polite conversation with a man you wish to impress. 'By the way, my half brother was hanged for murder, and Monk could have asked for clemency, but he didn't. I hate him for that and wish to engineer his destruction if I can! I intend to use you to that end.' Not the sort of thing you say at the dinner table."

Wingfield was on his feet, his face darkened by outrage.

"Yes, yes," Lyndon said with a wave of his hand. "Sir Oliver, I am inclined to grant you certain leeway, considering the desperate state of your case, but you stray too far. This observation of yours sounds close to irrelevant."

"My lord, it is most relevant," Rathbone said humbly. "I believe Mr. Clive, unaware of Mr. McNab's emotional investment in Mr. Monk's downfall, may inadvertently have given him information that prompted Mr. McNab's further action."

"Then you must demonstrate that, Sir Oliver," Lyndon warned.

"Yes, my lord. I shall." He turned again to Clive. "Sir, might you have mentioned your suspicions that Commander Monk, or someone very like him, could have been involved in the murder of Piers Astley, your right-hand man in the early days of the gold rush in California?"

Clive stood absolutely motionless. He stared down at Rathbone.

Wingfield fidgeted as if waiting to object but unable to think of any cause. He would look ineffectual if he were overruled.

"Mr. Clive?" Rathbone repeated.

"I doubt it," Clive responded. "But it is possible. Mr. Monk was there. And unfortunately Mr. Astley's killer was never found."

"So I understand," Rathbone agreed. "That must be very hard for you, and especially so for Mrs. Clive."

"Is that a question?" Wingfield demanded from his seat.

"I will put that another way," Rathbone said smoothly, and without turning to acknowledge Wingfield. "Did you ever give up hope of one day finding out who killed Mr. Astley, even if you could not prosecute him, because perhaps he is in a different country?"

"I did not keep up the pursuit," Clive answered. "I imagined that whoever it was would be in California, but quite definitely not in London. It is a painful subject I prefer, for my wife's sake, not to follow when there is little realistic hope of solving it. And, as you point out, even with proof, you would have no jurisdiction over it."

"Exactly," Rathbone agreed. "But it would be indicative of a man's character, wouldn't it?"

"Of course." Clive attempted to look puzzled again, and he must have been aware of what Rathbone was leading to.

"Therefore something Mr. McNab would be happy to have said of Mr. Monk?" Rathbone continued.

"You will have to ask Mr. McNab that."

"I shall. But you have no idea who killed Piers Astley, Mr. Clive?"

"None at all." Clive shook his head. "I was at the assay office forty miles away from the saloon where he was shot."

"Yes, with a Mr. Belknap, I believe."

"Exactly."

"You were able to swear to his presence at the assay office when he was accused of a totally unrelated crime some distance away. Which meant, of course, that he was able to swear to your presence also."

Again Wingfield stirred, and then decided to keep silent.

Beata was watching so intently that it was several moments before she noticed the small boy beside her, in ill-fitting clothes scrubbed clean too many times. He pulled at her elbow again.

"Missus," he said urgently. "Yer gotta listen, Missus." His blue eyes were wide and frightened, and he was missing a front tooth. He looked perhaps six or seven years old.

"Worm?" she said tentatively. She had seen him a couple of times at the clinic in Portpool Lane, and Oliver had told her how bravely he had conducted himself in the rescue of Hester from the farm at which she had been held captive only a short while ago.

"Yes." His face relaxed at her recognition of who he was. "Dr. Crow said as yer gotta ask Mr. Sir Oliver to keep it going as long as he can, 'cos we're finding proof as Mr. wot got drownded din't set up the fight on the ship. It were McNab 'isself, an' all, wi' Mad Lammond, but we got someone as'll swear to it."

She hesitated. How could she explain to the child that the truth didn't matter, it was what Monk had believed that would hang him?

"Please, Missus! Yer gotta tell 'im. Dr. Crow says!"

"I will," she promised. "Will Dr. Crow come with the proof?"

"Yeah. 'E says it in't no good Miss Hester doin' it, 'cos they won't listen to 'er."

The man in the next seat was glaring at them.

"I'll tell him," she promised, and with a quick flashing smile the urchin was gone.

Rathbone was still questioning Aaron Clive. "Piers Astley's killer was never caught?" he asked.

Clive shook his head. "Unfortunately not."

"Could pursuing the truth about Mr. Astley's death be why your wife spoke alone and urgently with Mr. McNab?"

Wingfield stood up. "My lord, this is all repetitive and entirely irrelevant to the charge of murder against the accused. Mr. Monk was seen to strike Mr. Pettifer when he was in the water, as a result of which Mr. Pettifer was unable to save himself, and he drowned. Whether Mr. Clive knew who killed Mr. Astley is of no importance whatever. Sir Oliver is wasting the court's time in an effort to direct our attention away from the facts. It is a very simple case, my lord. And the accused is very clearly guilty."

Mr. Justice Lyndon looked at Rathbone.

Rathbone was very pale. Beata knew what it cost him to keep his composure. She felt for the first time the crushing weight of isolation for a man fighting a battle with every eye upon him, another man's life the prize to be won or lost, and no weapons in his hands. With Ingram she had never appreciated that. It had been more like a game, win or lose. If he had exulted over a win, she saw it; if he had ever grieved over a loss, even wept over it, and felt a wave of guilt or self-doubt, she had no idea.

She must get Worm's message to Rathbone but she could think of no way to do so. He was standing in the center of the floor alone.

"My lord," Rathbone began, "there is no question that Mr. Monk and Mr. Pettifer struggled with each other in the water. Mr. Pettifer panicked and lashed out at the very man who was trying to save his life. He was insane with fear. It is not an uncommon thing to happen. Mr. Monk struck him to keep him from drowning them both. His intent was to render him temporarily unable to strike back, until he could pull him ashore, and save him from drowning in the river. If he had wished him dead, he would simply have stood on the wharf and left him to drown by himself."

There was a murmur of agreement around the gallery, and a couple of the jurors nodded.

"The whole question of guilt rather than misfortune rests upon Mr. McNab's accusation that Mr. Monk hated Mr. Pettifer over incidents that happened in the past," he continued. "To prove that charge untrue, we must examine the past. The very recent past includes Mr. McNab's curious visits to Mrs. Clive. It also includes this idea of a conspiracy to rob Mr. Clive, which Mr. McNab insists that Mr. Monk believed, or pretended to believe. And of course, the escape of two prisoners held by Customs . . . Mr. McNab's men . . . one of whom, Mr. Blount, ended up both drowned and shot! The second, Mr. Owen, was closely involved in Mr. Pettifer's death."

Wingfield rose again. "My lord, Mr. Owen was a considerable distance from Mr. Pettifer when he drowned. If you believe the evidence of Mr. Monk's own man, Mr. Hooper, and of Mr. Gillander, who observed the incident from the deck of his ship, then Mr. Owen was swimming strongly away from Mr. Pettifer when he drowned."

Rathbone smiled. "I was referring to the fight on the wharf, my lord. If Mr. Owen had not escaped and led the chase to the wharf, then jumped into the river, taking the fight into the water, then no one would have drowned."

"Just so," Lyndon agreed.

Beata was aching for Rathbone to question Clive further, and she saw the chance slipping out of his hands. He had killed Piers Astley! That was Miriam's whole purpose for having colluded with McNab in the first place.

Who else could he call? What was it that Crow could tell anyone? If he did not arrive soon then it would all be in vain.

"Thank you, Mr. Clive," Rathbone said firmly. "Please could you wait there in case my learned friend has anything to ask you?"

Beata was desperate. How could she get a message to Rathbone? She did not carry a pencil or paper to make notes, even if she could have stood up and walked over to give it to him.

Wingfield rose and walked out into the area before the witness stand.

"Mr. Clive, you have been very patient with us. May I ask you, did the accused inform you of this . . . conspiracy theory of his? Did he warn you in any way?"

"Yes," Clive agreed. "But vaguely. He did not seem to have any details, except that it might involve specialist skills, such as forgery, and explosives."

Wingfield's eyebrows rose. "Forgery and explosives. It sounds very grand, and very violent. Did you believe him that you were in any danger?"

Clive sounded a little weary.

"Frankly, I thought it very unlikely. Anything as extreme as explosives would alert the whole neighborhood, and very probably damage the exact goods that a thief would value."

"So a little far-fetched?" Wingfield smiled. "You must have wondered about his professional judgment?"

Clive shrugged ruefully. "I regret to say that I did," he said.

"Would it be fair to say further that you had a higher regard for Mr. McNab's professional judgment?"

"Yes, it would."

"Thank you, sir. That is all I have to ask you."

Beata stood up and started to move along the row toward the end so she could reach Rathbone and at last deliver the message.

"That's my foot you've stood on!" a large women said accusingly.

"I'm so sorry," Beata tried to adjust her weight and step aside.

"You'll wait your turn!" her husband said angrily. "We're all hungry, you know."

"I need to deliver—" Beata tried.

The husband stood up, completely blocking the way.

Beata drew in her breath to protest again, and knew it was pointless. By the time she finally reached the aisle all she was able to do was catch an usher's attention.

"Yes, ma'am?" he said politely.

"I'm the widow of the late Mr. Justice York. Will you please tell Sir Oliver Rathbone that I have received a message that further evidence is on its way. This is of extreme importance."

He looked at her blankly.

She was desperate. She hated to remind the man of her position as Ingram's wife, but she saw no alternative.

"I am sure you remember Mr. Justice York," she said sharply. "He presided in this courtroom often enough."

"Oh! Yes, yes, of course, ma'am. I'm sorry . . . I didn't recognize you. Of course. I'll do it right away." And he retreated from his embarrassment without further comment.

"Thank you," she murmured with relief.

THE AFTERNOON BEGAN WITH Rathbone recalling Fin Gillander.

"Mr. Gillander," he began. "You have already sworn to tell the exact truth, without fear or favor. Will you please now tell the court about the occasion on which you saw Mr. Monk after Mr. Pettifer's death and the escape of Mr. Owen?"

"Yes, sir," Gillander replied meekly. He recounted in exact detail Monk's coming to the *Summer Wind* and asking about Owen, who had claimed to be Pettifer, and exactly what Gillander had said and done as a result.

It was more inclusive than necessary, and Wingfield rose several times to complain that Rathbone was wasting time with issues that did not matter. They made not the slightest difference to Monk's guilt or innocence. Rathbone argued every point, which all took up more time than if Wingfield had simply ignored the time-wasting. He must surely have been aware of that? Was he trying to disturb Rathbone's concentration, or simply to make him look desperate?

If that were so, Beata felt as if Wingfield were succeeding, and she hurt inside, with a deep, painful knot in her stomach, for the humiliation Rathbone was suffering, and must know it, but at least it proved that he had received the message.

"Did you find Mr. Monk to be a good seaman when you went down the river on the *Summer Wind,* looking for . . . what was it you said? Some information as to where Mr. Owen had gone, and who might have helped him?"

"Yes, he was very good," Gillander replied with slight surprise.

"You had not expected him to be?" Rathbone's eyebrows rose.

"I knew he was," Gillander answered. "My surprise was that you should ask. Of course he's good. We've hit some pretty rough seas together." He smiled, his handsome face lighting up like a child's with joy at the ultimate adventure, the risk of pitting all against the raw forces of nature.

Wingfield rolled his eyes. "All very dramatic, I'm sure, and possibly a reason to take with a pinch of skepticism anything Mr. Gillander might say in defense of the accused. Sir Oliver has rather made my point for me."

To Beata, his voice was ineffably smug. Where was Crow? Why was he taking so long to arrive? There was nothing she could say or do, and her helplessness ached inside her like a wound.

"Not yet, my lord," Rathbone replied. "Mr. Gillander, did Mr. Monk speak to you about this conspiracy that, according to Mr. McNab, and Mr. Clive, he feared?"

"He told me about the possibility of a robbery, sir. But most pressingly he needed to find out who shot Mr. Blount, and if there was any connection between Mr. Blount and Mr. Owen, other than that both escaped from the custody of Mr. McNab's men. He thought maybe there wasn't."

"There wasn't?" Rathbone said with surprise. "Then he didn't believe in the conspiracy?"

"No, I don't think so. But it's his job to be certain. He had to look into it, no matter how unlikely it was. After all, he'd look a fool if it were real and he hadn't bothered."

"Indeed he would," Rathbone agreed. "And did he find anything?"

"Yes. Found a fellow in the Deptford area, hiding out in a stinking old warehouse, oozing down into the mud. He said Mr. Owen had got out of it to France, as fast as he could, because he was scared stiff of Mr. McNab. He also told us that it was Mr. Pettifer himself who drowned Mr. Blount."

"Told us?" Rathbone asked, with raised eyebrows.

"Yes, sir. Commander Monk, and me," Gillander explained.

"Drowned him?" Rathbone said, as if with surprise. "Who shot him?"

"Not certain, sir. Customs man, but could have been another one."

"How interesting," Rathbone murmured, almost as if to himself. "I begin to see sense in all of this."

"That's a great deal more than I do, my lord!" Wingfield protested. "What Sir Oliver tells us he sees, or thinks he begins to see, is neither here nor there. With respect, my lord, how long are we to endure this charade?"

"Until I say otherwise, Mr. Wingfield," the judge snapped, but his patience was wearing thin also, and Rathbone had to be conscious of that.

"My lord," Rathbone said meekly, "I will have a witness with crucial evidence on this tomorrow, but may I, in the meantime, call Lady York, widow of the late Mr. Justice Ingram York, to the stand? I regret that she has been in court throughout most of this case, and therefore already heard the evidence presented, but I have only just appreciated that she has evidence of her own knowledge that may clear up much."

He had not wanted to call Beata but he was desperate for anything to play for time.

Wingfield threw his hand up in the air. "My lord, what on earth can the respectable widow of an eminent judge know of the stinking slums of Deptford, or what some drunken sot has to say on the drowning of an escaped forger? This is beyond preposterous."

"Sir Oliver?" the judge asked skeptically.

Rathbone still looked a little pale, and he did not move with his usual grace. "I don't imagine Lady York knows anything of Deptford, my lord. I did not mean to suggest that she did. But she does know a great deal about San Francisco in the gold rush days, since she lived there herself. And she has been acquainted with Miriam Astley, as she was then, and with Piers Astley, whose death seems to haunt these proceedings, and with Aaron Clive, the king of that society. She may also have had some knowledge of both Mr. Gillander in his youth, and of William Monk. I think the court may find her information pertinent in several ways."

"Does Lady York still have the acquaintance of Mr. and Mrs. Clive, Sir Oliver? And is she well enough, after her recent bereavement, to take the witness stand?"

"She still has the acquaintance of Mr. and Mrs. Clive," Rathbone answered. "Indeed, since her bereavement they are the only close friends she has visited regularly, in connection with the endowment of a chair at a university in the name of the late Sir Ingram York. And she is quite well."

"Then proceed, but I warn you that if you are wasting the court's time, I will not take an agreeable view of it. It may all be very dramatic, but this is not a theater, Sir Oliver, and a man's life is at stake."

"Just so, my lord. Thank you."

Beata was conducted across the floor by the same usher to whom she had given the message. She took the stand and was sworn. She felt a trifle giddy. She had not realized that the steps up to the witness box were so narrow, or so steep. She did not resist the impulse to hold on to the rail in front of her. She knew she must have looked nervous.

"Lady York," Rathbone began gently. She must not smile at him as if she knew him. She must appear impartial. "I believe you lived in San Francisco for some time, including a year of the gold rush that we are all familiar with, of 1849. Is that so?"

"Yes."

"During that time, did you know some of the people now involved in this trial, specifically the accused, William Monk? Or Piers Astley, who was murdered in 1850? Or Fin Gillander, who owns the schooner

Summer Wind, and the then Miriam Astley, and her present husband, Aaron Clive?"

"Yes, I knew all of them except William Monk. I knew him only by sight, and by reputation."

"Indeed? And what was his reputation?"

"As a brave man, a good sailor, but not someone you wanted to cross. Though he was unusual in that he was looking for adventure, not gold. Rather like Fin Gillander." Should she tell the whole truth? Rathbone had not asked her for it. But it was part of the story. She knew that now better than he did. "Except that Fin, like a lot of men, was in love with Miriam Astley. He was about twenty, and she was more than that, as was I. But it was quite hopeless, and he knew it, because she had never loved anyone else but her husband."

"Her husband then, Piers Astley, or her husband now, Aaron Clive?"

"Her husband then, Piers Astley."

"The man who was murdered?"

"Yes."

"Why do you mention them, Lady York? Are you somehow suggesting that Fin Gillander had something to do with his death?"

"No. I'm sure he had not. Nor had Mr. Monk. Miriam knows now who killed him, and she has evidence that is proof to her, beyond question." She took a deep breath and heard the gasps of a hundred people around the room.

Rathbone's voice brought her back to the moment.

"Lady York, if she has proof of someone's guilt, why does she not accuse him and have him charged?"

"Because it is proof only to her. You do not shoot at a bear unless you are sure you are going to kill it. If you only wound it, then it will kill you."

There was a ripple of nervous laughter around the room, then a wash of silence, like a returning wave.

"Do I take it that the person who killed Piers Astley has great power?" Rathbone asked. "And they would destroy Mrs. Clive were she to accuse them, and fail to get them convicted?"

"Yes." She had no hesitation now. "That is why she wanted to involve Mr. Monk in the case. She believed he had the power to win a conviction. Of course she did not at that time know that Mr. McNab was exercising his passion for revenge against Mr. Monk, for the hanging of his half brother for a crime which he unquestionably did commit." She took another deep breath. She must make a good job of this: no half measures. "I was married to a lawyer and judge for years. It was not difficult to look up the records of the case. I knew where to look and what to ask. There was no question of Rob Nairn's guilt. Mr. Monk might have asked for leniency, but it would not have been granted."

"Let me understand this, Lady York. Mrs. Clive was seeking justice, or if you prefer, revenge, for the murder of her first husband. At the same time Mr. McNab was seeking revenge against Mr. Monk for not having requested clemency for his half brother. And to this end they were each using the other?"

"Yes. Briefly."

"Taking these issues one at a time, how was Mr. McNab hoping to be revenged on Mr. Monk?" Rathbone asked her.

She drew in her breath, hesitating as long as she could. She glanced around the room. Please heaven Crow would turn up soon. She could not string this out much further.

"By setting up what appeared to be a monstrous conspiracy to rob Aaron Clive, and when Mr. Monk had warned Mr. Clive of it, it would turn out to be a hoax, and Mr. Monk would look like a fool," she replied. She could feel the jurors' eyes upon her and hear the whisper of slight movement from their seats.

"Do you have some evidence of this?" Rathbone looked dubious.

"No, but you do," she told him. "It has already been given in court. It concerns the escapes of both Mr. Blount and Mr. Owen from McNab's custody, which is not the coincidence it appears. And then Mr. Blount's death, and Mr. Owen's escape from London altogether."

"But where is this conspiracy then?" Rathbone looked puzzled. Surely he was pretending that for effect?

"Then Mr. Pettifer drowned in the river, while Mr. Monk was trying to rescue him," she answered to fill the yawning silence. "Mr. McNab could not have foreseen that, but it was a far simpler and more powerful revenge than he could have created. He abandoned the conspiracy and accused Mr. Monk of having killed Mr. Pettifer on purpose."

Rathbone made a gesture of confusion with his hands.

"But all the evidence of Mr. Monk's hatred for Mr. Pettifer because of the gunrunning ship fiasco, and Mr. Orme's death!" he protested. "What about that?"

"We have only Mr. McNab's word that it was Mr. Pettifer behind the events that led to Mr. Orme's death," she replied. She was desperate now, arguing with Rathbone. How long would the judge let her do that? "What if Mr. Pettifer were no more than a lieutenant, carrying out Mr. McNab's orders . . . just as he appears to be?" she went on.

"It makes sense, Lady York, but that is very far from proof! What proof have you of any of this?"

She felt as vulnerable as a black fly on the middle of a huge, white plate. When she spoke her voice was hoarse, almost whispering. "You will have to ask Dr. Crow's witness for that. Or Miriam Clive herself."

"Thank you, Lady York. I shall do both."

At last Wingfield stood up. She had temporarily forgotten that of course he would have the opportunity to cross-question her as well. Rathbone could not protect her from that.

She faced him as if he had been a spider, of the sort that eats flies. She found herself gulping for breath, and he had not even spoken.

"I am sorry you are placed in this predicament, Lady York," Wingfield said gently. "First of all, may I offer you my condolences on the death of your late husband. He was a very fine man. I knew him well, and he will be deeply missed."

Was that a smirk on his face? She felt the blood burn up her cheeks at the thought that Ingram might have boasted to such a man of the things he had caused her to do! Would she ever live that down? Was he mentioning Ingram now on purpose? A warning to her of what he knew?

She stared at him with defiance, even hatred, as if he were Ingram. They even had the same color of eyes!

He was waiting for her to thank him.

"Thank you," she said coldly.

"I am sure you are deeply distressed," he went on, his voice even gentler, and now holding a little pity.

Good God! She knew what he was going to do! He was going to suggest to the court that her mind was unhinged by grief, and she was not to be taken seriously.

Very deliberately she smiled back at him. She must not, she would not, let him win.

"Fortunately for me I have had considerable time to become used to the idea, Mr. Wingfield. Ingram was ailing far more than most people knew for some time before he had his seizure. In fact, I have been prepared for widowhood for nearly two years. And I am well provided for, both financially and with good friends. I consider myself most fortunate. And poor Ingram is at last at peace. But while I thank you for your courtesy, I am sure the court is interested only in the truth of this case. What is it you wish to know?" She smiled back at him now with exactly the same gentle patronage he had exercised toward her. She hoped he recognized it.

"I am puzzled by what you are referring to as 'Dr. Crow's witness,'" he said, but perhaps not with quite the overwhelming confidence he had had before. "What was it regarding?"

She would have to make it up! "The death of Mr. Blount, which appears to have begun the idea of a conspiracy," she replied.

"And the reference to crows?" he pressed.

She raised her eyebrows a little, as if his ignorance surprised her. "I believe it is the slang term for a doctor, among some people."

"People you know, Lady York?" he asked incredulously.

"Affectionately, yes. Is that of relevance, Mr. Wingfield?"

He considered pressing it again, and changed his mind.

She prayed fervently that Crow's witness would turn up very soon. She was struggling to think of anything more to say.

There was a moment's rather stiff silence. An usher crossed the floor to speak to Rathbone. Suddenly the tension in the room mounted, as if a tingle of excitement had rippled through the air. All the jurors were facing him as Rathbone smiled.

"My lord, Dr. Crow's witness has arrived. I would like to excuse Lady York and call Albert Tucker to the stand."

Lyndon bit his lip and leaned a little forward behind his magnificent carved bench.

"This had better be relevant, Sir Oliver. I share Mr. Wingfield's dislike of theatrics!" There was a touch of sarcasm to his tone. He disliked Wingfield's own theatrics just as much. "If Mr. Wingfield has finished his questions you are excused, with our thanks, Lady York."

Wingfield agreed and with overwhelming relief she thanked him and, grasping the rail, came carefully down the stairs and across the floor to take her seat again.

Albert Tucker came in conducted by another usher, and took the stand. He was a lean man wearing a blue pea coat. He had a weather-beaten face and narrow, blue eyes, as though he were permanently squinting against the light reflected off the water.

He swore to his name and his occupation as a lighterman on the Thames.

Rathbone came straight to the point. He knew the court's patience was wearing thin.

"Did you pull the body of a dead man out of the river, who was later identified as Blount?"

"Yes, sir. Me and Willis, sir. We reported 'im straightaway."

"To the River Police?"

He shook his head. "No sir. 'E were drownded. Weren't no reason not ter give 'im straight to the Customs, since 'e were escaped from them, like."

"How did you know that his name was Blount, or that he had escaped from the custody of the Customs service?" Rathbone asked curiously.

"'Cos they bin asking after 'im. I seen 'im before, anyway. 'Anging around the waterfront, like, where 'e practiced 'is business."

"And when you pulled him out of the water, he was dead?"

"Yeah. Drownded."

"Not shot?" Rathbone affected surprise.

"No, sir, just drownded."

"Are you quite certain of that, Mr. Tucker? Because when Mr. McNab called in the River Police, specifically Mr. Monk, Mr. Blount was quite definitely shot in the back."

"Yes, sir. But Mr. Blount weren't shot when Mr. Willis an' me pulled 'im out o' the water an' gave 'im ter Mr. McNab."

Rathbone looked astonished.

"How can you be sure? Did you examine him? Did he have a coat on? Might you not have missed a bullet hole, particularly if the water had washed away any blood, as it might?"

"No, sir." Tucker looked a little uncomfortable. He shifted his weight from one foot to the other.

Rathbone looked totally unperturbed. Did he really feel it, or was it a desperate mask? "How can you be?" he asked.

"Can I turn around, me lord?" Tucker asked the judge. He, too, looked unhappy now.

"If it serves some purpose," Lyndon said.

Tucker turned around slowly in a full circle until he was facing Rathbone again. In the gallery one could have heard a pin drop.

Tucker swallowed. "This is the coat," he said quietly. "It were a very good coat, an' Blount didn't need it ter get buried in! Willis and I tossed a coin for it! I won. It fits me better anyway. 'E'll get the next one."

"It certainly has no holes in it," Rathbone agreed. "It was . . . brave of you to wear it here, in the circumstances. Did it not worry you that his lordship might take a dim view of your stealing the coat off a dead man?"

Tucker gulped hard and shivered. "Yeah . . . it did. Reason I din't come forward before. But now I know as Mr. Monk's in trouble, an' it were Mr. McNab as had've shot Blount, even though 'e were as dead as a fish anyway. Dr. Crow told me as I must say wot I know."

"Did he offer you any reward for doing this?" Rathbone inquired.

"No, sir."

"Or punishment if you did not?"

"No, sir."

"Thank you, Mr. Tucker. Will you please remain there so my learned friend Mr. Wingfield may question you also."

Tucker looked extremely unhappy, but he had no choice.

Wingfield rose to his feet and walked over toward the stand. He looked up at Tucker as if regarding some piece of refuse that had been left by the tide.

"Do you often steal from the dead, Mr. Tucker?" he asked.

There was a gasp around the gallery.

"You never bin poor an' cold, or yer wouldn't ask like that," Tucker replied, his chin raised a little. "It were flotsam, washed up on the tide, like. 'E didn't need it ter be buried in. 'E were perfectly decent as 'e were. Didn't take 'is shirt nor 'is trousers."

"His boots, perhaps?" Wingfield asked sarcastically.

Tucker glared at him. "As if I'd take a man's boots!" he said outraged.

"So you say." Wingfield managed by the inflection of his voice to patronize a man he physically had to look up at. "And you are willing to come here in his coat, and swear, in front of Mr. Justice Lyndon, that the coat you are wearing is the same one you took off the corpse of Mr. Blount, who was both drowned and shot first?"

"'E could 'a drowned by accident," Tucker pointed out. "An' 'e weren't shot until Mr. McNab got a hold of 'im. I reckon 'e did that so 'e 'ad a reason to call Mr. Monk in."

"And I reckon that Mr. Monk's dubious friends up and down the riverbank are lying to gain credit with the River Police, which they will expect to be repaid in kind!" Wingfield snapped back at him.

Tucker was insulted. He gripped the rail and leaned forward, his face pinched with anger. "If I wanted ter do that, Mister, I'd 'ave said I saw McNab shoot the corpse. An' yer got no right ter call me a liar when I'm tellin' the sworn truth."

"You wouldn't know the sworn truth if it bit you!" Wingfield said almost under his breath, but the closer members of the jury must have heard him, as he returned to his seat.

Rathbone hesitated, then rose to his feet and stepped forward.

"Mr. Tucker, have you ever been convicted of lying, to anyone?"

Beata closed her eyes and held her breath.

"No, sir," Tucker said firmly. "Willis 'as. That's why Dr. Crow said as it should be me as comes 'ere, wearin' the coat so you could see it yourself."

Rathbone let out a sigh. "Thank you, Mr. Tucker. As far as I am concerned, you are free to go."

Mr. Justice Lyndon smiled with bleak humor. "I would take that chance, Mr. Tucker, if I were you. Keep warm in your dead man's coat. It's a shame to waste a good garment."

Tucker thanked him and made his escape.

"My lord, I have one more witness only," Rathbone said, glancing at the tall windows and the fading sun beyond them. "I believe I can be brief."

"Then call your witness, Sir Oliver," Lyndon replied.

"I call Miriam Clive to the stand."

There were several moments of hesitation. People craned their necks round to watch. Then there was a gasp of indrawn breath as she appeared. Until now, for most of the court, she had been a creature of legend. Finally they saw her, and she met all their expectations. She had always been beautiful, but with her face pale with fear and her head high she was breathtaking. As if she were going to her own execution, she walked up the aisle between the rows, not once glancing to either side. She crossed the open space of the floor and mounted the steps. She swore to her identity, and that she would tell the truth, all of it, and nothing else. Then she faced Rathbone as she would have the headsman with the ax already in his hand. She was dressed in a burgundy so dark it was almost black, and her luxuriant hair was drawn away from her face to emphasize her high cheekbones and her marvelous eyes.

Even Rathbone was impressed. Beata saw it in his very slight hesitation. She was barely aware that her own hands were so tightly clenched they hurt. What would Miriam say? She had been waiting for years for this chance to damn Aaron!

Beata tried to remember what she had said, and what she had only thought to say. Did Oliver even believe her? Could he imagine, here in midwinter London, in the Old Bailey, what the heat of summer and gold had been like in the wild country of California twenty years ago? Gold fever was another world!

"Mrs. Clive," Rathbone began graciously, "I believe your first marriage was in California, before the gold rush of 1849?"

Wingfield was on his feet immediately. "This is irrelevant, my lord. Sir Oliver is wasting time again!"

"You opened the door to the past in San Francisco, at that time, Mr. Wingfield." Lyndon turned to Miriam. "You may answer the question, Mrs. Clive."

"Yes, it was." Her voice was almost expressionless. She was fighting to keep her emotions in control. Beata knew that, because she knew Miriam. Did she look vulnerable to the court, the jury, as if she barely kept from breaking? Or did they see her as rich and beautiful . . . spoiled by fate? How far that was from the truth. Her beauty had not been a blessing.

"To Piers Astley, who was very tragically killed in 1850?" Rathbone continued.

She cleared her throat. "Yes. He was shot to death in a saloon bar, about forty miles outside San Francisco."

"Was it a brawl of some kind? An accident?"

"No. It was in one of the back rooms, and he was alone with the man who murdered him," she replied. Now the emotion in her voice was raw and no one could have failed to hear it.

Rathbone kept his voice calm and level. "If you were not there, Mrs. Clive, how do you know this?"

Again the room was utterly silent.

"Witnesses," she said simply. "To the fact, not as to who fired the shot."

"I see. Do you know who it was?"

"I didn't at the time. I do now."

There was a gasp around the room like wind in piles of fallen leaves.

Wingfield half-rose in his seat, caught the judge's eye, and changed his mind. He sank back without interrupting.

"Was it William Monk?" Rathbone asked.

"No. I never thought it was. But I did at one time believe that he might have been able to help me prove the truth."

The judge leaned a little forward over his high, carved bench but he did not speak. None of the jurors appeared even to blink.

"But you discovered that in fact he knew nothing," Rathbone asked.

Beata held her breath. Be careful! Be careful!

"Yes . . ."

Rathbone went on before Miriam could add anything.

"Did Mr. McNab approach you about the matter, or did you approach him?" Rathbone asked.

Miriam winced very slightly. "No. When I heard from my husband that there was a degree of ill feeling between Mr. McNab and Mr. Monk, I approached Mr. McNab, very discreetly."

"To what end, Mrs. Clive?"

"To the end of persuading Mr. Monk to tell me what he knew about Piers's death. If he had been willing to speak, he would have done so at the time. I thought if Mr. McNab knew something against Mr. Monk I could maybe use it as leverage to persuade him to help me prove who had killed Piers."

"Let me understand clearly: You were prepared to use Mr. Monk to expose whoever killed your first husband? You already knew who it was, but you needed proof? Is that correct?"

"Yes." She was breathing very deeply, trying to steady herself.

"Did you explain any of this to Mr. McNab?" Rathbone continued.

"As much as necessary. He did not need a great deal. Until Mr. Pettifer's death, he was very keen indeed to convince Mr. Monk that there was a major conspiracy to rob my husband's warehouses."

"Until Mr. Pettifer's death?" Rathbone repeated with increased interest. "And after that?"

"After a while he let the matter drop," she replied. "I think that, unintentionally, Mr. Monk provided him with a far better means of revenge. He gave it to him as if it were a gift."

"So Mr. McNab no longer needed your assistance?"

"That is correct. And I no longer needed his," she added. "Mr. Monk had no idea who killed Piers."

"But you know?"

"Yes. I have known ever since I was brought the bloody shirt he was wearing when he died. I knew it was his because I stitched it myself. Most women can tell their own stitching, especially on a large piece of work. They know how they turn a collar, or set a sleeve."

Every eye in the room was on her.

"That was proof?" Rathbone said with surprise.

"No. The proof was in where it was found, and in whose possession." She stopped. It was obviously extremely difficult for her to keep any composure at all. Her body was shivering as if she were standing in an icy wind.

Beata had to imagine what it must have been like holding her husband's shirt, soaked in his blood. Even that thought made her head swim, and she felt sick.

"And that proved . . . ?" Rathbone's voice was hoarse.

"That, and a deed for land on the American River where there had been much gold found," she added.

"I see."

"Proof of death," she said, choking on her own words. The tears were now sliding down her cheeks. "And proof of payment for the act."

"And someone's guilt?" he asked.

The room was so still Beata could hear her own breathing.

"Yes. It was found in the belongings of a dead man. His name was Belknap. The man my husband, Aaron Clive, was with at the time of the murder of Piers, forty miles away."

"Are you saying that Mr. Belknap killed Piers Astley, and Aaron Clive lied to protect him?" Rathbone said incredulously.

"No . . . you fool!" she cried out in desperation. "He lied to protect Aaron! Belknap was committing a robbery miles away, as he was justly accused at the time! Aaron lied, saying he was with Belknap, supposedly to protect him. But it was actually so Belknap could protect Aaron! I only learned of it when Fin Gillander brought me the news that

Belknap was dead, and he had the shirt Piers was wearing when he was shot, which he had found and kept as evidence, plus the deed for the land that Aaron gave him, for his silence."

"Yes," Rathbone said very quietly. "I see. He kept it to safeguard his own life?"

"Yes!"

Rathbone turned to Wingfield. "I think that settles an old crime and a present tragedy. You can do nothing about the murder of Piers Astley, except clear all others of blame. What you do about Mr. McNab is your own affair. The Board of Customs will no doubt wish to question him regarding the sabotaging of the Thames River Police operation against the gunrunners, and the resulting death of Mr. Orme. But I trust you will now withdraw your charge against Commander Monk in the unfortunate drowning of Mr. Pettifer, who seems to have been an unsavory character, willingly misled by his superior, and drowned in spite of Monk's efforts to save him."

Lyndon was nodding slowly.

In the jury box all the men began to relax. A couple even smiled.

Around the gallery there was a sigh as tension was let slip. There were rustles of movement.

Wingfield rose to his feet.

"The Crown wishes to withdraw its case against William Monk, my lord. The other matters I would like to take under advisement, if the court pleases."

"Indeed," Mr. Justice Lyndon agreed. "The court does please." He looked up toward the dock. "Commander Monk, you are free to go."

Beata sat motionless, letting tears of relief fill her eyes and slip down her cheeks. She looked across at Rathbone and found that he was already looking at her.

15

It was dark when Monk awoke. For an instant he did not know where he was. He heard the banging somewhere below him. It sounded like someone trying to force a door. Fool. No one broke out of this kind of prison.

Then he realized he was warm, and the stench of soiled bodies and human waste was not there. The air smelled sweet.

He was at home! Hester was beside him. It wasn't a dream; he was definitely awake—wasn't he? Or was this an illusion, and he was going to seem to waken again and again, until he really awoke to reality, and find he was still in prison?

The banging on the door was still going on.

Hester stirred. It must have been the first night for ages that she had slept properly, but it penetrated even the depth of her sleep.

Monk heard feet on the stairs, light and rapid. Then he remembered. Scuff had been home last night, to celebrate.

The banging stopped. Scuff must have let someone in. Monk lay without moving. If the whole of London was on fire, tonight he did not care. His head ached; in fact his whole body ached. He could sleep all night and all the next day. Perhaps he would.

There was a sharp rap on the door.

"What is it?" Monk asked quietly, turning up the gaslight.

Scuff came in, wearing a nightshirt with a blanket around his shoulders. He was almost as tall as Monk now.

"Mr. Gillander's here," he replied. "He says can we come and help him. Clive has taken Miriam and he's gone out to sea. Mr. Gillander says he'll take her to France, or maybe he'll just dump her overboard."

Monk was instantly awake. He slid out of bed as Hester sat up, awake now, too.

"Yes, of course I'll come," Monk answered. "I'll get dressed and be down in three or four minutes. Tell him I'll be there."

"Yes, sir," Scuff said, going out and closing the door.

"I'm sorry," Monk told Hester. "She broke him. He won't forgive her for that. He'll probably kill her one day, but slowly. He'll make her suffer first."

She sat up. "Why didn't they arrest him last night?" She started to get out of bed.

"For what?" he asked.

She closed her eyes and sighed. "I don't know! I suppose she knew that, too!"

"Stay there." He pushed her gently back, and kissed her. "There's nothing you can do. You did it already, finding Tucker."

"Are you going to take Hooper?" she asked.

"There's no time. We can manage the *Summer Wind* with just two of us." He pulled on his clothes, the heaviest he could find: thick trousers, socks, sea boots, and a Guernsey sweater. He would get his pea coat from downstairs. There was no time to shave, although no need. He kissed her quickly. He hesitated a second, then let go of her and went to the door.

In the hall, the gaslight was turned up high. He went down the stairs and found Gillander, ashen-faced and unshaven, in the hall.

"She went to Lady York's house last night, but Clive broke in and took her. It was their footman that came to tell me. Are you ready?" He did not waste time in apologies for getting him out of bed.

Before Monk could answer Scuff came in, looking almost like a man in his thick, river-edge clothes and a pea coat not much different from Monk's. He, too, was wearing sea boots.

Monk drew in breath to say he could not come, but Gillander spoke first.

"Good man," he said briefly, then opened the door to the darkness outside. Scuff went straight after him, ahead of Monk.

There was a hansom at the curb and Gillander gave the driver instructions for the dockside as he swung in. Scuff and Monk followed him.

They rode in silence. There was nothing to ask because Gillander himself would know little until they reached the water. It did not matter now who had brought him the news, only how fast they could get the *Summer Wind* under sail and go after Clive.

The streets were dark and wet and the wind was rising. They moved as fast as they could. The cabbie must have a good horse to go at this speed.

They pulled up at the dockside and Gillander handed the driver a fistful of coins. It must have been a couple of pounds' worth! The man looked at it, saw the silver in the light of his carriage lamps, and thanked him.

The *Summer Wind* was moored close in and its rowing boat tied up at the foot of the steps. They went down carefully, knowing the wet stones would be slippery. Without a word they got into the boat and loosed it. Monk and Gillander took the oars, pulling together, falling into rhythm without a word.

They rowed toward the lee side of Gillander's ship. The river was already choppy and the sky overhead dense with cloud. The low moon in the west gave a little light so the other ships nearby rode on glimmering water, now and then catching a crest of white foam.

It was going to be a rough night. They would be able to recognize Clive's ship only by its rigging—if Gillander knew it. It was named the

Spindrift, and Monk reckoned it would be no more than a mile ahead of them. If the moon clouded over completely, they would see only its riding lights.

He had no more time to think. They shipped the oars and set about climbing up the ropes to board the schooner, then winched up the smaller rowboat and made it fast.

"We'll put up the foresail," Gillander said, looking at Monk. Then he turned to Scuff. "D'you know how to raise the anchor?"

"No, sir. I'm a doctor. I can sew but not sail," Scuff replied, regret in his voice.

"Please God we won't need those skills," Gillander answered him. "Just keep out of the way, and do as you're told."

Actually, Scuff had underestimated his own natural common sense. As they raised the foresail Gillander raised the anchor and steered them out into the mainstream of the river and the choppy tide. It was hard work. The wind was strong, and increasing all the time. It pulled hard as the sail filled and billowed out.

Gillander yelled, "Keep it short!" but Monk was already lashing the ropes. The ship plowed forward, slamming down hard on the water and sending the spray high.

It took several minutes to get it exactly right, Gillander at the wheel and Monk on the foredeck, now and then shouting back. They worked as one, as if it were long seasoned in habit. They passed many ships moored ready to unload their cargoes, in their turn. It was too early for the strings of barges to be moving yet, but of course there were the few ferries that ran all night.

Monk stared forward all the time into the darkness, watching, signaling what he saw. Gillander had told him that Clive's boat was also a two-master. It was swift and graceful, too: a sailor's ship. This was going to be a test of skills, and of courage. Who could sail closest to the wind? Who could turn and tack the most smoothly, judge the wind and the current exactly right? The navigation would be largely by sight, judging the distance of the lights, until they were clear of the Estuary. After that, in the open sea, only speed would matter.

The wind was increasing all the time, from the northeast. If it swung around it would make a difference, especially if it bore due west. Then it would be directly against them, beating them back toward the coast of England, where they would risk either running aground on the shoals, or striking the rocks and being broken into pieces.

It was getting a little lighter, the sky paling in the east.

Monk peered into the ever-moving shadows ahead. Was that the outline of a ship, or only wind patterns on the waves? Then he saw the green riding light. The red port light should be to the left of it. Only it was to the right! The ship was coming toward them.

He shouted back to Gillander, waving his arms.

Gillander pulled the wheel, throwing his weight against it. As they listed heavily to port, Monk had to scramble to gain his balance.

The other ship swept past them, twenty yards clear. It was a three-masted schooner heading south, toward the flat Kent shore, which they couldn't see in the gloom.

"Scuff!" Gillander shouted above the roar of the wind and water.

Scuff turned immediately. He was longing to help.

Gillander waved. "Go help Monk shorten sail, then tell him to come back here and take the wheel. I'm going to see if I can get the jib up, too. We need to go faster if we're to catch the *Spindrift*."

Scuff obeyed instantly.

Monk watched him. He knew by the stiffness of his arms and back that he was afraid. They all knew that a man overboard in this sea was lost. No matter how hard anyone tried, they would never come about in time and go back to the same spot to find a lost body in this heavy and pitching sea.

He clambered forward, conscious of the line about his waist, and finally reached Monk.

"He says to shorten the sail!" Scuff shouted.

Monk signaled that he had heard, and with gestures rather than words he instructed Scuff how to balance his weight, brace his body, and hold the rope.

Watching him, Gillander brought the ship around tighter into the wind and for a moment the sails felt slack. They worked hard and fast. Gillander swung them round again gently and the sail billowed out, hurling them sideways and all but pitching Monk over the side. He lunged forward and caught Scuff as he lost his footing. Spray flew up and stung their skin like pellets of ice. They were under way again, moving forward fast.

Ten minutes later they saw the riding lights of a two-masted schooner ahead of them. The light was clearer now, as the dawn was paling in the east, right above the prow. The other ship was moving fast, east by southeast, across the wind, as they were.

"The *Spindrift!*" Gillander shouted above the whine in the rigging, and the surge and break of the water. "That's her."

Monk felt as if time had disappeared. He was on the Barbary Coast again with the surge of the Pacific under the keel and the endless horizon stretching all the way up to the Arctic Ocean and the great white mountains of Alaska. Every man was alert with his skill, pitched against the sea, and yet in a way deeper than any understanding of the mind, at one with it.

On the land any man might be your enemy, your rival for fame or gold or the love of a woman. Out here he was your brother in war against the sea.

They worked together, Monk, Gillander, and Scuff, speeding forward, then keeling over, swinging the boom, righting up again, and tacking the other way. Tightening sail, driving forward, always closing the distance between them and the *Spindrift*. The wind was blowing harder, whipping up white crests on the back of every wave, hurling the *Summer Wind* forward. They were flung up, and jarred down again crashing on the water as if it were stone. How the ship did not break under the impact Monk would think about only afterward.

Then, he thought with amazement, does it matter? His vanished years might have all kinds of treasures, or ugly stretches haunted by loneliness and error. So has everyone else who has ever seized life and ridden it into the storms, and the light beyond. If he had forgotten the good, then he had forgotten the bad as well. He had come so close to absolute desolation standing in the dock, unable to speak for himself, afraid of everything, even the truth.

And his friends had saved him—partly because they cared, and partly because the truth was good, difficult, but so much brighter than he had feared. It was time to accept help, love, error, and be grateful for all of it.

They were closing on the *Spindrift*. What the devil was Gillander going to do when they caught up?

One more tack and, if they judged it exactly right, they would be alongside. Then what?

Monk waved his arms, pointing toward the ship now only a hundred yards ahead of them and to their right. He turned his hands up in a gesture of question.

Gillander took his right hand off the wheel and waved it in the air as if he had a sword in it.

Scuff gave a whoop of joy.

"You're going to stay here and hold the ship," Monk told him. "Someone has to." He saw Scuff's face drop. "And defend the ship against boarders," he added. "Don't know how many crew they've got. You'll be the only man here."

Scuff's face became very sober.

The broadening light was gray on the wave caps now, and dark, shining shadows ran across their unbroken backs and the white spume here and there was less fierce.

The *Spindrift* was fifty yards away.

Gillander beckoned to Scuff to go back to him where he was standing at the ship's wheel. Monk watched as Gillander placed Scuff's hands on the wheel and saw as his body stiffened to hold the violent pull against him. He threw his weight into it. The ship came into the wind again and righted itself.

Gillander gave a tiny gesture of salute, looking at Monk over Scuff's shoulder.

Monk went forward. He touched Scuff lightly in tacit approval, and felt him tense with pleasure.

"Go below to my cabin and get three cutlasses from the cupboard under the bunk," Gillander ordered Monk. "And be quick. You'd better take that pea coat off. You can't fight with your arms tied up in that thing."

The distance between the ships was closing fast. There was no time to argue. If he failed, Hester would never forgive him for this. And for taking Scuff! But if he failed he would be dead, so he would never know.

He gave one of the cutlasses to Scuff, sliding it through the side of his belt while his two hands were on the wheel.

"Only if someone boards the *Summer Wind!*" he said grimly.

Scuff grinned. "And if you an' Gillander get killed, I'm going to sail this back home by myself?"

"Don't be impertinent," Monk snapped back at him, suddenly appalled at the idea of his being terrified . . . hurt . . . alone.

He forced the thought out of his mind. Loving anyone made him such a hostage to terror . . . and pain.

He gave the second cutlass to Gillander and kept the third. It felt strange in his hand, unfamiliar.

They were only twenty yards from the *Spindrift* now. He could quite clearly see Clive on the deck, and one other man. There could be more, with at least one at the wheel. They would have weapons, too, maybe cutlasses, or—far worse—guns. Although one would need extraordinarily good luck to hit anybody on the pitching decks of either ship.

Gillander had the cutlass in his belt and a grappling iron on a long rope in his hands. He clearly meant to come close enough to the *Spindrift* to hurl it, so it caught on the rail and the two ships could be lashed together. The maneuvering would have to be precise. If they were going in opposite directions at more than a few yards a minute, the rope would snap and recoil back on whoever threw it, possibly dragging them into the sea.

Monk strode forward to Gillander. "You steer," he ordered. "It needs more than luck to do this. I'll throw the grapple."

Gillander stood still for a moment. They were fifteen yards away and closing. The wind had dropped and the sun was rising fast.

Ten yards.

Gillander took the wheel and Monk held the grapple, watching carefully where the length of its rope lay.

"Keep back!" he ordered Scuff. "Right over there!"

Scuff blinked, then realized that Monk was talking about standing on the rope coiled lying on the deck, which would take him over with it. He obeyed instantly.

Ten yards. Five. Monk threw the grapple and it hooked on to the rail. He lashed it to the deck stanchion and threw his weight against it, tying it fast.

Gillander ordered Scuff to take the wheel, then he leaned sideways and grasped the lines to lower the sail yet farther. Immediately the ship lost way. The two were no more than a couple of yards apart, then crashing sides, and locked together.

Gillander leaped aboard the *Spindrift*, cutlass in hand. Monk tightened and lashed the ropes again, and jumped to the deck of the *Spindrift* himself. He landed heavily as the roll of the deck dropped it down, then up again.

There was a man not a yard in front of him, saber high. He lunged forward. As if it were second nature, Monk sidestepped and parried. All the aches of exhaustion fell away from him like a discarded garment. The blood surged in his veins and he was almost dizzy with energy. All the fights he'd ever had were unrolling inside him now, memory in the muscle and the bone. He swung round and slashed at the man, altering his weight, moving easily, striking and defending, seeing blood where he had scored a mark. Next moment his own arm stung and he saw a thin red streak on his sleeve. There was little pain, only irritation that he had allowed it to happen. He knew better than this!

He swung, jabbed, and then swung the other way. The man yelled in fury, lunging forward, blood all over his shoulder. Monk sliced the opposite way and the man fell.

Gillander was on the other side of the deck, facing the other crewman, fighting hard. Even as Monk watched, the two of them moved dangerously, almost elegantly, around the closed deck hatch, every step closer to the rail and the sea.

Monk could not intervene; the blades were sweeping and striking, clashing and then disengaging. They were both good, clever, desperate. Life and death were the prizes.

Monk glanced at the *Summer Wind*. Scuff was still clinging to the wheel, his face white in the cold dawn light. Gillander leaped over the hatch cover, swung around like a dancer, and sliced open the other man's chest. He staggered back, jackknifed over the rail, and plunged into the sea.

Gillander turned back to face the deck, and saw Monk. There was no one else there. Clive and Miriam must be below—if Miriam was still alive. This was the moment of knowing.

Clive was clever. He would make them go below, where he was waiting for them. He knew the layout of the ship; he might well have a musket, or any other kind of firearm. And he had Miriam.

Would he harm her?

Did any part of him love her? Or was she just beauty to him, an appetite, albeit a consuming one?

He looked across at Gillander.

Gillander was grim-faced. For the first time Monk saw fear in his eyes. He knew it was not for himself; it was for Miriam.

Monk looked across at Scuff. "Wait here!" he shouted. "That's an order. When we come back up, we'll need your help. Understand?"

"Yes . . ." Scuff, too, was afraid now.

Gillander went first, reaching the hatch before Monk and going straight down the steps, cutlass at the ready. He must have appreciated the chances of being shot before he reached the bottom. Any man would. But he did not hesitate.

Monk followed on his heels.

It took him a moment to adjust to the dimmer light, but he could make out the cabin. Gillander was standing in front of him, with the cutlass at the ready. There was no one else there.

Gillander remained motionless for less than a minute. Then he put his hand on the door between the cabin they were in, and the next space, which would probably be the galley. He opened it softly. That, too, was empty. Clive and Miriam had to be in the cabin beyond.

Monk froze. If Clive heard them, above the creaking of timbers and the sound of the water, which was getting louder as the wind rose again, then he would shoot. If it were one of his own crew, still alive, they would call out to reassure him. And he would take the chance anyway.

Gillander held up his hand to warn Monk to stay back, then he kicked the door in with his leg high, heel hard, and stepped back immediately. He was only just in time. A shot went past him and crashed into the galley wall behind him, then another.

Monk stepped forward with his own cutlass held high. Aaron Clive stood in the center of the large cabin, holding Miriam in front of him so any careless shot would have caught her first. Her hair was wild, long, a dark cloud around her white face. Her eyes were wide, but it was not only from terror, but from a kind of exultation as well. Aaron was revealed for exactly what he was: clever, marvelously brave, and yet corrupted by pride and appetite. He had imagined himself invincible; fate would grant him whatever he wanted, if he wanted it enough. Astley had only stood in his way.

No one spoke. Words were unnecessary now. Clive stared at Monk, and Monk knew he would sacrifice Miriam if necessary. And they all knew that Gillander would never risk that. No justice would ever be bought at the price of Miriam's life. It was not a weighing of ideals. He had loved her since he had first seen her when he was barely twenty.

Clive smiled. If one did not look at his eyes, his face still had all the old charm.

He could not shoot Miriam. If she were dead he had no shield. They all knew that, too.

Then Monk saw the small, sharp sailmaker's knife in Clive's other hand, his arm tightly around Miriam, holding her to him. It fit neatly in his palm, the light on its short, curved blade.

"Go back," Clive said quietly. "I won't kill her. She's no use to any of us dead. But I will cut her, and it will hurt." As if to demonstrate he put the blade a little higher and deliberately sliced the fabric of her sleeve from elbow to wrist. Then just as carefully, as no one moved, he cut the flesh, and the blood oozed through in a long, scarlet line, which grew thicker all the time.

Miriam gave a moan and fell slack in his arms, all her weight against him.

He was taken by surprise. He had not meant to cut so deeply.

Gillander let out a cry and lunged forward, stopping short only as he collided with Monk.

Clive was bent forward, dragged down by Miriam's weight. In that instant of surprise, she turned, violently alive again, grasped his hand holding the blade, and pushed forward with all her strength. The knife went up into his arm, high, near the shoulder, and the blood spurted out of him.

His arm fell limp and she scrambled away from him, out of his reach, gasping for breath. Gillander went to her immediately, calling her name, fumbling to reach her petticoat and tear off a length of it to bind her arm.

Monk went to Clive, who was now covered in blood, his face ashen white. The blood was gushing from his upper arm. His other hand was covered with it and it drenched his jacket. It was bright red arterial blood, and there was nothing that could stop it. Monk had seen such wounds before, on the battlefield in America, at the beginning of their civil war. He would do what he could to bind it up, but it was pointless. It was merciful, but no use.

He heard Gillander go to the cabin door and shout for Scuff. Monk would have stopped him if he had been quick enough. He didn't want Scuff to try to save Clive, and fail.

That was stupid. Scuff had seen death already in his training to be a doctor. Yet the instinct to protect him from it was powerful, aching inside him as if he, too, had been injured.

Monk looked at Clive's face. For a moment their eyes met. Clive did not look frightened, just puzzled, then his life slipped away, leaving him completely blank.

Monk stood up slowly. He was stiff, and sad. He turned to look at Miriam just as Gillander came back in with Scuff on his heels. Scuff was frightened, and cold, but now he was faced with something he understood. He gave Monk a quick nod, then bent to look at Miriam's wound. He spoke to her gently as he took out the small cloth bag he had brought with him, and found a tiny bottle of spirit, a needle, linen thread, and some clean lint. He seemed as if he knew what he was doing, and for a moment he looked so like Hester: his hands, thin and strong, the way he bent his head, the air of assurance, whether it was real or not.

Miriam smiled at him as he started to work.

Gillander looked up at Monk. "Weather's rising again. We can't get two ships back in this."

Monk was praying over and over in his mind: Please God, we can get one back! He spoke to Scuff. "Make that as good as you need to so we can get back on the other ship. Do the finishing bits afterward."

"I know," Scuff said quietly. "It's fine. We'll be ready." He turned for an instant and gave Monk a beautiful smile.

Monk was choked with gratitude. He felt the tears prick in his eyes as he went through the galley and the outer cabin and up the steps to the deck.

The wind was high, whipping spray up onto the deck, the whitecaps racing past. Gillander was right. They could not save both ships. With no one at the helm, two dead men on board, and one lost in the sea, the Spindrift would founder in the storm and go down, all hands lost.

But Aaron Clive had been lost for a long time, perhaps since Zachary had died.

Five minutes later, Gillander helped Miriam up onto the deck of the Spindrift, then over the side to the Summer Wind. She was pale, but quite composed. Scuff had stitched her wound and there was barely any new blood on the bandage.

They unlashed the ropes and pulled the grapples back. With sail half-raised, they let the sea pull them apart.

Miriam went below, and Scuff came back up on deck to take the wheel as Monk and Gillander raised a short, tight mainsail. They turned the ship back into the storm, heading westward and home, unaware of anything except a deep abiding victory within.

For more murder and mystery on the river Thames, turn the page to sample the next installment in the bestselling William Monk series,

AN ECHO OF MURDER

"IT'S A BAD ONE, sir." The policeman shook his head as he stepped back on the wharf, allowing Commander Monk of the Thames River Police to reach the top of the stone stairs up from the water. Monk moved onto the dock itself. Hooper had made fast the two-oar police boat they had come in and was hard behind him.

To the south, the Pool of London was already busy. Huge cranes lifted loads of bales from ships' holds and swung them ponderously over to the docks. The water was congested with boats at anchor, waiting their turns; barges loading; ferries going back and forth from one side of the river to the other. Black masts were a tangle of lines against the backdrop of the city and its smoke.

"Unusually bad?" Monk asked. "Who is he?"

"He's one o' them Hungarians."

"Hungarians?" Monk's curiosity was piqued.

"Yes, sir. Got a few of them around 'ere. Not thousands, like, but enough."

The policeman led them past stacks of timber into a storage bay, then opened the door to one of the warehouses.

Monk followed, and Hooper after him.

Inside was just like any other warehouse—packed with timber, unopened boxes and bales of goods—except that no one was working.

The policeman observed Monk's glance. "Sent 'em home. Only make it more muddled," he added. "Best they don't see any of it."

"Was it one of them who found him?" Monk asked.

"No, sir. Didn't know 'e was even there. Thought 'e were at 'ome, where 'e should 'a been."

Monk was beside him now, keeping step across the floor and to the stairs that led up to the offices.

"So who did?"

"A Mr. Dob—something. I can't say them names right."

"Lead the way," Monk directed. "I suppose you've called the police surgeon?"

"Oh, yes, sir. And I didn't touch a thing, believe me!"

Monk felt a chill of premonition, but he made no reply.

At the top of the stairs he followed a short passage, then came to a door. There were low voices murmuring inside. The policeman knocked once, then opened it and stood back for Monk to go in.

The room was fairly large for an office, and the light was good. Monk had seen death before. It was a large part of his job. But this was more violent than usual and the raw smell of blood filled the air. It seemed to be over everything, as if the poor man had staggered and fallen against the chairs, the table and even the walls. Now he lay on his back on the floor, and the army rifle with its fixed bayonet was sticking up from his chest like a broken mast, crooked and looking as if it would fall awry at any moment.

Monk blinked.

The middle-aged man kneeling on the floor beside the body turned and looked up at Monk. "Commander Monk. Thought they'd send for you," he said drily. "Not a job any man'd keep, if he could push it off on someone else. Place opens on to the water, so I suppose it's yours."

"Good morning, Dr. Hyde," Monk said bleakly. He had known and respected the police surgeon for some time. "What can you tell me, other than that?"

"Dead about two hours, I would say. Not entirely a medical opinion. Could be longer, except that the warehouse itself was closed until six, and he hasn't been here all night, so he must have come since then. No way in here except up these stairs."

"But at least an hour and a half?" Monk pressed him. It was a tight time period, and that should help.

"Still warm," Hyde answered. "And the first workers got here about an hour ago. Your friend here," he gestured to the policeman, "will tell you that none of the men on the warehouse floor came up here. So if it was them, then they're all in it, lying their heads off. You could try them, of course." He looked back at the corpse. "Looks plain enough. Bayonet through the chest. Bled to death in a few minutes."

Monk looked around the blood-spattered room.

"I didn't say immediately!" Hyde snapped. "And there are cuts on his hands and arms. In fact all the fingers on his right hand are broken."

"A fight?" Monk was hopeful. This man was big, heavy. Whoever fought with him should have a few good bruises as well, possibly more than that.

"Not much of one." Hyde pulled his face into an expression of disgust. "One man armed with a fixed bayonet, and the other apparently with nothing."

"But his fist was damaged," Monk argued. "So at least he got in one pretty good blow."

"You don't listen, man! I said his fingers were broken. All of them, and it looks deliberate. Not evenly, as they more likely would be if he hit something. Dislocated and broken, like deliberate mutilation."

Monk said nothing. It was conscious brutality, not the result of hot temper, more like deliberate torture.

Hyde grunted and looked back again at the corpse. "I'll give you the rifle and bayonet when I've taken it out of him, at the morgue. There is more to the wound than just this. Don't know what, but that's up to you.

If there's only one wound, then God knows what happened. There's blood on all those candles over there"—he gestured to several tables and ledges—"and those torn-up bits of paper. But none on his hands. I suppose you noticed that?"

Monk had not. But he had noticed that the man's mouth was badly disfigured, and covered with blood.

"Is that more than just bruising?" he asked. "A punch in the mouth, against his own teeth?"

Hyde bent closer, and was silent for several moments. "No," he said at last. He swallowed. "His lips have been cut off, after death. They're stuffed in his mouth. At least I think that's what's in there. God help us."

"Who is he?" Monk asked.

The other man in the room came forward. He was of average height, and ordinary build. In fact, there was nothing unusual about him until he spoke. His voice was penetrating, even when quietly used, and his eyes were an extraordinarily clear and piercing blue. He looked at Monk in a way that might have been deferential. "His name was Imrus Fodor, sir. I knew him only slightly, but we Hungarians are not so many here in this part of London that we are strangers to each other." He spoke English with barely any accent.

"Thank you." Monk looked at the man steadily. "How do you come to be here, Mr. . . . ?"

"Dobokai, sir, Antal Dobokai. I am a pharmacist. I have a small shop on Mercer Street. I came to deliver a potion to poor . . . Fodor. For his feet." He held up a brown paper bag.

"Do you normally make your own deliveries?" Monk asked curiously. "And at this hour of the morning?"

"If I am not busy, yes. It is a small service. It pays in loyalty, and I do not dislike the walk, especially at this time of the year." Dobokai's eyes did not waver for an instant. There was such an intensity of emotion in him that Monk found it hard to look away. But if he had set out to perform a small kindness, and come in to find this bloody carnage, it was hardly surprising he was emotionally raw. Any sane man would be.

"I'm sorry you had to discover this." Monk meant it. If he found it shocking himself, what must this ordinary domestic chemist feel, when it had happened to a man he knew? But better to ask the questions now, while the memory was part of his immediate experience, than have to revisit it later. "Can you tell me what happened from the time you left your own premises?"

Dobokai blinked; his concentration was obvious, and intense. He managed to continue while Hyde's assistants came in and put the body on a stretcher. They maneuvered around so as not to bump into anything, and carried the body out. Hyde followed immediately after them, leaving Monk alone with Dobokai and the policeman. Monk knew the young man would be making a plan of the building, and finding every possible way anyone could have come in or out.

"I woke early," Dobokai said quietly. "At about six I decided to collect some of the medicines that needed delivering today. I put Fodor's potion in a bag." He opened another bag and showed Monk several screws of white powder.

"And then . . . ?" Monk prompted.

"I know that Mrs. Stanley rises early too. Can't sleep, poor woman. I delivered her opium at about half-past six—"

"Where does she live?" Monk interrupted.

"On Tarling Street, right near the crossroads."

"And then?"

"I took Mr. Dawkins his laudanum. He lives a little farther down, on Martha Street," Dobokai replied. "Then I stopped at the Hungarian café on the corner of the High Street and had a cup of coffee and a pastry. I knew they wouldn't be open for business here until eight o'clock, which is when I arrived."

Monk turned to the policeman. "Did any of the men arrive here early?"

"No, sir. I asked them, but according to what they say, they all came at the same time, eight o'clock exactly. The dead man was very strict. Bit of a martinet about time. Dock any man who was late."

Dobokai interrupted. "But he very rarely kept them late, and if he did, he paid well for it."

"And all the men came here together?" Monk pressed.

"Yes, sir, that's what they said—all of them," the policeman agreed. "Looks like he was killed before anyone else got here. Agrees with what the doc said. Sorry, sir, the police surgeon," he amended.

"But you came up here, Mr. Dobokai?" Monk reaffirmed. "Just after eight. Were the workers all here?"

"Yes. I . . . I went up to give him the potion, and I found . . . this." His eyes flickered around the room, then back again at Monk. He had a naturally sallow complexion but now he looked ill.

"Did you happen to notice the men working downstairs when you passed them? Was there anyone you knew?" It was perhaps a foolish question, but sometimes people recalled more than they expected to, even trivia that seemed of no importance.

"Yes, sir," Dobokai replied, a little color returning to his face. "There were seven men. I know them by sight, but that's all."

Monk was surprised at the exact number. "Whereabouts? Perhaps you will draw a sketch for the constable?"

"Two were on the big bench just inside the door," Dobokai answered without hesitation. "One standing in the middle of the floor. And four along the bench at the back. They had tools out. Three wood saws and the last one had a pair of pliers in his . . . left hand."

"You are unusually observant. Thank you."

"Not a day I'll forget," Dobokai said quietly. "Poor Fodor. Before you ask me, I have no idea who would have done this to him. He seemed a very ordinary sort of man to me. Lived alone. His wife's dead. Worked hard to build his business up, and he was doing well. I think . . . I think you've got a lunatic here. The place is . . ." He turned around slowly, looking at the blood, the broken candles, their wicks scarlet as if they had been dipped in the dead man's wounds. There must have been six-teen or seventeen of them, all different shapes and sizes. "What sane man could do this?" he asked helplessly. "I will help you to solve this. I know them. I will translate for you, for those whose English is not good. Anything—"

"Thank you," Monk cut him off. "If I need your help, I shall ask you, and be grateful for it." He understood Dobokai's fear, his need to feel that he was doing something, not just standing by. "First we shall speak to the men. I'll have someone go through Fodor's business accounts, monies due, owed, and so on. That may tell us something."

Dobokai looked at him skeptically. "This is how you settle overdue debts in England? I have been here in your country for many years, Commander. Before I was in London, I was in Yorkshire. Good steel-making country. Good people. This is not business, not English business."

Monk looked into Dobokai's remarkable, clear blue eyes, and realized his error. He had underestimated this man. "No, of course it isn't," he agreed. "We have to go through the motions, just to exclude the possibility. But you are right. This is hatred, a terrible, uncontrolled passion to destroy. But I don't want to frighten people if I can avoid it. And we must find out all we can. Looking into his business is as good a way to start as any other. It will allow us to ask questions."

"I see. I see," Dobokai said quickly. "A way in. Of course. I should have understood. Yes. You cannot tell people there is a monster loose; they will panic. I shall tell no one how . . . what a horror this is. You will ask people what they have seen, and bit by bit you will work it out." He looked around the room again. "Such hatred," he whispered, not to Monk, but to himself.

Monk had the powerful feeling that Dobokai was realizing something that he had never seen before, not fully, not like this. In due course, perhaps he, Monk, would find out what it was.

"Thank you, Mr. Dobokai," he said more gently. "We'll stay here a little longer, speak to the workers, the neighbors, and see if anybody has noticed anything different. In case we need you, leave your exact address with Mr. Hooper, outside, and let us know if you think of anything further."

"Yes," Dobokai agreed. "Yes, of course." Now he was unsurprisingly quite relieved to excuse himself and leave the awful room.

Monk looked around again, alone now. Everything he saw—the splashes of blood, the blood-daubed candles, two of them a dark purple, close to blue, the torn-up paper, which looked like it might be a torn-up letter of some kind—all of it spoke of rage, absolutely out of control, almost beyond sanity. What sane man does this to another?

But where had such depth of feeling come from that no one had seen it? Or perhaps they had? If he looked in the right place, surely he would find something to tell him that Fodor himself had been aware of it. And there would be others who could help, colleagues of Fodor, friends. Such hatred does not spring into being without a deep foundation.

Hooper came back from questioning the employees, and searching the building for traces of entry or exit. He and Monk had worked together for some time now, two or three years at least. Hooper was a big man, quietly spoken, but there was a depth of both intelligence and emotion beneath his controlled manner; Monk had seen it in extraordinary loyalty. When everyone else had considered Monk guilty of error, and worse, Hooper had risked his own life to save him, not to mention his career to defend him.

"Sir?" Hooper asked.

"Oh . . . yes." Monk swung round to face him. "Learn anything?"

"Nothing that looks useful," Hooper replied ruefully. "No one broke in. Can't climb up from the water, anyway. Back entrance locked and bolted from the inside."

"So we're starting with the entire community to pick from," Monk concluded.

"Dobokai . . ."

"Right. That is, if he was really mixing ointment for the dead man's feet. Have to check it." He looked around the room. "You'd think someone who hated this violently would be pretty clear the moment we saw him. Probably baying at the moon, with blood on his teeth. But he can't be. He'll probably look like anyone else . . . most of the time."

Hooper shrugged. It was true. Obvious eccentrics were sometimes the sanest people of all—and repressed, obedient followers, when they finally snapped, could have unimaginable monsters inside them . . . or not.

"Have to see what we can find out about Imrus Fodor, poor devil,"

Monk said. "I suppose most of his neighbors and customers will speak English?"

FODOR'S HOUSE WAS PLEASANT, ordinary on the outside, like all those along the street, but inside unusually comfortable, and definitely full of character. They had found his door keys in his office at the warehouse, so breaking in was unnecessary. They stood in the hall and stared around.

"Not English," Hooper said, but there was interest in his voice, even a degree of respect.

Monk looked at the paintings on the walls. Several of them were of horsemen in dress he had never seen before. One was of a city he did not recognize. It had old-fashioned outlines, foreign to England, but was very beautiful, like a creation of the imagination rather than from history. He also noticed a beautiful, gentle painting of a mother and child, surrounded in gold.

"He wasn't a poor man," Hooper observed, looking now at the furniture. "That hall table would fetch a good price. And the mirror above it, too. Good glass, and the carving is perfect."

Monk started through the other rooms, touching very little, but gathering a strong impression of the dead man's taste, and very considerable expenditure on his home. He knew quality and style, and clearly had the means to indulge them. And yet there was no extravagance and no sense of making an effort to impress. Nothing was new. Interesting. Had he brought them with him from Hungary? Or was their acquisition from something uglier? Obtained via blackmail? There had been the sort of hatred in Fodor's death that speaks of someone over whom he had a power. Was it to hurt, to rob, to destroy? Why now? That was always the question with any violent crime—why now?

"Have to look very carefully into his last few days," Monk said. "Last week or two. What happened that a man who lived in a house like this suddenly got attacked as he did, with such hatred?"

But a careful search of the rest of the house turned up nothing that seemed to tell of an unusual event. There was no diary, nothing marked on the calendar on the kitchen wall, no notes, letters, or invitations.

"Start next door," Monk said, looking up and down the street. "Seems well kept, as if there's somebody there a lot of the time."

Hooper smiled. "Yes, sir. I saw the curtains twitch."

"Right. I'll go this way," Monk said. "You go that." He pointed in the other direction. "See you at the station."

Hooper gave a half salute, and walked away.

They asked the neighbors all sorts of seemingly ordinary questions, trying to find anything unusual, or at the very least what they thought or felt about Imrus Fodor.

"Nice enough man," Mrs. Harris said, one door down to the right. She was about fifty, perhaps a year or two older than the victim. "Not that I knew him, of course. Hungarian, he was." She added that as if it were an explanation.

"Did he speak good English?" Monk asked.

"Ah . . . well, yes, I suppose so. But for all that, he wasn't like us. Couldn't be, could he?"

Sometimes Monk chose to be obstructive, to see how an interviewee changed, what they said when they were off guard with annoyance. He decided to use this strategy now.

"I don't know," he replied. "I don't think I've even known a Hungarian. What are they like?" He kept his expression polite with some difficulty.

"Like?" she said stiffly. "I don't know what you mean."

"You said he was not like us," he reminded her.

"Well, he wasn't English, was he!" she snapped.

"I believe not."

"You ever met an Englishman called 'Fodor'?" She raised her eyebrows.

"No. Was he rude to you? Untidy? Disrespectful? Unclean? Noisy? Did you ever see him the worse for drink? Did he have women coming and going in the house?"

She looked taken aback. "Well . . . no. Except Mrs. Durridge, of course. She came and cleaned for him, and might have cooked, for all I know."

He got little more from Mrs. Harris, or the next people he spoke to. The man behind the counter at the corner tobacconist's was more forthright, however.

"Not enough work around here for us, never mind all the foreigners coming in," he said darkly. "Not that he was bad," he added. "Took on a few workers, 'e did, but mostly 'is own, like. More foreigners. But what do you expect? Foreign newspapers they've got, too. Print them right 'ere. That pharmacist fellow, Dobokai, 'as something to do with that. Not any idea what they're saying about us. Can't read a word of it. Could be anything."

"Perhaps it's news from Hungary?" Monk suggested.

The man grunted. "They're different, that's all. And now look what's 'appened! Got himself murdered. Don't want that kind of thing 'ere."

"We don't need any more," Monk agreed. "We've got enough of our own without help."

The man looked at him narrowly. "What's it to you, then?"

"Police," Monk replied. "Want to find out who did this to him, and get them put away as soon as possible."

"Right. You do that!"

"Need your help. I don't know the area here," Monk replied.

"Where do you live, then? You foreign, too?"

"Other side of the river," Monk replied. "Just about straight across from here. Up from the Greenwich Stairs a bit."

"Well, what do you want to know?"

Monk surprised himself. "What do you know about Antal Dobokai?"

"Interesting fellow . . ." The tobacconist gave it some consideration. "Quiet. But underneath it, thinking all the time. Educated. But in Hungary, o' course, where 'e comes from. Do sums in 'is 'ead faster than most of us can on paper, an' always right. Was an architect once, so rumor 'as it. Harder to find work over 'ere. We got our own. But seems 'e's doing all right. Why? You think 'e done it?" There was both skepticism and amusement in his face.

"No," Monk replied. "So far it looks as if he's the one man who couldn't have."

"Why's that, then?"

"Time. Can't be in two places at once."

"Bad thing. You're police: Was it as bad as talk 'as it?"

"Pretty ugly. Someone hated him, or was out of his mind in some way or other. Is there strong feeling in the community? Rivalries? Feuds?"

The man looked slightly surprised. "They're different, I suppose, them Hungarians, but civil enough, if you're civil to them. Don't bother me. Of course, there's always them that don't like anyone who's different, dress different, act different, like. Stick-in-the-mud, like. Like old Sallis around the corner. 'Good enough for my father, and 'is father before 'im, good enough for me,' 'e'll say. Like change is an insult."

"Did you know Fodor?"

"Some. Nice enough. Always got a good word or two. Never walks right by you, like some. But then they're all different, like we are."

We, and them. Monk noticed it over and over. He stayed a little longer, then moved on a block or so and asked a greengrocer, then a cobbler. It was late afternoon and he had learned nothing unexpected when he met up with Hooper again.

"Not much help," Hooper said, shaking his head. "Known locally, especially among the other Hungarians. Quite a few of them in the area. All come to the same place. Reckon I'd do the same if I had to live in some other country. Not like I would! Why'd they come here? Ones I spoke to were doing well enough. Why not stay at home, where you're just like anyone else?"

"Did you ask them?"

Hooper smiled ruefully. "Enough people been asking that, like they'd no right to be here. Got nothing useful, sir. Everyone says what you'd expect them to. He was all right, but still a foreigner." He shook his head. "This was someone who knew him well and hated him, or is a madman."

Monk had reluctantly reached the same conclusion. He wished Hooper had argued with him, and yet if he had, Monk would have thought less of him. It was too easy to evade a truth because you did not like it.

"Or someone who hated incomers," Hooper added. "Felt a bit of that. Some people find change threatening."

"Then they should go and live out in the countryside," Monk said tartly. "The city's changing all the time. That's what's both good and bad about it. I heard the same, but it's just grumbling, as some people grumble about the weather."

"Somebody hated the poor devil," Hooper said as they began to walk. The sun was lowering in the sky, pavements already partially in shadow. "Perhaps we should get Dobokai to help us? He might pick up inflections we miss. He knows the people and he speaks the language. Most of them seem to have pretty fair English, but they still speak to one another in Hungarian. We might be missing something."

"I think I'm missing everything," Monk said with a touch of bitterness. "It's not a random lunatic. There was hatred in that room; deep, irrational, personal hatred. Whoever it was drove a bayonet through his heart, extinguished candles in his blood, broke his teeth and his right hand. And they hacked off his lips. We've got something terrible there, Hooper, whether it's English or Hungarian or something we haven't looked at yet. Wonder what the candles mean. Nobody lights seventeen candles just to see by. Did you notice two of them were a dark, purplish blue color? Does that mean something? Or was it just what he had? There's no panic yet, but if we don't solve this murder, there will be. Word will spread, and no doubt get worse in the telling."

"Yes, sir, I know," Hooper said quietly, keeping in step with Monk so exactly he did not need to raise his voice. "You'll be putting more men on it tomorrow?" It was barely a question.

"Yes, all we can spare."

MONK ARRIVED HOME LATE, although it was still light. No lamps were lit yet in the street as he walked up the hill from the ferry. As he turned on Paradise Place and looked back, the sun was making a polished shield of the still water of the river, marked here and there by the black hulls of moored ships and the masts barely moving against the backdrop of the sky above the city. The air was still warm. There was no wind to rustle the heavy leaves of the trees in Southwark Park. Violence seemed a distant nightmare.

He walked the last few steps and went in at his own door.

Hester heard him and came into the hall from the kitchen. She was not a traditionally beautiful woman, perhaps a little too thin, and certainly there was far too much courage in her face, and too much intelligence for her demeanor to be comfortable to most men. There had been a time, long ago, when he had found it aggressive. Now it was what he loved in her the most.

He went straight to her and hugged her, surprising her by the fierceness of his grip.

After a moment she pulled away, concern in her eyes.

He knew right away that she could not have heard of the murder in Shadwell.

"You didn't go to the clinic today?" he asked.

The shadow in her eyes was immediate. The clinic was in Portpool Lane, to the north of the river. She had founded it several years ago, to take in and treat women off the streets who were ill or injured. It was her final role as a nurse, which had begun with Florence Nightingale, and the Crimean War. Now others ran the clinic, but she still took part.

"Sorry," he said. "I meant you haven't been out, or you would have seen the headlines in the evening papers. We had a pretty terrible murder in Shadwell, just along from the Wapping Station."

"On the river?" She turned and led the way back to the kitchen. The kettle would be on the hob, as it always was at this time in the evening.

"Just off it, but practically on the Shadwell New Basin. Regular police were glad to get rid of it. The victim works with boats. Hungarian. There's a bit of a community there. Just a few hundred, at the most."

Hester pulled the kettle onto the hottest part of the stove, which was stoked and lit only for water and cooking. It was more than warm enough in the house, so it wasn't needed for heating. The only thing Monk wanted immediately was hot, fresh tea. Hester had no need to ask.

"Cold beef and bubble and squeak for dinner?" she asked. "And I've got apple pie."

It was exactly what he wanted, especially the pie.

ANNE PERRY is the bestselling author of two acclaimed series set in Victorian England: the William Monk novels, including *An Echo of Murder* and *Revenge in a Cold River,* and the Charlotte and Thomas Pitt novels, including *Murder on the Serpentine* and *Treachery at Lancaster Gate.* She is also the author of a series of five World War I novels, as well as twelve holiday novels, most recently *A Christmas Message,* and a historical novel, *The Sheen on the Silk,* set in the Ottoman Empire. Anne Perry lives in Los Angeles and Scotland.

anneperry.co.uk

To inquire about booking Anne Perry for a speaking engagement, please contact the Penguin Random House Speakers Bureau at speakers@penguinrandomhouse.com.